D0261519

THE MAN IN THE BUNKER

Rory Clements was born on the edge of England in Dover. After a career in national newspapers, he now writes full time in a quiet corner of Norfolk, where he lives with his wife, the artist Naomi Clements Wright, and their family. He won the CWA Ellis Peters Historical Award in 2010 for his second novel, *Revenger*, and the CWA Historical Dagger in 2018 for *Nucleus*. Three of his other novels – *Martyr*, *Prince* and *The Heretics* – have been shortlisted for awards.

To receive exclusive news about Rory's writing, join his Readers' Club at www.bit.ly/RoryClementsClub and to find out more go to www.roryclements.co.uk.

Also by Rory Clements

Martyr

Revenger

Prince

Traitor

The Heretics

The Queen's Man

Holy Spy

The Man in the Snow (*ebook novella*)

Corpus

Nucleus

Nemesis

Hitler's Secret

A Prince and a Spy

THE MAN IN THE BUNKER

RORY CLEMENTS

ZAFFRE

First published in the UK in 2022 by
ZAFFRE
An imprint of Bonnier Books UK
4th Floor, Victoria House, Bloomsbury Square, London, WC1B 4DA
Owned by Bonnier Books
Sveavägen 56, Stockholm, Sweden

A CIP catalogue record for this book is
available from the British Library.

Hardback ISBN: 978–1–83877–765–4
Trade paperback ISBN: 978–1–83877–766–1

Also available as an ebook and an audiobook

1 3 5 7 9 10 8 6 4 2

Typeset by IDSUK (Data Connection) Ltd
Printed and bound in Great Britain by Clays Ltd, Elcograf S.p.A.

Zaffre is an imprint of Bonnier Books UK
www.bonnierbooks.co.uk

For Madeleine, with love

Chapter 1

They skirted the slumped remains of a Panzer, its blackened gun barrel twisted sideways like the crook of an elbow. Collingham stuck a cigarette in his mouth and inspected the packet. 'God damn it, we're clean out, Mr Harper.'

'I'll stop there.' The driver nodded towards a ramshackle stall at the side of the road, fifty yards beyond the tank. A few miles away, threatening cloud banked over the Alps, but here in the foothills and lakes of southern Bavaria, the sky was clear and bright.

In another time, Randy Collingham could imagine coming here for a holiday, but he'd have to disregard the darkness bred and nurtured in these pretty villages and towns, and he wasn't sure that he could stomach that. Too many horrors lurked beneath the surface of those still waters and in those snow-capped peaks.

He got out of the passenger seat, leaving the door open, and strode towards the rickety trestle table on which random items were laid out to tempt buyers: an old box camera, a Hitler Youth dagger, two bottles of milk, a large bottle of beer, an Iron Cross medal, a typewriter and some potatoes. The stallholder was a thin woman in her fifties. Her dress was tattered and torn and her left eye was haunted and restless. The right eye was missing; beneath the empty socket, scars rained down across her cheek.

'*Zigaretten, bitte. Haben sie Zigaretten?*' Collingham said. He knew she'd have some stashed away; cigarettes and dollars were the only universally respected currencies in the ruins of the Third Reich.

'Five dollars,' she said in English. 'For pack of ten.'

THE MAN IN THE BUNKER | 2

'You're not allowed to use dollars, only scrip.'

She sneered. 'Keep your scrip.'

'OK, two dollars for pack of twenty.'

She shook her head then looked away.

'What make you got, Fräulein?' Broad and tall, he towered over her. The conqueror and the conquered. But he could see she did not fear him. Did not even respect him. Good, he liked that defiance.

'English cigarettes. Very best – straight from Naafi.'

'OK three dollars – for twenty.'

'Eight dollars.'

'What? I pay a fraction of that at the PX!'

'Then go to the PX, Ami. I got kids to feed.'

Collingham took out his wallet and slapped down a five-dollar bill. 'You drive a hard bargain, sister. Take it or leave it.'

The woman shrugged, pulled out a single pack of Senior Service from her concealed stash behind the table, tore open the seal and removed eight cigarettes. 'Twelve *zigaretten* for five dollars. A bargain, yes?'

The American laughed and accepted her offer; he could no longer do the arithmetic. He shoved the pack of twelve into his shirt pocket.

The woman touched the medal, then the dagger. 'You like souvenir, Ami? Perhaps you like Nazi guns? I got a Luger, full working order with bullets – only twenty-five to you.'

'Not today, lady.' He walked back to the car, climbed in and pulled the door shut. 'Come on, Mr Harper, let's go and catch ourselves a retired dictator.'

There was a lot of blood on the road. A boy in leather shorts was kneeling beside a girl in a dirndl, her body splayed awkwardly.

Two bikes, one of them twisted and broken, lay a few feet away on the verge. Collingham's eyes were fixed on the girl. She wasn't moving. Even from two hundred yards away he feared she was dead.

'Stop the car, Mr Harper.'

'Are you sure, sir?'

'Of course, I'm sure.'

They had only gone two miles since haggling for cigarettes. The road was clear of traffic. Apart from the occasional wreckage of tanks and other vehicles, this region south of Munich was largely undamaged by the mass bombing in the last weeks of the war, and so there was little to detract from the beauty of the countryside. Randy Collingham wound down the window and tossed out the stub of his cigarette. He was in a hurry, but not so much that he wouldn't stop to help an injured child. As a father of three, how could he do otherwise?

Agent Denis Harper pulled the big black Opel Käpitan to a halt. The boy in the lederhosen rose to his feet and the two men in the car could see the horror in the lad's face. That and something else – relief, perhaps, that assistance had at last arrived.

The boy was running to them, begging for help. '*Hilf mir bitte. Hilf mir.*' His tanned chest was bare beneath the straps that held up his leather shorts. '*Meine Zwillingsschwester ist verletzt.*' My twin sister is injured.

Collingham tried to comfort him, told him they would do what they could, then he pushed forward and knelt beside the girl. Her head was roughly bandaged by the boy's white shirt, now red with blood. She was covered in blood, on her arms, legs and face. Her fair, braided hair was thick with gore. He couldn't see what injuries she had. Her chest was moving, but her eyes remained closed and she seemed to be unconscious. Touching her throat with the back of his hand, he felt a pulse. He turned to the boy and spoke in fluent German. 'What happened?'

'We were cycling home. A lorry clipped her. It didn't stop. Perhaps he didn't know what he'd done.'

'Well, she's alive, but we're not medics. We'll take her to hospital.'

'Yes, please, sir, her head is bad.'

Special Agent Collingham was weighing his options – Third Army HQ at Bad Tölz or the CIC medical centre at Garmisch? Maybe the latter; it was closer. 'Come on, help us carry her to the car. Gently.'

The conflict in Europe had been over for almost four months. The blackouts were gone and the lights were on. It had been a good war for Special Agent Randy Collingham, but he had lost friends. Parachuted behind enemy lines in late 1943, his language skills had served him well. So had his expertise in sabotage. He had evaded the Gestapo, but good comrades had not been so fortunate and he had scores to settle. This mission, to find the most wanted man in the world, could go a long way to getting even. And then he'd go home to North Carolina and hope that Jill and the kids recognised him.

In the meantime, there had to be a place for compassion and humanity, otherwise what had the fight been about? Whatever the reluctant Harper might have to say on the matter, Collingham was not a man to walk on by. Harper was a colder fish; he had no one back in the States and would happily carry on here. But the slaughter had stopped. Life had to start again – the sort of life where neighbour helped neighbour and men didn't ignore the suffering of those less fortunate.

'Agent Harper, help us.'

The two men and the boy raised the girl's limp body and eased her into the rear seat of the big car. Collingham's head told him they had to get to the hospital at speed; his heart told him he should be trying to administer some aid, clean up her wounds to see what injuries she had sustained. His head won. Time was crucial. Both for the girl – and for their mission.

'Drive, Mr Harper.'

They were in the front passenger seat. The children – probably aged twelve or thirteen – were on the bench seat behind them. Collingham tore his white shirt into strips and handed them to the boy to use as more bandages to staunch the bleeding.

'*Danke sehr.*'

They were the last words Randy Collingham heard. A single bullet drove a hole into the back of his skull, deep into his brain. A second bullet came a split second later, entering Denis Harper's head at an almost identical angle. The two men slumped forward in their seats. The horn was blaring, the car sliding right onto the verge, just past the bicycles.

The girl in the dirndl was sitting up now, grinning as she wiped the coagulating pig's blood from her pretty face and fair hair. 'We did it, Siggy.'

'It was easy, Hildy. You were wonderful. Come, let's get our bikes. Time to go.'

Chapter 2

Peace. At last it really felt like peace. Johnny was riding on Wilde's shoulders, madly waving his arms in the air as they galloped along Grantchester Meadow. Johnny was laughing himself silly and so was his father.

It had been a very special day. He had shown the boy his rooms in college, introduced him to the porters and Bobby the gyp – his college servant – and then he had taken him to the boxing gym in the south of the town. Johnny had put on a tattered pair of boy's gloves – the smallest available, but still far too big for a five-year-old – and together they had spent half an hour giving the punchbag a good hammering.

'The lad'll be beating you soon, Prof,' the trainer had said, grinning broadly.

'Don't I know it, Joe. He's a tough one.' Pride surged through Wilde's heart. This was every man's dream, a son who could protect himself in an unkind world.

'Not a bad size for his age. I wager he'll be a middleweight like you.'

Wilde and his son had been Joe Spinks's only two customers. The trainer had told them it had been reasonably busy in the gym during the last two years of the war when the area was packed with servicemen, many of them American, but now everyone seemed to have other matters on their mind. Men were being demobbed, people were restarting careers or education, life was returning to normal with a rush.

'I'll tell my new undergraduates about the place, Joe. Bound to be one or two of them who fancy a bit of sparring. You'll soon build up again.'

'And you'll bring your boy here regular? Can't start them too young, you know.'

'That might not be the way Mrs Wilde sees it, I'm afraid. I'll talk to her.' He knew what her answer would be, of course. *Wait until he's a bit older, Tom. Let him choose for himself. He's too young.*

'What about yourself, Prof?'

'Oh, I'll come along, but I may not be in great condition.'

'You look lean enough to me.' Joe ranged his eyes over Wilde's six-foot frame. 'Barely eleven stone. You're verging on beanpole.'

Wilde knew it was true. His trousers were, indeed, a little on the loose side, but he wasn't alone in that after six years of wartime rationing. Still, he felt strong enough. He appraised Spinks, a former champion. 'You look as if you've lost a couple of pounds yourself, Joe.'

After the gym, Wilde and his son had walked hand in hand towards the river. Cambridge was slowly regaining its mellow, peaceful pre-war character. There were still bombsites, of course – houses turned to rubble, roads badly damaged – and it would almost certainly be like that for years to come, but at least the sandbags around public buildings had been removed.

They ambled along beside the Cam to Grantchester for a glass of lemonade, cheese sandwiches and a slice of cake, all of which Lydia had packed for them. It was a warm day, but few people were out enjoying the meadow. At the village of Grantchester, they played catch with an old, threadbare tennis ball, then lazed by the river, looking for frogs and fish, and tossing a bit of crust to the ducks. Best of all was a dazzling multicoloured light that flashed before their eyes under the overhanging trees.

'What was that, Daddy?'

'You've just seen your first kingfisher, Johnny. The most special bird in the world.'

'But where did it come from? Where did it go?'

'It came from its secret nest and it's gone to catch fish for its supper. Come on, let's go home and tell Mummy about it.'

Wilde had spent most of the past three years in central London in a senior advisory role with the Office of Strategic Services – America's wartime intelligence outfit. He had been given no title and he hadn't wanted one, for he still thought of himself as a professor of history.

Yet it had been a fine time, starting small with a handful of enthusiastic but inexperienced amateurs, and ending up with a vibrant powerhouse of intellect and ideas. Some of them wore uniform, some dusty sports jackets and soup-stained ties, some wore smart skirts or flowery summer dresses. For the most part, rank didn't count, nor did gender. After a shaky start in 1942, they had become an effective intelligence unit.

He would miss the clever, charming, oddball bunch of men and women at the top of the organisation. And he would never forget the courageous operatives who volunteered to be parachuted behind enemy lines, sometimes to their death. They had all been bold, innovative people – and his years with them had, in many ways, been the time of his life.

But that was then, and this was now. This was the peace and he wanted to put the war behind him. In college, the blackouts were gone, the static water tank had been removed from the old court and the civil servants who had taken up residence for the duration were moving back to Whitehall.

Wilde had quit the OSS and was preparing for the Michaelmas term. He still wasn't entirely sure how many undergraduates he would have; he supposed most of them would be battle-hardened ex-servicemen who had postponed or interrupted their courses for the duration of the war. Some would have scars and medals for valour, some would have nightmares. They would include captains and majors who had grown accustomed to giving orders rather than receiving instruction. They would be very unlike the fresh-faced young men straight from school that had been his usual intake. Could be interesting. How would the disparate groups get on with each other?

He was also dusting down the book he had been writing on the Jesuit priests who risked their lives coming to England in the late sixteenth century. He was only a third of the way through the work, but he felt full of energy for the task ahead. It was a story well worth telling, a natural rounding-off to the successful books he had written on Walsingham and Cecil from the same period.

His publisher had been calling him these past two weeks. 'The public are hungry for new works, Tom. They've had enough of Nazis and all that jazz. They want some solid English history. The Tudors are the thing. But keep it shortish – paper's in extremely short supply.' Well, that was all fine but it wasn't going to be ready any time soon. He'd have to go through all his research again, so it would be eighteen months at the very least, but more like two years.

Wilde lived with his wife Lydia in an old house called *Cornflowers* in the north-east of Cambridge. They had been married only three years having happily endured the reproachful glares of certain neighbours during several years of 'living in sin'.

The most interesting time was the birth of Johnny outside wedlock. Wilde and Lydia laughed merrily at the pursed lips and stiffening shoulders that greeted them when they walked out with the baby. But not all their neighbours were like that.

Perhaps it was the war and the loosening of stiff Victorian morality that made their domestic arrangements acceptable to more and more people. In the end, though, they had succumbed to marriage, perhaps as much for Johnny's sake as their own.

As father and son neared home, Wilde noticed a big American car by the kerb at their front gate. It was a soft-top Packard, black with white-wall tyres and expansive running boards. Johnny was impressed. 'Look at that car, Daddy. It's huge!'

'So it is.' It was a beautiful machine, but Wilde wasn't at all sure he was glad to see it. At a guess, the occupants were now in his house and he was thinking hard as to their identity and the purpose of their visit. Perhaps it was a social visit from one of the boys at Grosvenor Street, London headquarters of the OSS. His instinct, however, suggested otherwise. Surely, the guys he worked with would have phoned ahead to see if it was OK to drop in. Wilde didn't much like any of the alternatives that came to mind.

Lydia was already opening the door as they climbed the steps.

'That's good service,' Wilde said. 'Very prompt. You could be a hotel doorman – or woman.'

'I saw you through the window. You have visitors, Tom.' Her eyes drifted up to the heavens.

'Yes, I rather thought I might. Your expression suggests it's not good news.'

'There are three of them. Three men – one of whom I know. Do you want to guess?'

He detected a note of resignation. 'Not bloody Eaton?'

'Got it in one.'

Good grief, Philip Eaton. He thought he had seen the last of him. At times in these past years, he had seemed like a sort of harbinger of doom. There had been a time when he had arrived with welcome tidings, but in general that was not the case.

'What does he want?'

'You, obviously. I don't have good feelings. One of them, the one smoking a smelly pipe, brought me a present – a box of French perfume and American makeup. What would I do with lipstick and eyeliner, Tom?'

'Well, I suppose it was well meant. You wore some at our wedding as I recall.'

'I think he was trying to soften up the little woman, get in my good books so I'd go along with whatever dreadful plans they have for you. But he gave me two pairs of nylons, too, so I'll forgive him.'

'I suppose I have no option but to find out what they want.'

Lydia stood back to let him pass. 'They're in the kitchen, drinking the last of our coffee. I'll let them introduce themselves.'

He lifted up his son and handed him to Lydia. 'Go with Mummy, Johnny.'

She plonked the boy on her hip. 'Just remember, Tom, whatever it is they want, say no. You've done your bit. You're a college professor again. And a husband. And a father. And don't forget, we've got Doris babysitting tonight and we're going to the cinema.'

'Of course.'

'It's Judy Garland's new film.'

'Message received and understood.'

'Really? Well, that would be a first.'

Three men were sitting at the kitchen table with cups in front of them. It was a spacious room, with plenty of light from a large window and a good-sized table in the middle of the tiled floor.

Despite the presence of an American refrigerator, however, the place was looking a little sad and unmodernised. Paintwork was peeling and nothing had been done about it in the war years. In fact the whole house was a little like that; comfortable but a bit shabby. Much like England itself.

The visitors at the table had obviously been talking but fell silent as Wilde entered the room. Two of them rose to their feet. Only Philip Eaton remained seated, but that was excusable. His left leg had been badly injured in a road incident in the last year before the war, and he had also lost his left arm. He looked frail. Wilde nodded to him but didn't smile.

'Hello, Wilde.'

'Eaton, this is a surprise.' Not a *pleasant* surprise. Wilde was not at all pleased to see him. Above all else, he wanted nothing to disturb his new-found peace.

'Forgive us for turning up unannounced, old man. But I'm afraid this is all rather urgent. Do you know Allen Dulles? He's OSS like you.'

Wilde turned his attention to the man indicated. Of course, he knew the name and he knew plenty about him; they had had dealings at a distance, by wire and encrypted messages, when Wilde was working at Grosvenor Street in London and Dulles was heading the Office of Strategic Services bureau in Switzerland. Wilde knew that during the war Dulles had run agents deep within the Reich, gathering intelligence and causing varying degrees of disruption among the Nazi high command.

The fact that the war was over didn't mean an end to intelligence-gathering, however. Wilde knew that Allen Welsh Dulles – known to close colleagues as AWD – was now in charge of the OSS in the American sector of Germany, ensuring that the Nazis stayed beaten.

He had heard a great deal about Dulles's reputation. His brilliant mind, his attention to fine detail and his honest dealing were legendary. So, too, was his less respectable side: his philandering and his cruel neglect of his wife.

He never even bothered to make much of a secret of that.

It was said that his wife, Clover, accepted that there would always be other women in his life, and that his secretaries would often be his lovers. That didn't mean his behaviour didn't hurt.

To everyone else, he was charm personified.

The man was tall, athletic and handsome, with clear eyes and a dark moustache. He wore a smart grey civilian suit and tie, and the stem of a pipe was clenched between his teeth. A thin stream of fragrant smoke emerged from betwen his lips. 'Mr Wilde,' he said, extending his right hand. 'How do you do?'

'I'm well, thank you.' He accepted Dulles's firm handshake. 'And honoured by your presence. Somehow I feel as though I already know you.'

'Likewise, Mr Wilde.'

'Were you just passing through?'

Dulles and Eaton both ignored the question, instead turning to the third visitor. 'This is Colonel John Appache,' Dulles said. 'He's with the Counter Intelligence Corps in Garmisch, in the mountains of southern Bavaria. We have flown over together.'

Wilde went through the same formalities with Appache. Shaking hands, exchanging the conventional pleasantries. Unlike the other two men, Appache was in uniform – US Army with the full-bird silver eagle insignia on his epaulettes. He was a couple of inches shorter than Dulles and seemed a few years younger. Wilde put him at late thirties. Crew-cut fair hair, good teeth and skin – typical US college kid twenty years on, a boy turned man without pausing to take breath, let alone change his style. Without any evidence, he found himself surmising that the colonel had probably played quarterback. He had the assurance and swagger.

'Well, gentlemen, you're obviously all here for a reason,' Wilde said at last. These were big guns; Eaton was a senior member of MI6 and this was definitely not a social call. 'Which one of you would like to explain. Eaton, you perhaps?'

'This is a joint initiative, Wilde. I'm here as British liaison, so I'll leave the initial spiel to Mr Dulles.'

Dulles pulled out his chair and sat down. 'OK, let's talk business.'

Wilde found himself positioned directly opposite Dulles, who had removed his pipe from his mouth and was cupping it in his left hand. The OSS chief smiled warmly at him. 'I'll get straight to the point. We have reason to believe that Hitler is alive and hiding out in Bavaria, southern Germany. We want you to find him.'

Wilde frowned in the echoing silence, waiting for the punchline. They had to be joking, of course. But they weren't laughing. Perhaps he had misheard – or misunderstood. 'Could you repeat what you just said, Mr Dulles?'

'You heard me.'

'I thought for a moment there you said you wanted me to find Hitler.'

'That's it. Got it in one.'

'You want *me* to find Adolf Hitler?'

'How many times do I have to say it? Yes, I want you to track down Hitler and bring him in. Clear now?'

Wilde burst out laughing. But he wasn't really amused. His laughter subsided almost as soon as it began. This wasn't funny. For pity's sake, what were these three men doing here?

He turned his gaze to the British secret service man. 'Come on, Eaton, tell me the truth. This is some kind of elaborate joke, yes? Why don't you slap me, wake me up . . .'

'It's exactly what Mr Dulles says it is. We want you to perform one last service for the Allies.'

'Good God, it's not even April the first. Who put you up to this?'

Eaton merely shrugged, with the hint of a grimace at the corners of his mouth.

'OK,' Dulles continued. 'I can see why you might need a little persuading. But Hitler *is* alive and we have to get him. You're the man for the job.'

He shook his head. 'No, I'm a college professor, a husband and a father. I teach history to spotty youths. My spying days are over and I'm enjoying being back in civilian life. My wife is hoping to start a medical degree course. I'm preparing for a new intake of undergraduates. I have a book to write, and a son whom I would very much like to get to know.' He paused. 'Anyway, what makes you think the bastard Hitler is even alive?'

'What makes you think he's dead?' the colonel said.

'The Russians found his burnt remains outside the bunker in the centre of Berlin.'

'Not quite so. No body was found – only a few bones and ashes, which could have been anyone's.'

'I thought he was identified from dental records.'

'Oh, some bridgework was identified as his by his dentist, but who knows the truth? The dental piece could have been faked easily enough, or the dentist could be lying. These are not difficult tasks for a regime that subjugated most of Europe.'

'Surely others in the bunker testified that Hitler and his mistress had killed themselves.'

'Most of them haven't even been found, and those who have spoken are dyed-in-the-wool Nazis. They'd say whatever the Führer told them to say. And there are other things. In particular, there are doubts from the Soviet side, the people who supposedly found Hitler's remains. If they were so certain about it, why did Stalin tell President Truman that he didn't believe Hitler was dead.'

'Did Stalin really say that?'

'Yes,' Dulles said. 'Yes, he did, at the Potsdam Conference. And the same message came from Marshal Zhukov and Commissar Andrey Vyshinsky when they met the press in June. And there's plenty of other evidence, which I will lay out in due course.' He sighed heavily. 'But first off, am I right in thinking you knew Randy Collingham?'

'What do you mean *knew*? Of course I know Randy. He was with us at Grosvenor Street for a few months. He's a good man.'

Dulles's eyes flickered towards Colonel Appache.

'Special Agent Collingham is dead,' the colonel said. 'So is Agent Denis Harper, who was working with him.'

'Dear God, are you serious?'

'I'm afraid so,' Appache said flatly. 'They were killed in their car. I saw their bodies. They were both shot in the back of the head and so we have to assume that an assassin had secreted himself in the rear of their vehicle, though no one can be sure how that could have happened. Strangely, the back seat was streaked with blood so it is possible the killer himself had been bleeding – and there was blood on the road a couple of hundred yards behind the car.'

'The thing is,' Dulles said, 'we believe Collingham and Harper were closing in on Hitler. They had a contact and it's likely they were on their way to meet him, or her. Unfortunately, we don't have a name or location for this person.'

John Appache cut in: 'Unfortunately Collingham and Harper weren't good team players, if you know what I mean – very poor at passing on operational details. That's why we don't know their intended destination on the day they died.'

'I can see your problem,' Wilde said. Inside, he was thinking, *but it's not my problem.*

'To be honest, I don't quite agree with Mr Dulles,' Appache continued. 'I never really believed Hitler was alive, and I thought Collingham and Harper were getting nowhere. But the murders of Randy and Denis suggest I was wrong. It is almost certain that they died because they were getting close, and Hitler's protectors had to stop them in their tracks.'

'I'm so sorry. It's terrible news.' Wilde felt sick to the pit of his stomach that a brave man like Collingham should have survived the war only to fall to an enemy bullet in the first months of the peace. The same for Denis Harper, a man he had met once but didn't know well.

'The killer left a taunting message,' Dulles continued. 'It said "*Es lebe den Führer*". Written in block capitals on a piece of paper neatly deposited among the bloodstains on the rear seat.'

'Long live the Führer.' Wilde sighed; this was bloody grim news.

'Also, strips had been torn off Collingham's shirt. Makeshift bandages, perhaps?'

A thought struck Wilde. 'Perhaps they were helping a man they thought was injured – a man who had smeared himself with blood. They put him in the back of the car to take him to hospital, then wham.'

Dulles nodded. 'We had the same thought. Anyway, I don't want Collingham and Harper to have died in vain. Nor do I want the mass murderer Adolf Hitler to evade justice. That's why we're here today. You can find him, Wilde.'

'No.' He shook his head firmly. 'I'm very sorry, but none of this has anything to do with me, sad as I am at the loss of two good men. The war is over and I'm keen to return to some sort of normality. Anyway,' he continued. 'I ask again – why would you come to me?'

'Well, you're a historian,' Dulles said. 'And I know of no group of people less likely to have the wool pulled over their eyes than historians. You delve and you delve to get to some semblance of the truth – and even then you are sceptical. And rightly so in the case of Hitler. We have eyewitnesses who insist he died in battle in the Tiergarten, others who say he is in Spain, Brazil or somewhere in the Baltic.'

'But you need an intelligence officer for this.'

'That's what you've been doing most of the war, isn't it? And a great job, too, by all accounts.'

'You don't need me. Europe is swarming with military intelligence officers. You're spoilt for choice.'

'That's not quite accurate,' Dulles said. 'We need all the intelligence officers we can get. The de-Nazification process is immense and will take years. There are still hundreds of thousands of Nazis or former Nazis to be questioned and assessed – and we're very short of German speakers. Honestly, there's not a man or woman to spare. I'm told you speak pretty good German these days, and this isn't the sort of mission where you can wander around with a local interpreter in tow.'

'And you have a score to settle, don't you?' Eaton said. It was his first contribution. 'As far back as 1936, friends of yours died, even your students, thanks to Hitler and his grisly band of criminals. To me, that's a compelling argument. Oh, and by the way, you wouldn't be alone in this operation.'

'Are you coming with me then, Eaton?'

'I honestly wish I could, but I'm not walking well. And the lack of a left arm doesn't help. No, you will be accompanied by a young lieutenant named Mozes Heck. You will both be co-opted to the US Counter Intelligence Corps in Garmisch. Heck is a Dutch Jew, who escaped to England in a small sailing dinghy in 1940 and joined the British Army. He knows Bavaria well, having lived there during much of his early life when his father worked in Munich as a physician. The family moved back to Amsterdam, but that didn't save them. They were all deported east in 1943 and, as far as we know, none of them survived. Mo Heck wants to find Hitler very badly. His strengths are his courage, his motivation, his fluent German and his knowledge of Bavaria and the Tyrol. He is good with a gun and has a visceral loathing of Nazis. You will make a formidable team.'

'Where is he now?'

'Back in Bavaria,' the colonel said. 'Desperately trawling his way through the displaced persons camps looking for any clue as to the fate of his family. Also hunting for Nazis posing as refugees. He's very effective but a bit headstrong – which is one of the main reasons we need a man like you.'

'*A man like me*? I'm not sure what that means.'

'Mature,' Dulles said. 'Grounded. Steeped in tradecraft. Sensitive to the political reality of a country occupied by four powers who might not always see eye to eye. Analytical and inquiring. Heck is a good, courageous man, but he needs guidance. You'll be taking the lead, Professor Wilde. You'll keep him in line.'

'You want me to be Don Quixote in this mad quest – which would make Mr Heck my Sancho Panza.'

'But you won't be tilting at windmills,' Dulles insisted. 'It is almost certainly pertinent that Collingham and Harper had mountain gear in the trunk of the car: hiking boots, ropes, crampons, that sort of thing. We have reason to believe that Hitler is in the Alps. This is real and it's dangerous. Hitler must have people protecting him and they haven't lost their taste for bloodshed. Once you start asking questions, they will know, and they will do all in their power to stop you.'

'You know, Mr Dulles, you are not making this a very attractive proposition.'

'Not attractive? To be the man who brings Adolf Hitler to book? There are millions who would love the chance. You have it.'

Except he didn't want it. He wanted to be a husband, a father and a historian. Anyway, he knew he'd never get a crazy idea like this past Lydia. 'Yes, of course, I would like to see him dealt with,' he said tentatively. 'We all would. But someone else is going to have to bring him in.'

'When you are in Bavaria,' the colonel said, as though he hadn't heard Wilde rejecting the mission, 'I will be close at hand at CIC Garmisch to supply you with all your needs – men for a raid when you have identified the hideout, specialist equipment, weapons, anything. Of course we're close to the Austrian border, which is now partly French zone. They are aware of our undertaking, but not involved. They will not be a hindrance.'

It was time to bring this conversation to a halt. Wilde rose from his chair, and his guests did likewise, Eaton struggling to push himself up with his right hand on the edge of the table.

'I'm sorry,' he said. 'I'm not doing it.'

'You want justice, Professor Wilde?' Dulles asked.

'Naturally. But the answer is no, and that's the end of the matter.'

'I want justice very badly. I lost friends to that monster – as did you. Look, at least think it over, won't you? Sleep on it.'

'The answer will be the same tomorrow, and the day after.'

Dulles sighed heavily and met Wilde's eyes full on. 'OK, Professor,' he said at last. 'I must accept your decision.'

'Thank you.'

'But the mission aside, I have to say it has been a real pleasure to meet you after all the great work you've done.'

'Likewise. And good luck to whoever gets the job.'

Dulles removed his pipe and shook his head slowly. 'You know, we weren't flattering you. There is no one else suitable for this task. It could take quite a while finding someone, and by then the trail might have gone cold.'

'Just out of interest, what will you do with Adolf if you find him?'

None of the three men answered.

As the visitors were leaving, Eaton clutched Wilde's arm. 'I'm staying in Cambridge tonight, at Templeman's. I'll call you in the morning if that's all right. It would be good to catch up, chat about old times.'

'Of course. I'll be in college later, but join us here for coffee, if you like.'

'That would be a pleasure.'

With the door closed, Lydia gave her husband a long hard look which seemed to say, *What was that all about, Tom?* Then, after he had explained what was being asked of him and his response, she just shook her head and said, 'I give up. I married you for better or worse, so do what you have to do.'

'Wait a minute, didn't you hear what I said? I turned them down.'

'Of course you did.'

'I'm serious. I refused point blank. A categorical no.'

'You turned down the chance to catch Adolf bloody Hitler?'

He shrugged and found himself laughing. 'Sounds ridiculous, doesn't it?'

They had an early supper, then went to the cinema, without once returning to the subject of the proposed mission. When they got home, Johnny had gone to bed and Wilde walked Doris home. By eleven, he and Lydia were in bed, making love.

Afterwards, they lay in silence, both wide awake and aware of the simmering tension between them. Lydia made the first move, turning to him and taking him in her arms. 'I suppose you should do it,' she said at last.

'I don't want to.'

'I know, but someone has to, don't they? The world can't let the hideous swine off the hook.'

'But not me. I've done my bit. We both have.'

'True.'

They were silent again. 'However,' she said after a couple of minutes.

'There is no *however*. I am preparing for Michaelmas. There's going to be a difficult new intake of students. I haven't taught in over three years and I need to be on top of my game. Also, I have a book to write.'

'But you wouldn't be away long, would you? It's August and the term doesn't start until October.'

'Are you trying to persuade me to accept their mad mission, Mrs Wilde?'

'It would be quite an achievement – to bring the tyrant to justice. That would be something to tell our grandchildren.'

He turned to the side table and switched on the lamp, then sat up against the headboard. 'You know, Lydia, one of the main reasons I turned down this insane mission was because I thought you would be dead set against it. I thought you wanted us to be a proper family again.'

'I do. Yes, of course, I do. But this . . . this is different. And there would be no danger, would there? The Nazis have been beaten to a pulp.'

He hadn't told her about the deaths of Randy Collingham and Denis Harper and something still held him back. 'Sometimes, Lydia, I really don't think I understand you at all.'

'Whereas I understand you perfectly, Tom. And I know you would be hell to live with if you turned down this opportunity. Anyway, it's obvious you're going to say yes eventually. Eaton knows it – which is why he's hanging about in Cambridge.'

He was silent again. This felt like a trap.

'And I'm told southern Germany is very beautiful at this time of year,' Lydia continued. 'Just think of it as a lovely late-summer holiday to refresh you in time for the new term.'

Chapter 3

Eaton arrived at nine the next morning in a ministry car with a driver. Wilde helped him up the steps into the house and guided him towards the sitting room.

'Well?' he said.

'Well what?'

'You've changed your mind, haven't you, Wilde? I knew you would.'

'Am I that obvious?'

'Let's just say we both know each other pretty well, old boy. The good and the bad bits, perhaps.' He lowered his voice. 'How has Mrs Wilde taken the news – or haven't you broken it to her yet?'

'Actually, it was Lydia who persuaded me I should take it on.'

'Then good on her.'

'Wonderful the effect a couple of pairs of nylons can have.'

'Very funny. But if she really has moved your position, then perhaps we could take our coffee in the garden. Sorry to be a nuisance, Wilde, but could you give me a hand. My damned leg really plays up some days, and this is one of them.'

'The garden? I suppose you believe our house is bugged.'

'I have to tell you things which are extremely sensitive.'

'Tea, Philip?' Lydia said, as her husband guided their guest into the garden.

'Oh God, yes,' Wilde said. 'I clean forgot – we're out of coffee.'

'Tea would be delightful, Mrs Wilde. And how was the film?'

'Lovely, but Judy didn't sing at all.' She suddenly laughed. 'Oh, Philip, we've known each other the best part of a decade – can't we move on to first names? You and Tom are like a pair of snotty prep school boys. Infantile major and Ridiculous minor.'

Wilde and Eaton looked at each other questioningly. 'I think she might be right,' Wilde said.

'Yes, I think she probably is . . . Tom. Can I call you that?'

'At last!' Lydia laughed. 'The Edwardian age is finally dead and buried. Welcome to the twentieth century, boys.'

'And am I correct in thinking you are signed up for a medical degree?'

'Well, not quite, but I've applied and it all seems possible so far.'

'Given up on the poetry publishing business, eh?'

'I don't think there's much call for poetry volumes at the moment, Philip. So hopefully Barts beckons. My father worked there, which means I'm banking on them taking that into account. Nepotism goes a long way. A lot will depend on the movements of darling Tom and the hiring of a reliable nanny, of course. We're not keen on the idea of a boarding school for a five-year-old. Oh, and my esteemed husband and master has given me his permission to begin my studies. What a lucky girl I am!'

'More fool him, Lydia. All those handsome young doctors . . .'

Wilde groaned. 'As if the esteemed husband would ever have any say in the matter!' He knew this refrain by heart. Medicine was something she had wanted to do for six years, but pregnancy, motherhood and the war had conspired against her. Now, with the boy ready for school and the war over, he owed it to her to do everything in his power to ease the path. There would be plenty of others after places, of course – demobbed officers set on a vocation that had been put on hold. Still, even with all the walls to break down she must be in with a chance, and she had been assiduously reading the latest edition of *Black's Medical Dictionary* in her spare moments.

The large garden had once been a place of delight with gorgeous flowers and a little summerhouse. Like gardens up and down the land, it was now a rather forlorn-looking vegetable patch with dust, mud, nettles. And, of course, the ubiquitous Anderson shelter – a sunken semi-cylinder of zinc-coated corrugated steel – which no longer served any purpose other than as a playhouse for Johnny. There was, however, a rather mossy old teak table and chairs, where they now sat. And the day was pleasantly warm with late-summer sun.

'So what now, Eaton?'

'To start with, you and I are going to Godmanchester.'

'That doesn't tell me much.'

'I couldn't tell you about it indoors. It's our most closely guarded secret, you see. Godmanchester is where it all started, Tom. It's where we learnt that Hitler is likely to be in the Alps – southern Bavaria or the Austrian Tyrol. We had been looking for him beforehand, ever since VE Day, of course, but this was the first serious inkling we had of a location.'

'Godmanchester is a little town twenty miles or so from here. What on earth has that to do with Hitler or the Alps?'

'You won't have heard of Operation Epsilon?'

'No.'

'And nor should you have. It's top secret. Highest level.'

'Tell me more.'

'There's a large old house in Godmanchester, name of Farm Hall. At the moment it's a bit like a rest home or country hotel, with only ten guests – each one of them a brilliant German scientist. Actually, "guests" isn't quite the correct word. "Prisoners" would be more appropriate, because however comfortable their accommodation might be, they aren't checking out any time soon.'

Lydia arrived with the tea and Eaton stopped talking.

'Don't let me interrupt you, Philip,' she said, placing the tray on the table.

'If I could include you in this, Lydia my dear, I would.'

'You boys carry on with your whispering.' She smiled sweetly at them both. 'I'll go and play with Johnny – at least there'll be some rather more adult conversation with him.'

When she was out of earshot, Eaton threw Wilde a meaningful glance. 'It does seem to me, Tom, that your delightful wife is even more fiery than usual.'

'Like the rest of us, she was hoping that the war was over. Despite what you might think, she was actually rather glad to have her husband back. Anyway, we're not here to discuss my domestic woes. Tell me about these ten scientists and their relevance to Adolf Hitler's whereabouts.'

'Specifically, they're all particle physicists.'

'Ah, the atom bomb.'

'Indeed. Until recently the bomb was the best kept secret among the Allies. Anyway, Hiroshima and Nagasaki has changed everything. Now the whole world knows about it.'

'I'm failing to see what this has to do with finding Hitler.'

'Bear with me, Tom. What no one in the West knew was how far the Nazis had got with their own attempts to develop the A-bomb – and what, if anything, we could learn from them. That's where Farm Hall comes in. Among the guests being held there, we have some big and important names: Otto Hahn, for instance – the man who discovered fission. Werner Heisenberg, Paul Harteck, Max von Laue, Kurt Diebner. They are all brilliant men and they have been there since early July –

nearly two months. And do you know what? We have been listening to every word they have uttered since they arrived.'

'They're bugged?'

Eaton grinned. 'Oh yes. Every bloody room. Wires in the walls, wires beneath floorboards. They can't go anywhere without being overheard. The place was fitted out as the ultimate recording studio even before they arrived.'

'Surely they must suspect we're listening. I mean they are not stupid.'

'You'd be surprised. Clever men can be astonishingly innocent to the ways of the world. Very early on, Kurt Diebner suggested to Heisenberg that perhaps they were being bugged. Heisenberg laughed the idea off. He said the British weren't smart enough to bug them, they were too old-fashioned for such things and had learnt nothing of Gestapo methods. I suppose we should be flattered that he thinks we're less ruthless than Hitler's boys, but it really was very naive of him. Rather unworldly bunch, our German scientists.'

'And have our listeners discovered much?'

'They've discovered that the Germans had not progressed as far as we had feared, which was a great relief. We had to be sure that the Nazis didn't have a bomb secreted somewhere. There is still a lot of edginess in Moscow, Washington and London regarding the possibility that Nazism isn't quite dead and buried.'

'But you're saying the Germans were way behind us?'

Eaton nodded. 'When news of Hiroshima came through, our German guests were dumbfounded. They thought it must be some kind of massive conventional device. And then, when the true nature of the bomb became known to them, they were incredulous. Utter disbelief. They had no suspicion that the Allies had got anywhere near building one.'

'Perhaps they shouldn't have been so hasty sacking and exiling all their brilliant Jewish physicists.'

'Quite. But they still had some talented men – and apart from anything else we wanted to discover exactly what they knew in case their researches could be of assistance to our own scientists. Also, we wanted to keep them away from the Soviets.'

'Ah . . . the entente looking less than cordial, is it?'

Eaton bridled. 'Not at all. Truman alerted Stalin to the bomb when they met at Potsdam. But it's understandable that America wants to keep its edge. That's realpolitik.'

'And Hitler's part in this?' Wilde was becoming impatient. 'I'm pretty sure my mission as outlined to me has nothing to do with atom bombs.'

'Indeed not. The thing is, the men inside that building have not confined themselves to talking science. They have been talking about their wives back home, the food they have been fed, the roses in the lovely Farm Hall gardens, the fate of their friends and of Germany itself – and of course their own part in it all. Much of their conversation has been pretty mundane and dull, truth be told. Most of all they have been wondering a great deal why they are being held and what is to become of them.'

Wilde sipped his tea and offered Eaton a biscuit, which he declined.

'The scientists are mostly apolitical,' Eaton continued, 'so they don't feel they are war criminals and don't understand why they can't go home. Some of them even appear to be rather happy that the Allies won. But not all. One of them – the aforementioned Kurt Diebner – remains a hardline Nazi, though he will deny it. A couple of others are also suspect.'

'And?'

'And there have been little whispered conversations between Diebner and his loyal chums.'

'Go on.' This had to be the crunch.

'Well, as you must know, there have been plenty of newspaper stories about the fate of Hitler. You know the sort of thing: did he really die in the bunker? Has he escaped to Spain or South America by submarine? The scientists are given the newspapers every day – and one of these stories put Diebner into a rage. "How can they print this shit?" he told the rather grim young Dr Horst Korsching. "Do they really not know where he is? God in heaven, I thought these Amis and British were brighter than that." "Do *you* know where he is then, Herr Diebner?" Korsching demanded. Diebner snorted. "Of course I do. I know exactly where he is. He is in his spiritual home, waiting to rise again." Professor Korsching pressed him. "Please, Diebner, this is big news. Won't you tell me more?" "All I can say is, think of the Alpenfestung," Diebner replied after a pause. "He will be protected to the death."'

'I see. But why trust Diebner?'

'I have no doubts, but you'll get to talk to him yourself, Tom. Then you can make up your own mind.'

'Did Randy Collingham interrogate him?'

'He couldn't, because it was reckoned that to do so would give away the whole of Operation Epsilon. None of the scientists could be allowed to think they were being eavesdropped. Things have changed a bit since then, however. Firstly, there is the time factor. That conversation between Diebner and Korsching took place before Hiroshima and is now weeks old. Also, we have acquired the bulk of their secret knowledge – such as it is – about nuclear fission.'

'So can we now interrogate Diebner?'

'If we're subtle, we can. He needs to think he's not being picked out for special treatment, particularly not for anything he might have said, because that would be a clear indication they were being bugged. Which is why we will go in and interview each of the ten men individually. They will be told that every senior member of the former German regime now being held in POW camps and other holding centres, is being questioned about Hitler's whereabouts. In nine of the cases at Farm Hall, we will just go through the motions. With Diebner, we will apply the third degree.'

'It could work – if he really knows anything.'

'There are a lot of ifs.' Eaton began to struggle to his feet.

'Wait. Tell me more about the Alpenfestung? The Alpine Fortress. I've heard of it, of course.'

'Oh, fairy-tale stuff. The Nazis planned a vast mountain redoubt – most of the Austrian and German Alps from Feldkirch in the west to Graz in the east, and from Salzburg in the north to Villach in the south. The idea was that with a couple of SS divisions high in the mountains, Hitler and his faithful disciples could hold out for years until they were strong enough to drive down into Germany and rebuild the Reich. It didn't quite happen like that, of course. There are no SS divisions in the Alps. That doesn't mean Hitler doesn't have his own little citadel there. We believe Collingham and Harper died because they had found it. Now you have to pick up the baton.'

'And you think Herr Diebner might know more?'

'It has to be worth a try. He was close to the top Nazis, especially Himmler.'

'Then let's go.'

At the door, Wilde hugged Johnny and tried to kiss Lydia on the lips, but she turned away and proffered nothing but her cheek. 'Well,' he said, 'I'll see you soon.'

'If we haven't moved away.'

He slung his valise in the back of the black Riley and was climbing in beside it when he felt the touch of Lydia's hand on his shoulder. He turned around and she took him in her arms and kissed him properly. 'I'm sorry, Tom,' she said when she came up for air, her chin nestling on his shoulder. 'I know you're doing the right thing – and I'd do the same myself given half a chance. Just make sure you give Adolf a bloody nose for me – and for all the poor souls he slaughtered.'

'I will.'

'Oh, and tell the bastard what we think of him.'

Chapter 4

Just under an hour later, the Riley drew up at the side of an unremarkable road named West Street leading out of the tiny ancient town of Godmanchester. On their left stood a tall and broad manor house, its frontage open to the road but with brick walls enclosing its land on either side. 'This is Farm Hall,' Eaton said. 'Queen Anne at an educated guess. Intelligence used it as a safe house for enemy agents and various others during the show.' He tapped the driver on his shoulder. 'Wait for us here if you would.'

The driver nodded, then Wilde helped Eaton out of the car and handed him his walking stick.

Inside the building, they were welcomed into the rather spartan and smoky office of Major T. H. Rittner, the British officer in charge of the house. 'No one is quite sure what the T. H. stands for,' Eaton had confided to Wilde beforehand. 'Everyone assumes he has a Christian name, but no one knows what it is. He's simply T. H. – even to his closest friends and family.'

'Welcome, gentlemen, welcome,' the major said by way of introduction. 'CSDIC HQ told me you were coming and they have authorised me to allow you to speak with my professors.'

'CSDIC?' Wilde said, shaking the officer's hand.

'Combined Services Detailed Interrogation Centre,' Major Rittner informed him. 'The fellows behind the operation here at Farm Hall. Anyway, you must be Professor Wilde – and of course I know Mr Eaton. Can I get you tea or coffee?'

They both declined the offer and placed themselves in the seats Rittner indicated.

'I was going to suggest you use this office for your interviews,' Rittner said. 'Would that suit you?'

'Could we not talk in their own rooms?' Wilde suggested. 'They might be more comfortable, and if they are at their ease they might let something slip.'

Rittner turned to Eaton. 'What do you think? At the moment, they're all in the garden or in one of the sitting rooms playing the piano or reading. Breaking their routine will inevitably cause a stir. Whether they are accompanied one by one to their rooms or here, there will be a lot of consternation. Some of these men are pretty emotional and close to the edge. Any disruption to their daily lives raises their hopes of release, then they fall into a slough of despond when it's not forthcoming.'

'On balance, I think this office might be the right place,' Eaton said. He focused his gaze on Wilde. 'Keep it businesslike from the start. Sorry, Tom.'

'Not at all. The major's right.' Wilde had taken to Rittner instantly. He was efficient, professional and protective of his scientists. He would do all in his power to make their lives better, within reason, but would clearly brook no nonsense from them. A good officer.

'I'll make myself scarce,' Rittner said. 'I have worked hard to build a decent relationship with these men and I don't want to put it in jeopardy if they become resentful. I do have one strict condition: there must be no questions of a scientific nature. Nor must they be given the slightest hint that they are being listened to by electronic means. I hope that's clear. And please go easy on them. My professors are not war criminals; they are honourable men. Mostly, that is.'

Wilde was pretty sure that Rittner knew that Kurt Diebner was the only one who really interested them.

The major read his mind. 'Let me mark your card regarding Herr Dr Diebner. In a word, he is cunning.'

'Cunning as opposed to simply brilliant?' Wilde asked.

'Well, both of course. They're all brilliant here. I haven't the faintest idea what they're talking about when they start discussing heavy water and isotopes. But of my ten professors, Diebner is the one I have least time for. Oh, he's a charming, reasonable man to my face, but I don't for a moment believe he is sincere. I'm convinced he knows he is being listened to. At times it seems to me that he is actually talking *to* the microphone, saying things he wants us to hear – excusing himself to us for his Nazi past. Trying to make out he was never really one of them, that being a party member was simply a professional necessity. It's when he whispers that it gets interesting.'

'Is he still a Nazi?' Wilde asked.

The major shrugged. 'I honestly don't know. I'm sure you'll find him jolly friendly, but don't be fooled. He'd stab you in the kidneys when your back was turned. He did say he would never have anything more to do with the Nazi Party, but he was playing to the gallery. The fact is, he *was* a staunch party member – right up until the end. Of my ten professors, Diebner and Dr Erich Bagge were the only paid-up members of the Nazi Party.' The major paused, then smiled wistfully. 'There you have it – my honest opinion. I don't like Diebner.'

They came in a random order and Wilde and Eaton spoke to them in a mixture of German and English, depending on their fluency. Wilde explained that the questioning was merely routine and was being applied to all senior members of the German regime currently detained by the Americans and

British, which ran into hundreds of men. It was simply that the fate of Hitler had never been confirmed and they were seeking clues from anyone who might have known him or might have some clue as to his whereabouts, however tentative.

The first in was Erich Bagge, a serious, bespectacled young man in his early thirties. He wore a striped tie and his shoulders were stiff. He was clearly nervous. He shook his head vigorously when offered tea and biscuits. Wilde explained that he was not being accused of anything and nor was he being singled out in any way. It was simply a fact-finding mission.

'But I have never met Hitler,' Bagge protested.

'And no one has ever spoken to you about where he might be?'

'I have read the papers, of course. The Russians said he shot himself in the bunker with his new wife. Other newspapers since then have suggested he escaped and might be hiding abroad.'

'Thank you, Dr Bagge,' Wilde said. 'That's all we wanted to know. You may go now.'

Bagge was wringing his hands. He seemed close to tears and had not moved from his seat.

'Is something the matter, Doctor?' Wilde asked.

'This is unbearable, this captivity, sir. How long must we stay here? I am terrified for my wife and daughters. They are in the French sector, and I heard their soldiers have been raping our women in my hometown of Hechingen. What has happened to my wife and my girls? I can't bear it. Please, can you get me out of here?'

'I will make inquiries on your behalf,' Eaton said. 'Major Rittner will give me your home details.'

'Thank you, sir, thank you. You know I never wished to join the Nazi Party. It was my mother – she applied on my behalf in

1936, and I was accepted. What could I do? They were in power then. If I had quit the party I would have lost my career, probably been consigned to Dachau. I hated them.'

'We understand,' Wilde said.

Professor Werner Heisenberg was next. Rittner had told Wilde that this was the most cooperative of the professors and that he genuinely wished to help the Allies. If Diebner had whispered anything to him about Hitler's whereabouts, there would be a good chance he would reveal it. The problem was, Heisenberg and Diebner were not on the best of terms.

'If I believed Hitler was alive and if I knew where he was, I would go and kill him myself, Mr Wilde.' Heisenberg smiled warmly. 'It would be my pleasure.'

'Do you believe he is alive?'

The German scientist thought for a moment, then spread his hands. 'Of course it is possible. Likely even. There are still plenty of Nazis in Germany and other countries who would happily give him shelter. But why do you ask *me* these questions? Has someone said something?'

'As I explained,' Eaton said, 'we are questioning all senior Germans, whether or not they were ever party members. You are all just names that must be ticked off. Who knows, someone might have something useful to tell us.'

'Well, I wish you the best of luck.'

'What about your colleagues here?'

'Oh, I'm sure that the only one of us who might be able to help you is Dr Diebner. He claims to repent his Nazi past, but I don't believe a word of it. If anyone here has any idea of Hitler's whereabouts, Diebner is your man.'

'Should we tell him you said that?' Wilde asked.

'Tell him what you like. He is a despicable man.'

Wilde could see the strain in Heisenberg's eyes. This confinement was taking a toll on him. 'Is everything all right, Professor?' he asked. 'These must be difficult days for you.'

'Yes, it is hard for all of us. The hardest thing was learning that the Americans were so far ahead of us with their device. They made us look small and backward. We were all astonished when we heard about the bomb in Japan. In Germany, we were nowhere near . . .'

'Were you really trying?' Wilde said, then remembered the stricture: no science. 'Forget I asked that,' he said. For a moment, he felt for the man. He knew how humiliated Heisenberg had been by America's success and his own failure; Otto Hahn had been recorded calling him a second-rater, to his face. Perhaps the truth was that he, Heisenberg, was *surrounded* by second-raters.

'One more thing,' Eaton said. 'We know you never joined the Nazi Party, but you wanted Germany to win the war. That would have made the Nazis all-powerful, would it not?'

'I didn't want them to beat the West, but I wanted them to destroy Bolshevism.'

Wilde and Eaton looked at each other. Wilde could no longer bear to listen to the man's triangulation. Heisenberg had had every opportunity to leave Germany before the war, but had chosen to stay. 'Thank you, Professor,' Wilde said. 'That will be all.'

Heisenberg rose from his chair. 'Then I shall go back to my reading in the rose garden. It has been a pleasure to meet you two gentlemen. Life here is very tedious and anything that breaks up the monotony is welcome. I just want to get back to my work.'

Kurt Diebner was the third man to arrive.

He had a smooth, unprepossessing face and sloped forehead, a little like Himmler, but without the moustache. His hair was brushed back severely, flat to his head, and he wore round spectacles.

His eyes shifted between his two interrogators, seeking clues as to their significance, and the nature of the meeting.

'Take a seat, Dr Diebner,' Wilde said. Eaton had warned him to go easy on the man because he had threatened suicide in the past, but Wilde wasn't about to hold back. He wanted to be in control of this interview. 'I am Thomas Wilde, and my colleague is Mr Philip Eaton.'

'Good day to you, gentlemen,' Diebner said.

'And to you, Doctor. This is a straightforward chat and one that is being conducted with all senior members of the late German administration. As you can imagine, there is much interest in the fate of Adolf Hitler. Is he dead or is he alive – and if he is alive, where is he?'

'Of course. I can understand why you need to know that.'

'So we have a simple question for you all: do you have any information that might be able to assist us?'

Diebner nodded his head slowly, then his mouth broke into an unctuous little smile. 'If I were to know anything, why would I wish to help you?'

'That's easy,' Wilde said. 'The Third Reich – of which you were an integral part – is dead. It is possible you might have regrets that you ever joined the party or worked on behalf of such a monstrous regime. It is possible you might wish to become accepted in the new scientific world, free of racial distinctions and the taint of cruelty.'

'Yes, I can see that.'

'And so any assistance would go a great way towards your rehabilitation. It would serve to convince people that you regret your Nazi past. So I ask again, do you know anyhing about the fate of Adolf Hitler?'

'You have asked the same question of Bagge and Heisenberg?'

'Yes.'

'And what did they say?'

'That is confidential – except for one thing. Professor Heisenberg said that if anyone in this house had any idea about Hitler's whereabouts, it would probably be you.'

Diebner laughed, but his left eye twitched unpleasantly. 'That was nice of the professor, putting me on the spot.'

Wilde and Eaton said nothing. They waited. The office wall clock ticked in the silence.

'Very well, it is possible I do know something.'

'Go on.'

'What would I get in return?'

'Your reputation as a decent human being.'

'Yes, I see that. And that is worth a lot.'

'Well?' Wilde said.

'Very well, I believe he is alive – and that he is in southern Bavaria.'

'Why do you say that?'

'Something I heard once from Reichsführer Himmler. Have you heard of the Alpenfestung?'

'Go on.'

'It was supposed to be Hitler's alpine fortress, where, with two or three SS divisions, he would hold out for years until he had grown powerful enough to drive out Germany's enemies. Of course, it never happened. Hitler wasn't really that interested, because he thought he could still win the war. But Himmler told me that a different, greatly scaled-down version of the fortress had been planned instead. I don't know the detail, but I imagine a secret bunker like the one in Berlin. Somewhere he could hide out indefinitely, perhaps directing a guerrilla war against the occupying armies.'

'You *imagine*? So you don't know?'

'No, I don't know for certain. But I believe it is likely. From what I read in the newspapers, his so-called suicide in the Berlin bunker had all the hallmarks of being staged. It would have been easily fabricated. No, I don't believe he is dead. Does that help?'

'Not much,' Wilde said. 'Anybody could make up stuff about a secret Alpine bunker. The cheaper newspapers spout rubbish like that all the time.'

Diebner stiffened perceptibly. 'But I am not making it up. This is what Himmler told me. I remember the date. March the twelfth this year, a few weeks before the end. He even mentioned that if it came to it, Hitler's disappearance would be camouflaged by a fake suicide.'

'What about the stories that he would go abroad, to Spain or South America, by plane or submarine?'

'I don't believe Hitler would ever leave his homeland. There are still many people who love him in Bavaria and Austria. He knew he would be protected there.'

'Who might know the precise location, do you think?'

'Someone involved in the Alpenfestung planning. If any of them is alive, of course. Franz Hofer, perhaps. Is he alive? He was the Tyrol Gauleiter.'

Wilde glanced at Eaton, who shrugged. 'I could find out.'

Diebner warmed to his theme. 'Or Schellenberg,' he said. 'Walter Schellenberg, he was certainly involved. But I repeat, Himmler was specific: southern Bavaria. Hitler is there.'

Chapter 5

Lilly Marais woke just before dawn to feed her baby and to milk the cow. It was the same ritual every day, however cold the weather, however dark the mornings. At least she had had a good night's sleep, undisturbed by Nathalie. She switched on her bedside lamp and it threw out a weak yellow glow.

It was bitter this morning. Ice streaked the inside of the tiny window. She huddled into her threadbare dressing gown, combed back her long golden hair with her fingers, then crossed the room to the old apple box that served as a crib. There was a good little cot in the house – the baby pink one her own mother had used all those years ago – but that was forbidden her. It was an unpleasant sanction, but Lilly shrugged it off; the important thing was that her baby was healthy and thriving.

Her breasts were swollen, ready to give the child her first feed of the day. She reached down to pick her up from the blankets, but then she froze.

Nathalie wasn't there.

Were her eyes deceiving her? The light was very poor. She picked up the tangled pile of blankets, but they were empty. Her fingernails scraped frantically at the rough edges of the wooden box, as though the baby was curled up in a corner. Where was she?

Perhaps her mother had come to collect her. Lilly left the box and went to the door. Lifting the latch, she stepped outside onto the short landing.

'Mama?' she called down the staircase.

There was no reply, and yet she could hear sounds from below, and the lights were on. She called again, louder this time. 'Mama, is Nathalie with you?' Unslippered, her feet icy cold on the bare boards, she hurried downstairs to the kitchen. Her mother was at the range, stirring a pot. She did not look around as her daughter entered the room.

'Mama?' Lilly said, perturbed by her mother's failure to respond. 'Where is Nathalie?'

'Ask your father,' the woman said, still without turning around. Her voice was flat. Something was not right.

'Is she with him? Where is he? Where has he taken her?'

'He's in the yard.'

Lilly felt her heart beating faster. Her mother's refusal to look at her told her that something was very wrong. They had had so many fights these past months. Her father's refusal to let her use the family cot was just one of their many points of conflict. One day, her father had even spat on the ground in front of the baby.

Her boots were in the corner, but she didn't wait to put them on. Instead she opened the back door onto the paved yard between the house and the smithy where her father worked.

The first faint winter light was just beginning to emerge across the icy field that bordered the yard on the east side. Two electric wall lights added a cold glow to the mud-streaked cobblestones.

Papa was there, in the centre of the yard, standing with his hands on his hips, legs astride as if he had been waiting all night for her. He wore his sleeveless leather jerkin, his muscular blacksmith's arms bare despite the cold. Those huge muscles that had once seemed so safe and protective now felt alien and threatening. Nor was her father alone. Thirty or more men clustered around him, as well as a few women. She knew them all; they were all residents of the commune. She had known them all her life. Some of them had been her school friends. She felt faint and nauseous. She thought she was going to be sick. There was still no sign of Nathalie.

The man at her father's right side took a step forward. He was the mayor, Jean Étienne.

'Lilly Marais,' he said. 'You have been tried by the people of Ste-Estelle-sur-Seine and found guilty of the crime of treason and unlawful congress with the enemy, against the state of France and the good name of this commune.'

'Where is my daughter? Where is Nathalie?' She saw her father glancing across the courtyard. What was he looking at? Oh God, where was her baby? Why was he looking at the well?

Lilly Marais was twenty. She knew that she was beautiful; with her flaxen hair and clear skin. She was the fairest maid in all Ste-Estelle-sur-Seine, perhaps the whole of Normandy. She had always attracted the most attention from the boys in her year and even the older ones. More than that, many had commented on her sweet nature, even the other girls and women, and she had enjoyed popularity both in school and the wider community.

They had still seemed to love her when she met the dashing German officer. Julius had charmed her, taken her dancing in the officers' mess and to good restaurants in Rouen, given her a gold necklace. He had made sure that she never went hungry, by providing her with wonderful foodstuffs, most of which she had passed on to her family and neighbours. They had been happy enough to accept her largesse, and smilingly called her German lover 'the generous one'. No one had insulted her. Not to her face at least.

But that was then, and this was now. The Germans had been driven from France by the Americans and British, and her lover was gone.

How quickly the worm turned.

Now she was scorned openly. No one in the commune spoke to her, not even her father, the blacksmith. Only Mama showed her any affection, but that was done discreetly when Papa was not around.

What no one cared about was the nature of her relationship with the baby's father. It was true love and he had promised to marry her, but that carried no weight in Ste-Estelle-sur-Seine. The change had come about six months ago, three weeks before Nathalie's birth, when the Allies came and the Germans lost ground. Lilly was heartbroken. Not because of the arrival of the British, but because Julius was gone – and he hadn't even seen her child. How he would have loved his beautiful daughter.

The mayor indicated a wooden chair in the centre of the courtyard. She hadn't noticed it. 'Sit down, Lilly Marais.'

She made no move. Her eyes were pleading. 'I beg you, where is my baby? Where is Nathalie?'

'You will sit.'

'My baby! My baby! Please, where is she?' Please God, why had Papa been looking at the well?

'That's enough. The bastard child is where it should be.' It was her father speaking now. He strode forward. He was not a tall man, but he was immensely strong. He picked her up as if she was an infant and thrust her down on the wooden chair.

Two women were coming forward: the stout figures of Françoise Dupont and Nicole Étienne. Her father was behind the chair now, holding her arms back so that she couldn't rise and couldn't resist.

'No, no.' She was crying. She knew what they were going to do but she didn't care about her hair. All she cared about was Nathalie.

The women were powerful and rough, their skin calloused by physical work. They had the strength of peasants who had laboured hard all their lives. Their hands could twist a chicken's neck or wield a knife to a pig's throat without apparent effort.

Françoise Dupont grasped her hair at the back and hacked at it with shears. She was the baker's wife and Lilly had always thought of her as kind-hearted. Nicole Étienne was the mayor's wife. Lilly had never liked her. She had a cut-throat razor in her hand and as Lilly's golden tresses fell, Nicole shaved her head close, with no soap or oil to smooth the blade's savage passage across her scalp. The blade cut into her skin, taking flesh with the hair. Lilly cried out but no one moved to help her.

And yet they had all collaborated in one way or another. All had accepted German rule. No one had joined the Resistance – at least not until a few weeks before the Allies came ashore. All had smiled at the German soldiers when they encountered them in the street. All she had done was fall in love. And the romances she read told her that true love knew no national frontiers.

More women were approaching, crowding around, mobbing her, calling her foul names, spitting at her or at the ground by her bare feet. One of them had a pair of scissors and began cutting her dressing gown and nightdress away, exposing her breasts. Others grasped the material in their bony fingers and ripped at it, shredding it, pulling it away from her slim body until she was completely naked.

She was shivering, not from the cold but from fear for Nathalie. What had they done with her? Why had Mama said nothing in the kitchen? Why didn't she stop this? Why had she allowed Nathalie to be taken?

'Now stand up, Lilly Marais,' the mayor said. Her father pulled her to her feet, still holding her hands tight behind her back. Her fair hair was strewn on the ground. Her bare body – the body that the German officer loved – was open to all the people. She felt blood trickling down her forehead, into her eyes and down her cheeks.

The mayor took something from one of the other men. Lilly saw that it was a wooden placard with a piece of string attached at both ends. It had four words: *Nazi whore, collaborator, slut.* Without ceremony, this was thrust over her head, so that it hung around her neck, resting on her breasts.

'Now march,' the mayor said. He swept his arm wide to indicate all the assembled village folk. 'Let the good people of Ste-Estelle-sur-Seine see your shame. Let them know what becomes of those who defile themselves.'

Her father released her hands, then pushed her in the back. 'Walk, damn you. You are no longer my daughter. I disown you from this day forward and you are banished from ever entering my home again.'

She clasped her hands together and fell to her knees in front of her father and the mayor, and the women with the shears and the razor and the scissors. 'I implore you, where is my child?'

'You will never see her again,' Jean Étienne said. 'That is our sentence.'

Chapter 6

August 1945

As Tom Wilde and Philip Eaton travelled to London by ministry car, the MI6 man explained all he knew about Walter Schellenberg. 'He was Himmler's sidekick, the worst sort of Nazi. Smooth, handsome, arrogant. Whatever he says to excuse himself, he must have known of all the atrocities. He was up to his neck in it. We call him The Shell – because that's what he is, an empty shell. A hollow man.'

Wilde allowed Eaton to talk on, but in fact he already knew a great deal about the German from his own work with the OSS. Schellenberg had risen through the ranks of the SD secret service – the Sicherheitdienst. By the end of the war, he was an SS-Brigadeführer and head of foreign intelligence, answerable only to Himmler and Hitler.

'I suggest we try appealing to his vanity,' Eaton said. 'These types love to feel important. Play it by ear, see what works best. Remember, he's desperate to save his own skin, so we have leverage.'

'I'd like to do it alone,' Wilde said.

'Are you sure?'

'I'll make him believe I'm on his side, that I understand that like a good soldier he was only obeying orders. One man can form a bond with another. Two men will always look official. Can I try it? If I get nowhere alone, join me.'

'As you will. Remember, this interview is a very special privilege. He has been in London since July and no more than one or two people have been allowed to interrogate him. He is the source of much of what we know about the inner workings of the SD.'

It had been mere chance that Schellenberg happened to be in custody in London. When Diebner referred to him at Farm Hall, he could have had no idea whether he was alive or dead, let alone that he was held by the British.

'I believe he's quite cooperative,' Eaton continued. 'Singing like a canary to save himself from the noose. He has been desperately presenting himself as a peacemaker for a long time now – even before the war ended he saw which way the wind was blowing and tried to negotiate a treaty.'

'Did Randy Collingham talk to him?'

'No, he didn't have that luxury. Look, you might get on with Schellenberg, but he's slippery as hell. When he was first arrested in Sweden he was telling anyone who would listen that Himmler had had Hitler poisoned. Then he ditched that story when investigators demanded evidence. He considers himself an intellectual, which I suppose he is – up to a point. He's a university chap like you, Tom.'

'History?'

'Law. He also speaks fluent English. He has never been popular with my office because he organised the capture of two of our chaps at Venlo in Holland in the early months of the war. Agreed to meet our men in the guise of a member of the anti-Hitler underground, then grabbed them. Egregious behaviour on neutral territory, but that's the Nazis for you.'

'Not cricket, eh?' Wilde raised a mocking eyebrow. MI6 would have found it difficult to live down the abduction of two of their officers in such circumstances.

The Shell had been brought by car from his sparse cell at Camp 020 in west London to the OSS offices on Grosvenor Street. He was sitting alone in a room that was bare save for a table and three hard-backed chairs. An armed Marine stood inside the door, legs akimbo, hands behind his back.

This large building had been ill-equipped and almost deserted when it was set up as the OSS London bureau in the summer of 1942. Wilde and Phillips and the other founders of the operation had rattled around, but, within a couple of years, the place was so packed there was scarcely enough room to squeeze in another typewriter.

Now, with demobilisation, the place was thinning out again. It was a good location for a quiet interview.

The German was wearing civilian clothes – a light grey or beige suit, which was a little too big for his slender frame. He had a plain tie, white shirt and black shoes that shone. He looked ridiculously young, his dark hair oiled back from his forehead like a matinee idol, but he didn't look well.

Perhaps it was his treatment in captivity that was wearing him down.

Wilde had visited Camp 020, and he knew that it was a harsh place. Captured German agents had been housed there during the war, and now it was used to confine various senior Nazis for prolonged interrogation. He knew that some of the techniques used there didn't stop very short of torture: prisoners were bawled at, subjected to long periods of isolation in darkness or glaring light and given cold baths. Wilde had heard, too, of mock executions.

Now, here in the more pleasant surroundings of Grosvenor Street, he introduced himself. 'I am Professor Thomas Wilde of Cambridge University but today I will be asking you a few questions on behalf of the Office of Strategic Services.'

The German struggled up from his chair and bowed briskly. 'It is my pleasure to meet you.'

'Likewise,' Wilde said, though the word stuck in his craw. Whatever Schellenberg's alleged efforts to broker a peace deal and save concentration camp inmates towards the end of the war, he had been right-hand man to Himmler. Nothing could excuse that. He turned to the Marine. 'Wait outside if you would, soldier.'

'Yes, sir.' The Marine did a sharp about-turn, exited the room and closed the door behind him.

'Now, Herr Schellenberg, sit down.'

'Thank you, sir.'

They sat opposite each other. Wilde noticed that the room stank of sweat, the sort of smell you get in a sickbay when men are feverish. 'Would you like water or a cup of tea?'

'That would be kind, sir. Tea, if I may.'

'I'll have it fixed in a short while.'

'You know, Professor, I have heard a great deal about you. You were famous at Prinz-Albrecht-Strasse. We had a thick file on you in our SD records. I recall you had made a deadly enemy of our Gestapo leader, Heinrich Müller. He discussed organising an effort to assassinate you.'

'Well, that didn't go too well, did it. What became of Herr Müller?'

Schellenberg shrugged and his thin, bow-shaped lips formed a half-smile which made him look unpleasantly self-satisfied. A film of sweat coated his broad brow. 'I have no idea. Is that why you're here – to find Müller?'

'No. I want to find Adolf Hitler. Tell me, Herr Schellenberg, how do you like to be addressed these days? General or plain mister?'

'I would like to be called Herr Doctor, if that suits you. I am a doctor of law and proud of my doctorate. I hope one day to enter academia if I am allowed. I am not so proud of having been an SS officer.'

'Are you being treated well? If you don't mind my saying so, you look rather ill. Have you been seen by doctors since you arrived in England?'

'Oh yes, I have been seen by doctors. Apparently I am *der hypochonder*, you know – feigning sickness.'

'Hypochondriac.'

'Yes, that is the word. But you are correct – I am ill. I have had a severe gut problem for years, but it is worse now. So I hope you will excuse me if I need the lavatory in a hurry.'

'Of course. It is two doors away along the corridor.'

'Thank you. My captors have no idea how hard this imprisonment is for me. I am at the edge of despair.'

'I'm sorry about that. In other circumstances, I would suggest we adjourn this meeting until a later date, but I am on a tight schedule.'

'That is all right, Professor – I would much rather be here with you than in my cell at Latchmere House. I think I should be in a hospital, not a prison.'

'What are the rations like?'

'Not good.'

Wilde nodded. 'OK, well, if you answer my questions faithfully, I'll go easy on you today – and I'll have some good food brought for your lunch. That might help to build you up a bit.'

'Thank you, sir.'

'So tell me – Hitler?'

'I believe he is dead.'

'What makes you say that?'

'It was announced. He died in the bunker.'

'Perhaps that was a carefully constructed lie. If Hitler was escaping somewhere it would be in his interests to make out he had killed himself.' Wilde handed his clean white handkerchief to Schellenberg, who thanked him and mopped his brow.

'Yes, it would be in his interests, but I sincerely hope he is dead. The world has surely had enough of him.'

'You swore allegiance to the man.'

'Like millions of others. But I was a young fool, only twenty-two when I enlisted in the SS, and I was carried along on a wave. Which among us can claim to have made no errors at such an age?'

Wilde watched the man. He seemed genuine enough, like a puppy keen to please its new master. And yet his hands moved constantly, just below the table. His voice had a curious metallic tone and his English, though good, was stiff.

'I would not call complicity in mass murder a mere *error*,' Wilde said.

'Professor Wilde, please. I joined the party because I needed the money. My family was not rich. Anyway, I was no more than an office boy when those terrible decisions were being made. Yes, I rose to great power by the end of the war. But by then the worst of the damage had already been done by other men. Talk to Count Bernadotte, if you wish. You know the Swedish diplomat? He will tell you I was instrumental in negotiating for the lives of thousands of Jews.'

'I'm not here to talk about that.'

'No, no, of course not. You want to talk about Hitler. Well, hopefully he has gone to the devil, his maker.' Suddenly, the German grinned. 'Would you not prefer to talk about Coco Chanel? Many people seem intrigued by my love affair with darling Coco.'

Wilde sighed and allowed the man a conspiratorial smile. 'I'm sure it's a fascinating story, but perhaps some other time.'

'Our affair lasted two years. Did you know that? Of course, she was a little old for me, but she was still beautiful. Perhaps you think it ungentlemanly of me to draw comparisons between our ages . . .'

Wilde raised his hand, palm forward. 'Enough, Dr Schellenberg, you're straying from the subject.'

'Forgive me.'

'You are an educated man, so it must have pained you to have to work with Hitler and his mindless thugs. Wouldn't you like to help me bring him to justice – the last chapter in this sorry tale of cruelty and murder? I know you have already done a great deal to assist the British and Americans. Finding Hitler would be a final feather in your cap, would it not? Proof that you are truly no longer a Nazi. When you come to trial for war crimes, it would go a long way towards mitigating your sentence.'

'I understand, Professor. The thing is, I had very little to do with Hitler on a day-to-day basis. I don't think he liked me much. Intellectuals made him feel uneasy. A little inadequate or inferior, perhaps.'

'You're still skirting the issue.'

'The point is I was not in the bunker in his last days. You need to speak to those who were there: Bormann, Müller if you can find him, two or three generals such as Jodl, Krebs and Burgdorf. Linge, his servant, and Kempka, his driver. And the secretaries, of course. I don't know what became of them? Did any survive, or did the Soviets slaughter them?'

Wilde had a small notepad and pencil and made a note of the names. He looked up at Schellenberg. 'Actually, Herr Doctor,

I don't want to talk with you about the bunker. I want to know about the Alpenfestung. You were deeply involved in that . . .'

He waved the very concept of involvement away with an extravagant display of his hands, like swatting flies. Then he laughed. 'The Alpenfestung? Do you believe in that?'

'I don't know. You tell me.'

'Nothing happened. Hitler did not want anything done about it. He was determined to defend Berlin and fight to the end. That's what I was told.'

'From what I understand, you were involved in the original Alpenfestung planning on the orders of Himmler. I believe it was first proposed at the end of 1943, after the defeats at Stalingrad and Kursk, when it became clear Germany could not win the war. Is that correct?'

'That is essentially the case. But—'

'Forget the buts for the moment. The idea was that you would hold the mountains between southern Bavaria, through Austria to the Italian border, and that it could be held with a relatively small army of highly trained, dug-in troops. This redoubt would have huge stocks of food and munitions and prepare for the long haul.'

'Yes, but it was all fake. We produced plans and Goebbels let them be leaked to the world. It was done to demoralise our enemies.'

And it had worked, Wilde knew. The Allied powers had fallen for the deception and it had delayed the advance of the Sixth Army in the south. In the end, resistance by the Nazis was remarkably light in Bavaria and Austria. However, that was not necessarily the end of the story. 'You see, Herr Dr Schellenberg, I readily accept your statement that the redoubt wasn't built, but that doesn't mean the work didn't start. And, if nothing else, the Nazis were extremely good at constructing and concealing reinforced concrete fortifications.'

Schellenberg nodded. 'It is a fair point, sir.'

'Well? Is there a Führerbunker in the Alps?'

'Not to my knowledge.'

'And yet you were the man charged by Himmler with planning this thing.'

'But nothing happened!'

'Just for a moment imagine that something had happened. Where would the effort have been concentrated? At Hitler's Berghof at Obersalzberg?'

'That would have been foolish. All Germany's enemies knew about the place. We would have sought somewhere far better hidden and more difficult to attack.'

Of course they would. Schellenberg wiped the sweat from his forehead again. It was time for a break. 'I'll get that tea,' Wilde said. 'Or perhaps you would prefer coffee.'

'Yes, coffee, please. I would like that. Thank you.'

They had coffee and they went over the questions for another hour. Then they had lunch of pork chops and fried potatoes, accompanied by a glass of wine. The German plainly appreciated the food and drink, but Wilde realised he was getting nowhere. After lunch, he questioned him further and harder. Schellenberg knew little of use. The Alpenfestung had never happened. Full stop.

In frustration, Wilde leant across the table.

'Give me something, Herr Dr Schellenberg. Give me something that will have made this day worthwhile. Something that will help persuade your judges that you did your best to assist me in discovering the true fate of Adolf Hitler. You know the alternative.' The threat was implicit. It was time to get tough.

Schellenberg didn't reply, but his hands were shaking.

Wilde pushed his face closer. 'I've treated you well, but enough is enough. This is your last chance.'

The German general closed his eyes and for a moment Wilde wondered whether he was weeping. The man's breathing was shallow and fast.

'Schellenberg?'

He opened his eyes and blinked. 'Do you have a pen and paper, sir?'

Wilde handed over his notepad and pencil. Schellenberg took the pencil in his trembling right hand and began to write, then handed the notepad back to Wilde.

There were three words: *August Jaeger, Almrosen.*

'This is a name and a place, right?'

Schellenberg nodded. 'Jaeger is a cousin of mine, on my mother's side. He lives in the village of Almrosen, just across the border in Austria, but not so far from Garmisch. He is a mountain guide. In the First World War he was a hero in the Alpine war on the Italian front.'

'And?'

'In June 1944 after the Allies invaded Normandy, Himmler became very agitated and wanted solid plans for a retreat to the Alps. He wanted to know where it would be best to set up headquarters for an Alpenfestung. I suggested my cousin as an adviser. No one knows those mountains better than August Jaeger.'

'So what happened?'

Schellenberg shook his head. 'As far as I know nothing happened. I was no longer involved in the Alpenfestung. I had more important work to do.'

'As far as you know . . .'

'Indeed. It is possible someone *did* contact him and ask for his thoughts. He would certainly be able to make suggestions for places where Hitler could hide.'

'Then I guess I had better go and talk to your cousin. Do you have a more specific address for him? House name or number? Street?'

'No. But Almrosen is tiny. Everyone in the village will know him and his house is the largest. But please, Professor, do not tell him or anyone else that I provided his name. I hope one day to return to civilian life and I am certain there will be resentment aimed at those who have helped the Allies.'

Wilde rose to leave. 'I'll see how it goes, Dr Schellenberg. But I'm not making any promises.'

The Shell also stood. His whole body shaking, he reached across to give the sweat-soaked handkerchief back to his interrogator.

'Keep it,' Wilde said.

Chapter 7

Mozes Heck had been Albert Rothstein's constant companion for four days. It was the way he held his cigarette and the way he looked at the canteen food that confirmed Heck's interest. That and the casual throwaway line of Jerzy, the boy with the camera.

Making friends with Rothstein had been difficult at first. Heck had used the direct approach. 'Hey, what is your name? You always seem to be alone,' he had said by way of introduction as they waited in line at the food counter.

Rothstein had shied away, startled at the unwanted intrusion on his personal space.

Heck was undeterred. He smiled, then clapped Rothstein on the shoulder. A gesture of understanding between two young men who had suffered the horrors of war. 'Don't worry, friend. We're all on the same side now. No one's going to hurt you. No guards here.'

They were in the Apfelwald displaced persons camp, located in the middle of a forest near Garmisch. It was one of hundreds of refuges dotted around Europe. Some were the size of towns and all were temporary home to the millions of people thrown to the winds by the war.

Many of those living here had been slave labourers interned in concentration camps, others were survivors of the death camps.

Volunteers from the Red Cross and the United Nations Relief and Rehabilitation Administration worked tirelessly to improve their lot. And things were getting better. Having lived through the horrors of the Nazi regime, the people here did their utmost to recreate some sort of normality. They planted flowers in pots and created intricate hanging baskets bursting with blooms. Their barrack-room accommodation began to feel almost homely.

In the months since liberation, the former prisoners had put on weight and had started to live and love again. But where would they go from here? When would their predicament end? 'Excuse me,' Rothstein had said when Mozes Heck first approached him. 'I just wish to get my food and eat alone, if you don't mind.'

'Don't be like that. Come on, what's your name?' Heck asked again. He had noted the accent; Rothstein was undoubtedly German.

'My name is Rothstein,' the man conceded with a sigh. 'Albert Rothstein. But honestly, I don't want to talk right now.'

'I'm Mozes Heck. Call me Mo.' His voice softened. 'Where were you held, Albert? You were in a KZ, right?'

'Auschwitz-Birkenau in Poland. Have you heard of it? Now if you'll excuse me, I don't wish to talk anymore . . .'

'Everyone's heard of Auschwitz, Albert. That must have been terrible for you.'

That was how it began, but not how it ended. Mozes Heck had been persistent. He had a big voice and a powerful personality that could win people over, however aloof they might be at first. Rothstein could not resist him

Over the next two days, Heck inveigled his way into Rothstein's life. Soon they were taking meals together in the canteen and drinking beers together late into the night. Rothstein gave up his attempts to shrug off his new companion's attentions and after a while he actually seemed to enjoy Heck's company.

Their conversation had become easy and light. Heck made jokes, laughed a lot about the needy Amis, the raping Reds, the stiff Brits and the sexually inadequate Nazis, and slapped

Rothstein on the back. Occasionally, he punched him gently on the upper arm to make a point. They talked of the cowboy film presently showing in the camp cinema and decided to watch it together. It was called *Stagecoach* and starred a young man named John Wayne. Afterwards, they discussed its finer points into the early hours.

They smoked cigarettes together and Heck spoke of his life before the war. He was from Amsterdam, he said, his father had been a doctor and his mother was a writer of pulp fiction, published under the name of Sam Heck, because it sounded international and helped her sales in America. He had two younger sisters, who would now be nineteen and seventeen, and a brother – the baby of the family – who would be twelve. They were well off financially and could have emigrated before the Nazi invasion, but they kept putting it off and then, when the Germans arrived, it was too late.

They had been carted away by the Nazis in the middle of the night. Heck knew from friends that they had been taken to the Westerbork transit camp in northern Holland, but after that the trail had gone cold. As far as he knew, none of them had survived. And yet he lived in hope that he was wrong, that one day a notice would go up on the Apfelwald notifications board saying that one of them was alive and was trying to make contact. It was a faint hope.

'And how did *you* survive, Mo?'

Heck waved the question away. 'Ah, that is a story for another time. But what about you and your family, Albert? Did any of them make it through the war?'

Rothstein did not seem keen on the subject, but Heck was insistent. 'Come on, Albert, at least tell me where you are from? You're German, yes?'

'Yes, from Stuttgart. I was a Lutheran, but I was classified as Jewish; my mother was a Jew on both sides of her family, whereas my father was a Christian, his Jewish mother having converted. I was brought up a Lutheran, so I know little of my Jewish heritage. The prayers, the festivals, the workings of the synagogue . . . I do not know them. Nor am I circumcised. My father would not allow it.'

'So being Christian didn't protect you from the fucking Nazis?'

'No. The law said I was a Mischling Jew, so that was that. I was put on a transport east; first to the ghetto in Krakow, then later on to Auschwitz.'

'And your parents?'

Rothstein shrugged, then looked down at the ground and slowly shook his head. 'Same story as you, I think, Mo.'

'Have you been back there – to Stuttgart?'

'Yes, but there was nothing there. No family, the house destroyed. I walked to Munich because I had cousins there, but they were gone, too.'

'Tell me about Auschwitz, Albert.'

Again he shook his head and was silent.

'Ah, no one wants to talk about it,' Heck said. 'And no one wants to listen. No one wants to hear our stories. They want to put all the misery behind them and get on with their lives. They want to get married, have babies, plan their futures in Palestine or New York or wherever. But not me. I want to know these stories, for I believe they must be heard.' He pulled out his leather-bound journal from his bag of khaki webbing and flicked through it. 'This is history and someone must write it down so that it is not forgotten. Surely you agree?'

'Yes, Mo, you are right. But not now. Maybe another day.'

They were sitting with their backs to a wooden shack in the far corner of the DP camp. Men, women and children ambled past without looking at them. Both were smoking American cigarettes. Heck was in tattered trousers held up by a length of cord tied around his waist. He had a grubby open-necked white shirt and his sleeves rolled up to show his tanned arms. Unlike Rothstein, he had no tattoos.

Rothstein wore an old suit, jacket buttoned up despite the warmth of the summer's day.

'Show me the mark, Albert. Your number.'

Rothstein frowned. 'What do you mean?'

'Your Auschwitz number. The tattoo on your forearm. I want to see it. Please. I need to witness these things. I need to hear your testimony – what you saw there. The murders, the Zyklon B, the crematoria.'

Without waiting for Rothstein to comply, Heck stubbed out his cigarette into the ground and then grasped Rothstein's arm and rolled back the sleeves of his jacket and shirt. The tattoo was there – B9658. Heck peered closely at the mark. 'It looks almost new, as though it were done yesterday.'

'It was done two years ago.'

'It is a badge of honour for you, and a badge of shame for your SS tormentors.'

'I suppose so.'

'I do not have one, but perhaps my family did. Perhaps not. Perhaps they went straight to the gas chamber. I still have no idea of their fate. Did you ever come across anyone called Heck at Auschwitz-Birkenau, Albert?'

Rothstein shook his head and tried to draw his hand back, but Heck was holding him in a firm grip.

'No,' he said. 'I knew no one called Heck. Now, please, Mo, let me go. You're hurting me.'

Heck ignored the plea. 'You've come out of it well, Albert. You must have put on quite a bit of weight. How long were you there?'

'Two years, as I have already told you. I was very thin and sick at liberation. I think I came close to death. You cannot imagine the horrors of the place.'

'Were you whipped?'

He hesitated, then shook his head.

'What were you doing there at Auschwitz? I believe they made you work hard for your gruel if you were considered strong enough not to be gassed. What was your work? Tell me about your days. I will write the history of these years and I need to hear your testimony. Don't be shy with me. Tell me everything.'

'I've had enough of this, Mo. You said you were my friend, but you are hurting me.'

'No, no, tell me about your work at the camp. Your labour day by day. Were you *Sonderkommando*, or shipped out to one of the factories?'

'I . . . I worked in a mine.'

'Mining what, may I ask?'

'Coal. I shovelled coal into carts at the Janina mine at Libiaz, two hours walk to the north-east of Auschwitz. It was so cold in the winter and my shoes were falling apart.'

'Now recite Kaddish for me.'

Rothstein looked uncomfortable. 'What is that? I do not know what that is.'

'Why, Kaddish is the Jewish prayer for the dying. Every Jew can say it. How can you not know what it is?'

'But I told you, I was not brought up a Jew. I am Lutheran but of Jewish stock.'

'Of course, I forgot. How foolish of me.'

'I have had enough of this, Mo. You are treating me abominably. Please, let go of my arm.'

'Take off your jacket and shirt, Albert. I want to see what those damned Nazis did to you. What scars they left on your poor young body.'

'I don't know what you mean?'

'The Nazis, they hit everyone, they whip you and beat you with rifle butts. You must have suffered many injuries. Everyone did. Let me see the scars.'

'No, I wasn't whipped.'

'I want you to strip to your waist, that's all. I want to see your whole upper body. Will you do that for me? This is important. I am going to write a work of great scholarship. I need the evidence.'

Rothstein managed at last to pull his arm away from Heck's grip and began scrabbling to his feet. 'No, you are crazy. Why would you ask such a thing?'

Heck, too, was on his feet now. He flipped open his bag and pulled out a pistol. He thrust it up close to Rothstein's face. 'Just do it, Albert. If you are who you say, you have nothing to hide from me.'

'I won't do it.' He was holding his arms tight around his body, as though he was naked already and trying desperately to cover his modesty or protect himself from humiliation.

Heck pushed his face within an inch of Rothstein's and bared his teeth. 'You see I have a suspicious mind. It is difficult not to have doubts about people when your family has been wiped from the face of the earth. And you know, Albert Rothstein, your tattooed number looks very fresh and clear. I have seen other Auschwitz tattoos and they are not so neat. There are other things about you, too. The way you hold your cigarette, like a Hollywood movie star. KZ survivors hide their cigarette, cupped in the palm of their hand, because smoking in the camps was punishable by death and they're still scared. They will always be scared, if they live to be a hundred. Also, you don't *look* at other people's food. But all the survivors do. They can't take their eyes off someone else's plate or bowl, especially if they think they have been given a larger ration in the canteen. It's natural when you have been fed nothing but a half-litre of cabbage water every day for two years.'

'I have fought against these things, Mo. I am trying hard to get back to normal. I want to rid myself of the nightmares, not keep reliving them.'

Heck ignored his protestations. 'And then there is my little friend Jerzy. Do you know him, the boy with the camera?'

'No. I know no little boy.'

'He knows you. He remembers you from Krakow. He says you weren't one of the Jews being marched to the transport. He says you were Waffen-SS and you looked very smart in your uniform. He says you smiled at him and gave him a sweet from your pocket, then carried on driving the Jews to their graves.'

Rothstein was sweating now, his eyes swivelling, looking for a way out of this, somewhere to run. But he had already worked out that Mozes Heck was a great deal fitter, faster and stronger than him. There were plenty of people around, but no one who could help him. 'This is nonsense,' he said. 'Utter nonsense. Why would you listen to such things from a stupid boy.'

Heck pushed the muzzle hard into Rothstein's damp forehead. 'Take off your shirt and jacket or I will shoot you like a dog.'

The man who called himself Rothstein backed off from the gun, and suddenly twisted into a run, but Heck was much too quick for him and brought him down with a flying tackle to the legs. He pulled the gun back and smacked it hard into Rothstein's temple with the butt. There was an audible crack and the German flopped forward, stunned by the blow. Heck knelt behind him and dragged off his jacket, then tore the shirt away and grasped his white left arm.

'What is this, Rothstein?'

He gripped his prey's head in an armlock.

Rothstein's mouth was open, his eyes scrunched up. 'My head,' he gasped. 'You hit me.'

'Did I?' He smacked him again on the head, this time on the other temple. Then he held the muzzle of the pistol to the second tattoo on his arm. This one was higher up from the tattooed number, near the elbow. There were two letters: AB. 'This looks like your blood type, Rothstein, or whatever your true name is. Why do you have your blood type tattooed there? As far as I know only the Waffen-SS have their blood group on their arm.'

'Please, I beg you. You are mistaken . . . I never hurt a soul.'

Heck pulled the trigger and the German SS soldier screamed.

Chapter 8

Wilde looked at the scene with astonishment and horror. His hand went to the shoulder holster, concealed beneath his jacket, and his fingers gripped the butt of the pistol. Then he changed his mind and slid the weapon back.

He turned to Colonel Appache at his side. 'What was that?'

'That was Lieutenant Heck shooting someone.'

They were twenty yards from the unfolding incident and Wilde watched with incredulity. Now he was moving forward. He pushed past the man with the smoking pistol and knelt beside the injured man. He was screaming and groaning, clutching the remains of his shattered arm as blood flowed into the dust.

'Get help, Colonel.'

Appache hesitated as though he balked at the thought of being ordered about by a college professor, but then he nodded and bustled away. Wilde bunched up the injured man's shirt and tied it as a tourniquet around his upper arm to staunch the blood. There was little more he could do. 'Hang on, Mister,' he said in German. 'Help's on its way.'

He was in the shadow of the gunman, Lieutenant Heck, and turned to get a proper look at him. Heck had the darkest, thickest eyebrows – *eyebrow* – that Wilde had ever seen. It ranged across his brow like an unbroken hedge of black foliage. He was looking down at them, the gun held casually in his right hand. He was grinning.

'You're Heck?'

'I guess you're Wilde.'

It was not an auspicious meeting.

'What in the name of all that's holy have you done here?'

'This man—' he waved his weapon in the direction of the crumpled bleeding mess of Rothstein '—was posing as a refugee, but he is SS. He was trying to escape so I shot him. He had an SS blood tattoo, so I removed it for him. Anyone would have done the same.'

The whole scene had a surreal quality. On a dusty patch not fifty yards away, a group of boys were playing football and didn't bother to stop at the sound of gunfire. Men, women and children strolled past going about their business without taking any heed of a man bleeding and groaning in pain. Not far away, a woman squatted down to piss without even lifting her skirt, let alone find somewhere private.

Wilde couldn't take it all in. He had come here to this camp with Colonel Appache from the nearby Counter Intelligence Corps base in Garmisch, having flown from RAF Northolt to the US-held airfield at Schongau. It now seemed that this man with the smoking gun and the insane eyebrow was the one he was supposed to team up with.

Mozes Heck stepped forward and gave the bleeding man a casual kick in the ribs.

'Have you lost your mind, Lieutenant?'

Colonel Appache appeared at the corner of the building. Two men were with him, carrying a stretcher, and they immediately took charge, assessing the wounded man and then gently easing him onto the canvas and raising him up.

Heck laughed. 'Well, I've got an appetite. I think I'll go and find some lunch.'

'Wait, Heck,' Appache said. 'This is Professor Wilde.'

'Yes, we've just met.' He shoved the pistol back in its pack then offered his hand.

Wilde took it. What else, he wondered, was he supposed to do? Apart from the remarkable eyebrow and the lack of concern over having shot a man, the other thing he noticed was the clipped accent.

One of the camp residents came up to see what was going on. He looked vaguely interested as the stretcher bearers went about their business, then grunted and wandered away. At last Wilde began to understand; such sights had become commonplace to these people.

Death and pain had become normal everyday occurrences.

'Did you really need to shoot him, Lieutenant Heck?' Wilde said.

The Dutchman's smile broadened. 'No. I could have strangled him or cut his throat. Do you have a preference? He was lucky you came along because I would have finished the bastard.'

'He wasn't even armed!'

The centre of Heck's eyebrow creased up in feigned bewilderment and he met Wilde's gaze. 'Do you think he worried about things like that when he shot defenceless women and children? Where have you been for the past six years, Professor?'

Wilde wasn't about to give details of his war service to this man.

'You know,' Heck continued, 'if the Nazis don't like getting shot they shouldn't go around Europe shooting other people. They're hardly in a position to complain now.'

Wilde couldn't let Heck's comment pass unremarked. 'But we have to show we're better than them, Lieutenant. We must demonstrate that the rule of law is there to be upheld. That's what the war was about. We have to learn to forgive, if not forget.'

Heck pulled a pack of cigarettes from his pocket and shoved one in his mouth. Casually smoking, he ambled alongside

Wilde and Appache as they walked across the centre of the camp. 'When your family has been murdered by Nazis, then you can come and tell me what I can and can't do to them.' He took a deep drag and blew out a cloud of smoke. 'Does that sound fair?'

'This hatred and murder has to end.'

'God damn it,' Appache said, 'stop the rabbiting won't you. This sounds like a college debating chamber.'

Heck laughed. 'The hatred and murder will end when the murderers are all dead. I want these fucking Nazis to suffer so badly that no one is ever tempted to try such atrocities against my people ever again.'

Wilde had nothing left to say.

'Now I'm going to see my little friend Jerzy, to thank him and tell him that his nightmare is over. I'll see you later – when you have disposed of that piece of filth.'

Heck strolled away, bag over his shoulder, hands in pockets.

The camp was alive with flies. Wilde tried to swat them, but it made no difference. It was a short walk to the medical centre, a large building that would have been the camp's administration block when the place was still run by the Nazis as a concentration camp. Now, a Red Cross sign outside signified the change of function.

On the drive from Garmisch, Colonel Appache had explained to Wilde that Apfelwald had housed slave labourers forced to work for the big Bavarian war industries. 'I believe many died of disease, malnutrition and maltreatment. Few were found alive when our troops arrived. Now it is home to refugees from all over Europe: Jews, Greeks, Italians, Russians, Poles, French. Name a language and it's probably spoken here.'

Now, outside the medical centre, the colonel addressed Wilde. 'I guess you're wondering what you've got yourself into here, feller. Well, I think we mentioned that Lieutenant Heck is headstrong. You've just seen what headstrong looks like in action.'

'I can't work with a man like that.'

'Oh, he'll be a pussycat with you. He only shoots Nazis.'

'He needs to be put on a charge.'

'Save it, Wilde. This isn't your snotty Cambridge college now. This is real life, this is the detritus of war, right here, and it ain't perfect. So live with it – and do the job you've agreed to do.'

A woman in a white coat emerged from the medical building, nodded to Appache and then glanced at Wilde. 'Are you anything to do with this?'

'No, Dr Gray,' Appache said. 'This is Mr Wilde and he did not do the shooting.'

'Well, who exactly are you then, and what are you doing here?'

'I'm an American intelligence officer, and I'm with Colonel Appache.'

'That explains nothing.'

'I'm sorry, it's all I can tell you.'

From her accent, he guessed she was middle-class English. Her hair was red and her face a mass of freckles. 'Anyway,' she said, 'you may or may not be pleased to know that the patient is being cleaned up and the duty surgeon will remove the bullet shortly. In the meantime, I'd like one of you to tell me what happened.'

'One of your inmates did the deed,' Appache said. 'Apparently he discovered the bastard was an SS man posing as a Jew. He got off lightly.'

The doctor bristled. 'Forgive me. There are no inmates here. They are refugees. Or you can just call them residents. And I can promise you the injured man did not get off lightly, as you put it. He is badly wounded and still in grave danger.'

Appache looked bored. 'I'm told he had an SS blood-type tattoo. It's been removed.'

'I want the gunman's name.'

'No can help, Doctor,' Appache said. 'And don't waste too much of your precious time on the case. Bandage his wounds and get him transferred to an SS internment camp as soon as he's good to go. I'll tell Major Derrick before I leave and he will arrange an armed escort. I hope that's clear, Dr Gray.'

The woman frowned. 'You seem to think you can give me orders, Colonel Appache, but you're mistaken. As you know very well, I'm in charge of the Red Cross here in Apfelwald.' She turned to Wilde.

Appache turned away from her dismissively. 'I'm going to leave you now, Wilde. I have five thousand satanic Nazis to interrogate at POW Camp Eight, and that's going to take a few goddamned months more. You have met our mutual friend, so it's up to you two now. Let's see what you're made of. One word of advice, if you find youself in Flint Kaserne – that's Third Army HQ at Bad Tölz – avoid General Patton at all costs. He hates smooth-talking academics and smart-ass intellectuals, and he'll have you booted back to London before you can blink. He doesn't know you're here and I don't want him to know. We'll meet back at Garmisch this evening, say six o'clock, for a final briefing. The lieutenant has the use of a jeep and will drive you. OK?'

Wilde nodded. He rather doubted he would be working with Heck by the day's end, but this wasn't the time for that conversation.

'And keep me in the loop. I won't tolerate mavericks in my command area. I don't want a repeat of the Collingham and Harper debacle. If, God forbid, something happens to either of you, I need to know what track you were on. Capisce?'

Wilde smiled half-heartedly. He wasn't here to be told what to do by this colonel. Appache was here to help him, not order him about. He had accepted a mission from Dulles, chief of the OSS in Germany, and he would do things his own way. Or not at all.

Appache nodded to the doctor. 'Don't forget, stitch up the Nazi and ship him out.'

'I beg your pardon?'

'You heard me.' Appache saluted sharply, then he was gone.

The doctor watched him marching away with a perplexed expression, then turned her attention to Wilde. 'Perhaps *you* have a civil tongue in your head. Your friend was rather abrupt. Are you going to tell me what this is all about?'

'I can't, and it's not really my place to apologise for the colonel. But I am sorry.'

'Well, that's something.' Suddenly she softened. 'Look, why don't you come into my office and have a cup of proper English tea. You look as if you need one. And do you know what, you look rather familiar.'

Chapter 9

Wilde spent an hour chatting with Angie Gray. In her little office, she had an electric kettle and all the other accoutrements of tea-making. He was happy to sit down on an old bench and relax for a while; the journey here from England by USAF transport and then jeep had been gruelling.

When he told her that he taught at Cambridge, her eyes lit up. 'I studied history there myself, before transferring to a medical degree at Edinburgh.'

'Perhaps that was before my time?'

'No, I was in Newnham for a year – and I now realise who you are,' she said, beaming. 'I attended one of your lectures. Elizabethan sea power, as I recall. But then I changed my mind and turned to medicine.'

'Oh dear, that sounds as though I put you off.'

'Not at all. Your talk was marvellous. But the die had already been cast. I loved Cambridge, but I wanted to be a doctor even more.'

She wanted to know everything about him, about the town – how it had fared during the war and whether it was going to be up and running again as a university in the coming Michaelmas term. She talked fondly about her three terms there, the dances at Dorothy's, the May balls she gatecrashed, her growing realisation that she had to swap to medicine.

Wilde told her about Lydia's plan, and Angie Gray was encouraging. 'Tell her she has to do it, Professor. She won't regret it.'

He changed the subject to her work at Apfelwald.

'You know this place might not be Cambridge, but it is rather like a small town – a very cosmopolitan town,' she said.

'Or that's how it *should* operate. The main organisational work is done by various organisations: the Red Cross, of course, the UNRRA – that's the United Nations Relief and Rehabilitation Administration – and the American Jewish Joint Distribution Committee. But it's all under the auspices of the American military.'

'Does that work well?'

'I don't see eye to eye with Major Derrick. He seems to think he's running a prison camp. Keeps guards at the gate and tries to stop the residents coming and going as they please. Half the bloody guards are Germans, and who knows what *they* did in the war. The refugees don't like that side of the arrangement one bit. The sooner they are allowed to form their own camp committee to run the place the better. Oh, and the major is a frightful anti-Semite and thinks the Jews are dirty and uncivilised. Just like our ghastly military governor here in Bavaria.'

'You mean General Patton.'

'Of course. He's in overall control of this camp and all the other DPs, like the huge one at Föhrenwald, but he simply can't get a grip. I just don't think he's interested. Do you know what Patton said about the poor Jews? He called them "lower than animals".'

'That's shameful.'

'Of course it is. Dear God, anyone would look worse for wear if they had been through what our Jews have suffered! The problem is Major Derrick takes his line. He's new out from the States, and that makes a big difference. Most of the troops who were here at liberation had a lot of sympathy for the people they freed because they saw exactly what had been done to them by the Nazis. But many of those fighting men have gone home now and the new intake are not so understanding. When they see a child pull down its pants and defecate in public without shame, they can't understand the experiences that have led to such practices.'

'It makes me wish I could help.'

'But you can't.' It was a statement of fact, not an accusation. She sighed. 'At least the other half of the guard detail is made up of black American GIs. I have found every one of them more polite and less arrogant than Major Derrick. Maybe he'll learn a thing or two from them.'

'What will happen to the refugees?'

Her helpless shrug told all. 'Who knows? At the moment many of the stronger and younger ones go out in the day to help with the harvests on local farms; they get bread, milk and beer as pay, which improves their diet.'

'And in the long term?'

'Some have tried to return to their homes in Poland and Hungary and elsewhere – only to be stoned and driven out by the local people who have appropriated their homes and farms. Even in Holland and Germany many of them can't go back. One family used to have a fine apartment in Munich but it was confiscated and given to a Nazi family. The son asked his father why they can't go home and the man just said "mustn't make trouble, my boy". He had tears in his eyes.'

'Good God, that's outrageous.'

'His wife told me all this, and she is in despair. But how do you go home when you know what all your former neighbours really think of you, even when they now deny they were ever Nazis? So these people are left in limbo, hoping for visas to England or America. One problem is that Jews are not classified simply as Jews, but by nationality. So the Polish Jews are supposed to go back to Poland and the Romanian Jews are told they must return to Romania. But they won't go because they have nothing to go back to. They only want America, Britain or Palestine. Zionism is burgeoning – encouraged by the Jewish Brigade.'

'Not easy to solve.'

'No, but despite all the bloody flies and the smell, this place is generally pretty clean and orderly now. We've got rid of the disease. The people live in makeshift cubicles in the barrack blocks and each family's space is partitioned from their neighbours by flimsy sheets hung from hooks in the ceiling. Some of them put pictures up and have vases of flowers. They have even started bringing out their own newspaper here and staging their own plays. They have schools and a synagogue and a church. For the foreseeable future this is their home.'

'And where do you call home, Dr Gray?'

'For a few more days, this is home. After that, who knows? I rather like the thought of Paris. But if you mean, where do I come from, it's Malaya. My parents managed to escape to India just before the Japanese arrived and are now in Bangalore.'

'So your posting here is almost up?'

'I've been here nearly three months and it's enough. You can't imagine what it was like when I arrived. People were dying by the dozen. The stench was unbearable, the conditions were foul – typhus, dysentery and starvation. We were living among corpses, and even those who were alive looked like corpses. But you'd be amazed how health returns, and it's been wonderful to see. You cannot believe the joy of the women when they get their first period in years. It means life, fertility, a future.'

'And they get enough to eat?'

'There's enough food at the moment. The American Jewish Joint Distribution Committee is very efficient. I fear for the winter, though.' She grimaced at the thought of what might lie ahead. 'This place is almost full and we get new refugees every day. Other camps are coming into being all over Bavaria – hundreds of them to house the millions of Germans driven out of their homes in Sudetenland, Silesia, Pomerania and East Prussia. Anyway, Professor, it has been a pleasure chatting to you. If you're passing again do come in for a cuppa. I love hearing about Cambridge.'

'And I'd very much like to know more about your medical journey, Dr Gray. I'm sure your story will give great encouragement to Lydia.'

'Tell her not to take no for an answer. What branch of medicine attracts her?'

'She's undecided.'

'Well, if you like, I'll write to her and give her a few tips and one or two names.'

'She'd love that. And thank you for your hospitality. I'm sorry we got off to a rough start.'

'Oh well, it wasn't you, Professor – it's these military types. What can one do?'

She was staring at him hard. There was something in her eyes but it was difficult to discern what exactly. For a moment he thought she was laughing at him, but that was absurd.

'You know, Mr Wilde – *Professor* Wilde – I still don't have the faintest idea what you are doing in my DP camp. Nor have you told me who's behind the shooting? Should I be involving Major Derrick in this?'

'That's up to you.' He rose from his chair. 'Thank you for the tea, Dr Gray.'

'Can I call you Tom? And you call me Angie? Everyone here is so bloody formal in that Germanic way – Frau Doctor this, Herr Professor that . . . I'm rather tired of it.'

'My pleasure, Angie.'

She smiled. 'By the way, have you got a good supply of chlorine pills? Not safe to drink the water without them.'

'Then I'd better stick to beer and schnapps.'

She raised an eyebrow, then opened a cupboard pulled out a small brown bottle. 'Here, my treat. Just drop one into the glass if you're ever desperate enough to drink H_2O.' She handed him the pills. 'Oh, and would I be right in thinking it was that madman Mo Heck who shot our new patient?'

'No comment.'

'Heck's been hanging around here two weeks now. Claims he's a refugee from Amsterdam searching for his family. But he's too well fed. He's hunting SS men.'

'Maybe, but the bit about his family's true. He believes they were murdered in one of the death camps.'

Wilde met up with Heck five minutes later outside the cook-house. He assumed the Dutchman had avoided going to the medical centre so as not to be identified or have to face any sort of inquiry. He was sitting on the ground, knees bunched up to his chest and a skinny, obviously malnourished boy of about thirteen was filming him with a home movie camera which Wilde recognised as a Kodak 8, the exact same one that he had at home.

'What kept you, Professor?' Heck said.

'I was shooting the breeze with the doctor.'

'Is the fucking Nazi alive or dead?'

'Still alive.'

'That's a shame. I'll fix him later.'

'Not a good idea, Lieutenant Heck. We have other things to do and it won't help if you're in court on a murder charge. Now, let's make our way to CIC Garmisch.'

'First meet my friend Jerzy. Jerzy Krakow, because he comes from Krakow. Either he doesn't know his real name or he doesn't care to use it.'

Wilde saw that the boy had now turned the camera lens in his direction. He kept the device up to his eye, seemingly filming constantly. He nodded to him. 'Hello, Jerzy, I'm Tom.'

'Hi, Tom,' the boy said with a strong Eastern European accent, without removing the camera. 'You want smile for me, boss?'

Wilde gave him a smile. The boy gave him a thumbs-up, then wandered off, the camera still clutched to his face.

Heck jumped to his feet. 'He sees the whole world through that lens, Professor. But he doesn't have any film.'

'Is his family here?'

'No. They were murdered by the fucking Nazis. He spent the war in the countryside, working on a farm. Then he walked and hitched here. He wants to go to Hollywood. He's friendly with the doc and she's been helping him with his English. He had already learnt some at home and now he gets by OK. He's a fast learner.'

Chapter 10

They picked up the jeep from the camp pound and drove south at a steady speed. It was a US Army vehicle, complete with five-pointed white star and canvas canopy. 'What's your usual car, Professor?' Heck demanded over the thunderous rush of wind and the noise of the road. 'This a bit basic for your tastes?'

Wilde laughed. He knew he was being tested. 'I ride a motor-bike. Rudge Special 500cc. Getting on a bit now, but she's reliable and I like her.'

'Never heard of it. Top speed?'

'About a hundred.'

'KPH?'

'MPH.'

'Not bad. Not bad at all. Better than this Yankee pile of crap.'

Wilde looked at his watch. It was just after 3 p.m. 'Do you think we could go and see where Randy Collingham and Denis Harper were ambushed?' he asked. 'Is that far from here?'

Without reply, Heck threw the jeep into a violent U-turn.

The speeds and cornering became ever more reckless. Wilde knew what it was about, of course. Heck was still angry with him for his reaction to the shooting of the SS man. Now, in retaliation, he was trying Wilde's nerve.

They came down a steep incline into an area of dark green forest, then cruised past the still waters of a nameless lake, up another rise, past a derelict tank and a roadside stall, and a little while later, the jeep skidded to a halt, almost throwing Wilde over the bonnet.

'This is the place,' Heck said. 'Have a look round, but there's not a lot to see.'

They both climbed out of the vehicle. Any blood on the road had long since washed away in the rain.

'If Collingham and Harper were ambushed here, maybe Hitler's hideout is not so far away,' Wilde suggested.

'Would they shit on their own doorstep?'

'It's possible.'

Heck looked doubtful. 'One thing is certain – the killer must have had knowledge of their movements. He must have known who they were and where they were going.'

'What about that stall a mile or two back?' Wilde said. 'Perhaps the stallholder saw something. Has she been interrogated?'

'I don't know. Let's go talk to her.'

They got back into the car and Heck drove them back up the road. The stall was run by a one-eyed woman in rags who looked as though she hadn't eaten in days. The stub of a cigarette hung from a corner of her mouth. 'Let me talk to her,' Wilde said. 'You are clearly very handy with a gun, Mr Heck, but you are also a little bit . . .'

'Intimidating?'

'Couldn't have chosen a better word.'

'I've been told it's the eyebrow. Like it or not, it's here to stay.'

Wilde approached the woman and asked her in German if she had been here when two men were killed in a car along the road.

'Are you Ami?'

'Yes, I'm American.'

'The two men who were killed, it was a great tragedy. Everyone in these parts was shocked.'

That sounded like a lie. Too many people hereabouts had been killed in violent circumstances to worry about the fate of two American soldiers. 'Had you seen them driving past?' he asked.

'It's possible. I don't really take much notice of which cars go past. I heard two shots, but they were muffled and distant and I thought there was a hunter in the woods. Lots of hunters around because there isn't much food rations for Germans. It was only an hour later when all the Ami jeeps came racing up that I heard what had happened. Truly a tragedy. Were the men friends of yours?'

'Yes, actually, they were.' He was looking at her and her wares, laid out on the table. She was clearly talkative, but that could mean anything. Her clothes were shabby and her solitary eye didn't stray from him for a moment. 'Do you do much trade here, *gnädige Frau*?'

'It's a good spot. There are no shops or bars nearby so I am the only place to get a little food or a beer. People stop because they are thirsty or they like to look at souvenirs. Amis like the Nazi stuff.'

'And where do you live?'

'There's a village, two kilometres through the woods. That's my home. Why? Why do you ask these questions?'

Suddenly, Heck lunged forward and snatched the cigarette from her mouth. It was a stunted, crumpled thing that had long since gone out. He studied it closely. 'What make are these? Stolen Yankee cigarettes, yes? I could haul you in for this.'

'No, sir, they are legal. British cigarettes – Senior Service from Naafi in English sector. They sell them to a friend of mine. I give him a good price. You want some?'

'The Americans who died had half a pack of Senior Service. They must have bought them here.'

The woman looked confused, her one eye blinking frantically, and suddenly her loquacity deserted her. Struggling for an answer, she backed away from her table – and from the imposing figure of Heck.

'Well?' Wilde demanded. 'Did the Americans stop here before they were shot?'

'I don't know. How should I know? People stop here ... I don't know who they are.'

Wilde put his arm out to hold Heck back. 'Two Amis, lady. You must have seen them that day, and you must know it. You sold them cigarettes. What happened? Was there someone else here – someone who climbed in the back of the car while they weren't looking?'

She shook her head violently. 'No, that didn't happen. I'm certain. I would have seen.'

'So you admit they did stop here. Did you mention this to the military police investigators?'

'No one has asked me before, mister.'

'Well, you should have volunteered any knowledge you had,' Heck said. 'Oh, I forgot, Germans don't think shooting for-eigners is a crime, do they?'

Her eye blazed at this. She spat on the ground. A dirty, brown spit as though she had been chewing tobacco. Then she threw back her head defiantly. 'You think it's a good idea to get involved in such things, mister? You think Nazis all bad, Amis all good? You don't know nothing. Yes, I heard the shots, but I saw noth-ing and know nothing. The killer didn't get into their car while they were here buying cigarettes. Whoever he is, I didn't see him.'

'I don't believe you,' Heck said.

Wilde tried to calm the confrontation. 'Look, dear lady, there must have been other cars, other people on the road. Think hard. Someone shot my friends.'

'I saw nothing.'

Wilde exchanged glances with Heck and noted the cold fury in his eyes. He shook his head almost impeceptibly as if to say,

No, Heck, don't reach for your gun, don't threaten this woman with violence.

'Let's take her in. She needs the third degree,' Heck said.

'Surely if she was involved, she wouldn't still be here, would she?' Wilde replied. He really wanted to defuse this before the situation got out of hand. He reached into his jacket pocket and removed his notepad and pen, then put them on the trestle table among the Nazi memorabilia and the miscellaneous items of food. 'Write your name and address on that.'

'Why should I do that?'

'Because if you don't, we'll place you under arrest and find you a nice cold cell in Garmisch while inquiries are being pursued. Your choice.'

She hesitated then, with great reluctance, scratched a name and address on the page, before pushing the small pad back across the table to Wilde. He saw the name Zimmer, Birgit Zimmer. The name of her town or village was Kochel-am-See which, she said, was only two kilometres from the road. 'It's not a big place; everyone knows me,' she said.

'And you think that's OK?' Heck said to Wilde. 'You think she's really put her own fucking address there.'

'Your guess is as good as mine.'

'Hey,' the woman said, this time in broken English, her antagonism gone like a summer squall. 'Give me your names and way to get in touch with you. If I hear anything, I make contact, yes? Perhaps there's a reward to find this killer . . .'

Heck raised a questioning eyebrow. Wilde nodded, then handed the notepad to his companion. Heck wrote hurriedly, then tore out the sheet and gave it to the woman. 'Call that number, sister, and ask for us. If we're not there, leave a message and we'll get back to you.'

She smiled for the first time. 'I do that. Good to help Amis. Amis save us from Hitler. Damned crazy teetotal vegetarian.' She held up a pocket watch and offered it to Heck. 'This is for you, mister. Fine watch.'

'Thanks anyway,' Heck said. 'But I'm really not interested.'

Wilde was interested, though – interested in the way the woman had changed her tune, from downright hostilty to feigned friendliness.

'Is free gift.'

'Well, if you want to give me something, how about that?' Heck pointed at the box camera.

'This?' She picked it up, then pushed it towards him. 'Of course. Take it, sir. Take it with my gratitude for all you do for us.'

'Got any film for it?'

'No, sir, I'm sorry, sir. Maybe in Munich you get some, or from your PX.'

Heck took the camera and grinned. 'A nice little present for my very good friend Jerzy from Krakow,' he said to Wilde.

Frau Zimmer reached beneath her table and pulled out an ornate plate with gold edging and a rustic scene in the middle, and offered it to Wilde. 'Here, sir, Meissen. Very expensive. You sell for many dollars in America, or nice present for your wife.'

Wilde shook his head and turned to Heck. 'Let's go.'

'You know Frau Zimmer just gave you a bribe, Lieutenant Heck?'

'Now why would she have done that? Do you think she's guilty of something?'

'Maybe. Or perhaps she's just scared. We're occupying her country. We're the rulers now. We can do what we want – even shoot people, Lieutenant Heck – and the Germans can't do a damn thing about it.'

Chapter 11

Heck drove slower so they could talk. 'Do you have a plan, Professor? Where do we go from here?'

Yes, Wilde had a plan. First he wanted to talk to August Jaeger, the alpine guide and cousin of Himmler's right-hand man Walter Schellenberg. It was a long shot, but in the absence of any other leads he had to be worth a try.

'Do you know a place called Almrosen?'

'No.'

Wilde looked at his watch. They had already missed their meeting with Colonel Appache, but what the hell. 'It's up in the mountains, not too far from here, maybe twenty miles, across the border in the Tyrol. It's in the French zone, but I have been led to believe that won't be a problem.'

'Never underestimate the talent of the French to make things difficult, Professor.'

'There's a man we should talk to there, a mountain guide. It's probable that Himmler's department consulted him when they were in the initial phase of planning an Alpine redoubt.'

'And how does that help?'

Wilde gave him a mystified look. Was it not obvious how that might help? He let the thought go. 'Well, it may not, but do you have any other ideas, Lieutenant Heck?'

'We go back to the beginning. We talk to everyone who was close to Hitler. Someone will know where he is.'

'Yes, I had that in mind, too. But the mountain man first.'

'You're the chief.'

They drove without talking for a while as the roads took them into higher territory and the mountains crowded steep and dark, stealing the late afternoon light. Wilde broke the silence. 'Do you feel certain he is alive?'

'A man like Hitler? Oh yes, he's alive. He's a snivelling coward. He's crawled into a hole somewhere, cowering, biding his time. Also, he has plenty of followers who would go to great lengths to keep him safe and hidden.'

'Then we'll find him.'

'Who's the guy in Almrosen?'

'His name is August Jaeger.'

'Another fucking Nazi, no doubt. So he will keep shtum. But hey, let's go give him a hard time.'

For the rest of the journey, Wilde tried to get to know Heck better. The Dutchman told him about his escape from the Netherlands soon after the German invasion of his country in May 1940. When it became obvious that the Nazi force was irresistible, he and two Amsterdam school friends hitched a ride to the coast, where they stole a small sailing boat and cast off into the North Sea. 'We knew nothing of navigation and only one of us had a vague idea how to sail. But we were lucky. The weather was on our side and we weren't spotted by German patrols.'

'You made it all the way to England?'

'The Royal Navy picked us up.' He laughed. 'I was just under seventeen, yet I looked a lot older. I had no passport, but the British accepted me as twenty and allowed me to enlist.'

'The eyebrow?'

'The eyebrow. You noticed that?' He grinned at Wilde. 'Yes, it put years on me. My friends looked younger and were packed off to foster homes and school. I joined the First Battalion Suffolk Regiment and learnt how to shoot guns, kill with a bayonet and march. The training was laughably easy and I excelled because I wanted badly to become a good soldier. But it was dull stuff for four years. We were stuck in England until last June and I was a lonely private saying, "Yes, sir, no, sir, three bags full, sir." Then came D-Day and my real life began. My chance to kill fucking Nazis. Every last fucking one of them.'

'For a Dutchman you have an interesting grasp of Anglo-Saxon.'

'Oh I learnt a lot more words than that in the barrack room. Too strong for your delicate college ears, eh?'

'I think I'll probably survive. So from the barrack room and the lower ranks, how did you become a lieutenant?'

'By January this year I'd made sergeant and so I thought I might as well apply for a commission. I had as good an education as any of the British officers and I reckoned I could do the job better than most of them. For some reason they accepted me. So here I am: Lieutenant Heck at your service.'

'And still just twenty-two? Good for you.'

'I could almost be one of your students, Professor.'

'Indeed you could. Maybe you will one day.' Heck was a paradox. He had an obvious zest for life and the possibility of a great future stretching out ahead of him, but the path he was on could as well lead to the gallows. A vengeful heart throbbed within the young man's breast.

Wilde wanted to know more. 'Your family, Lieutenant Heck: when did you learn about your parents' fate? Maybe you don't want to talk about it . . .'

'Oh, I want to talk about it. I want the world to know about it. There must be no forgetting and no forgiveness.'

'You've chosen a hard path.'

'I didn't choose it. The fucking Nazis chose it. In May this year, I went home, five years after I last saw them. A neighbour told me they had been rounded up and sent on a transport to

Westerbork. From there, they must have been sent eastwards, maybe Auschwitz. I don't know. I have had no word of them, so I must assume they are dead. I go around the DP camps, looking at the noticeboards, talking to survivors, trying to find any clue as to their fate. Apart from that, what can I say?'

No tears came, but his voice was breaking

'I understand, Heck.'

'No, you'll never understand. You can't unless it happens to those you love. My beautiful, ridiculously clever sisters, my brilliant little brother the violinist and funnyman.' He snorted. 'That's enough. You want me to be soft like you, but I won't be soft.'

'OK.'

They had been climbing steadily into the high Tyrol and it was getting dark. The only traffic they encountered was military: jeeps, troop carriers, armoured patrols. Most of the roads in southern Germany and Austria were untouched by war, but some were in a bad way. Military wrecks had simply been bulldozed to the side of the road, and the occasional crater scarred the highway where a bomb had removed a whole section. These had been hastily and poorly repaired. Military police checkpoints delayed them three times. Bridges both large and small were invariably damaged, but at least they were now passable.

It was slow going and the jeep was seriously underpowered. Now, in Austria, there was less damage, but the road was single track, poorly maintained and deathly quiet. They had been stopped briefly at the border between southern Bavaria and the French zone, but Wilde's diplomatic passport and the easy lie that they were making their way to Italy via the Brenner Pass had seen them waved through.

They had turned off the main road down a high-banked valley. Green pastures darkened with the setting of the sun, a river of melt water rushed at their side. Above them, mountains towered, their dazzling glaciers reflecting the last of the light.

Wilde had taken over the driving, and as they traversed a small town, he estimated they were twenty minutes short of Almrosen. 'This rattlebox jeep wasn't designed for these inclines. What say we stop the night here?' he said, slowing down outside a large building that had the welcoming look of a guest house. 'We've already missed the colonel.'

'That'll put his nose out of joint.' Heck laughed.

'You don't like him?'

'Did I say that?'

'Just an impression I get.'

The headlights of the jeep illuminated a sign at the door saying 'Der Kuhhaus', along with a fresco of a cow with a bell and a large painted edelweiss flower; music was filtering out into the cool night air. 'I suppose it'll be too late to call on our mountain guide anyway. Let's see if we can get some food here and a couple of rooms.'

'A beer, too,' Heck said. 'What is this village?'

'I saw a sign that said Grünegg.' Wilde was already parking the jeep, directly in front of the building. 'Looks a nice prosperous place; doesn't seem to have been affected much by the war.'

They knocked at the door, but there was no reply, so they pushed it open and walked in. They found themselves in a large room, lit by candles and packed with tables, all of which appeared to be occupied by grey-haired men in Tyrolean leather shorts and close-collared jackets, and women in colourful dirndls, all clapping and singing along to a tune played by a woman with an accordion. She was accompanied by the deep notes of a double bass played by a man with a long grey walrus moustache. Most of those present were women. One or two looked in the direction of the newcomers, but then turned back to their beer and clapping.

A woman dressed like everyone else but with a leather money-belt slung across her hip approached them with a smile. Heck did the talking. 'We need food and we need rooms for the night. Can you help us?'

'Of course. We have bread and sausage or you can have spätzle.' She looked at her wristwatch. 'You are a little late, but it will be fine.'

'I'll take the spätzle,' Heck said.

'And I'll take the bread and sausage,' Wilde said. 'Also a beer and a brandy.'

The woman's expression changed. Just a fraction, but it definitely changed. 'Ah, you are Ami – American?'

'I'm not, my friend is,' Heck said. 'Does that make a difference, Fräulein?'

'No, no, of course not, sir. Just from your accent I thought you were Bavarian.'

'I lived a lot of my early life in these parts.'

'Now, I understand, sir. Let me find you a table and bring you your food and drink. I hope you enjoy the music.'

The food was good, so was the beer and brandy. Wilde began to feel mellow. Then the folk dancers came on in their knee-length tasselled lederhosen and long socks, slapping their thighs, smacking the soles of their shoes and stamping their feet while the crowd all clapped in time. The dancers – six of them – were all boys, none of whom could have been more than twelve years old.

A man, who was clearly the proprietor, came up and bowed graciously to Wilde and Heck. He had thin grey hair and a barrel chest. The flesh of his face was thick and muscled – the mark of a man whose diet had always been predominantly meat. 'Good evening, gentlemen,' he said in heavily accented English. 'Do you like the *schuhplattler*?'

'The dancing?' Wilde said. 'Yes, it's fine.'

'And you, sir?' he said to Heck.

'Not my sort of thing, fellow.'

'May I sit with you a moment? It is not often we get honoured American guests.'

'Take a seat,' Wilde said.

The man introduced himself as Heinrich Stifter and ordered more brandy, on the house. As the dancing finished, the audience clapped appreciatively. Stifter shook his head. 'Half our young dancers are dead. Look around the room – women of all ages but only old men and boys. That's what the war did – that's the legacy of those German bloody Nazis across the border. Sent our young men to their deaths.'

'Where are the other half?'

'Prisoner of war camps, trying to stay alive.'

'So, no Nazis here in Grünegg, eh, Herr Stifter?' Heck said.

The scepticism in his voice was very obvious to Wilde.

'Oh, you know, one or two among the older folk, but I'm sure they have now seen the error of their ways. But tell me, gentlemen, you do not look like soldiers.'

'What do soldiers look like?' Heck said.

'Well, they wear uniforms. Are you perhaps vacationing?'

'What we're doing is our business.'

'Of course, of course. But we love to have Ami guests here and we would like many more. I was just thinking that if you were US Army, you could tell your friends about our beer and music and food – our *gemütlichkeit*, our friendly atmosphere. And we want to get skiing again this winter. Perfect for your Ami friends for a weekend of sport. Can I offer you more brandy, gentlemen? Or a little home-made plum schnapps?'

'I think I've had enough,' Wilde said.

'You know, Herr Stifter, you all look pretty well fed here? How come you have food when everyone else seems to be starving?'

'This is a farming community, sir. Farmers always have food. It is the way of the world, I think. I'm sure that in England and America the farmers ate better than the city-dwellers.'

'Perhaps you'd show us to our rooms,' Heck said. 'I don't want to hear about your well-fed bellies.'

Wilde noted the darkness in his eyes. Was it the brandy – or the display of Tyrolean culture, as though nothing had changed in six years, as though millions had not died. As though life could go on regardless.

'Of course, sir.'

'Oh, and by the way. You mentioned the Nazis across the border in Germany. Perhaps you hadn't heard, but one Adolf Hitler was an Austrian and legend has it that he, too, was a Nazi. Just fancy that.'

Stifter bowed deeply. 'Your point is well made, sir.'

Heck rose, pushing his chair back so that it fell clattering to the floor behind him. Wilde rose, too, and they followed Stifter towards a door to the reception hall and staircase. Just then, the accordionist struck up a new tune and Wilde heard the scraping of chairs as the whole room rose to their feet.

As one, they burst into song. Wilde and Heck turned back. On the little platform beside the accordionist, a thin man of middle years with greying hair was leading the singing.

'*Die Fahne hoch! Die Reihen fest geschlossen!*'

Heck looked at Wilde with intent. 'Do you hear that?'

The strains sounded vaguely familiar. 'What is it?'

'Goddamn, can't you hear it? *Raise the flag! . . .The ranks tightly closed!* The flag is the swastika. They're singing the fucking Horst Wessel song. The only thing missing is the Hitler salute. They're all fucking Nazis.'

He was carrying his bag and pulled out his pistol. Without hesitation, he strode into the centre of the large room, surrounded by forty or fifty men and women all standing to attention. He raised the pistol and fired a shot into the ceiling. The sound was deafening in the enclosed space and brought the singing to an immediate halt.

'Get out,' he shouted in German. 'Get out every one of you, because if you don't I'll shoot you all, and anyone left alive I'll have arrested and held as an enemy combatant. Do you all understand?'

There was murmuring, but little movement among the crowd. To encourage them, he fired another shot, this time lower into one of the walls. 'The next one will be in someone's head,' he roared.

Wilde could only look on and wonder how this was going to end. He had a pistol, too, but he kept it holstered. The two of them were hugely outnumbered, and who could tell what weapons these men had secreted about them? Wilde's eyes strayed to the grey-haired lead singer and saw a look of deadly loathing.

The proprietor, meanwhile, was standing in front of Heck now. 'You cannot do this! You have no right.'

Heck pushed the muzzle of his pistol into the Austrian's face. 'I have every right, mister. That song is banned in Austria and Germany. You thought we'd be too damned stupid to know, didn't you, you smug Nazi bastard. So tell all your fascist friends to go home right now, or you'll be the first to get a bullet. Do it!'

Heinrich Stifter looked murderous, not scared. For a moment Wilde thought he would try to punch Heck, but thankfully he managed to hold in his fury because Wilde was pretty sure the Austrian would have ended up dead.

Then Stifter turned away and reached out his arms, patting his palms downwards in a gesture designed to calm his guests. He was red-faced and as taut as a cable, but he managed to speak in measured tones. 'Do as he says, friends. Go home now. Leave me to deal with this and we will meet again soon. Thank you for your custom. Sleep well, friends.'

Within a minute, the guests were all gone, leaving just Wilde and Heck and Stifter and the woman who had first welcomed them. Was she his daughter or wife?

'Now then,' Heck said. 'You were about to show us to our rooms, Herr Stifter.'

'Surely you do not expect to stay here after what you have done?'

'Well, you can be sure I'm not sleeping outdoors, so yes, we're staying. And we want a damned good breakfast. Eggs, bacon, your best bread, butter, real coffee. The works. Got it, mister?'

'If you insist.'

'Oh yes, I insist. You really don't want to know what the alternative is.'

They were given adjoining rooms.

'Is this wise, staying here?' Wilde said after the proprietor had departed with yet another deep and insincere bow.

Heck laughed. 'You worried the boys in the leather shorts are going to come and do for us in the night?'

'Aren't you? The problem is, Lieutenant Heck, that you have announced our arrival in rather a dramatic fashion. If anyone in these parts knows the whereabouts of Hitler, they now know about us too.' The fate of Collingham and Harper did not need mentioning.

'Think of it as flushing him out, like beaters on a shoot.'

'I really don't think that strategy will work in this case. News will travel like fire in this part of the world. You might already have scared August Jaeger away.'

'Then we'll be certain he knows something. And we'll find him.'

It was a futile discussion. Wilde was becoming painfully aware of the reasoning behind the decision to use him as a counterpoint to the headstrong Dutchman. He was less sure that he was up to the task. In fact, he was rapidly coming to the conclusion that while they might have individual strengths, they were never going to make a team.

'Well, goodnight, Lieutenant.'

'And goodnight yourself, Professor.'

Wilde paused with his hand on the door handle to his room. 'You know, Heck, for a minute back there, I really thought you were about to shoot our host in the head.'

'I was.'

Chapter 12

Wilde slept fully clothed except for his shoes, with his Walther under the pillow. His room was a pleasant, pine-scented chamber with a balcony, a large bed with duvet, and a basin with hot and cold water. He woke with the dawn, rested, and looked out through a picture window on to a magnificent mountain panorama. God, this place was beautiful. Maybe the Führer really was close by. If he loved the Alps as much as it was said, he could find no better place to live out his days.

At breakfast, their host, Heinrich Stifter, was a chastened man. He served them with grace, fawning over them as he brought all the food Heck had commanded, along with cheeses, sliced sausage and a bowl of fruit.

'Forgive me,' he said, bowing his head. 'I beg you to forgive all of us for the events of last night. We have all lost children in the terrible war and it is hard to shrug off old loyalties like an overcoat. I myself lost both my sons on the Eastern Front. I realise it was wrong of us to have sung that song, especially with two honoured guests in the room, but it was merely meant as a tribute to those we have lost, not to the criminals who held our country in thrall to their accursed ideology.'

'OK,' Wilde said.

Heck shook his head. 'No, it's not OK. I'm going to have you hauled in for de-Nazification, Herr Stifter, along with everyone else in this godforsaken village. You are very lucky I didn't kill you last night.'

'Yes, sir, I understand. And please, accept the rooms and your food at my expense.'

Heck said no more to the Austrian, simply pushed away his plate and cup and stood up. 'Let's go, Professor. Work to be done.'

The last part of the drive became steeper and more dangerous, around a series of hairpin bends that zigzagged up the side of a mountain. The road was in bad condition. Rockfalls had narrowed the way, but Heck – who had taken over the wheel once more – seemed unconcerned by the precipitous edges they had to negotiate.

Finally, they got to Almrosen. It was a collection of no more than twenty buildings, one of which was the onion-domed church, and two of which were bombed-out ruins. The houses that had survived the war were all pretty Alpine chalets with balconies, beautifully decorated with boxes overflowing with masses of red geraniums. A place barely touched by war compared to the cities, but still with its own evidence of the hostile years.

'Where does your friend live, Professor?'

Wilde had no idea. Walter 'The Shell' Schellenberg had told him no more than the name of the village and the fact that cousin Jaeger lived in the largest house. 'I don't even know if he's still living here, Lieutenant Heck. Schellenberg hadn't been in contact with him for many years.'

'Then we'll knock on a few doors and find him.'

The first house they came to was answered by a plump, grim-faced young farm wife wearing a bloodstained apron. In one hand she was holding a scrawny chicken by the legs, blood dripping from the neck where until a few moments ago its head had been attached. In the other hand she had a sharp knife. Her arms were bare and muscled.

'August Jaeger,' Wilde said. 'Where is he?'

She pointed to a house further up the single street, on the right-hand side.

'Is he in?'

'Maybe, I don't know.'

They left the jeep and strolled up the deserted street. The house the woman had pointed out was a large and very old timber chalet, its wood darkened with age. Wilde thought it was magnificent. The front door was overtopped by a vast set of antlers. He knew that Heck had his pistol out, and was holding it concealed in his jacket pocket. Wilde, too, had his Walther fully loaded and close at hand beneath his jacket.

Wilde knocked at the door, but there was no answer. They waited a few moments, then Heck took out his pistol, stepped forward and hammered with the butt of the gun. When no one came, he lifted the latch and discovered the door was open.

They both stepped inside the darkened hallway. Slippers, shoes and boots were clustered neatly on the floor to their side. Wilde called out, 'Hello, Herr Jaeger!' No reply. 'I get the feeling he's not here, Lieutenant Heck.'

'Then why is his front door open?'

'Country folk. They don't lock up because they know and trust their neighbours.'

They began searching the house, room by room. It was ranged over three floors and seemed as large inside as it had appeared from the outside. It was so spacious it could easily be a guest house or hotel, Wilde reflected. The main room was decorated with more antlers. Snowshoes and skis and old bows that might have been hundreds of years old were displayed on the wall over an immense stone fireplace.

A large, exquisitely detailed map of the Austrian Alps was laid out on the table. Next to it, tidily arranged, were fine-nibbed pens and an inkwell. Wilde studied the map and realised it was a hand-drawn work in progress and was signed '*Jaeger, A.*' So he was a cartographer as well as a mountain guide. Schellenberg had been correct in one matter at least: it would be hard to find a man with more knowledge of these mountains if an *Alpenfestung* was ever being seriously planned.

Heck had wandered off into other rooms. Suddenly, Wilde heard a noise behind him and turned. Someone was standing in the doorway looking at him. It was the woman from down the road, only now she had discarded the dead chicken and the knife and the bloody apron. She had also donned a white cap to hold her fair hair in place.

She smiled awkwardly at him. '*Grüss Gott*,' she said by way of greeting. 'You said you were looking for Herr Jaeger?' She spoke in an Austrian version of German which Wilde struggled with.

'That's right. You pointed us in this direction. Isn't this his home?'

'Indeed, sir. But he is not here. No one in Almrosen has seen him in more than a week.'

'Isn't that a little worrying?'

She shrugged her powerful shoulders. A real mountain woman, thought Wilde. 'Not so much. He often disappears into the mountains for long periods, sometimes taking hikers and climbers, sometimes just on his own to do a bit of hunting and trail-finding.'

The lieutenant had reappeared and looked suspiciously at the woman. Wilde couldn't fail to see the tension in him and could sense that he was holding his concealed pistol with an unnecessarily tight grip. Wilde repeated what the woman had told him about August Jaeger's tendency to disappear into the mountains for extended periods.

'What sort of timescale are we talking about, Fräulein?' Heck demanded.

She shrugged again. 'Days, weeks, even months. He comes and goes without telling anyone. But tell me, kind sirs, why do you want him? Are you climbers?'

'Maybe,' Heck said. 'We were told he might be able to help us with a tour we want to make.'

'He would be your man. No man in Austria knows the mountains better than Herr Jaeger. I could ask him to contact you if you like. Would you care to leave your details? I could get him to call you when he returns. I see from your vehicle that you are US Army.'

Wilde and Heck caught each other's eye. Both of them realised that if Jaeger wasn't here they had made a long journey for nothing. They certainly couldn't hang around here for days on end, and looking for him in the mountains would be pointless.

Did it make sense to give this woman a contact number? She seemed straight enough. But so did almost everyone when confronted with armed members of the occupying powers. Wilde wrote his name and the CIC telephone number on a piece of paper and handed it to her.

'Does Jaeger live here alone?' Heck asked.

'Yes, sir, since his mother died two years ago.'

'How old is Jaeger?'

'Fifty-five, I think. No, fifty-six.'

'It's a big house for one person,' Wilde said. 'Does he have no wife, no children?'

'Yes, it is too big, but his family has owned this house and lived here for many generations. He had a wife, of course – Margarethe – but she died in childbirth twenty years ago. The child died, too. But there was an elder boy, Franz. He died at Monte Cassino. Herr Jaeger has no one left.'

Wilde felt a sudden pang. His first wife, Charlotte had also died in childbirth many years ago. He was married again with a fine boy, but the pain of that first loss could never be completely erased.

There was silence for a few moments. Motes of dust caught in a shaft of sunlight from an east-facing window. This house had the stillness of a museum, or a church.

Heck broke the moment. 'Is there anywhere in the village we could get a cup of coffee?'

'I'm sorry, sir. There is no cafe. Nor do we have a Gasthof or hotel. But, if you wish, I could offer you coffee.' Her mouth dropped and she looked apologetic. 'But it is ersatz – acorns – and I am sure you Amis are used to real coffee.'

'I'll give it a go,' Wilde said. 'Could you bring it to us here? We have come a long way to see Herr Jaeger and I'd like to stay here an hour or two, just in case he turns up.'

She bowed again and disappeared.

'This is like a ghost house,' Heck said. 'Did you trust her?'

'I don't know, but she seems a decent woman and her story makes sense.'

'Does it?'

'You don't think so, Heck?'

'I don't trust a single fucking German or Austrian. You saw those bastards last night with the Horst Wessel song. The only things missing were the Sieg Heils.'

They continued looking around the house. Wilde spent a long time gazing at the map on the table, as though he would see a mark that told him where Hitler was hiding out. *Here lies buried treasure.* But, of course, there was no such clue. All the map told him was that the Alps were vast, and trying to find anything without directions or hints would be nigh on impossible. No wonder the German high command had considered turning these forbidding mountains into a fortress.

The woman returned with their acorn coffee. It tasted nothing like the real thing, but it wasn't too bad. She bowed and was about to leave when Wilde stopped her.

'I believe Herr Jaeger is related to Walter Schellenberg. You must know him from his visits.'

She looked puzzled. Or worried, perhaps. 'Who?' she said.

'Schellenberg. SS-Brigadeführer Schellenberg. Himmler's right-hand man.'

She froze and then shook her head stiffly. 'No, sir, I have not heard of such a man. I am sure he is not known in Almrosen.'

'That's funny, he told me he came here. A visit by an SS general would have been a big event. Didn't you put out the flags for him?'

'No, forgive me, sir, I have lived here all my life and this thing has never happened. There has never been an SS general here. And I have not heard of this man you mention. August Jaeger has never spoken of him.'

'Well, that's a shame.' Wilde put down the coffee, then returned to the table and carefully folded up the map. He wanted to study it more; if Jaeger knew anything, this might just hold the secret. Either way, he'd likely want it back, so it might prompt him to make contact. 'Tell Herr Jaeger I will return this to him when I see him. Don't forget to tell him to call. And thank you for the coffee. It was fine.'

She was helpless to prevent him taking the map, though her eyes followed it in horror. A theft was being committed before her very eyes and she was powerless to do anything about it.

Outside the front door, Wilde breathed deeply of the mountain air. 'What do you reckon now, Lieutenant Heck? Shall we look around? Take the village tour?'

'No, goddamn it, this has been a waste of time. At least in a wild goose chase, you know there's a goose. Let's talk to the people who knew Hitler best.'

'I agree. I particularly want to meet those who were with him to the end. Perhaps the bastard really did shoot himself in the bunker.'

Heck smiled. 'You don't believe that, Wilde.'

The jeep was getting short of fuel, but there would be enough to get them as far as Innsbruck, where they could bank on finding a French garrison to fill up. The road down from the high village of Almrosen was atrocious but the day was bright and there was no other traffic. Wilde was at the wheel.

Halfway down, there had been another rockfall. Wilde slowed to a crawl to skirt the boulders that littered the road. On his left, the fall-away was sheer, with a precipice of close to a thousand feet.

'Enjoying the drive, Professor?' Heck said. 'Let's see if you can keep us alive.'

'Was that a vote of confidence?'

'Take it how you will.'

Wilde glanced in the mirror. Some way back, he spotted another vehicle, a light-green truck loaded with tree trunks. He and Heck maintained silence; concentration was critical. One minor error would do for them.

He gave the mirror another cursory look. To his surprise, the light-green timber lorry seemed to be gaining on them. It was going too fast for the road and he felt a stab of anxiety. How would it cope with the rockfall debris? Perhaps the driver was familiar with this way, but such a vehicle would be difficult to control when it came to negotiating difficult terrain, and braking would be grindingly slow. Instinctively, Wilde put his foot down gently, to maintain distance.

'OK, Professor?' Heck had seemed to sense the tension in Wilde's hands.

Wilde's eyes flicked between the road and the mirror. 'What the hell is he doing?' he said under his breath as the green lorry swerved its way through the scattered boulders.

Heck hadn't seen the truck. Now he turned around. 'Goddamn it, Wilde, I don't think he can slow down. You're going to have to motor.'

That was impossible. The road was narrow and passing places were few and far between. To their right was sheer rock wall, to their left, the precipice.

Despite his misgivings, Wilde accelerated again, but even thirty miles an hour was too fast for this stretch and he felt a real stab of fear; they were approaching the most severe of the hairpins.

And then they saw the second truck, a heavy black lorry, growling up the mountain road, straight at them.

Chapter 13

Wilde couldn't brake. The truck following them was now gaining at an alarming speed and had swept through the rockfalls like a racing driver cutting through chicanes. If the jeep stopped now, they would simply be crushed against the rock wall or swept over the edge to certain death. But how could they find a way past the oncoming vehicle grinding its way uphill, its driver seemingly oblivious of the immediate peril facing all three vehicles.

The driver of the heavy black lorry displayed no sign of being aware of the danger, making no effort to pull in against the rock face to make way for the jeep. His steady, laborious progress did not alter. Perhaps he hadn't seen them. Perhaps he didn't have enough power to get up this road if he didn't make it in one go.

Wilde felt the sweat drip into his eyes.

What a stupid bloody way to die. Survive a war and plummet off a mountain precipice.

There was no time to talk, no time to consult with Lieutenant Mozes Heck, let alone say goodbye. No time even to pray.

A hundred yards ahead they somehow had to make an impossible turn at speed on the sharpest of the hairpins. Would the jeep even be able to corner at this speed? And then what? They would hit the oncoming black truck head on. Wilde glanced at the dials and saw his speed was thirty. He estimated the green timber lorry behind to be doing fifty or more. It would rear-end them in seconds, crushing them into the front end of the black truck, crumpling them like a cigarette packet. Or it would bulldoze them over the lip of the road down hundreds of feet to certain destruction.

Wilde eased the throttle and feathered the brakes. Not hard enough to stop but to slow down a fraction, just as he entered the bend, hugging the inside track against the rock face. The black truck was entering from the parallel side of the hairpin. Wilde had one chance, and it had to be timed to perfection. His eyes met the wide, frowning eyes of the driver of the black truck, then he bluffed and slid left, to the wrong side of the road, just as the oncoming truck made a swerve the other way, as if to hit the jeep and crush it into the rock face.

The offside panels of the jeep scraped and sparked against the side of the black truck. The nearside wheels of the jeep were almost completely over the cliff edge. A mere one or two centimetres of rubber gripped the road, throwing up dust and stones in a billowing fog.

Wilde held the line.

The black truck's tail moved off centre, a reaction to the driver's sudden swerve inwards, pushing the jeep to the edge. Wilde's rear nearside tyre lost contact with the road, hung out out over nothingness. Only momentum kept the vehicle on track. Time slowed down, almost stopped, but then, incredibly, the wheel was back in a rush, tyre burning from the sudden friction as it scorched across loose scree.

Wilde let out the throttle – and he was past the truck. He knew instantly that he had overcooked it; he lost control and the jeep lurched, skidding left and right. His hands fought the wheel as though it were a living thing. From some distant place he heard an explosion, but it was elsewhere, in a dream.

'Shit,' Heck said. His head was twisted, peering behind him and his voice little more than a whisper. Then, much louder, he exclaimed, '*Scheisse!*'

They were about to hit another hairpin, but Wilde didn't dare slow down. The rear wheels were dragging to the right and they were about to plough into the sheer wall of rock.

'Hey,' Heck said. 'Stop, Professor. We're OK.'

'What?'

'They hit each other. The two trucks. They hit each other and they've both gone over the edge.'

Wilde slowed, then ground to a halt.

'Good driving, Professor. Things were looking dicey there.' Heck jumped out of the jeep and loped back up the hill. Wilde applied the handbrake and followed him. The road at the hairpin was littered with rocks and pieces of metal. Long, swerving tracks of burnt rubber scarred the road where Wilde had fought to gain control.

He caught up with Heck and together they peered over the edge. Far below, they could see the last tumbling journey of the timber lorry and its cargo of trees, falling inexorably into a gorge at the foot of the mountain. The black lorry was a little to the side, cartwheeling – and then both vehicles came together, tangling obscenely like monsters mating as they hit the ground. There was another explosion, echoing and distant. The first one had been the sound of the two lorries colliding; this one was the flash and roar of petroleum igniting and engulfing the wreckage and the two drivers in a ball of flame. Black smoke rose upwards in a filthy cloud.

'What happened there?'

'I honestly don't know,' Wilde said.

'Were they trying to kill us? Didn't they see us? Didn't they see each other? What do we do now?'

Wilde shook his head. There was nothing they could do. He imagined the drivers in their cabs and hoped that the impact had killed them. The thought of them being incinerated alive was too much. He couldn't bear to watch any more, so he walked back to the jeep and climbed in the driver's seat and waited. After a couple of minutes Heck was with him.

'Do you want me to drive, Professor? You're sweating like a pig.'

Wilde held up his hands. They weren't shaking, not even a tremor. 'I think I'm OK. But a slug of whisky would go down well.'

Heck laughed. 'You know, Professor, I'm growing to like you. If I had a bottle of hooch it would be all yours, but I'm afraid I've nothing to give you but water. Oh, but I got these.' He fished the last of his cigarettes from his shirt pocket and tapped out a couple. 'I think you deserve one, don't you?'

'No, thanks, I'll wait for the whisky.'

They took the rest of the mountain road at a sedate pace. Heck put his feet up and smoked. At the bottom, where the mountain track joined the main valley road, they stopped and looked back towards the ravine where the two trucks had ended up. All they could see was the occasional lick of flame and the plume of black smoke.

Wilde switched off the engine.

'What are you doing, Professor?'

'I have to go and see.'

'No one could have survived that. Leave it to the locals – or the French. They must patrol this road, so they'll find it soon enough. God knows how they'll get to it, though. Must be a mile across impossible terrain.'

Wilde shrugged. 'I have to look.' He climbed from the road down a shallow incline of rock to a meadow. Cows turned to gaze at him without much enthusiasm or interest, their bells clanging and carrying on the breeze. He turned briefly and saw that Heck was following him. He waited for him, then they walked together, descending to a fast-flowing river and following its path towards the smoke.

It took them half an hour to reach the wreckage. The hike had not been as difficult as anticipated. The fire had burnt out, but smoke still spiralled from the blackened metal skeletons. The timber lorry's driver was still in his cab, his charred corpse slumped across the wheel, almost unrecognisable as a human being. The driver of the other vehicle had been thrown clear and lay fifty yards away, untouched by fire. He was old, well over sixty with thin grey hair. His age-lined eyes were open, staring sightlessly up through the smoke to the blue of the sky. His face seemed unmarked by the fall.

Wilde half wondered whether he might be one of the elderly men they had seen in the Kuhhaus pension at Grünegg the night before, but the face meant nothing. He felt for a pulse but didn't find one. Then he turned him over and saw that the man's ancient skull had been broken open like an egg, his brains spilling out.

'Dead,' Wilde said.

'Well, there's a surprise, Professor.'

He stared, frowning, at Heck's eyes. 'Are you really as callous as you make out, Lieutenant? Or is this just some game you've decided to play with me?'

Heck said nothing, simply turned away and began making his way back to the jeep. Wilde went with him; there really was nothing to be done, but he would have loathed himself if he hadn't looked.

They drove on northwards and some way to the west, back towards the Bavarian border. Wilde still couldn't make sense of what had happened. He couldn't get away from the gnawing suspicion that either one or both of the truck drivers had been on a mission to kill. He had detected something in the oncoming truck driver's wide, expressionless eyes, and he wasn't convinced that the last-second swerve had been done with the finest of motives.

In which case, to hell with the two men.

Back at CIC headquarters in Garmisch, the bustling market town and ski resort at which Hitler had hosted the winter Olympics in February 1936, they ate a meal of steak, mushrooms, fried potatoes and tomatoes. Good produce imported from America to feed the conquerors of a starving people. Wilde thought it was the best food he had ever eaten. In the absence of Scotch whisky, he could even appreciate the Kentucky rye that the barman suggested.

'There's something up there in Almrosen,' Heck said. 'I'm sure of it. That empty house, that woman, the trucks . . .'

Wilde couldn't disagree. But they were still no nearer their quarry. They might track down August Jaeger sooner or later, but what if he just shrugged his shoulders and feigned ignorance? In fact, why would he say anything else if he had been instrumental in helping the world's most wanted man to disappear?

The Gestapo might have ways of obtaining information under such circumstances, but Wilde didn't. And so without inside information, they had nothing.

Hunting for one man in the Alps would be no easier than finding a crow in a crow-black night.

'If they know something up there, I don't think they'll talk,' Wilde said. 'And if they don't know anything, we'll just be

wasting a lot of precious time. We both know what we have
to do now. We have to talk to the obvious suspects, the people
who were there, the ones who really know something. One of
them will break, because conspiracies never hold.'

After their meal and a chance to shower and change clothes,
they met Colonel Appache in his office. He had his jacket off
and his military shirtsleeves rolled up. He gave his visitors a
perfunctory salute, then spread himself out in his leather desk
chair and ran his fingers through his crew-cut hair. 'What
happened to you last night? We had a meeting planned.'

Wilde gave him a full report of their visit to Almrosen and
the incident of the two lorries. The colonel listened, but he
seemed rushed and distracted and soon began tapping his
fingers on the desk.

'Is that it?' Appache said when the story was finished.

'It seemed to mean something to us,' Wilde said, annoyed
by the colonel's apparent disinterest, even ennui. 'Of course it
would help if we could find August Jaeger and bring him in for
questioning. Also those men in the Kuhhaus at Grünegg . . .'

'Goddamn it, Professor Wilde, just because they're diehard
Nazis doesn't mean they're hiding Hitler. If we arrested and
interrogated every German and Austrian who still hankers
after the good old days of Hitlerdom, we'd have to intern half
the nation.'

It wasn't worth arguing. Wilde was beginning to understand
why Collingham and Harper had not bothered to brief the
colonel in any detail.

Appache pushed a sheet of paper across the table. 'These are
the people you should be talking to. They actually knew – or
perhaps *know* – the Führer. Their evidence is crucial. If they
know where Hitler is, it'll be your skill that gets the truth out

of them. That's what you're here for.' He directed the words at Wilde, then glanced at Heck. 'And I know you have your own methods, Lieutenant. But be careful. A GI has gone on trial for killing a German civilian. I don't want to see you in the dock. You do it the way Professor Wilde tells you. He may not have army rank, but on this mission he is your senior officer. Understand, son?'

Heck smiled, but didn't bother to reply.

Wilde looked at the paper. It had two names on it: Hugo Blaschke, dentist; Erich Kempka, driver. Fair enough. He already had the names on his own, rather more extensive, list.

'Dentist and driver,' the colonel drawled. 'You may think they're a bit low level, but they sure as damn were close to Hitler – particularly his driver Kempka. He was there at the end. He was the man who was ordered to find fuel to burn the bodies of Mr and Mrs Hitler. He supposedly found the two hundred gallons of gasoline to douse them. As for the dentist, he's the one who identified a piece of dental work found by the Soviets in the ashes outside the bunker as a bridge he had made for Hitler. They've been interviewed extensively, but we believe there's more there to be learnt. God go with you, gentlemen. Keep me informed.'

And with that, he rose from his desk and they were dismissed.

Chapter 14

Hitler's chauffeur, Erich Kempka, had been captured at Hintersee in Austria and had been moved around. Now, he was in a POW camp at Darmstadt, twenty-five miles south of Frankfurt, so Wilde and Heck hitched a ride on a USAF transport flight.

On landing at the airfield, a car was waiting for them and they were driven directly to the camp. They were still in the American zone and Wilde was shocked by the devastation he witnessed, far worse than the countryside and towns north of Munich. Almost the whole city of Darmstadt had been razed to the ground. Everywhere, women, children and men were scrabbling around the rubble and ashes, looking for food or coal and trying to find some sort of shelter. They were slow, ponderous and blank-eyed, like creatures from an old black-and-white Bela Lugosi movie.

It was as though they had given up all hope of a future. Many had limbs missing. From the car window, Wilde watched a small boy of about eight pushing a little girl in a wheelbarrow. It seemed likely that she was the boy's sister. Her flaxen hair was plaited in pigtails and her face was exquisite. She had one arm and no legs.

There was something else, too, a miasma; the sickly stench of death, of decaying bodies still buried in the ruins. That and the ubiquitous waft of disinfectant. Half a dozen women with knives were attacking a dead horse at the side of the road, cutting ragged haunches and slices for their supper. Crows picked at the meat alongside them. Even from the car, Wilde could tell that the meat was already rotten, like pheasant hung a great deal too long.

They stopped briefly at a junction and an old man tapped on the window then presented his hands, palms upwards in supplication. 'Cigarette, Ami, please. One cigarette.' The car drove on.

The prisoner of war camp was nothing but a series of vast open-air fields surrounded by tangles of barbed wire, guarded by bored American GIs with their weapons cradled casually in their arms; these sentinels knew their many thousands of prisoners were defeated and that they had nowhere else to go. If any of them wanted to escape, so what? Maybe they'd shoot them, maybe they'd just let them go.

Word had been telephoned ahead from CIC Garmisch that Wilde and Heck would be arriving, and so Erich Kempka had been brought to the administration block to wait for them. It was a grey, damp, dispiriting afternoon. Here on the outskirts of Darmstadt, the destruction was everywhere and inescapable.

An American officer introduced Wilde and Heck to Kempka, then said he'd have coffee and sandwiches sent to them.

'Just us,' Heck said. 'Not the prisoner.'

Kempka seemed to understand the gist of the English and looked disappointed.

'Understood,' the officer said. With a brisk nod to his guests, he said he'd leave them to it and went out to organise their refreshments.

'Coffee and sandwiches?' Kempka said. 'Some for me, please, kind sir. I'm not good at answering questions when I'm hungry. And I tell you, we are all as hungry as hell in this shithole camp. No shelter, no food, no cigarettes.'

'Answer our questions, give us information we haven't heard before, and I'll make sure you have some good food,' Wilde said. It had already been agreed that in this interview, he would lead the interrogation.

'And beer. I'd kiss your feet for a stein of beer.'

'All depends what you tell us. But don't push your luck, Herr Kempka.'

'Obersturmbannführer Kempka,' he said. 'That is my title. What you might call "lieutenant colonel", I believe.' He pronounced "lieutenant" the American way. Wilde noted the slight curl of the lips as though he had just smelt or tasted something unpleasant. Not quite a sneer, but not far off – and enough to make Heck begin to steam. The SS officer's arrogance was likely to make him boil over, which might be useful later, but not quite yet.

'Big title for a glorified taxi driver,' Heck said.

'In many ways I was the Führer's right-hand man.'

'Then where is he?' Wilde demanded.

'He's dead. I personally burnt his body, and that of his new wife, Frau Eva.' Kempka laughed. 'This is crazy, you know. How many times do I have to answer this question? I think I have been to every Ami base in Germany and every time I am asked this by you intelligence officers. Each time, I give the same answer, because it is the truth, and so I have no other answer to give.'

'You are laughing. Do you think there is something funny about all this?'

'It is amusing that I am asked so often what has happened to him when I saw him dead with my own eyes and keep telling everyone this.'

'No, you're wrong,' Wilde said, 'we have evidence that he's not dead.'

'OK.' The German shrugged. 'He's not dead then – if that's what you want to hear. Perhaps you can tell me where he is.'

Heck stepped forward, grabbed the slick young man by the collar and lifted him from his chair into the air. 'If you don't want to die here in this room, you piece of SS filth, you will answer us straight.' He flung him down to the floor. Wilde pulled Heck away, then helped the German back to his chair.

An orderly arrived holding a tray with a pot of coffee, two cups, milk, sugar and a plate of cheese and ham sandwiches. Wilde calmly poured two cups of coffee, handed one to Heck and sipped the other himself. He left the sandwiches on the table, just where Kempka could see them. The German stared at the food with desperate eyes.

Wilde started again. 'We want to hear your story all the way through, Herr Kempka. If you are persuasive, I may let you have a single sandwich. If you help us, I may even have more sandwiches brought – perhaps some bratwurst – and a litre of beer. How does that sound?'

'And cigarettes?'

'That depends on you. Go ahead.'

He was a slender, dark-haired man with a fresh face. Somehow he had managed to keep himself groomed. He was clean-shaven and his hair had been trimmed neatly. Wilde guessed that was a major part of the job: look good, drive safely, keep a high shine on the boss's car. Habits died hard.

'What is there to say? I am thirty-four, nearly thirty-five. I originally come from Oberhausen in the Ruhr. I was a motor mechanic, but I joined the Party in 1930 and in 1932 I was selected for the Führer's SS bodyguard detail in Munich, as stand-in driver when Schreck was indisposed. In 1936, after poor Schreck died, I was promoted to number one driver, and that was the role I carried out until the very end. Nor was I just his driver. I was also in charge of the Führer's private fleet of forty vehicles.'

'And you were always loyal to Hitler?'

'Always, and I still am. When I met Hitler I immediately came to admire him, and we developed a bond which lasted until the very end. I will never say a word against him. Shall I go on? Would you like to know about the many times I drove him on important missions?'

'No,' Wilde said. 'Cut to the bunker, April thirtieth this year.'

'Perhaps just one cigarette?'

Wilde didn't have any because he didn't smoke. He glanced towards his companion with a raised eyebrow. Heck took the hint and pulled a cigarette from the packet in his shirt pocket. He lit it, then dropped it on the floor so that Kempka had to go down on his knees and forage for it.

'Now then,' Wilde said after the SS officer had taken two long drags of the smoke. 'The bunker.'

'Thank you, thank you for the cigarette.' He bowed his head ingratiatingly towards Heck. Suddenly the bluster had dissipated; the SS superman had feet of clay and was prepared to grovel for scraps like a common beggar. 'Very well, it was one thirty in the afternoon. I was at the car pool, in the underground garages, when I received a call from Otto Günsche . . .'

'Who's he?'

'Hitler's adjutant.'

'And where is he now?' Wilde was taking notes.

'I don't know, Professor Wilde. Maybe dead, maybe taken by the Soviets. If I knew, I would tell you.'

'OK, carry on.'

'Otto asked me to bring gasoline to the bunker, to the garden exit. He said he wanted a lot, but he wouldn't tell me why it was needed. I asked him how much he wanted and he said at least two hundred litres. That was difficult. I am sure you can imagine how short our fuel supplies were at that time. Otto was insistent. He said I should siphon the tanks of all the vehicles in the car pool if necessary, so I did that and had the cans transported to the bunker straightaway.'

He paused for several more drags of the cigarette, holding the smoke deep in his lungs for as long as he could before expelling it with a gasp.

'Did you take the fuel to the bunker yourself, or send other men?'

'There were others. I could not carry two hundred litres alone. But I led the way. And when I arrived, I learnt that Hitler and Eva were dead. They had killed themselves in their room. Of course, I later learnt that Fräulein Braun had become Frau Hitler in the last hours of her life.'

'Who told you they were dead?'

'Otto told me. He was white with shock. He simply held up his hand, forefinger out like a pistol barrel, and held it to his mouth. And so I knew that the chief had shot himself. A little later, the door to Hitler's sitting room opened and his body was brought out by his physician, Dr Stumpfegger, and his valet, Heinz Linge.'

'You saw Hitler clearly? You saw his face?'

Kempka shook his head. 'No, the body was wrapped in a dark grey blanket. His face and torso were covered. But I saw his legs and recognised his black trousers, his shoes. His arm was hanging loose. At the top, I could also see his greying hair.'

'So you couldn't be sure it was Hitler?'

'Of course it was the Führer. I didn't need to see his face to recognise him after so many years together. Then Bormann came out of the room carrying Eva. I couldn't stand to see that because she was always a good friend to me and I knew how much she hated him, so I took her body from him and carried her up the stairs. It was not easy on the concrete steps, so when Otto Günsche saw I was struggling he assisted me.' Kempka sighed. 'Please, I am getting faint. A little food and drink, kind sirs. The rations in this camp are so poor. All we are given is black bread, a little sausage sometimes, cheese and butter. And we don't even have a roof over our head at night, did you know that? Men dig themselves into the ground for warmth. What will happen to us when winter comes?'

'I suspect you're a lot better off than the prisoners your people held in Bergen-Belsen or Auschwitz,' Wilde said.

Kempka was silent. He had no adequate response, but if he felt shame at what his beloved master had done, it was hard to detect.

'So you and your comrades carried Eva and Adolf upstairs from the bunker. What happened then?'

'We laid them on the ground, side by side, in a depression, about three metres from the entrance to the bunker and poured the petrol over them. This was difficult and dangerous because the Russians were shelling us all the time by then. God knows how none of us were killed or wounded.'

'Who was there?'

'Myself, Günsche, Linge, Stumpfegger, Bormann. Oh, and we had been joined by Reichsminister Goebbels. So there were six of us. But the shelling became so intense that it was too dangerous to venture out to light the fire to cremate the bodies. We huddled in the doorway, trying to work out how to do it. I found a rag, doused it in a little petrol, set it alight, and threw it. And the flames went up. As one, the six of us came to attention and saluted our fallen leader, then with our heads bowed, we quickly went back down into the bunker. And that was that. The end of a glorious age.'

'So six of you did this. Well, we know where you are, Kempka, and we know that Goebbels is dead and Bormann is missing. Do you know where he is?'

'I have no idea except that he tried to escape Berlin on foot.'

'What about the other three?'

'Linge left the bunker with me on May the first – the day after the Führer's death. But we became separated. I know that Stumpfegger was with Bormann, but I don't know what became of either of them. Probably dead, because the chance of evading the Soviets at that time was very slim. And, as I told you, I don't know where Günsche is. Perhaps you have more information?'

Wilde did not answer. In fact, he *did* know that both Linge and Günsche were in Soviet hands. He had no idea about Stumpfegger or Bormann though. He nodded to his companion. 'Do you have any questions for the prisoner, Lieutenant Heck?'

'I would just say that it is very convenient that you never saw Hitler's face, and that the other men who supposedly carried him to his cremation are either dead or missing. Very convenient. You are the only one in Allied hands who can tell us this story.'

'Can I just add, sir,' Kempka said, 'that I did go into the Führer's sitting room, and I saw the Führer's blood on the floor. Also his gun. So, whatever you care to believe, I am certain that someone died in that room. And I truly have no reason to believe that it was anyone other than the boss and his new wife. You know, he is painted now as some sort of devil, but to us he was like a kindly father. He was much loved by those who worked for him and saw him every day. His death is a great sadness and loss for the nation. If I believed for a moment that he was still alive, I would shout it from the rooftops.'

Wilde saw Heck's fists bunching and quickly tried to put a stop to the chauffeur's paean to his leader. 'There were many other people in the bunker?'

'Of course. Dozens of senior officers, generals, guards, secretaries, cooks. It was like a vast underground garrison. And no one had any doubt what had happened. None of them. They had all been told by Hitler that he intended to kill himself, and all were agreed that that was what had happened. The Goebbels family had no doubts – they followed their master to the next world.'

'Hitler could have escaped. He could have been flown out of Berlin hours earlier, and you could have burnt the body of an impostor, dressed in his uniform.'

'But that would not have been his way. He would never have cowered away like a rat. He wanted to die in the front line and he insisted that his remains be destroyed. He told us clearly that he would never allow his body to be displayed in a glass case by the Russians so that it could be mocked and spat on by everyone for years to come.'

Wilde handed the plate of sandwiches to Kempka, who hesitated only a moment before greedily thrusting them into his mouth. Wilde signalled to Heck. 'Come with me a moment, Lieutenant.' They left Kempka stuffing his face under the watchful eye of an armed guard, then retreated outside the office. 'What do you think?'

'I think I want to shoot the bastard in the face. He smirks at us; he bullshits us.'

'You're right. He's an unreliable witness. But that doesn't mean he's not telling the truth – as he sees it. However, he plainly couldn't identify Hitler from his trousers and a lick of grey hair. No one could, whatever he says. So he was relying on the word of the men who wrapped the body in the blanket. We know their names: Bormann, Linge, Dr Stumpfegger and Günsche. Two are missing, two are with the Soviets. None of them is available to be questioned. A very convenient fact.'

'I agree.'

'It means that Kempka wasn't in on the conspiracy – otherwise he would simply lie and tell us that he saw Hitler's face.'

'That tells us that Hitler didn't trust him enough to be involved in his disappearance. He's nothing more than a stooge. The problem is, we're now at a dead end – unless we can persuade the Russians to let us talk to Günsche and Linge.'

'There's the dentist, of course, Hugo Blaschke. He has testi-fied that the bridgework found in a jawbone in the ashes out-side the bunker was made by him for Hitler,' Wilde said.

'Of course he'd say that. That's what he has been told to say. Talking to him is pointless.'

'But what if he's an integral part of the conspiracy. I mean, if Hitler in his hideout has toothache, Blaschke is the man he'll send for.'

Heck dismissed the idea. 'We're clutching at straws. I can't be bothered to talk to a fucking Nazi dentist. If Hitler needs him, they'll go and get him and take him, blindfold, to the hide-out. They're not going to trust a man like that with knowledge of his whereabouts.'

Wilde realised Heck was probably right, which put Blaschke at the bottom of the list of those to be interrogated. 'Come on, let's give Kempka one last going-over. I have another question for the bastard.'

'Can I threaten him?'

'If you think it would help. But don't kill him.'

Heck shrugged. 'If you say not. But I'd very much like to.'

They returned to the room. All the sandwiches had gone. 'One more thing, Kempka,' Wilde said. 'You were driving Hitler for many years. Most of it was on official business, I am sure. But what about the other times – when he was relaxing?'

'The boss liked to relax at Obersalzberg – at his house there, the Berghof.'

'Oh, we know that. But where else? He loved southern Bavaria and his native Austria, I believe. What were his favourite outings? I'm told he liked to be driven around at high speed in his supercharged Mercedes. Where did he demand to be taken on a sunny afternoon outing? What were his favourite lakes, villages and mountains?'

Kempka seemed to be thinking. Heck tossed him another lit cigarette, as he might toss a treat to a dog.

'He certainly liked the lakes – Walchensee, Chiemsee. He loved the mountains of the Tyrol. He always told me that mountains recharged his batteries.'

'Any towns or resorts in particular? Did you ever go to a place called Grünegg? Or Almrosen?'

Kempka's expression didn't change. 'I don't know those places,' he said. 'But I can tell you this: he once told me he wanted his body to be laid out on top of the Wildspitze, like a Teuton warrior king, so that his flesh could feed the eagles.'

Chapter 15

'Phone for you, Professor Wilde.'

'Who is it?'

'Mr Dulles, calling from Berlin.'

'Thank you.'

Wilde and Heck were in the US Army canteen in the Darm-stadt base, a huge functional building that had been thrown up in great haste. They had been discussing their next move. Both agreed that there was little more to be gained from Erich Kempka, a man of huge self-regard but very little intelligence. If others around Hitler wanted to pull the wool over his eyes, it would have been a simple matter.

Now the call from Allen Dulles had come through and Wilde went into the office to take the phone. 'Hello, Mr Dulles.'

'Professor Wilde, I heard you were near Darmstadt and that you've been given the chance to talk with Hitler's driver. Piece of work, huh?'

'Indeed. A convenient idiot.'

'Quite.'

'Is there any chance of talking to Linge and Günsche? If there's a conspiracy, then they're in on it. Won't the Russians cooperate with us?'

'Could be tricky but I'll see what I can do. In the meantime, how's it going? Lieutenant Heck killed anyone yet?' He chuckled.

'He's come close.'

'Well, that's why you're there – to keep him in line. He's a good man, but understandably vengeful. Oh, by the way, Colonel Appache told me about your little excursion into the French zone. Sounded interesting.'

'It was frustrating, not to mention hairy.'

'Well you're alive, and that's the important thing. Anyway, the reason I called is that you're not far from Camp Sibert at Oberursel, a little way north of Frankfurt. Why not drive down and talk to Hanna Reitsch? You've heard of her, I take it?'

'Of course.' Hanna Reitsch was Germany's most famous aviatrix. She had set many flight records and had worked as a test pilot. It was said that Hitler was mesmerised by her.

'We have her interned for interrogation and de-Nazification. It's possible she effected Hitler's escape from the bunker. She flew from central Berlin not long before his supposed suicide, the last flight out. If anyone got him out by plane, it had to be her. And we know she was in the bunker in the last days of April.'

'What does she say?'

'She denies it, of course, and she has undergone many hours of interrogation. But you, Professor, will discover the flaw in her testimony. You and Lieutenant Heck.'

'OK, we'll try.'

'Organise a car, drive up to the interrogation centre and weave your magic. In the meantime, I'll fix transport and visas to get you to Berlin. The Russians may or may not grant access to their prisoners, but if they do, it would be better to have you *in situ* so you can act fast before they change their mind. They're a fickle bunch, the Reds.'

The drive to Oberursel showed them more of the terrible destruction wrought on Germany. Roads were cratered, bridges hastily repaired but not properly rebuilt, checkpoints commonplace, town centres shattered and shops boarded up. Makeshift markets had sprung up everywhere – sometimes single stallholders like Birgit Zimmer's pathetic collection of bric-a-brac on a remote roadside in Bavaria, sometimes groups of people throwing up tables full of food, old clothes or random items in bombed-out squares and streets.

Heck had asked that he be allowed to lead the questioning this time. Wilde wasn't happy, but Heck pushed his case. 'You think I am not subtle, Professor. But I am when need be. Had the Nazis not invaded the Netherlands, I would have gone to university to study literature. At least try me.'

'OK, but remember, there is no suggestion that this woman is a war criminal. She's not SS.'

'I understand that, and I accept that you are the boss. If it's not working, butt in.'

Hanna Reitsch was not what Wilde expected. Strong, small, smiling, not pretty but strangely magnetic. They met her in the camp commander's comfortable sitting room. Reitsch wore a smart red suit, pearl earrings, and had somehow managed to get her short fair hair permed. Neat and businesslike, it enfolded her scalp and temples like a military helmet.

At thirty-three years old, feted in Germany and abroad for her remarkable flying skill, she was clearly a woman who enjoyed her star quality and would never present anything but her best face to the world.

She seemed particularly interested in Wilde and he assumed it was his position as a Cambridge professor that impressed her. He could imagine her as the sort of person who immediately latched on to the most important person in the room, anyone who could in any way advance her career or interests. 'I must say, you don't look like a professor, Mr Wilde.'

'I'm not quite sure what a professor looks like – or whether I should feel flattered or insulted.'

'I mean, you look more physical than the usual type. German professors are all bent and weedy with thinning hair and thick spectacles.'

Wilde knew when he was being manipulated and shut down the flattery by indicating to Heck that it was time to change the subject and get on to more important matters. 'Lieutenant, over to you.'

Heck put his first question. 'Perhaps you would tell us about your final trip to Berlin, Frau Reitsch.'

The Dutchman's voice was calm and soft. Wilde was pleasantly surprised.

'You know, of course, that I have been all through these events already – on several occasions?'

'Indeed we do, but we would like to hear it from you for ourselves. Otherwise it's all hearsay.'

'To what end, may I ask?'

'We want to find Hitler.'

She sighed. 'You know, I sincerely wish he was alive. I wish I had been able to persuade him to leave the bunker and come with me, but he wouldn't leave.'

'Then tell us every detail of your trip and your meetings with him. That last flight out of Berlin.'

'Of course.' A smile lit up her face. Her large eyes sparkled. 'I like nothing better than to talk about flying. So, I was with General Robert Ritter von Greim . . .'

'Your lover?' Heck asked.

She laughed. 'So people say, but I would never talk about such things, even if they were true. But it is no secret that Robert and I were close. Anyway, in the final days of the war, Goering was dismissed as head of the Luftwaffe and Ritter von Greim was promoted in his place. Not that there was much left of the Luftwaffe to command, you understand. The Führer wanted to see him to give him his orders, but Robert was in Munich. The question was how to get into Berlin when it was almost completely overrun by the Red Army? All we had left was a few hundred metres around the Führerbunker and the Chancellery.'

'What did you do?'

'Well, Robert was undeterred. He would have been within his rights to say such a journey was impossible but he was utterly loyal to Hitler and I was loyal to both of them. Together, Ritter von Greim and I flew from Munich to the large airbase at Rechlin, north of Berlin. We commandeered a Focke-Wulf and flew on to Gatow on the western outskirts of Berlin.'

'But you were flying through enemy airspace – surely you were attacked?'

'Of course, but we had a fighter escort, forty strong. We were damaged but lucky because we managed to land safely. Many of the brave fighter pilots who escorted us were not so fortunate.'

'All for the vanity of one man.'

She gave him a death stare, then moved on with her tale. 'With the Focke-Wulf out of commission, we transferred to a Fieseler Storch for the last leg into the city centre.'

'Wasn't that suicidal?'

'It was war. You are a soldier, Lieutenant. Soldiers put their lives on the line and never question an order.'

'Carry on.'

'Robert Ritter von Greim was at the controls and we flew at treetop level. Very soon we came under intense fire again and Robert was badly injured in the foot. Maybe a bullet or shrapnel from flak, I don't know. But he was in intense pain, bleeding badly and was in danger of losing consciousness. He could no longer fly and so I had to lean over him and stretch for the controls, which was not at all easy. The plane was struck many times by bullets. Fuel streamed from the tanks, but I suffered no hits myself. Soon our fuel tanks registered completely empty and I knew I had to glide in to land. But where? And then, amid the rubble and the uprooted trees, I spotted a small, flat space in what remained of the Tiergarten, just behind the Brandenburg Gate. The area was deserted – just a wasteland of dust and debris. The Soviet shelling was constant and shrapnel was raining on us, a torrential downpour of metal and high explosives.'

'So you landed safely, then just walked through this bombardment to the bunker in company with a badly injured man?'

'No, no. Once again our luck held. A Wehrmacht truck was weaving through the destruction and I managed to flag it down. They drove us up Unter den Linden right to the Reich Chancellery. Everyone in the bunker was astonished to see us, for they could not believe anyone had managed to reach them.'

'You met Hitler?'

'Of course. He came to the field hospital where Ritter von Greim was being treated by Dr Stumpfegger. The Führer looked in a bad way – very grey and old. He was stooped and trembling, but he took Robert by the hands and thanked him from his heart, rewarding him for his staunch patriotism and courage by promoting him from general to field marshal and commander-in-chief of the Luftwaffe. Then he turned to me with tears in his eyes and called me a brave woman and said "There is still loyalty and courage in the world." That meant more to me than any medals or prizes. You know, even as a test pilot, I was always a civilian, but I loved my country above all else, as I am sure you two gentlemen do with yours. The Fatherland was everything to me and it still is – so to be praised like that by the greatest German of all time was the finest honour that could be bestowed.'

Wilde had been listening to the exchange in silence. Heck was keeping his composure as he had promised, but how long would he be able to keep his cool in the face of this unapologetic Nazi? When would the swear words or threats come tumbling from his mouth?

Suddenly, Heck changed the subject. 'What do you think of Jews, Frau Reitsch?'

She looked taken aback. 'Why do you ask?'

'Curiosity.'

'I have nothing against them. Why, are you one?'

'Does it matter if I am?'

'No. I just wondered. I know crimes were committed against them, terrible crimes, but they were not my responsibility. I knew nothing of such things and I am certain the Führer didn't either. Nor did Ritter von Greim.'

'But you won the Iron Cross? That doesn't sound like the sort of reward given to a civilian.'

'I was awarded it twice, in fact. Second class and first class. For my work as a test pilot, you see. Not for doing any harm to anyone.'

Wilde could see she was becoming flustered. She talked faster and with greater animation. Sometimes her face formed into a smile, but it looked rehearsed and insincere. Her hands were agitated and her big eyes darted between her two interrogators.

'So let's get back to the bunker,' Heck said. 'You were there how long?'

'Two days – April twenty-sixth to the twenty-eighth. We left two days before the Führer and his bride took their lives.'

'What did you do during your time in the bunker?'

'Well I ate and I slept, of course. I played with the beautiful Goebbels children, and I read stories to them. I became very friendly with their mother, Magda. I also got to know Eva Braun – Eva Hitler, of course. She was very sweet to me. Everywhere in that bunker there was a terrible atmosphere of doom. It felt like a sarcophagus. But then, out of nowhere, there was dancing and drinking and laughing. A lot of drinking, and then tears and gloom.'

'You saw Hitler again?'

'Once more, alone in his sitting room, and he looked even worse. He handed me two cyanide capsules and said they were to give me the choice of what to do. The Führer said that he was determined that he and Eva would take their own lives and their bodies would be reduced to ash. Saying farewell to him was the most terrible thing I have ever had to do.'

'How did you get out?'

'With great difficulty. The shelling had become incessant so that even the depths of the bunker shook. Concrete and plaster fell all around us and the explosions were deafening. Robert Ritter von Greim and I had decided we would stay until the end and share the fate of everyone else, but Hitler had other plans. He believed Himmler had betrayed him and he wanted Robert to go and have him punished for trying to do a deal independently with the Allies. That seemed impossible. Getting in to Berlin was difficult enough – how were we to get out again?'

'But you did?'

She nodded vigorously, grinning with uneven teeth. 'It was night-time. Field Marshal Ritter von Greim was in a bad way and had to be helped up from the bunker; he was on crutches and it was very difficult for him. At last we got out of the bunker and into the open air. It wasn't dark. The whole city was lit by flames. All we could do was wait for a lull in the shelling. When there were a few moments of relative quiet, we hurriedly climbed aboard a Panzer waiting for us in the Voss-strasse, and the nerve-shattering journey began. Among fire, thick smoke, acrid dust and a deafening hail of shrapnel and bullets, the tank negotiated its way towards the zoo, which was nowhere near the place we had left our damaged Fieseler Storch. I confess I was terrifed that we must be heading straight into the Soviet lines and would all be killed. But the tank crew knew what they were doing, and from the zoo we crossed the wasteland of Tiergarten to the Victory Column where the flight control was based. Miraculously this was still in German hands, and a two-seater Arado 96 trainer plane was waiting for us there. It had been flown in specially for us from Rechlin and was concealed in a concrete bombproof shelter.'

'A two-seater?' Heck asked. 'So just enough room for you and Adolf Hitler?'

'No, no, please don't put words in my mouth. The Führer was not with us. I am small so Ritter von Greim and I managed to squeeze together in the single rear seat, and the pilot who had brought the AR96 to Berlin sat in front of us at the controls.'

'So it was a three-seater?'

'In effect, but only because of my size. It was designed for two.'

'Why didn't you fly it yourself? That way you could have taken your lover, von Greim, and your beloved Führer.'

'I wish he had been with us, but he wouldn't come. That is an end to the matter.'

'OK, what then?'

'We took off. It was a cold, eerie night, but our young pilot was full of courage. He ascended as steeply as he could, but we instantly came under attack. Below us, Berlin was in flames, smoke and fire billowing from half the city. Within minutes, we had shot through the flak into the thick cloud cover. Once we were above the clouds, the sky was starlit and clear of enemy aircraft, and we were free.'

Wilde and Heck looked at each other with the same obvious doubts in mind. Heck signalled Wilde to take over the questioning.

'Why didn't you carry someone more important than the young pilot?'

'That would not have been fair on him. He risked his life to come for us.'

'Since when did Nazis give a damn about fairness or a young man's life?'

'I don't understand.'

'I mean Hitler was happy to sacrifice millions of his own people and even more millions from other countries or races in his insane war. None of you Nazis gave a damn who lived and who died. So why didn't *you* fly the machine instead of some anonymous young pilot? He was just cannon fodder to Hitler, wasn't he? Why not leave the pilot to stew and take Hitler himself? Or Bormann? Or Goebbels? Or one of his pet generals? You can surely see our problem, Frau Reitsch.'

'If you don't believe me, you don't believe me. There is nothing I can do about that.'

'So where did you fly?'

'Rechlin first, then to Plön. They are both in northern Germany.'

'Why Plön?' Wilde asked.

'Because Admiral Dönitz was in Plön. And when the Führer died, he assumed command of the Reich government.'

'Then you moved on again – very quickly.'

'Indeed, we had several stops until we arrived at Zell-am-See in the Alps.'

'And within a few days you and Field Marshal Ritter von Greim were in Kitzbühel in the Tyrol, which is where you were arrested by the American Army. So why there? Why didn't you stay in the north of Germany?'

'We had messages to convey from the bunker, and we wished to surrender to the Amis, not the Reds. There was no other motive.'

'What messages?'

'Private letters to loved ones from those who were about to die.'

'Where are they now, these letters?'

'We delivered them, as promised.'

'But Greim didn't surrender, did he? He took the cyanide pill.'

'He was very sick. The damage to his foot caused extreme pain and the outlook was poor.'

'I suggest you arrived in the Alps because that was Hitler's preferred destination. That's where you flew him and helped him to his mountain hideout.'

She threw her hands in the air. Her wiry body twisted so she was looking away from them, not meeting their eyes. 'I have heard this nonsense so many times! Why will no one believe me? Nothing I say will convince you, so this is all pointless.'

'You can surely understand our doubts, Frau Reitsch: we have no proof that Hitler is dead. The evidence is flimsy at best. We have the word of his driver, who didn't see the face of the man he supposedly burnt. The Russians just found a few ashes and a dental plate, which a dentist conveniently identified as one that he himself made for Hitler. And that's it. Even Stalin doesn't believe he's dead.'

'Then find him and I will believe he is alive. More than that, I will rejoice.'

For the first time, Wilde noticed Heck shifting in his seat. He was beginning to wonder how far to trust the lieutenant's assurances of self-control. Time to move on with the questioning.

'What do you know of the villages of Grünegg and Almrosen?'

'Well, I have been to both of them. They are very pretty Tyrolean resorts and high farming communities. Why?'

'Did you ever meet a man named August Jaeger in Almrosen. He's a mountain guide.' For the first time, Wilde detected some hesitation in Hanna Reitsch, some doubt perhaps over what to say. 'Well?'

She nodded slowly. 'Yes, I have met August Jaeger. He is a fine man, well thought of by all who love the mountains.'

'So he's a friend?'

'I don't know him well enough to call him that.'

'If anyone was going to find some sort of hideout or concealed fortress in the Alps, he'd be the man, right?'

'If . . . if . . . if . . . this is all crazy conjecture, Professor. Why not speak to August? Ask him.'

'We will, but I'm interested to hear that you're his friend. When did you last meet him?'

'I don't know. Maybe two, three years ago. I like to ski in that part of the world. Have you heard of ski touring, when you move from mountain to mountain over long distances? I like that very much, and he is a good companion and guide.'

'Sounds like a very close friend,' Heck said, returning to the conversation. 'Did you ever visit Wildspitze with him?'

'The high mountain? No, I am certain we never went that far. Wildspitze must be a hundred and fifty kilometres from

Almrosen. Easy for a man like August Jaeger, but not so easy for me. Why do you mention Wildspitze?'

Wilde ignored her question. 'You know it, though?'

'I have flown over it, yes. It is a beautiful mountain, second highest in Austria, I believe.'

Heck pushed back his chair and got to his feet. 'Come on, Professor, this woman is going to give us nothing.'

Chapter 16

Wilde and Heck arrived in Berlin late at night at the OSS bureau in the Dahlem suburb and were welcomed by Richard Helms, who had been waiting up for them. Wilde knew him well from the last months of the war when he arrived to man the German desk at 70 Grosvenor Street – OSS headquarters in London.

They shook hands warmly and then Helms introduced himself to Heck. 'I have to apologise,' he said. 'AWD has had to go to Wiesbaden, so you're stuck with me. He asked me to ensure you were provided for and given every assistance. We have set aside quarters for you here.'

'Any word from the Soviets?' Wilde asked. 'We want to speak to two of their prisoners – Otto Günsche and Heinz Linge.'

'Nothing as yet,' Helms said. 'But quick decisions are not in the Soviet playbook. Everything has to go via Moscow, usually to Beria, then back. You might be left hanging for a few days. Sorry about that. Oh, and I heard you had a conversation with the pocket flying machine, Hanna Reitsch. How did that go?'

'Interesting,' Wilde said. 'She thought she wasn't giving anything away, but in fact she was. She was obviously harbouring a secret, and enjoying every minute of it. Thought she was taunting us. If anyone flew her beloved Hitler out of Berlin, it was her.'

And then, of course, there was her link to the mountain guide August Jaeger. That question had caught her unawares.

The Office of Strategic Services had outposts in Munich, Wiesbaden, Frankfurt and, most recently, this one in Berlin. It was housed in a large private villa on the pleasant Foehrenweg street, one of the less bombed areas of the city. It even had a hint of the pre-war greenery and suburban tranquillity that, in Third Reich days, must have been what attracted Wehrmacht General Ludwig Beck to make the place his home.

Beck was dead, of course, having shot himself when the July Plot against Hitler failed, but his house still stood untouched and was conveniently situated in the American sector, just south and east of the wooded outlying district of Grunewald.

Wilde was itching to get on with the inquiry. The idea of waiting around in Berlin kicking his heels hoping for a response from the Russians was unsettling.

'When – if – they do come through with assistance, Tom, a word of warning,' Helms said, as they settled down with drinks in the comfortable mess. 'Yes, they're our allies, yes we smile at each other in public and take hard liquor together. But there's plenty more beneath the surface, as time will tell. What I'm saying is, don't trust the bastards an inch.'

It was a warning Wilde didn't really need. He had his own suspicions about Stalin's true intentions in the post-war world. Why was it, he wondered, that the Soviets knew everything that was going on within the OSS, but that the OSS had zero information from Moscow?

One day that would have to change.

They were allocated rooms, which contained nothing but a single bed along with a small table and a hard-backed chair and a handbasin. 'Sorry about the lack of creature comforts, folks,' Helms had said. 'The Russians stripped the city before we arrived. Took everything of value back to Moscow. Heavy machinery, whole factories, vehicles, furniture from places like this, the lot. They see it as reparations, or what our forefathers would have called the spoils of war. But try the

Wiesbaden bureau if you get the chance, Tom. That's a sight more comfortable. We've taken over the Henkel fizzy wine factory and some fine local villas. Germany's answer to champagne flows like water. Also a little R and R at the five-star Hotel Nassauer Hof for OSS and CIC guys. Not quite so well provisioned here yet.'

'We'll manage,' Wilde said.

'You'll find this little bar the cosiest place. So make full use of it. Better stay around here at night. Out there in the big bad remains of a once great city, there are some desperate people: Soviet deserters, unreconstructed Nazis who haven't had their fill of killing, black marketeers, looters, whores and thieves. One thing they all have in common is that they'll shoot you or shiv you for the price of a cigarette. And there's no shortage of serious weaponry on the streets.'

'I'll bear that in mind.'

'On the positive side, the Soviets have done a good job getting things moving. Electricity, clean water, basic rationing. The problem starts after dark when the desperate and the dispossessed come out and defy the curfew. It's kill or be killed. The people stink. They haven't seen soap in months and their clothes are in shreds. And in the worst of the heat, the gardens and canals reek of corpses.'

Heck said he was tired and would go straight to bed, but Wilde stayed down in the bar and had a couple more whiskies with his old colleague. They talked about the situation in the new Berlin, split four ways since early July, about the atomic bombs that had ended the war in Japan a few days earlier, and Stalin's desperation to acquire a nuclear weapon of his own. On a lighter note, Helms told Wilde that their brilliant friend Julia McWilliams from the London bureau had hooked up with fellow OSS operative Paul Child in Ceylon and the rumour was they would be marrying.

Wilde was delighted. 'About bloody time a good woman nabbed the old boy. They'll make a wonderful couple.'

'They'll get fat,' Helms said, laughing.

'Fat and happy.' Wilde laughed too, then yawned. 'Well, I think it's finally time to hit the sack.'

'Goodnight, Tom. Look, I know this is frustrating for you, but I'm hoping we can trade interview for interview with the Soviets. We've got people they're desperate to talk to, so let's see how it goes.'

Wilde slept well and woke late, at 10 a.m. But he wasn't concerned. If the Russians had made contact, Richard Helms would have had him woken. He wandered along to the bathroom, shaved and had a quick bath, then returned to his room. Dressing in a clean white shirt, socks and underwear from his light valise, he made his way downstairs to the communal dining room, which was empty save for a single waiter. He gave him an order for a pot of black coffee and a full English, then asked him if his companion, Lieutenant Heck, had taken his breakfast yet.

'Yes, sir, he came early. About six-thirty, I believe.'

'Thank you.'

'Can I bring you a newspaper, sir? *Washington Post*? *New York Times*? I'm afraid they're all a day or two out of date.'

'Those two would do me fine. Couple of London ones would be good, too, if you can rustle them up.'

He devoured the news and his breakfast with equal hunger. He loved newspapers almost as much as he loved black coffee. After eating his fill, he wandered back upstairs and knocked on

Lieutenant Heck's door. When there was no reply, he turned the handle and looked in the room. It was empty, but Heck's case was there and the bed had clearly been slept in. Wilde went to his own room, found his toiletries bag and went along to the bathroom to brush his teeth. For the first time in a couple of days he felt like a new man. Clean body, clean clothes, full belly.

Ten minutes later, he found Richard Helms in his office. 'Any word, Richard?'

'Well, something, but not quite what you want.. You have been assigned a guy named Boris Minsky. He will meet you, listen to your needs, and see how they can help.'

'Who is he? What's his position?'

'Officially, he's attached to the Kommandatura, the four-power body governing Berlin, as one of the senior Soviet representatives. In reality, of course, he's SMERSH – Soviet counter-intelligence – so you'll have to take everything he says with a pinch of salt. Anyway, we're not in a position to argue, I'm afraid, so go meet him and see if you can get anywhere. At least you won't have to hang around here. I've accepted a lunchtime meeting on your behalf. A late lunch or early supper, depending on your point of view. The Russians have decided in their wisdom to put their sector of Berlin on Moscow time. So it'll be about 2 p.m. here in our sector – 4 p.m., I suppose, to Comrade Minsky. Go figure, Tom.'

'Where do we meet?'

'At the Kommandatura building. I'll have a driver take you.'

'Thanks. And by the way, have you seen Lieutenant Heck this morning? He had an early breakfast. Where would he be, do you think?'

'I saw him. He said he was going out for a walk. But that was three or four hours ago. Is he in his room?'

'No.'

'Well, feel free to have a look around the place. He must be back by now.'

'Actually, I'd like a sober half-hour talk with you, Richard. Legend had it in London that you once met Hitler . . .'

'That's not legend, Tom, that's the God's honest truth. I had lunch with the guy.'

'In which case I'd very much like to get your take on him. Everything I've heard so far is from people who thought the bastard was God's gift to Germany. So I want *your* instinct: suicide or escape? Hiding in his homeland or a foreign country? That sort of thing. I promise I won't hold you to it.'

Helms smiled. He had dark, swept-back hair and habitually wore a happy-go-lucky grin. It seemed to Wilde that he looked more like an estate agent than a spy chief. But maybe that was his secret. It had to be a plus to go unnoticed in the dark world of espionage. 'Let's go sit down with some coffee then, Tom. Let me reminisce to my heart's content.'

Helms had been a young reporter for United Press who was in the right place at the right time covering the Nuremberg annual rally in 1936 when he was given an invitation for lunch with the Führer on the following day.

'I was picked up in a big open-top Mercedes with a Polish reporter and some Nazi bigwig, and we were taken to listen to a speech by Hitler.' Then they followed his car to the old Nuremberg Castle where they were introduced to Hitler.

'I'm ashamed to say it, because I always loathed Nazism, but he was an impressive man. He understood politics, he had a firm handshake, a smile for every guest and an easy manner. But you know he didn't look so good close up. His skin was poor, his hair greying, and he mumbled his words when he spoke to you. Only his eyes commanded attention, his blue eyes, they were something. Brilliant and bright.'

'What did you learn about his character?'

'He didn't suffer doubts. When discussing world affairs, you or I might say, "I think the UN is a great idea" or "I believe Truman will make a fine president." But Hitler wouldn't say that, even if he thought it – which I confess is unlikely – because he never prefaced any of his opinions with the words "I think" or "I believe". That's what I noticed about him. He stated opinions as bald facts.'

'So, the moment of truth: suicide or escape?'

Helms gave a shrug and smiled. 'Honestly, I don't know. I have no doubts he was or is a brave man in his own warped way. Brave enough to shoot himself without a moment's hesitation. But also, hard, cruel and insanely iron-willed. So yes, he would go into hiding if he thought for a moment that he could lead a counter-offensive like Napoleon after Elba. He would not kill himself while he held the slightest hope of ultimate victory.'

'Homeland or abroad?'

'Homeland, without a doubt.'

Wilde glanced at his watch. They had been talking much longer than planned. Still no sign of Heck. 'Check with your team, would you, Richard? Perhaps someone has seen him or maybe he told someone his plans. If he's not with us soon, I'm going to have to meet Comrade Minsky alone.'

'We have a couple of army uniforms. You should wear one.'

'Do I need to?'

'No one messes with you if you're in uniform in this city.'

'I'll take my chances, Richard.' It would feel wrong to Wilde to wear uniform when he had never been enlisted.

At 1.40, there was still no sign of Lieutenant Heck and Wilde decided to go without him. He wasn't worried about his colleague; if anyone could look after himself, it was Mo Heck. And though he couldn't explain it to himself, he also had the feeling that this was a mission he would like to conduct alone.

The driver dropped him off in a broad tree-lined street, outside the monolithic slab of a building that housed the Kommandatura. Four flags fluttered in the breeze – the Stars and Stripes, the Hammer and Sickle, the Union Flag and the Tricolour. He went through to reception and was informed that Mr Minsky would be a little late.

Wilde took a seat. He knew this trick: gain a negotiating advantage by keeping the other guy waiting. It didn't worry him in the least. The place was incredibly busy, with representatives of all four powers, many in uniform, plenty more in suits, as well as Germans picked as administrators of the city's new order. Apart from a few secretaries, the Germans were almost all men, and they all looked uneasy, aware that they were answerable to the occupiers in everything they did. Wilde closed his eyes, sat back and relaxed.

A few minutes later, he emerged from his reverie to find a short, plump, entirely bald, chubby-faced man looking down at him.

'Professor Wilde?' the man said with a large grin and a magnificently thick Russian accent, like a Hollywood version of how a hard-smoking Red Army officer should sound.

'Colonel General?' He rose to his feet, hand out.

'No formality here, we are comrades-in-arms,' he growled and then, instead of shaking hands, Minsky hugged Wilde like an old friend. His bald pate only came up to the American's chin and Wilde got a whiff of expensive cologne, mixed with stale smoke. When Minsky eventually released him, he stood back, pushing out his belly against his tight Red Army uniform and punched the air, like a victory salute. Two medals, one of them a star, were pinned to his tunic. 'This is a wonderful day. Come on, comrade Professor, let's go and eat and drink. Yes?'

'I'm afraid it's just me. My colleague Lieutenant Heck is indisposed.'

'Don't worry about that. More for us, eh? Come, we have a little taste of Moscow just around the corner – a little Russian restaurant in the heart of the fascist empire. And right from the start I want you to know that the people of the great Soviet Union and Comrade Stalin himself insist on paying for everything. It is an honour to have you as our guest, my friend.'

'Well, it's an honour to be here, Colonel General.'

'Today, we forget military ranks. I am your comrade, Professor. Nothing more.' Together, they strode out on the street. Minsky walked quickly for a man of about fifty with short legs, but Wilde kept up easily.

'So tell me, Comrade Minsky, where did you learn your English? Have you spent time in the West?'

'I was in England for a year back in 1913 to 1914. A great country, but, oh, the class divide. Your poor were so poor, your bourgeoisie so comfortable and smug. These English workers, why do they suffer serfdom still? Why do they allow themselves to be ruled by the capitalist bourgeoisie?'

Wilde couldn't help laughing. The thought of any twentieth-century Englishman submitting to serfdom was beyond ludicrous. 'Would you call Attlee and his new Labour government bourgeois? I thought they had some pretty radical ideas, comrade, but perhaps you know more about these things than I do.'

'Ah, now you are making fun of me, Professor. Of course, I am but an ignorant peasant from the Steppes. How can I possibly know about the way things are in your adopted country?'

'So what were you doing in England before the First World War?'

'Organising labour, evading the Tsar's secret police. What else was there to do? I needed to spend a little time abroad and England seemed the place.'

'And I suppose you left because of the war?'

'I had to go back to fight the Germans – and to organise a revolution.' Minsky laughed even louder, then slapped Wilde's arm and stopped outside a rather pleasant-looking little restaurant. 'Enough about me. We have fine Russian food to eat, and vodka to drink. Come inside, please.'

The dining area was crowded with loud-talking men and a few attractive young women. All of the men wore Red Army uniforms, and so did the women. The air was thick with pungent tobacco smoke and Wilde struggled not to cough.

A table laid with white linen and silver cutlery for three had been reserved for them in the corner. At a word from Minsky one of the place settings was quickly removed.

'Are you hungry, Comrade Professor?'

'I had a hearty breakfast, but more food sounds mighty fine. You've been told why I wanted to talk to you, I take it?'

'Of course. You want to find the house painter. And so do we. Comrade Stalin says he is alive and hiding. He believes he went by submarine to Argentina. So we must find him.'

'Well, I don't know about submarines and South America. But yes, we want to find him, too.'

Minsky grinned broadly and waved his fork at him. 'This is all for show, of course – this investigation of yours. We know the Americans and the British are keeping Hitler alive. Somewhere comfortable in the Home Counties most likely.'

'Good God, why would we do that?'

'To use against us, of course. Do you think we are fools?'

It was a question Wilde couldn't really answer, because if Minsky really believed that then, yes, maybe he was a fool.

'That doesn't sound very likely.'

'Ah, you and your anti-Soviet propaganda! We know your ways. You are even saying that our glorious Red Army soldiers have been raping German women, but that is absurd. Why would we rape women when we can buy anyone we want for two cigarettes or a can of beans? Anyway, we all have campaign wives, and we send our home wives Gretchen knickers to keep them happy. We're no worse than the Amis – I'm told they pay with nylons.'

Wilde didn't bother to argue. 'Anyway, Mr Minsky, putting your unfounded suspicions aside for the moment, my reason for meeting you is that I'm trying to talk to those who were with Hitler right to the end, especially those who supposedly saw his corpse burnt outside the bunker. I believe a couple of them are in the custody of the Soviet Union. Otto Günsche and Heinz Linge. Have you heard of them?'

'Indeed I have, but they are in Moscow now.' A waiter was hovering. 'Come on, let us order our food. Beluga caviar to start with. You like?'

'Oh, I can put up with it at a stretch.'

Minsky spoke in rapid Russian and the waiter scuttled away.

'Does everyone eat caviar in places like this in the people's paradise, comrade?'

'No, Professor, I am sure that you know they do not. They have been brought to starvation by the fascists stealing our livestock, burning our crops, slaughtering our land workers. I am eating here in this fine restaurant in honour of my esteemed guest. Any other day I would make do with beet or potato soup.'

They drank vodka, ate caviar with blinis, devoured tender beef Stroganoff and half a dozen other Russian dishes. Then drank more vodka. Wilde sipped his, aware that Minsky was keeping a close watch on him. The Russian himself drank copious amounts without discernible effect.

After the caviar course, Wilde complimented the dish and Minsky summoned the waiter over and said something in Russian. He returned with a large tin of caviar and handed it to Minsky who, in turn, offered it to Wilde. 'Here,' the Russian said. 'Take this home to your beautiful bourgeoise wife in Cambridge. I know very well how much you and your people have suffered.'

'Why do you mention Cambridge?'

'Because you live there. We know a great deal about you, Professor Wilde. Perhaps you like a wristwatch, too? I have many.'

'Thank you. No to the wristwatch, but the caviar would be greatly appreciated. It's a kind gift. I am sure my beautiful bourgeoise wife will be thrilled,' Wilde said, accepting the tin. He would give it to Helms back at the OSS bureau, where it could be logged and shared between the staff. No one could afford to be bribed by the Soviets. Bribery always led to blackmail. 'Tell me, though, perhaps you could do me another favour, too. You said Günsche and Linge were in Moscow – could I be flown there to interrogate them?'

They had finished the meal and were drinking thick Turkish coffee. Minsky was smoking American cigarettes, one after the other. He shrugged at the question. 'I will have to take advice from my superiors, Professor. But if you want my honest opinion, I would say that such a trip would not be sanctioned by the Kremlin. I can but ask though, eh?'

'I really need this. If anyone knows the truth about Hitler, it has to be someone who was there at the cremation. At least one of them must have been in on the conspiracy. The driver, Kempka, didn't see the corpse's face, but then *he* didn't wrap the body in the blanket and carry it. Günsche or Linge must know the truth. And if they do, they should have a pretty good idea where their boss is now.'

Minsky stubbed out the latest cigarette and rose. 'Come, comrade, let me take you for a little drive – I have something to show you.'

Wilde downed his coffee, which was surprisingly good, picked up his precious tin of beluga and followed his host. A large black car was waiting for them at the kerb. This had all been planned.

To the side of the restaurant facade, a blind beggar stretched out his trembling hands. Minsky was about to climb into the back of the car when he spotted the man and went back. He fished in his pocket and pulled out coins, which he placed carefully into the beggar's palms, closing his fingers around them. He said something in German which Wilde didn't catch, then returned to the car. 'Come, Comrade Professor, join me in the back. I swear no harm will befall you. May I call you Tom? I already feel I know you like a brother.'

'Where are we going?' Wilde said as he climbed in.

'A nice surprise trip. Wait and see.'

Chapter 17

There was birdsong and the sun was emerging from behind a solitary white cloud. Mozes Heck looked up at the blue of the sky and thought it was impossible. There shouldn't be colour in this city, not ever again. It should remain monochrome for all eternity. The grey of the concrete, the black depths of the woods and the canals, the white of the ash, the pallor of the skin, the darkness of the hearts.

He was standing in a street of rubble, outside a tenement block that had lost much of its roof and most of its windows but looked solid and inhabitable, perhaps bolstered and held up by the structures on either side. Most of the damage was on the other side of the road, where the buildings had collapsed. So this was Wolfsstrasse.

There was no sign to reveal the building's number or name, but he had counted down the existing numbers further along the street and had no doubt that this was number eighteen. He was in Charlottenburg in the heart of the English sector. Being in civilian clothes, he had been approached half a dozen times by British soldiers who took some convincing that he was one of them, even when he showed them his ID card and paybook. One sergeant threatened to take him in to have his identity checked. 'You ain't no bleeding British Army lieutenant, you're a bleeding 'Un,' the sergeant had said. Heck had pushed the muzzle of his pistol into the sergeant's face. 'Maybe this will convince you?' Only the intervention of a more senior British officer saved the situation, releasing Heck with a warning not to draw a gun on his men again.

Now he was here, in Miriam's street, outside her home. But he wanted to be sure. A thin woman with a headscarf was pushing a dusty pram past him. Her feet were shoeless, wrapped in rags and her face was almost obscured by the scarf. He stopped her, grasping her twig-like upper arm with his powerful hand. He looked in the pram and saw that the baby – or whatever it was she was transporting – was completely concealed by a bundle of grubby blankets. 'Excuse me,' he said in German. 'What house is this? What number?'

She shied away from him, her sunken eyes wide with fear.

'I'm not going to hurt you. Just tell me the number of this block.'

'Eighteen,' she said. 'Eighteen.' She tried to scurry away but he still held her.

'Is anyone living here?'

'Yes. Yes. Please, let me go. I must take my baby to the doctor.'

'You know the people who live here?'

'No, no. Perhaps. One or two.'

'Miriam Rabinowitz?'

'No. I don't know her. Please, let me go, sir. I was never a Nazi. I never hurt or denounced a Jew. I am so worried about my baby. He is so poorly.'

'Who mentioned Jews?'

'I thought you said you were looking for a Jewish lady, sir. The name you said . . .'

'So is she here in this tenement? Miriam, daughter of Solomon and Gila Rabinowitz. Big apartment on the first floor, I believe.'

She was shaking her head violently. 'I don't know this lady. I am not a Nazi. Please let me go.'

He released her. 'Go,' he said, and she pushed the pram away from him, along the road. He watched her a moment, then turned back to the building. Why was he holding back? Fear that she would be here or that she wouldn't? At last, he stepped through the rubble that had already been shovelled apart to allow a pathway to the front entrance.

There was no door on the hinges, and so he was able to enter. A woman in the hallway was brushing up dust and chips of plaster and scraps of old wallpaper into a pail. She looked at him with surly eyes, then turned back to her work without a word. The staircase had survived and so he climbed it. Wooden slats creaked beneath his feet and he wondered how safe this building really was.

He stopped on the broad landing. There were two doors to two apartments and a further staircase rising to higher floors. Reason told him that Miriam's flat was the one on his right because he knew from her letters that her front window looked out over the street. The door was intact and closed. This felt like the place she would have lived; he had never been here, but she had written to him often, and he felt that he knew her home intimately, for her prose was vivid and detailed. And yet the name on the door was Ganzen, not Rabinowitz. Had they changed their name out of fear, perhaps pretending that they were not Jews?

He stood outside the door for a full minute, his resolve deserting him. In battle, he had never experienced fear, only an overpowering hunger to avenge his family. He had never cared whether he lived or died. Now he was afraid of what he would find, or wouldn't. His hand went to the inside pocket of his jacket and touched the slim wallet holding her photograph and her last letter to him. This was crazy. Surely she couldn't be here? He combed his fingers through his hair, pulled back his shoulders and knocked.

He had met Miriam in the summer of 1937, when both families were on walking holidays in the Bernese Oberland in

Switzerland. They hadn't known each other but, by chance, the families were in the same beautiful hotel in the shadow of the white-capped Jungfrau, and they were both Jewish. Importantly, both their fathers were medical men, so when the restaurant manager called out at supper on the first night 'Please, is there a doctor in the house?' two hands went up, and the fathers looked at each other and smiled.

The need for a doctor was not life threatening – a sous-chef had scalded his arm – but the incident enabled the two families, the Hecks and the Rabinowitzes, to meet. They all hit it off straightaway, particularly Miriam and Mozes, who were both fourteen.

From that day on, Mozes Heck and Miriam Rabinowitz spent every waking hour together for two glorious, sun-filled weeks. They had much in common; he was strong and clever; she was pretty and clever. They made each other laugh.

After that intitial meeting, the families took all their meals together and walked the mountains together. Over supper each night their fathers talked about the increasing persecution of Jews in Germany. It was the reason Heck's father had moved them from Bavaria back to Amsterdam, their home city, a year earlier. Solomon Rabinowitz wouldn't have it, though. Berlin was his city, he said, and he was damned if some pipsqueak corporal with a loud voice and an ugly moustache was going to make him give up his beloved home and medical practice. 'They won't be there forever,' Rabinowitz said. 'It's just a matter of waiting them out. Germany is fundamentally a civilised country. You'll see.'

'But you can't even practise your craft, Solomon,' Maurice Heck replied.

'But I can still treat my own people – our people – and they need me, now more than ever.'

Mozes and Miriam heard these dark conversations, and they were old enough to understand. They had felt the coming darkness themselves. It seemed to them that Jews were being punished for some unspecified crime. Certainly, their lives had already changed. Miriam had been removed from her school and was being educated at home. More than that, they understood that the situation was dangerous.

But none of it really mattered to Mozes Heck and Miriam Rabinowitz. All they cared about was each other. At the end of the two weeks, they kissed. It was a new and thrilling experience for both of them. They took their addresses and wrote to each other at least once a week until May 1940.

After that, Heck escaped to England and heard no more, either from his own family or the Rabinowitzes. Often he wished that both sets of parents had had the sense back in 1937 to stay in Switzerland and seek asylum, or perhaps take a direct flight to London.

If only.

He raised his hand to knock at the door. He was aware of the 'U-boats', the Jews who had stayed in Berlin and other parts of Germany, avoiding deportation to the death camps by surviving beneath the surface. He was aware, too, that precious few of them had made it to the end of the war; too many Germans were prepared to denounce their neighbours.

And if by a miracle they had survived, where would they be now? Perhaps they had come home? Perhaps they had somehow managed to stay here all along. This tenement block, this apartment was the only lead he had.

He knocked, and heard scuttling inside, like rodents scurrying to their holes. He knocked again. This time he heard a voice from the other side of the door.

'Who is it?' A woman's voice.

'Heck. Mozes Heck, from the holiday in Switzerland.'

'Who?'

'Can you open the door, please?'

'Go away.'

Heck stood back. He certainly didn't recognise the voice. It wasn't Miriam or her mother, Gila, he was sure of that. 'I just want a minute of your time,' he said, his voice as low and unthreatening as possible. 'One minute. I can give you American dollars or English pounds for your time. I even have cigarettes.'

'Who are you?'

He tried the door handle. It turned and the door began to open, but the woman inside was pushing against it, trying to keep him out. Heck was far too strong for her and the woman fell back. Heck found himself standing inside a dark hallway, facing a curiously smart woman; a contrast to so many of the down-at-heel Berliners he had seen on his way here from Foehrenweg. She was wearing an expensive-looking suit of short jacket and knee-length skirt. Her hair was blonde and braided in a crown on top of her head. He estimated her age at forty, or perhaps a little more.

'How dare you come into my property like this.' It was not a question but an expression of outrage.

'I told you, I just want to take up a minute of your time.'

'Get out, whoever you are. We don't want your dollars or pounds. Go now.'

Heck had been brought up to respect women, but he elbowed this one aside and pushed through into the main room. It was far larger than he had expected and had two tall windows – still glazed – looking out over the street at the front. Remarkably, it was fully furnished, in the manner that Heck imagined the

Rabinowitzes would have had it, with dark furniture and rather formal but comfortable sofas.

He turned back to the woman and saw that she had a pistol in her hand, a Mauser semi-automatic. He laughed. 'Are you going to shoot me?'

'If necessary, yes, if you don't get out of my apartment this minute.'

'I'll get out when you tell me what has happened to the Rabinowitz family.'

'Who are they? I have no idea who you are talking about.'

'They are the people who used to live here. Solomon and Gila Rabinowitz, their daughter Miriam and their two boys.'

'I have always lived here.'

'I don't think so.' In one swift movement, he knocked her gun arm aside and the weapon fell from her grasp to the floor. Languidly, he picked it up. 'Nice weapon, eh?' He removed Miriam's last letter and picture from his pocket and carefully removed them from the slim wallet. He unfolded the single-sheet missive and pointed to the address at the top. 'There you go, lady. Number eighteen Wolfsstrasse. That rather shows you haven't always lived here.'

'Perhaps it's one of the other apartments.'

'No, it's this one. My friend described it precisely. And look at this.' He held up the photograph of Miriam. It had been taken in this very room. Even the curtains behind her were the same.

'That proves nothing,' the woman said. 'Your friend has written the wrong address. This is our home. It always has been. Are you Bavarian? You sound a little Bavarian.'

He ignored the question 'Who else is here?'

'No one. Just me.' Her face was hard, but suddenly she tried to soften it, perhaps in response to his possession of the gun.

'Look, please, I didn't mean to talk to you so sharply, but you know we have had many unwelcome visitors here: Russian soldiers, English soldiers. I have not always been able to fight them off.'

He heard a sound from the next room. 'I thought you said no one else was here.'

'That is just my father. He is old and senile. My husband is a prisoner of the Russians and may already be dead. My son was in the Volkssturm, and he is dead.'

Heck put the letter and picture back in his pocket, then gazed around the room. There were picture hooks but no pictures. Probably, they had hurriedly burned their portraits of the Führer, or hidden them beneath the floorboards to be brought out when he rose again in glory.

On the mantelpiece, however, Heck saw a small family photograph in a poorly made wooden frame, half-hidden behind a vase. He picked it up and saw that the mother in the picture was the woman. The man at her side wore an SS uniform and their child wore his Hitler Youth outfit. The man was clearly a senior officer, perhaps the equivalent of a colonel or a brigadier. Heck was not entirely au fait with SS ranks and insignia.

'It was a different time, sir,' the woman said.

'Indeed it was. A time when apartments were stolen from Jewish families and given to loyal murderers of the Third Reich.'

'That is not what happened. This apartment was unoccupied when we were shown it. It suited us. My husband and I come from Leipzig and his work brought him to Berlin, for he was based at Lichterfelde for a while. We needed somewhere to live so we could be near him.'

'Let's say hello to your father, shall we?'

'No, he is in bed, sick. He cannot move.'

'Don't worry, he doesn't have to move.' Heck walked to the first door on the left.

She came after him, clutched at his arm. 'Please, he is an old man. He doesn't know what is happening.'

Heck pushed the door open. A man of about sixty-five stood there in a brown shirt and swastika armband. He had a Hitler moustache and his arm shot out at an angle of forty-five degrees and stayed there, quivering. Heck turned back to the woman. 'This is your father?'

'He doesn't know the war has ended.'

Heck put his pistol to the man's head, but he didn't back off. 'Now tell me, one of you, what happened to the Rabinowitz family?'

'If I knew I would tell you,' the woman said.

'What is your name, lady?'

'Ganzen.'

'First name.'

'Ursula. Ursula Ganzen.'

'So, Frau Ganzen, where did the former occupiers of this apartment go?'

She closed her eyes and took a deep breath.

'Yes?'

'I believe they were told to report for deportation.'

'The date?'

'February 1942, I believe.'

'You keep saying believe, but in fact you know, because you were completely involved in it. It was in February 1942, because you wanted to move in then. I suppose you viewed the apartment before they had even left. Your husband was a senior SS officer at the Lichterfelde garrison. Such a man must have had his pick of Jewish apartments.'

The old man's arm was still held out stiffly, but his knees seemed to be giving way. Frau Ganzen's eyes were fixed on her feet but Heck could see no trace of shame or remorse in her features.

'Where were they taken?'

'I am not sure,' she said.

Heck lashed out at the old man, the sharp edge of the gun cracking the side of his head, knocking him back on to the bed.

'Please, don't hurt him.'

'Where?'

'Theresienstadt maybe, or Warsaw or Litzmannstadt. I really don't know. I didn't ask but I believe – *know* – that many Jews were relocated to those places. They were to be given new homes and work. Yes, I felt sorry for them, but everyone was doing it. They were going to be deported to a wonderful new life, and if we hadn't taken the apartment, then someone else would have.'

'Who was here when you visited?'

'The mother, the father, the sons.'

'And the daughter?'

'I didn't see the girl but I know there was one here because I saw some of her things. Maybe she was at school . . .'

'A Jew at a German school in 1942, Frau Ganzen? I don't think so, do you? She was eighteen or nineteen then.'

'Perhaps she was queuing for food or visiting friends. I beg you, sir, I don't know these things and I can't answer your questions. I know it's over, I know we lost and I am ashamed of my father for wearing his SA uniform and swastika, but he won't listen to me.'

Heck wanted very badly to shoot her. His hands were steady but his mouth was trembling. He took out the the picture of Miriam and showed it to the woman. 'This is for her, for Miriam Rabinowitz and her kind, generous family,' he said.

Then he put a bullet in the old man's head.

Ursula Ganzen emitted a low scream and fell to her knees.

'Now you won't have to feel ashamed of him. Now you will know what it means to lose all your family.'

She muttered something under her breath, perhaps not intended for him to hear. But he heard it. 'We should have killed more of you,' she said. 'We should have killed you all.'

Chapter 18

'Well here we are, Professor Wilde. This is where it all happened.'

They had passed the shell-battered edifice of the Branden-burg Gate – the Soviet flag flying on high – then turned right at a huge portrait of Stalin that now dominated the Tiergarten end of Unter den Linden, and the car had stopped on Wilhelmstrasse outside the ruins of the old Chancellery. Then they had made their way on foot to the bunker, picking their way through the rubble and shell craters. The circular observation tower was still remarkably intact, but the square tower housing the entrance had suffered more hits.

It stood, bleak and grey, in a sort of junkyard of old planks, ash, boulders, blackened earth and abandoned concrete mix-ers. Wilde had seen newspaper photographs of it and knew that the area enclosing the bunker had once been the Chancellery garden. All that grew now were weeds.

The bunker's construction was massive blocks of reinforced concrete several feet thick. Soviet shells and bullets and British bombs had cut chunks from the sloping roof and the blank, windowless walls, but could not penetrate.

The entrance doorway was open, its heavy steel door had come away from its hinges and lay flat on the ground like a gangplank to lead you in. One bored-looking Red Army soldier stood outside, rifle at the ready.

'So this is the Führerbunker.'

'Indeed, Professor. This is where Hitler made his last stand. Just like your Colonel Custer. But did Adolf live or did he die? Opinion in the Soviet Union is that he survived, that his supposed suicide and cremation was a carefully staged fraud so that we would not look for him.'

'Opinions in the West are divided.'

Minsky had brought two hurricane lamps. He lit them both, turned the wicks up to brilliant, and handed one to Wilde. 'Please, follow me in. This is the emergency exit, but it is the way Hitler's corpse was said to have been carried out. The main entrance is on the other side of the complex and is accessed by way of the Chancellery. The bunker beneath us goes deep down into the ground on two levels. Hitler's rooms are on the lower level and in all there are thirty rooms. I show you where it all happened. Perhaps you will find a souvenir. Some of Hitler's nail clippings, maybe, or Eva Braun's pretty pink lipstick. Come.'

Minsky flashed a card at the guard and he clicked his heels and let them pass without demur.

The first thing that assailed Wilde was a smell of damp, burnt wood and rotten vegetation. The antechamber to the complex had been partially destroyed by fire, so the walls were scorched and the guards' wooden table and chairs were charred.

No one had attempted to clear the place up. It must have looked very like this on May eighth, when the war ended. But why would anyone bother to clean or tidy such a place? Leave it just the way the Nazis left it, a squalid museum to man's wickedness.

The floor was littered with bits of paper. Wilde picked up a scrap and saw an official heading and, scratched at the bottom, Hitler's sloping signature.

'One for your autograph book, Professor?'

Wilde let the paper flutter to the floor. They made their way down concrete steps to a corridor. The light from the hurricane lamps flickered ghostly shapes against the blank grey walls and low ceilings. There were a series of doorways. Minsky indicated one and led him through into a collection of rooms of varying sizes. 'These ones on the left were used for the telephone exchange and for power generation. On the right, you have a maze of rooms used by Hitler and Eva, his mistress and latterly his wife, though that has never been confirmed to my knowledge. Where is their marriage certificate? Where is the cake?' He laughed. Wilde merely managed a polite, insincere smile.

The floor here was under a couple of inches of water. 'It will get a great deal worse when we get heavy autumn rains,' Minsky said. 'This part of the bunker is below the water table and there is now no power to pump out the flooding.'

A huge rat ran past Wilde's feet, its shadow from the hurricane lamp magnifying it into a cinematic monster.

Wilde was trying to imagine the scene here at the end of April. It must have been crowded and claustrophobic with no natural light, dank air, the stench of sweaty unwashed bodies and the encroaching roar of battle outside. The world closing in and all those present knowing that there was no hope of avoiding defeat, whatever their chief might say to the contrary. And with each passing hour, their chances of finding a way through enemy lines becoming smaller and smaller.

There were children, too. The five girls and a boy who were brought here to die by their parents, Dr Goebbels and his wife Magda. What made them think their six innocent babies deserved to be poisoned just because their parents' lives were about to be snuffed out? That had all happened here, within yards of where he now stood. His stomach churned.

'My God, this is grim,' Wilde said.

'No place to die, eh?'

'Can we see his rooms – the place he is said to have shot himself?'

'Of course. Come through here on the right.'

They went through small bedrooms, bathrooms and ante-rooms. Almost everything in the Führer's office had been broken apart and the stink of decay assailed the nostrils. His writing table had been upended. All the rooms still contained various articles of furniture – single beds, bunks, sodden carpets, overturned wardrobes and chests – their drawers all turned out and anything of immediate use such as cigarettes or brandy looted. Finally, Boris Minsky opened the door to Hitler's private sitting room.

It was remarkably small and undistinguished for a man who had wielded such power. Maybe fifteen feet by ten at the most. A door on one side led to a basic water closet and on the far side another door led to an oppressively cramped bedroom, little more than a cell with a single, metal-sprung bed. In the sitting room, there was a sofa, three chairs, a little writing desk and a table. The sofa was ranged against the rear wall. It was wooden framed with padded back, seat and armrests. Wilde held his hurricane lamp close to see the pattern; some Germanic folk scene of hunters or minstrels and a pair of fawns. He looked for bloodstains but couldn't see any.

'Just between the two of us, I have heard that the woman, Eva Braun, was slumped on the seat, her head to one side. They say she had taken a prussic acid capsule,' Minsky said.

Yes, that was what Wilde had been told by Philip Eaton in London, though he had not explained his source.

'And Hitler?'

'He was in the padded chair, close to her. His Walther revolver was on the floor – in fact two Walthers, of different calibres.'

'Where are they, the pistols?'

'Who knows? I expect they're in some soldier's pack. He probably thinks he has the gun that shot Hitler and will hand them down to his children and grandchildren. Hah, the gun that Hitler put to his temple! A bit of history, eh, Professor?'

'Was it not the mouth rather than the temple?'

'Günsche says temple. Anyway, we simply don't believe him. Maybe he found Eva Braun here and a man beside her with his brains blown out, but it wasn't Hitler. The general secretary is certain of that.'

'The general secretary? You mean Stalin, of course.'

Minsky grinned. 'Comrade Stalin is a man of the people. He doesn't need titles like president or king.'

'Have you met him?'

'Several times.'

'And what manner of man is he? I ask as an historian not an intelligence officer.'

'He is Henry VIII incarnate.'

Wilde was taken aback. It was a dangerously indiscreet thing for a Soviet security officer – or anyone else for that matter – to say. Wasn't it? Comparing Stalin to an English king? But he played along, assuming it was merely a joke. 'With fewer wives.'

Minsky's laugh echoed around the damp, dirty room. 'So far. Give him time! But, please, professor, don't tell anyone I said these things or we will both be shot. And don't forget, the official Soviet line is that Hitler did not die here.'

'Don't worry, you've made that clear enough.'

The Russian snorted. 'Uh, I have such a loose tongue. It will get me executed one day.'

Wilde wasn't so sure about the loose tongue. He rather thought that every word that came from Minsky's mouth was calculated, but he just smiled then crouched down to examine the seat in which Hitler might have died. The upholstery had the same rather sentimental pattern as the sofa. Not to Wilde's taste. But there was no bloodstain. And any blood on the floor would have been washed away.

'Heinz Linge, the valet, has a slightly different story,' Minsky said. 'He claims both Eva and Hitler were on the sofa. Have a look at the armrest on the left. There is a bloodstain, you see.'

Wilde studied it. There was certainly a stain, but whether it was blood was impossible to discern after four months.

'It is worth remembering,' Minsky continued, 'that both Günsche and Linge were fanatical SS officers. They would lie to the death to protect their master, so we should take their testimony with a pinch of salt and pepper.'

'Just salt.'

'Ah yes, the English idiom. I get mixed up after all these years away from that fine country.'

'On the matter of Linge and Günsche, though, I'd still very much like to talk to them, lies and all.'

'Don't get your hopes up, Professor. Come, do you wish to see the rest of the bunker? There are many more rooms.'

No, he didn't. He wanted to get out of this fetid labyrinth as fast as possible. There was nothing to be learnt here. But he said yes, he would be pleased to tour the remainder of the underground shelter.

The worst place was the room with bunk beds where the Goebbels children had slept and died. He didn't need Minsky to tell him that this was where it had happened, because it was manifest; here the ghosts were real. The very walls seemed to bleed with the tears of countless thousands of little boys and girls.

Whatever Goebbels and Hitler had done, their beautiful children had done nothing. Nor had the millions of other children who died or were maimed by the Nazis' insane ambitions of world conquest. Wilde was not a superstitious man. He did not believe in the occult, nor even an afterlife, yet he could hear the children's cries. He could feel the pain seeping through the concrete. He could smell the Zyklon B that killed mothers and babies and toddlers at Auschwitz, the carbon monoxide that killed young and old at Treblinka and Sobibor and Chelmno, and the bitter almonds of the cyanide that did for Heidrun, Hedwig, Holdine, Hildegard, Helga and their brother Helmut. The Goebbels children.

And he thought of his own boy, beautiful Johnny, full of laughter and joy back at home in Cambridge and his eyes filled with tears.

'Come, Professor. It is too much here. We go, yes?'

Wilde nodded. He couldn't speak.

On the way out, Minsky took Wilde's arm and moved his mouth close to his ear. 'One moment, Professor, let me show you this room.' It was the largest room they had been in. 'The diesel generators were here; we found a better use for them elsewhere.' He lowered his voice again. 'Can I trust you, Professor?'

'I hope so – it depends what you want.'

'You are a human being – I saw that just now. And I think we can help each other. No one is listening down here. Even our secret services cannot bug concrete four metres thick.'

'The only help I want, comrade, is an interview with Günsche or Linge – or both. Or perhaps you also have Bormann?'

'I'm sorry, that won't happen. And no, we don't have Bormann. Nor Dr Stumpfegger for that matter. Their disappearance is as mysterious to us as it is to you.'

'What about the two dental technicians from Blaschke's clinic? You told us they identified the bridge and jawbone as Hitler's. Can I talk to them at least?'

He shrugged. 'I know nothing about them. No, wait, I recall now – I'm afraid they too have been sent to Moscow. Anyway, their testimony was deemed unreliable.' He sighed. 'Look, I know I seem to be unhelpful, but these things are out of my hands. However, I do have access to another man who was here in the bunker until the very end. I think you might find him extremely helpful.'

'Who is he?'

'Hans Fritzsche, a senior official in the propaganda ministry. He has been in our custody in Moscow, but now he has been brought to Berlin because he will be standing trial with Goering and Ribbentrop and all the other senior Nazis at Nuremberg. He is a coward and he will do anything to save his skin. So he will talk.'

'What has he told you?'

'This and that. You know, we have not been as obsessed by the fate of Hitler as our Western Allies. As I mentioned, before, our intelligence services believe you have him in safe keeping.'

'And I'm sure you know that is nonsense. So take me to this man Fritzsche. I would like to talk to him.'

'But you have to give me something in return.'

'What do you want? Money? Cigarettes?'

Minsky smiled. 'Do I look that cheap, Professor?'

No, he didn't. He looked very high maintenance with expensive tastes. He was one of the lucky ones in Soviet Russia, one of the ones who survived the purges and the war and had access to the good things in life. His belly told you that. How long could his luck last?

'Go on. Tell me what you want. If it's feasible, then I'll help.'

'Give me your word that you will not breathe a word of this to anyone in Berlin. Not Helms or Dulles or Lieutenant Heck. Even if you say no to a deal, that must be clear.'

Wilde thought for a few moments. Did he have anything to lose by making such a vow? It had to be worth the risk. 'OK, I swear I won't tell a soul. This conversation never leaves this room.'

'Thank you, Professor. I believe you are trustworthy – perhaps too trustworthy for your own good. Anyway, during lunch you asked about my English and I told you the story of my time in England before the First World War.'

'You said you were avoiding the Tsar's secret police.'

'Yes, that's what I said. But it wasn't true. Nor was my life as a peasant in the Steppes. I am as bourgeois as you, Professor. My father was a wealthy merchant and I was studying at Cambridge University. My set of rooms was a joy, with a college servant keeping my fire burning all winter and my nearest neighbour an earl who invited me for shooting weekends at his great house. But with the war looming, I returned to Russia.'

'Interesting times.'

'Indeed. I could only get as far as St Petersburg – Leningrad, as we learnt to call it – and I was press-ganged into the army, as a private soldier. That suited me fine – I had no wish to be an officer, because they always get shot first. Towards the end of the war, when I saw the way things were going, I reinvented myself. I became the revolutionary peasant Boris Minsky, a name I stole from a dead soldier.'

'What was your real name?'

'That's not important. What matters is that I am beginning to fear for my safety. I feel the eyes of Beria and Abakumov on me. I can't keep them both happy – so if one doesn't do for me, the other will. I am caught in a vice between them. And so I want to get out. I *have* to get out, otherwise I know how this will end. You could help me.'

Wilde was astonished. 'Are you serious, Comrade Minsky?'

'Never more so. Specifically, I want to get to Cambridge, a place I loved. And I will need work, a roof over my head, money.'

'But you are a senior officer, Colonel General. A hero of the war. You have immense power of your own.'

'And did that save Kamenev and Zinoviev? And did it save Yezhov, the man who falsified the evidence against them? What of Yagoda, did his murders save him? And the most powerful of them all, Trotsky – did his power blunt the ice pick? When the worm turns in Moscow, there is no escape. And the bigger you are, the bigger the target you make. I have been expecting this for years. Now I know that my time is almost up. Perhaps I could survive Abakumov or Beria . . . but *both* of them? Two vials dripping poison into the general secretary's ear.'

'You're asking a lot.'

'And I give you plenty back. First your interview with Fritzsche. And then, when I am safely in England, I give your intelligence services all the secrets of the Soviet Union. One day soon you are going to need them.'

Chapter 19

'Why me?' Wilde asked.

'At Cambridge, I had a supervisor very much like you. A professor and a man of honour. There are no such men in my world. In my world, sons denounce fathers, friends denounce friends, wives denounce husbands, colleagues shoot colleagues in the head in cold cellars. But I know that men of honour exist in your world. And so I place my future in your hands.'

'You realise, of course, that I alone couldn't provide you with what you want? It is beyond my power, so I would have to seek assistance.'

'Of course. But you must be very careful, and very discreet. Do not mention my name until you are sure it is safe.'

'What about your family? Do you have a wife and children?'

'You let me worry about those things, Professor. I know what I have to do. Come on, time to go. I will fix your interview with Fritzsche and then we meet again.' He tossed something to Wilde, who instinctively put out his hand and caught it. 'There you go my friend, for your courage.'

Wilde looked at it and laughed. It was an Iron Cross, in its box.

'I found hundreds of them in Gestapo headquarters,' Minsky said. 'You have a son?'

'I do.' Wilde rather suspected that Minsky already knew that.

'Take it for him, Professor. Boys love medals, and guns, of course. Anyway, all the German heroes are dead.'

The woman with the headscarf and pram was still outside the house, walking in circles. She glanced at Heck but instead of backing away from him, she said, 'Are you a doctor? I must have a doctor for my baby.'

Heck had left Frau Ganzen clutching her dead father to her breast. It was the first time he had considered killing a woman, but something held him back, some need to show himself better than the Nazis. He knew it wasn't rational, for he had just killed a man in cold blood, but how could any of it make sense? All the nightmarish events of the past ten years were the stuff of the madhouse.

He stopped and watched the mother with the pram. She was so thin and bent, she looked like an old woman. But the bone structure was there, all too visible, and in a former life when food was plentiful and clothes were pretty, she must have been a good-looking young woman.

Having already stuffed his pistol into his belt, he had his hands in his trouser pockets. When she approached him, he leant over the pram to look at the child, though there was nothing he could do to help. The baby was still smothered in its blankets. 'I think you must give him a little air, dear lady,' he said. He smiled at her, then gently pulled back the dirt and grease-stained blankets.

'Oh,' he said. It was more an exhalation than an exclamation. It seemed the air had gone from his body. There was indeed a baby there, but it was a desiccated, mummified thing, a tiny scrap of leathery skin. It must have been dead for weeks. He looked back at the woman and saw hope in her eyes.

'Can you help us, sir? Please say you are doctor.'

He took her arm and began pushing the pram with her. 'Come, lady, let us see where we can find you some help. The British soldiers have doctors and nurses. What is your name, please?'

'He is called Jürgen, he is so sweet.'

'Your baby?'

'Of course.'

'And *your* name, lady?'

'Oh that's not important.'

They walked a few hundred yards, slowly. He slipped his hand into her pocket without her noticing, found her ration card, saw her name and replaced the card. As they walked, they made a curious couple. Some people looked at them with sullen faces filled with self-pity, others averted their eyes, minding their own business. Women, some with shovels, some with buckets, formed chains, clearing bricks and rubble away to prepare routes for trams and cars. Heck watched them with vague curiosity. They were called *trümmerfrauen* – debris women. They were paid a meagre seventy-two pfennigs an hour, but they had no option but to work – for if they refused, they didn't get ration cards. The idea that they would ever clear this devastation was laughable. Berlin was dead for ever.

A British checkpoint was waving military vehicles through at a crossroads. Heck approached them and flashed his ID.

'This woman needs help,' he said in English.

'Looks fit enough to me, chummy,' the grizzled sergeant replied.

'You call me *sir*, sergeant, and if I say the woman needs help, then you say, *Yes, sir*. Do you understand?'

'Yes, sir,' the sergeant said reluctantly, clearly unsure why he should be answerable to a man in civilian clothes with a foreign accent, especially one so young.

'There is a dead baby in her pram. She thinks it requires treatment. But it is the woman herself who requires treatment. Where can we find medical assistance for her?'

'That'll be at base, sir.'

'What's your name, Sergeant?'

'Wainwright, sir.'

'Coldstream Guards, yes? Well, Sergeant Wainwright, you will depute one of your men to take this woman to base and make sure she is seen by a doctor. Your man will explain the circumstances and see that the woman is looked after. I am holding you personally responsible. Is that understood?'

'Yes, sir. Where precisely would you like her to be taken? Mackenzie King barracks? Brigade HQ in Fehrbelliner Platz? Someone there will know what to do. Or the British Military Hospital, Spandau?'

'Go direct to the BMH by jeep. Tell them her name is believed to be Maria Dienstag. Mary Tuesday in English. Look after her and call me to let me know the outcome. Do you have a notebook?'

The sergeant handed over his small notepad and pencil.

Heck wrote his name and the telephone details at OSS. 'Good day, Sergeant. And remember, she may be German, but she has suffered enough.'

Minsky dropped Wilde back at OSS headquarters in Foehren-weg. They had agreed that the Russian's driver would pick him up at nine o'clock the next morning. Minsky said he wished Wilde to come alone.

The question now was, where was Lieutenant Heck? There had been no sign of him all day. It was worrying, but for the moment it could wait. First, he had a telephone call to make. He sought out Helms. 'Do we have a secure line here, Richard?'

'I hope so. We swept the place thoroughly before taking possession, and we hadn't mentioned to the Soviets or anyone else beforehand that we would be coming here. Why, are you worried about diehard Germans or our friends?'

'All of them. I need to call Eaton privately.'

'Well, I know better than to inquire what it's about. Use the phone in my office. There's a gramophone in there. I like to play a bit of Glenn Miller while I'm making important calls. A pleasant way to muffle my own voice, I find.'

'Thank you.'

'And I would be delighted if you and Heck could join me at my place for dinner. I have a local girl cooking and she does a great schnitzel.'

Wilde happily accepted the offer. Half an hour later he got a line through to Eaton at 54 Broadway, London.

'Hello, Tom, how are things in Deutschland?'

'Pretty wrecked actually, Philip. Can't see how they'll ever rebuild the place to be frank.'

'You can blame Bomber Harris for that. By the way, I like the accompaniment. Is that the divine Billie Holiday?'

'*What A Little Moonlight Can Do*. Can you hear me OK?'

'Just about. This is for my ears only I take it.'

'Indeed. I need your help. Your advice at least. I am in contact with an important member of Soviet intelligence. He wants political asylum in return for a great deal of information. What would the British line be?'

'You're an American, Wilde. Why not take this to Bill Donovan?'

'My man wants to come to England. Cambridge to be precise. He also wants money.'

'Well, he wouldn't be the first Russian in Cambridge. What sort of information is he offering?'

'In the first instance, he's offering help with my quest. After that I'm not certain – we've only had a preliminary discussion. Hang on, the record's ending.'

'Can we have some more Billie?'

'I was thinking Lester Young – *Lady Be Good.*'

'Perfect.'

Wilde switched the record, then picked up the phone again. 'As for what he could offer MI6, I have to be honest and tell you that I don't know. Also, this must be conditional on sharing with the OSS.'

'Naturally. I wouldn't have it any other way.'

'My man is very cagey, very nervous. He says he trusts me, but he's well aware that he's on extremely thin ice.'

'Has he said why he wants to give us all this wonderful information? Has he given up on communism?'

'I have no idea about his politics. He seems to think he is falling foul of Beria and Abakumov and if one doesn't put a bullet in his head, the other one will.'

'Ah, well, yes, I see his point of view. Definitely living on borrowed time if he's got those two fellows on his case. You say he trusts you, but do *you* trust him?'

'About as much as a rattlesnake.'

'Good. I'd be worried otherwise. Let me take advice – see what we can do.'

'I don't need to tell you how important discretion is in this matter.'

'Of course not, old boy. Your friend's secret is safe with me. But isn't this all rather interrupting your own work?'

That had indeed worried Wilde. But he had given his word to Minsky and would see it through. It would be good if at least something came of this mission, for he wasn't optimistic at the moment about his chances of finding Adolf Hitler. 'Can we talk tomorrow, Philip. I don't intend being in Berlin for more than a couple more days – at the most.'

'Of course, old boy. And I look forward to hearing what other music you can provide.'

Wilde replaced the phone and went to find Helms again. 'I'm getting worried about Heck. I have no idea where he's gone.'

Helms looked helpless. 'There are two or three million people in this city, swelling with refugees by the day. And the place is split into four zones. Where could anyone even begin looking?'

'I don't know.'

'Well, I'm sorry to offer simplistic philosophy, but all I can say is that if your colleague's dead, there's nothing to be done. And if he's alive, he'll make his own way back, and you can quiz him then. Come on, I think you need a pre-prandial, Tom.'

He did. Something to dispel the memory of that squalid underground cell where six children had died at the hands of their own parents.

Chapter 20

Heck had begun to suspect he was being followed even before he handed Maria Dienstag into the care of the soldiers. Now he was heading back towards Wolfsstrasse because he wanted to talk to the neighbours, and he was certain he had a tail.

He stopped. All he saw were resentful, cast-down faces. Even in civilian clothes, the older ones seemed to step as one, like a military unit. He looked for contrition or shame, but saw only bitterness and anger. No remorse for starting the war, just rage at losing it. At least the children laughed and ran and played. Defunct and burned-out artillery and military vehicles were their playgrounds. Perhaps there was a glimmer of hope for the generations to come.

A man in workmen's dungarees caught his eye, but he didn't break his step. Which one of these men and women was following him? Was he imagining it?

And then he saw the man. He was young and slender. He wore a trilby, perched low over his brow, and the clothes of a working man with a belt tied tight around his waist. He had stopped when Heck stopped. Now he was lighting the butt of a cigarette. Quickly, he glanced up, then just as rapidly lowered his eyes.

Heck moved towards him, but trilby man started to edge away. Two seconds later, he was running through a side street in the vague direction of Wolfsstrasse. Heck was fit, but so was the young man.

Trilby man raced around a corner into a small square filled with rubble which hadn't been even partially cleared; there was no way through, merely a mountain of bricks and concrete. The trilby hat was on the ground, spinning to a stop, but the man was nowhere to be seen. A group of laughing children was climbing in the half-buried hulk of a tram. A thin trail of smoke rose from the huge heap of debris.

Heck picked up the hat and tried to get his bearings, tried to see how his pursuer had disappeared. Suddenly, he spotted a woman's head, then her upper body, and within moments, she was on top of the mound of bricks looking about her as though afraid. Thin and haggard, in a light summer dress that would look pretty if she hadn't been so gaunt, the woman was walking tentatively towards Heck, stumbling occasionally over the debris that had once been proud buildings. Never once did she make eye contact.

He ignored her and moved to the place where she had emerged and found a concealed flight of steps down into a cellar. That must be where his pursuer had gone, because there was nowhere else. Pistol in hand, Heck looked down into the darkness and saw that there was actually a little light down there in the pit. He tossed the trilby like a discus down the steps into the gaping cellar entrance, then followed it down.

Mozes Heck wasn't easily shocked, but the scene he found seemed like one of the circles of hell. Dozens of women were crowded here, camped along a narrow basement lit by candles, little oil lamps and cooking fires. The stench of the farmyard hung heavy; sweat and manure and something like stale milk. Also, the familiar miasma of boiling cabbage. As he approached, the women receded deeper into the shadows.

Rodents scuttled before his feet. He scanned the dark corners, looking for his man, but could see only women. He began to wonder whether he had been mistaken about the sex of his pursuer. Now that he thought about it, he realised it could have been a woman in male clothing. He approached one of them, a girl in her late teens clutching a baby, but she hurried away.

He tried to talk to others, but they either fled or shrank into themselves, like hedgehogs.

He moved around, from corner to corner, looking for his pursuer or a second exit from this basement where he or she might have escaped. But he couldn't find a way out, nor any sign that his tail had even been here. Nothing. Nobody.

A woman was walking towards him. She was a great deal older than most of the others, grey-haired and tall, her shoulders unbowed. 'Who are you?' she demanded. 'What do you want with us?'

'A man came down here, just before me. I'm looking for him.'

'Are you German?'

'I am Dutch, but I am a British Army officer.'

'I see. A Dutch Britisher who speaks German with a southern accent. What a strange cosmopolitan place we have become. As to your question, the answer is no. I have seen no man coming through. There are only women and children here.'

'It might have been a woman in male clothing.'

'Do you *see* a woman in man's attire? There are none here. Nor would such a one be welcomed. Believe me, these women have had enough of men. Just your appearance has terrified them.'

Heck frowned at her. 'I did nothing, I threatened no one.'

She glanced at his gun.

'This is to protect myself.'

'Of course it is. What else would a gun be for?'

Her sarcasm was not lost on him, nor her bitterness.

'I'm not trying to scare you.'

'You don't. I have nothing left to lose. But these young people – they have plenty to fear, for themselves and for their children.'

'Were they safe under the Nazis?'

'Are you innocent or stupid? Do you have any idea what has befallen us since so-called liberation?'

'I don't have time for this. I am looking for someone.'

She swept her arm around the shadowy space. 'Look at them. Every one of them has been defiled in the most disgusting fashion, time and time again, sometimes twenty times in a day. I am almost seventy years old, yet I lost count of the times I was raped. One of the Ivans, an officer, raped me with the barrel of his pistol, laughing all the while, then fell into a drunken stupor at my feet. Many of my friends here have Russian babies in their belly. We almost all have gonorrhoea. And then there are the lice and the unseen wounds. A week does not go by without some poor, despairing soul taking her own life. Go to the canal any day of the week and you will see a woman's body floating by.'

'Perhaps your men did the same to the wives, mothers and daughters of the Ivans.'

'German soldiers are not animals.'

Heck might have argued the point, but he wanted this woman's assistance. 'Well, of course, I am sorry that these things have happened to you, lady, but things will improve now that the British have arrived. They are not vengeful, though they have reason enough. Nor are they out of control.'

'Tell them we need food, penicillin and abortions. When those things arrive, I will believe you.'

'Dear lady, is there another way out of this cellar? Another exit apart from the steps down which I came?'

'No, there is only one way in or out.'

'I will have to look around.'

She smiled then and he saw that her front teeth were missing. She noticed his look. 'Knocked out by the Ivan who defiled me with his gun,' she said.

'I'm sorry.'

'You are a polite young person, Dutchman. I will walk with you – my presence at your side will put my friends at ease.'

He went slowly with the unnamed grey-haired woman. He imagined that in a former life, she might have been a school-teacher. She stood silently by his side, protective like a mother hen as he approached the women and girls in turn.

Each of them had haunted eyes, made more anguished by the flickering of the candles and lanterns. They were sur-rounded by pathetic bags and belongings. Some cradled babes in their arms. But despite their destitution, he saw that they had comfort in the company of others caught in the same dreadful circumstances; they had made a home of this place, crafting beds for themselves and their small children out of old rags and cushions, anything they could find among the rubble of bombed-out homes.

They offered him nothing. If they had seen his pursuer, they weren't revealing it. If any one of them had been his pursuer, she had changed at speed into female clothes, and none of her friends was going to denounce her. Every question was met with a blank stare or a shake of the head. And there was no other exit. It was a helpless task.

He must have been mistaken. His pursuer was long gone.

'Thank you,' he said finally to the grey-haired woman. 'I hope you are given the assistance you need.' And even as he said it, he wondered what their husbands and fathers and sons had done in the war.

'Where have you been, Lieutenant Heck?' Wilde was aston-ished to see the young officer strolling through the front door of the OSS building, hands in the pockets of his trousers, as though he had just nipped outside for a quick breath of fresh air.

'Sightseeing while we waited on the Russians.'

'Well, the Russians were quicker than expected. You missed an interesting lunch.'

'Then you'll have to tell me all about it. Don't say you were worried about me, Professor.'

Wilde had just emerged from the office of Richard Helms. It had been agreed that they would meet up in half an hour and stroll to his villa for a reasonably early supper. 'Worried would be the wrong word, Heck. Curious about your vanishing act when we were supposed to be working together. Damn it, man, I thought you were committed to finding Hitler. Are you in this thing with me or not?'

'Everyone needs a day off.'

'That's no answer.'

'I can't explain any further.'

'Can't or won't?' He shook his head. 'Don't do it again. I have been assigned as your superior officer in this enterprise and you will obey me, or I will have you returned to your regiment. Is that understood?'

'I didn't think you would need me today.'

'That's not the point.' Wilde glanced at his watch. He considered leaving Heck here at the OSS base to stew, but then he softened. 'Come on, we're being treated to supper with Mr Helms at his villa. I can brief you on everything that happened then. But perhaps you'd like to dust yourself down and brush your hair first. You look as though you've been crawling through a dust bowl. We're to meet Richard down here in half an hour.'

'No, I'm going to my room because I have a journal to write. Please, give my compliments to Mr Helms.'

'But you must eat. Look, Heck, we need to talk.'

'We can talk at breakfast.'

'Very well, we'll meet at 7.30 a.m. Be there. It's your last chance.'

Heck brushed some of the dust from his shoulders, then grinned. 'Take your gun tonight, Professor. I was followed today and this place is almost certainly being watched. Someone really doesn't like us.'

Chapter 21

Helms's generous hospitality stretched into the early hours and Wilde was aware that he had imbibed too much red wine and whisky. 'I must take my leave,' he said at last.

'I'll get a car brought around.'

'Oh it's no distance, quarter of a mile tops. The walk will do me good.'

'No, it's not safe.'

'If you insist.'

'I do.'

Fifteen minutes later, he was in bed, crashed out. But he woke within a couple of hours and lay still, captured by a fitful waking dream in which his subconscious was telling him he was in the wrong place, that he should be in the mountains and lakes of southern Bavaria. His waking brain, however, told him there were still things to be learnt in this city. Berlin was where the Hitler story came to an abrupt end. So this was where it had to be picked up again.

In the morning, feeling worse for wear, he took a bracing shower, shaved and went down for breakfast. He was relieved to see that Heck was already there. After two coffees, they got down to business. Wilde told him about the offer he had of an interview with Hans Fritzsche. 'Have you heard of the man, Lieutenant Heck?'

'No.'

'He was one of Goebbels's team in the propaganda ministry. Also a well-known broadcaster, churning out Nazi drivel to the masses. I'm told by Minsky that he was in the bunker until the first of May, the day after Hitler's supposed suicide, and then handed himself over to the Russians, offering the surrender of Berlin to the Red Army. There's no suggestion he saw the body of Hitler or the cremation, but at least we have a senior man who was there at the end. I want to hear his story. There is a slight problem, though.'

'You don't want me there.'

'It's not me, it's Minsky.'

'Then you go alone, Professor.'

'I can force the issue if you want. I haven't agreed his terms yet.'

'Forget it, Professor. You go.'

'What will you do?'

Heck hesitated then shrugged. 'Well, I suppose I might as well come clean. I didn't tell you yesterday because I thought you wouldn't react well, but I was looking for a childhood friend, a Jewish girl and her family whom I met on holiday. We used to write to each other like pen pals. I went to her address. A fucking Nazi family had taken it over. So of course I fear the worst has befallen my friend and her family. But I'd like another day to myself to see if I can find out what became of them.'

'There must be noticeboards, like the one in the DP camp.'

'Yes, I'll try that. And hopefully I will find a helpful Red Cross station. Can the OSS lend me a vehicle and some petrol?'

'I'll ask Helms. But be back by six. I hope you find your friend.'

Heck took out the photograph of Miriam and placed it on the table in front of Wilde.

'She's lovely.'

'Yes.'

Wilde heard the choke in the Dutchman's voice, but he didn't look up. He didn't want to see the tears welling in the man's eyes.

Hans Fritzsche had been brought to the Kommandatura building from his military cell in the Soviet sector. Minsky had warned Wilde that the prisoner might look unhealthy. 'He has been imprisoned since early May, first in Berlin, then Moscow and now back in Berlin, so you will undoubtedly find him feeling sorry for himself.'

'I hope you're not saying he's been tortured, comrade.'

'Torture? That is a slur on the good name of the Soviet Union. Please don't say such things or your access to the prisoner will be revoked.'

'Forgive me. I am sure, of course, that Herr Fritzsche has been held in hotel-like conditions with three hearty meals a day and a feather bed.'

'Now that *would* be obscene treatment for a Nazi. No, he has been treated humanely with adequate food, nothing more. Probably very much like the men presently held by the Americans and British.'

When Wilde entered the room and saw the prisoner, he understood why Minsky had prepared him for the worst. Before coming here, he had examined the OSS files and discovered that Hans Fritzsche was a Rhinelander of forty-five years, but the man who struggled to his feet in front of him looked ten or fifteen years older than that. His shoulders were bony and cramped forward and he was unhealthily pale. His eyes rose to meet the newcomer, large and wide and entreating.

Minsky clicked his heels. 'And now, Professor, I leave you to do your interview alone. I know you are a professional, so I am sure you don't need me listening in. Just tap twice on the door if you require assistance.'

Wilde thanked him. He couldn't help being amused. Did Minsky think him a fool or naive? Or was it just a joke? He knew very well that Minsky would be listening in. Every word would be recorded, typed up and sent up the line to whoever in Moscow had authorised this meeting. Wilde took the seat opposite the prisoner and addressed him in German. 'Good day, Herr Fritzsche,' he said. 'Please sit down.'

'Thank you, sir.'

'Have you been told who I am?'

'No, sir. I have been told nothing.'

'I am Professor Thomas Wilde, representing the American and British governments in their quest to discover the true fate of Adolf Hitler, and I have been given permission by our Soviet friends to talk with you, as one of the last of the senior men to leave the Führerbunker in May of this year. Are you willing to answer some questions?'

'Yes, sir.'

'Good.' Wilde gave the man a brief smile. He was glad that he hadn't brought Heck here. Fritzsche might not react well to intimidation. Compliance could turn to defiance when confronted with hostility.

'To begin with, then, why were you in the bunker?'

'It is a question I have asked myself many times. Dr Goebbels insisted I be there, but I am not sure why he needed me. I wasn't actually in the Führerbunker the whole time, however. Much of my work could only be carried out in the remains of the ministry nearby – so I had to take my life in my hands to run between them.'

'You were chief of radio propaganda?'

'Yes, sir. I was director of the department.'

'And you also made propaganda broadcasts. Were you still doing this in the last days?'

'The opportunities became fewer and fewer. You could say I was the voice of Berlin, so as the city began to fall, my role diminished.'

'The voice of Berlin? You were the voice of Nazism. Isn't that the unvarnished truth?'

Firtzsche hesitated before answering.

'Well?'

'I suppose some might put it that way. But I wasn't important. I don't suppose Hitler even knew my name, and I swear that I had no knowledge of the atrocities discovered by the Allies.'

'Of course you didn't. None of you did.' Wilde couldn't help but understand why the obfuscation and denial of these Nazis made Mozes Heck so trigger-happy.

'I accept your sarcasm, Herr Professor. But I was a mere functionary, obeying orders from Dr Goebbels. It was Himmler and Kaltenbrunner and Müller who were the devils.'

'That's a matter for the court. That's not why I'm here.'

'But I have been told I am to be taken to Nuremberg to be tried for war crimes, and I don't understand why. If anything, I am the *victim* of a war crime, Professor. For weeks in Moscow, in the Lubyanka, I was incarcerated in a cell one metre square. I had to stand or sit down hunched up, even to sleep. My sole companion was a fly. At first I wanted to kill it, then it became my only friend. It was as if I was already in my grave – except at least in my true grave I would be lying down. In the Lubyanka I was kept in a standing coffin. My spine and joints have not recovered.'

'If you believe you have been mistreated, it is something you should bring up when you go to Nuremberg. You are to have legal representation there. Talk to your lawyer about these matters.'

'But why am I to be tried? Why am I classed with Goering and Streicher and Kaltenbrunner?'

Wilde had difficulty retaining his equanimity. This man was as cold as ice. He had supported a regime steeped in bloodlust and cruelty – yet here he was, complaining about *his* lot.

'Herr Fritzsche, all I want from you is your version of events in the last days of the bunker, particularly your recollections surrounding the supposed death and cremation of Hitler. Tell me about April thirtieth. Did you see Hitler's body?'

'No, sir, but I was told that he had shot himself and that his new wife had taken poison.'

'Did you see the funeral pyre?'

'No, sir. Not then.'

'What do you mean?'

'I mean, I did not see their bodies burning. But when I was a prisoner of the Russians they took me there and showed me ashes which they said were the remains. They also showed me photographs of corpses and asked me to identify them.'

'Were the photographs identifiable as Hitler and Eva Braun?'

'No, sir. Nor were they the same as the ashes I had seen. The pictures were of fully formed but burnt corpses. It was easy to identify Dr Goebbels, however. Also his wife Magda and their six children.'

'How many bodies did you see?'

'Fifteen. I counted them. Hitler and Fräulein Braun were not among them.'

Wilde stopped. Suddenly, tears had started coursing down the German's cheeks. Had he misjudged Fritzsche? Was this a cynical act, or did he actually have a heart? 'Herr Fritzsche, are you all right? Would you like to take a pause?'

'No, no. I want to talk to you. It is the shame I can't bear. I see the loathing in your eyes, Herr Professor. My guards have told me all about the atrocities: the death camps, the death marches, the murders of innocents. I fear my country is forever damned.'

Fritzsche wiped his sleeve across his tear-stained face and Wilde allowed him a few moments to compose himself.

'Very well,' he said at last. 'Let us move on. After you were told of Hitler's death, what happened?'

'I stayed in the bunker. Others either killed themselves or fled. Bormann was one of those who escaped. He went with Dr Stumpfegger and others.'

'So who at that time was the most senior government official left in the bunker?'

'I was, although there were also senior military men such as General Burgdorf. On May second, I made the decision that it was time to surrender Berlin to the Red Army before more damage and needless deaths occurred.'

'Were all those still present in the bunker agreed on this?'

'I took the decision unilaterally. There was chaos by then, so someone had to act.'

'And no one objected?'

He laughed through his tears. 'Burgdorf tried to shoot me, but a junior officer knocked the pistol from his hand. Then I went over to the Russian lines, to Marshal Zhukov and offered the surrender. I have been a prisoner ever since.'

'Did you believe the reports of Hitler's death?'

'That is a difficult question.'

'Yes or no will suffice.'

He bit his lip. 'I found it hard to believe. He was a godlike figure and it seemed impossible that he should be dead.'

'Did you actually have any sound reason for believing he was alive?'

'No, none. Just my gut telling me that he couldn't be dead. The Führer was immortal. He couldn't die, could he?'

'So if he was still alive, what might have happened to him?'

'Maybe he escaped the country. My Russian guards all believe he is alive. They try to taunt me by saying that he is enjoying cups of tea with Churchill in England while I am rotting away in my cell. Others say he is with Franco in Spain, planning his next move.'

'Did you see Hanna Reitsch, the famous aviatrix, in the bunker?'

'Yes, of course.'

'Did you see her leave?'

'No, but I heard she had gone.'

'And after she had gone, did you see Hitler again?'

Fritzsche shook his head.

'So Hitler could have gone with her?'

'I don't know. Perhaps it's possible. I have no evidence either way.' He took a breath. His watery eyes met Wilde's and his brow knitted slightly.

'Well, Fritzsche? You seemed to be about to say something more.'

'You know, now that I come to think of it, there was something else. Someone else was there at the same time as Hanna Reitsch.'

'You mean General Ritter von Griem?'

'No, not him. Someone I had never met but had heard of because of his famous exploits with the Waffen-SS. A man called Julius Boden. Standartenführer Boden.'

'So an SS colonel was there – was that unusual?'

'No, not unusual. The place was full of loyal SS men. But Boden's presence was different. He was a man of action, not a courtier so I was surprised to see him. Everyone in Germany admired him and I, personally, had broadcast reports about his daring and courage. He was like a movie star. Clever, brave, charming, handsome and athletic. He had it all. I believe that while at university in Göttingen, he was known as a great runner at eight hundred metres and might have gone to the 1940 Olympics. Women loved him.'

'Was he married?'

'No.'

'Parents? Where are they?'

'I'm sorry, I have no idea.'

'Apart from hero worship, Herr Fritzsche, why are you mentioning him now?'

'Because I saw him conversing with Hanna Reitsch. Talking secretly, like conspirators. And when she had gone, so had he.'

'Then it is possible they took Hitler together, is that what you're saying?'

'It has to be a possibility, Herr Professor. Doesn't it?'

'And where would I be likely to find Standardenführer Boden?'

'I have not the slightest idea. I don't even know if he is alive.'

'You said you were willing to talk to me, Herr Fritzsche. I took that to mean you would cooperate to the utmost of your ability. If you really do help me, it would demonstrate your remorse. It might even sway the judges at your trial. So try giving it a little more thought . . .'

His eyes were closed. He seemed to be thinking hard, either trying to dredge up a memory, or perhaps deciding what was safe to reveal. Suddenly, his eyes opened. 'You know there is someone who might – just might – be able to help you. Someone of the same wealthy Bavarian class. I am certain they were good friends.'

Chapter 22

Lieutenant Heck arrived at the British Military Hospital with the words of Sergeant Wainwright hot in his ears. They had spoken on the phone two hours earlier. 'My private delivered the German lady safe and sound to the BMH, Lieutenant.'

'Good man. Did she see a doctor?'

'Yes, she saw someone – a doctor or a nurse, I'm not sure which. Apparently they were extremely kind, even though they were worried that there was little they could do for the poor woman. They intended to sedate her and give her a good night's sleep before seeing a trick cyclist. In the meantime, they would take the dead child away for a proper burial.'

'Well, perhaps I'll call them myself.' There was something about Maria Dienstag that seemed to sum up the whole bloody horror of the past six years. Heck couldn't quite get her out of his mind.

'There was something else,' the sergeant said. 'My private told me the woman said something to him as he drove her to the clinic. She said, "I know where she is". He thought she was talking about the baby, but he had a strange feeling. I thought I should tell you, sir.'

I know where she is.

She wasn't talking about her baby, because the dead child was a boy.

'Did she say anything else?'

'Not that he mentioned, Lieutenant.'

Now Heck was here at the Military Hospital, an outfit set up at great speed in the two months that the British had been in Berlin. A nurse had told him that a psychiatrist, Dr Marsh, had worked on Maria Dienstag's case the previous evening and again this morning. In fact, he was with her now. The nurse placed a call through to the doctor and then directed Heck to his office and asked him to wait outside until summoned.

The door opened and Dr Marsh emerged. 'Ah, Lieutenant Heck, it's good of you to come. Will you join us? I'd like a few words with you in the presence of the patient. You and I will speak English, which she doesn't understand. Are you all right with that?' He was.

'You will notice that she looks a little different. Beneath her headscarf, her hair was alive with lice and we had to shave it off and disinfect her. We have given her another scarf to make her look presentable, but I'm just telling you this so you don't stare too obviously or look startled.'

'I understand.'

'How old do you think she is?'

She obviously couldn't be as old as she looked, but he really had no idea. 'Thirty-five?' he suggested.

'Twenty-three,' the psychiatrist said. 'She's worn out, mentally and physically.' Dr Marsh was a kindly man in his late thirties, but he too looked exhausted, as though the war and its aftermath had taken a great toll. Heck followed him into the office.

'Do sit down, Lieutenant.'

Heck smiled at Maria Dienstag and sat beside her on the doctor's couch. He reached out and took her bony hand. 'Are you OK, Frau Dienstag?' he said in German.

She nodded stiffly. Her hand was limp in his but she didn't try to pull it away.

The pram stood at her side.

'Don't worry, it's empty,' the doctor said in English. 'Now then, Lieutenant, I want to include you in this because I have no other point of contact for the woman. No next of kin, no friend. I don't think anyone has taken any interest in her in the recent past. She's clearly not well, but you had already deduced that. Sadly, she has the same condition as many other people in this accursed city – indeed this whole blighted continent – death of child, death of husband, despair. And no one to look after her. I would love to send her to a good sanatorium in Switzerland, but my resources are severely limited.'

'Of course.'

'It's been difficult to make her talk, but I got a few things out of her. Remember, she's not mad, she's fragile. Crucially, she now accepts that her child is dead. I have shown her that the pram is empty and we have talked it through, and she is beginning to come to terms with it. The problem is, she just can't bear it. The little boy was her only link to her late husband and to a better life. But I had to be blunt with her because the fact of the death can't be altered.'

'Is there anything you can do for her?'

'Last night when she came in, she allowed a nurse to examine her for VD and she was in the clear, so that was something. She wouldn't eat, kept saying we had to give milk to her baby. I thought it best to sedate her so we could get her away from the pram while she slept. This morning the pram and blankets were there but she didn't notice the baby was gone. We gave her coffee for breakfast. It was all she would take.'

'Is there a name for her condition?'

Dr Marsh smiled. Despite the world-weary lines, his eyes were still warm. If the war had disillusioned him, it hadn't killed his humanity. 'I don't think any psychiatric term explains her condition better than the old terms: grief, bereavement. A condition as old as mankind. Apart from that I believe she is perfectly sane.'

'So what then? We send her back out into the ruins to throw herself into the canal or hang herself from a beam?'

'I hope not because I had an idea which might help and I have already put it in motion. There is an undamaged church nearby and I happen to have met the priest, who is a decent old fellow. He told me the Nazis had closed it down and now it is open for worship again. First thing this morning I went and had a chat with him and he agreed to perform a little funeral for the baby. No time to get a coffin, I'm afraid, but we can swaddle the child in a shroud. I'll ask a couple of nurses to come along and I'd like you there to comfort her.'

'Will that help?'

'I really think it might. It should make the death seem real to her, however hard that might be. A funeral proves to the living that their loved ones meant something. And only in accepting loss can we begin to live our lives again. And there's more – the priest has said he will take her in and look after her. He hasn't got much in the way of food or other essentials, so if there is any way of getting funds or rations to him, all to the good. That's it, I'm afraid. I can offer nothing else.'

'Thank you, Doctor. That's more than I could have hoped for.'

'Well, she's lucky she met you. Can you afford to stay with her for a few hours, Lieutenant? It would do her a lot of good to get a meal inside her. The small Naafi here isn't too bad. Sausages and mash with a cuppa, that kind of thing. They're a good bunch so I'm sure they'll let her in. Just mention my name if need be.'

Heck took her out into the gardens and sat with her under a broad sycamore tree. They had left the pram in Dr Marsh's office and Heck assumed they wouldn't see it again. 'Did you understand any of what the doctor told me?' he asked in German.

She shook her head.

He told her everything, all the while holding her hand in his – that they would have a little service in the church for Jürgen, with a priest. And if she liked the priest, he would look after her for a while. 'Would that suit you, Frau Dienstag?'

She said nothing.

'Well, let's see.'

A little later, he took her to the Naafi, which had been set up in a marquee in the gardens of the hospital. They were fed corned beef, carrots and boiled potatoes, with a thin gravy. At first she looked at it as if it were poison. Heck began eating, and then so did she. In the DP camps he had seen many survivors of the concentration camps eating with their fingers, but this woman used her knife and fork, holding them delicately like a lady. She was clearly hungry, but she didn't eat greedily.

'You said "I know where she is", Frau Dienstag. What did you mean?'

She stopped eating and her eyes met his for the first time.

'Frau Dienstag? Maria?'

'You think I am a crazy woman?'

'No, I don't think that, nor does the doctor. You're sad, that's all. You have every right to be.'

'I think I *have* been crazy. I knew my baby was dead, but I didn't want to know. It was too much for me. God asks too much of us.'

'He's asked too much of everyone these past years.'

They sat in companionable silence for a few minutes. Heck smiled at the woman, and after a while, she smiled back.

'Yes,' she said, 'I saw her. I liked her very much.'

'Who are you talking about?'

'Your friend, Miriam. The Jewish girl. The one you were looking for. She stayed with me two nights, but it was too dangerous, so she had to be moved on.'

'Is this true? She stayed with you? When, Frau Dienstag, when was this?'

She hesitated again, and then the words simply spilled out of her, words that had been held inside too long.

'When her family was taken away to Grunewald Station to be loaded on to the train east. She saw them going and ran to me and I looked after her for as long as I could safely do so.'

'You said she was moved on. Where to?'

'She had to become a U-boat.'

'She went underground?'

'Yes. It was safer for her. All my friends knew the terrible fate the Nazis had in store for the Jews.'

'Where did she go after leaving you?'

'I wasn't allowed to know. They told me it was safer that way.'

'But who took her?'

'The Red Orchestra, of course. My friends. But I think they are all dead now. All my friends are gone. They were rounded up three years ago and murdered in Plötzensee Prison. Some hanged, some guillotined, some simply strangled or shot without trial in dark cellars. Murdered by Hitler and Himmler for speaking the truth.'

'What of your husband?'

'We escaped the first arrests and went underground with false papers and survived until January this year, then Johann was arrested and taken before the People's Court. Judge Freisler sentenced him to death. I am told he was guillotined.'

'I'm sorry, Frau Dienstag.'

There were no tears in her eyes. A little smile played around her mouth. 'He had worked in the Air Ministry and he was very like you, sir. Not in looks, but something else. I can't describe it, but you remind me of him.' Suddenly she shrank away from him and her hand slipped from his grasp. 'You don't expect anything from me, do you? All the soldiers in this city, they offer bread and soap and cigarettes but I always know what they want in return.'

'No, I want nothing like that from you.'

'Yes, you are very like my Johann. He was angry like you.'

'Do you think I'm angry?'

'Of course. You have reason, don't you?'

He shrugged. Angry with the Nazis, yes. But who wouldn't be? 'So your friends in this so-called Red Orchestra . . .'

'That is what the Gestapo called us because some of us were communists. Not all though. We were just people who hated Nazis. That was the one thing that bound us together. We printed leaflets and posters to tell the people what was truly happening in the East. And we helped fugitive Jews.'

'So the Red Orchestra – your friends – looked after Miriam?'

'They would have moved her from house to house every few days. Perhaps they found a remote farm in the countryside where she could be kept safe. But after the arrests of August 1942, who knows? When I said I know where she is, I meant I know that she escaped the initial round-up. Whether she survived, I cannot say. When I walk these streets it surprises me that anyone is alive.'

'So you never saw her again?'

'No. But I would very much like to. She was a lovely girl. I lived just across the road from her in Wolfsstrasse, though my home is no more. We had long conversations, and she told me about a pen friend she had, a Dutch boy. I think she was a little in love with him.'

Chapter 23

Wilde and Heck met as planned at 6 p.m. 'We have to get to Nuremberg as soon as possible,' Wilde said. 'Helms has fixed us a flight from Gatow at 7 a.m.'

'Are you going to explain any of that, Professor?'

'I discovered something in my interrogation of Fritzsche.' He outlined his talk with the Soviet prisoner, and his revelation that an SS man named Julius Boden had quietly appeared in the bunker, then just as silently vanished at the same time as Hanna Reitsch. 'Fritzsche also told me that Baldur von Schirach may be able to tell me more about the mysterious Mr Boden.'

'Baldur von Schirach? Oh, I know all about him. He founded the Hitler Youth, then became governor of Vienna. The worst kind of fucking Nazi. Signed the deportation orders to ship out Vienna's Jews to the camps. I would like to kill him.'

'Well, you won't. He's locked away, facing trial for war crimes.'

'You're right, Professor, I won't. Because I'm not coming with you. Not tomorrow, anyway. I still have business here in Berlin. Can you do the Nuremberg thing alone?'

'How long do you need?'

'Two days.'

'I'll give you twenty-four hours, but then you follow me. I really feel we're making progress, and we have to press it. My nose tells me Boden is the key: the SS war hero who would do anything for his master.'

Heck nodded. 'All right. Twenty-four hours it is then. And tonight?'

'Do what you want, Lieutenant Heck. I'm going to the cabaret.'

The resourcefulness of some people never failed to astonish Wilde. In the middle of the London Blitz, parties had raged around Soho and Mayfair. For many, life was lived more fully and intensely than ever before. Love affairs were more electrifying – and shorter. Music was louder and more rousing. Dancing was frenzied, and booze flowed through the night and into the day.

And here at the Kabaret Lola? How did such a place exist in the wasteland of Berlin?

The greeter at the door looked Wilde up and down. 'OK, let me guess, you Ami?'

'Right first time.'

'Amis, Ivans, Tommies, I can always tell.'

'And the French?'

'Ah, they don't come here. They're too busy beating up German women.'

'I take it that's meant as a joke?'

'Not for the German women it's not. And this is my second guess – you're not in uniform and you speak German, so that means you're spy or diplomat. Same thing, huh?'

'Whatever you say.'

'And you know that Hitler was a British spy? He can take off his false moustache now, and get a knighthood for destroying Germany.'

Wilde managed a smile. The greeter at the Kabaret Lola had one leg with a pirate-style wooden peg where his right one had once been. He was tall and dressed all in black, save for a thin silver tie. He held out his hand. 'Ten cigarettes or ten dollars, take your pick, Ami.'

Wilde gave him the ten dollars and made his way into the warm, dimly lit interior of the dilapidated dance hall. Tables were full, the air was thick with smoke, music and loud conversations. On a small stage framed by crimson curtains, a dance troupe of young women in fishnets and tight bodices cavorted with energy and promise while an ancient chanteuse in a slinky dress growled an old jazz number into the microphone. Wilde wanted to laugh. It was as if the last twelve years had never happened, as though a time machine had transported him back to the bohemian days of the Weimar Republic.

He looked around for Boris Minsky, but there was no sign of him. The Russian had passed him a note at the end of the meeting with Fritzsche. It simply said 'Kabaret Lola 10 p.m.' Back at the OSS, Wilde quickly established that there was only one Kabaret Lola and that it was in Kreuzberg in the American sector – not far from both the Russian and British zones.

A waitress in a similar skimpy outfit to the dancers showed him to a table for two and took his order for a large whisky. The dancers finished their number and the peg-legged greeter came on stage and took the mike from the singer. He had drumsticks and began humming 'Deutschland Uber Alles' while tapping out the beat on his wooden leg. Then he grinned. 'Everyone happy? Amis, Ivans, Tommies? You all like our pretty Gretchens?'

The room was packed with men in uniform and girls fawning over them. The tables were overflowing with beer and various other dubious alcoholic concoctions sourced from the black market. Everyone was talking and drinking, kissing and groping, no one was paying attention to their host, but he carried on anyway, in thickly accented English for his predominantly American and British audience. As Wilde seemed to be the only one listening, he focused his attention on him.

'You heard about the Gretchen with two Ivans in her bed? It was her first quiet night of the summer.'

No one laughed. The waitress arrived with his whisky and hovered. Wilde fished out a coin and handed it to her. 'You like I stay, Ami? I like fun.'

The voice of the greeter boomed through the mike. 'Remember, *Meine Damen und Herren*, no fraternisation! Strict orders of General Eisenhower. All agreed? *Jawohl*, no fraternisation. But he didn't say nothing about fornication, did he?'

'Thank you,' Wilde said to the waitress, 'But no. I'm waiting for someone.'

'You waiting for another girl? I'm better jig-a-jig, mister. Twenty cigarettes, that's all.'

'No, I'm waiting for a friend.'

'I can find boy for you.'

Wilde shook his head and gave her another coin. 'Just bring some vodka for my friend. He'll be here soon.'

Reluctantly the girl accepted the coin, gave a little bow of the head and disappeared.

On stage, the one-legged greeter was failing badly. 'Before Hitler came to power, kids used to say, "What's for supper, *Mutti*?" Now they say, "What's for potato?" Hey, you're a tough crowd. No one thinks I'm funny. Let's bring back the dancing girls.'

With that, the band struck up again and the girls reappeared. Wilde felt a tap on his shoulder.

'Comrade Professor, good to see you, my friend.'

Wilde half rose from his chair and shook Minsky's hand. 'This is quite a place.'

'Just don't tell Abakumov that I'm here. He'll think I'm bourgeois and decadent. And certainly don't tell Beria or he'll come snatch all the girls for himself.'

'Now that's funny.'

'Funny enough to get shot for?'

'Maybe not. I've ordered you vodka.'

'You see, you already know me. We are like old friends.'

The vodka arrived, Minsky downed it in one and ordered the girl to bring back a whole bottle, as well as a botle of whisky.

'Nice and noisy in here, Comrade Professor. We can talk without being overheard. But you can be sure we are being watched, so just be a little cautious, OK?'

'Well if you're being watched surely you are in grave danger just by meeting me?'

'International relations. I'm spying on you, getting you drunk to discover your next move. So tell me, my friend, how did your little talk with the Nazi go? Did he tell you where Hitler's hiding?'

'Are you suggesting you don't already know exactly what Hans Fritzsche told me?'

'Now, how would I know that? You had a private conversation.'

Wilde laughed. 'So SMERSH has never bugged a room. Well, well, it's good to hear you're so trusting. But tell me, what do you know about SS Standartenführer Julius Boden?'

Minsky shrugged. 'I can tell you that he is not in Soviet hands, if that is any help.'

'But you've heard of him?'

'Not before today. But back to my problem. I have to trust you, comrade Ami. I am putting my life in your hands. What moves have you made?'

Wilde had spoken with Eaton earlier in the evening. 'OK, this is the situation,' Eaton had said. 'If you can get your Russian to Bad Oeynhausen, I'll meet you and take over from you. I'll transport him to England for debriefing in a safe house. You can make him one promise: we will not send him back to the Soviets. But there are sticking points. Money is the main one. Also we will need to know his name sooner rather than later. The other thing is that all this must be done without the Soviets knowing that we are in any way involved. They are, lest you forget, our allies and so we cannot be seen to be working against them.'

'It is agreed that we work together on this, MI6 and OSS?' Wilde said. 'All information gained from him shared?' Wilde was feeling conflicted. Going straight to MI6 ahead of his OSS chiefs was uncomfortable, as if he was crossing an invisible line.

'Naturally.'

'I have one worry. Getting him out in secret. I'm pretty sure he's got a shadow. He went to great lengths to speak to me where we could not possibly be overheard.'

'I'll rely on your judgement, Tom.'

Wilde conveyed an edited version of this to Minsky. He seemed disappointed by the refusal to offer money, but remained undeterred. 'I can discuss that when I am in England. Serious horse-trading. Money for secrets. The more you pay, the more you get.'

'The other thing is that they need your name.'

The dancers were finishing their high-kicking routine and the bottles of vodka and whisky were arriving.

'No, they can't know that yet.'

'You know, I'm doing my best here, Comrade Minsky, but you're not making things easy.'

'As soon as they know my name it will leak back to Moscow.'

'Oh come now, you're not suggesting there are any Soviet spies in the British secret services.'

'You believe what you want, Mr Wilde.'

Wilde sighed heavily. His mind was already in Nuremberg, and he really didn't need this complication. 'Can you at least get yourself to Bad Oeynhausen?'

'No, you have to get me there! I can't travel a hundred miles through Soviet-held territory without raising suspicion. There will be roadblocks everywhere. You have to fly me out on an RAF or USAF transport, Mr Wilde. There is no other way.'

'This is going to take time. My London contact will have to arrange such a flight. The problem is I don't have the necessary time. I'm flying to Nuremberg in the morning.'

'I don't have time either. I have had information that I am to be recalled to Moscow at any moment, and I know exactly what that means.' He held up his forefinger like the pistol of a gun, but surreptitiously. 'If it happens, my blood will be on your hands.'

'That's ridiculous. Your blood will be on the hands of who-ever shoots you.' Wilde began to get up from the table. 'I've had enough of this. I've done all I can, and I have a job of work to do elsewhere. Goodnight, Mr Minsky, and good luck.'

Minsky's hand gripped Wilde's wrist. 'Wait, forget the money. And tell me the name of the British officer you have been dealing with.'

'Philip Eaton? Do you know him?'

'No, but you trust him?'

Did he? Wilde was never quite sure. But he had had no one else to go to. He did not answer Minsky's question, if it *was* a question. 'He will fly to Bad Oeynhausen and meet you.

Another thought, comrade – if you really fear your liquidation is imminent, could you go into hiding here in Berlin, in one of the western sectors, perhaps?'

'I will think about it.' Minsky ran a hand over his bald pate. Was he frightened? He looked cool enough.

'You could come with me now. I can't offer you accommodation, but I could lend you civilian clothes. You could hide out in a cellar somewhere, or in the woods.'

'No, I can't do that.'

Wilde sat down again and poured himself a last whisky. 'It's your life, comrade. If I could take you with me tomorrow, I would. But I can't. A flight out for you will have to be approved.'

Minsky grasped the bottle of vodka by the neck and stood up, knocking his chair over in the process. 'I am going now. Helms doesn't know about this, does he?'

'No, I told you that. Only Eaton.'

'So when you have fixed my exit and when you are back in Berlin, get Helms to make contact as before. This time he is to say that Professor Wilde sends his thanks to Colonel General Minsky for his assistance. That's all. Then I will know and I will find my way to you.'

'That could be a while.'

'I know, but better to get it right.'

'Good luck, comrade.'

Minsky snorted. 'I don't trust luck. I trust my pistol.'

Wilde watched him go, weaving his way through the tables, and wondered whether he was being taken for a fool. Something wasn't right about Boris Minsky. His story made sense, of course; he knew only too well the callous disregard for life of men like Viktor Abakumov, the head of SMERSH, and Lavrentiy Beria, head of state security. Both loved the finer things in life, including women. Both distrusted everyone, including each other, and would put a bullet in the head of friends and enemies alike on the say-so of a solitary informant with a grudge.

The OSS lacked spies in Moscow, but word seaped through anyway, nuggets of gossip from diplomats about the peccadilloes of the senior men in the Kremlin. In the circumstances, Wilde knew all he needed to know about these men. So Minsky's fear that his time was almost up sounded all too genuine. And if he had secrets to impart, well that was a major reason to assist him. Why then did Wilde have such doubts about the man?

As Minsky vanished from view, Wilde noticed another movement among the crowd. A small, slender man with slick hair was rising to his feet and making his way towards the door. From this distance he looked for all the world like Josef Goebbels, except younger and without the limp. So that was Colonel General Minsky's tail.

The waitress came with the reckoning for two bottles of spirits. Wilde handed over a wad of dollars and poured himself another Scotch. He'd watch another dance and listen to a couple more songs. He'd paid enough for the pleasure.

Chapter 24

Wilde had parked the borrowed jeep directly outside the front of the hall, having secured a space among a group of twenty or more service vehicles scattered across the road with the arrogance of the conqueror. At the doorway, the comedian with the peg leg and the silver tie smiled broadly. 'Going already, Yankee? Don't like my jokes, huh?'

'Some of us have work to do.'

'Of course. Locking up bloody Nazis, finding Bormann, finding Müller . . .'

'Finding Hitler.'

'Hitler Schmitler, he's drinking schnapps with the Fräuleins down in Buenos Aires. Laughing at us.'

Wilde walked on. He was thinking that Comrade Minsky already owed him for the booze. Well, perhaps the lead in Nuremberg would pay off. His eyes scanned the moonlit street. This wasn't as bad as most areas of the city centre. A few houses down, no glass in windows and roofs a rarity, but the rubble had been tidied up nicely by the *trümmerfrauen* with their buckets. Wilde stopped a moment, breathing in the cool air after the fug of the dance hall. He had his hand in his jacket pocket, gripping the handle of his automatic.

The jeep was open top. He climbed into the driver's seat. Now his hand was off the pistol to take the wheel. At first he didn't see the slender watcher from the cabaret, nor did he see the sniper prostrate on the roof, rifle poking down.

The watcher was a few paces up the road. He wasn't big, but he looked as lithe as a dancer. He combed his palm through his hair, then identified Wilde by nodding in his direction. It was then that Wilde saw him, but he didn't see the gunman.

A shot rang out, followed by a second one. Wilde fell side-ways into the passenger seat.

Mozes Heck had almost no time to aim and the merest sliver of a target – nothing but a pair of eyes, a forehead and a shock of hair. His right arm went up, his left hand gripping his right wrist, and he fired without thought, as he had done so often in the heat of battle this past year. His aim was invariably better that way.

Don't think, shoot. Thinking loses split seconds. The difference between life and death.

The head had disappeared from view but Heck's pistol remained at arm's length for a few moments, just in case he was wrong. Just in case he had missed. But if the sniper on the roof was still alive, he wasn't showing himself. The little man was still there, though, and he was moving away down the street, running. He would recognise that smooth loping style any-where; it was the man who had been following him yesterday, the one with the trilby.

Heck wanted to go after him, but first he had to help Wilde.

Wilde had felt the wind across his brow, then heard the metallic smack of the bullet carving a hole into the dashboard. Finally, he heard the crack of the shot, then another. As he threw himself down across the seats, he knew he was alive and almost certain that he hadn't been hit.

He crawled snake-like, head down, out into the road on the far side of the jeep and went into a low crouch. The automatic pistol was in his hand now. He heard footsteps. Hard leather on asphalt. He ranged the barrel of the Walther, his finger about to pull the trigger the moment the man came to his side of the vehicle. He wouldn't have time to negotiate.

A voice came from somewhere nearby. 'Don't shoot, Professor.'

Heck? Lieutenant Heck? What in the name of God was he doing here, and why was he shooting at him? 'Drop your damned weapon, Heck.'

'Take it easy. You're OK.'

'Throw it out. Throw the gun out where I can see it.'

Heck laughed. 'I'm not the one firing at you. There's a sniper on the roof. He fired, I took him out.'

'Still, do as I say.'

The pistol slid along the ground towards Wilde. 'OK, now step towards me.'

And then Wilde saw the crazy eyebrow, like a thick charcoal line across his brow. Heck was walking around the side of the jeep, arms up, grinning. 'Happy now, Professor?'

'What the hell are you doing here, Lieutenant Heck?'

'Saving your life. But the question is: what are *you* doing here, Professor? No, save that for later. I want to check on our sniper.' Heck picked up his pistol, put it into his pocket and began ascending a pile of rubble at the side of the Kabaret Lola building. At the top of the bricks and concrete, he managed to get a foothold on the downpipe that ran down the side of the dance hall, and shinned up to the top.

He saw the figure of a man at the edge of the flat roof and approached slowly, gun ready for the slightest threat. His eyes scanned the area around him; there was no sign of anyone else. The sniper lay stunned and unmoving on the parapet, head slumped across his hunting rifle. He had had a superb vantage point to take out anyone approaching the vehicles in the street below and it was difficult to see how he had missed Wilde. Either his rifle was badly calibrated, or Heck's movement distracted him at the last second.

Heck pulled the man's head back. In the silvery light a brutal crimson line seemed to indicate that his shot had cut a groove upwards through the front of the man's skull, from just above the eyes, following the slope of the brow, but that it hadn't passed into the brain. He was still alive, but dazed.

'Who are you?' Heck pulled the man back roughly by the hair and thrust his pistol square into his face. The man's eyes did not open, but he grunted something unintelligible. He was a thin, underfed man in Wehrmacht field grey, with grey hair. Certainly not a young man, perhaps forty or fifty. 'Who are you working for? Where's fucking Hitler?'

Heck smacked his pistol into the side of the sniper's head. He let out a prolonged groan, his lungs deflating, his jaw drooping, his eyes clenched in pain.

'It sounds as if he's alive.'

Heck looked up and saw Wilde silhouetted against the moon. 'Oh, he's alive.'

'Get him up. We'll take him in.'

'Fuck that,' Heck said. He pushed the hard-edged muzzle of his pistol into the man's open mouth, shattering teeth with the violence of the act. 'Who are you? I won't ask again.'

The man made a strange retching, choking sound.

'He can't answer with your gun in his mouth, Heck.' Wilde reached down and tentatively cupped the Dutchman's gun hand, gently pulling it away from the would-be assassin's mouth. 'Let me take that.'

Heck allowed Wilde to take hold of the pistol, then he dragged the sniper away from the lip of the roof by the collar of his jacket. In the centre of the flat roof, there was a doorway leading to interior stairs. The door was open and electric light streamed out. Heck forced the man against the wall to the side of the door, his legs sprawled before him, his head lolling. Blood from his head wound flowed down across his eyes and cheeks.

'Last chance.'

Words, low and growling, emerged from the injured man's mouth. Blood bubbled from his mouth where the gunsight had cut him.

'What did you say?' Heck had his right hand at the man's throat.

The sniper's eyes opened and met Heck's through a film of red. 'I said go to hell, Jew.' The words were muffled by the blood, but Heck heard them clearly enough. He drove his left hand hard into the would-be killer's abdomen. He gasped again and a serene smile crossed the man's bloody lips.

Wilde reached out and pulled Heck away. 'That's enough.'

'OK, we'll do it your way, Wilde.'

Heck pulled the would-be killer to his feet. And then, in one unstoppable movement, he lifted him above his head like a weightlifter raising a heavy barbell, leant backwards, then lunged forwards, throwing the gunman over the side of the roof down into the street. There was no cry, no scream, just the sound of the body hitting rocks and bricks and road. The sound of flesh and bone being broken apart.

'Jesus, Heck!' Not for the first time, Wilde was stunned into incomprehension by his companion's insane bloodlust.

'He would have killed you.'

'But we needed the bastard alive, Lieutenant Heck! We needed to question him.'

'He wouldn't have talked.'

'We'll never know, will we? And you're going to be up on a murder charge!'

Heck was incredulous. 'A German killed in Berlin in 1945? Who's going to be interested? More importantly, did you see the other man, the little accomplice?'

Yes, he had seen him. Both in the hall and outside. Minsky's shadow. 'He looked a little like Goebbels.'

'He moves quicker than fucking Goebbels.'

'Shit,' Wilde said. Who had been trying to kill him? Why would a man following Minsky want him dead?

'But we know one thing at least,' Heck continued. 'Our corpse was a German, not Russian. I thought that might interest you, Professor, seeing the company you keep.'

Chapter 25

They made their own separate ways back to the OSS base at Foehrenweg. Wilde arrived first and waited in the communal anteroom for Heck to appear. He knew he would have been dead but for the Dutchman's intervention and yet he was furious, too. What was Heck doing there at the Kabaret Lola? He had a lot of explaining to do.

Wilde glared at him as he strode through the door. 'Well?' he demanded.

'Well what?'

'Why were you there? Were you following me?'

'Yes, I was, fortunately for you. You were keeping things from me and I didn't like it.'

'If I want your assistance, I'll tell you.'

'Are you serious, Professor?'

'You seem to be forgetting who's in command.'

'Yes, sir, master professor. Please, let me lick your boots.'

Wilde stared at him hard, then suddenly his mouth creased in a laugh. This was absurd. 'I'm sorry, Lieutenant, I know you saved my life.'

'I'm glad you understand that.'

'It's just been a rather fraught night. There are matters I would happily discuss with you, but I am under an obligation to maintain silence. I'm sorry.'

'Clearly something to do with the Russians. I take it that was Comrade Minsky with you in the cabaret.'

'You saw us?'

'Yes, and I saw the little man watching you. Yesterday he was following me.'

Wilde felt the sting of humiliation. Was he losing his touch? He hadn't even seen Heck in the hall and he was under the false impression that the slim, slick-haired watcher was observing Minsky, not him. He nodded. 'I should have been more aware.'

'Well, you're alive, so that's OK.'

'But I really do wish you hadn't killed the bloody sniper. We need information. Badly. If someone is trying to kill one of us, it is likely they are trying to protect Hitler.'

'Maybe the Ivans want to kill you, too. Have you upset Minsky?'

No, he hadn't. But he had colluded with him.

'Don't worry, chief. The sniper was German. He was wearing field grey and he spoke German with a German accent.'

'He looked vaguely familiar,' Wilde said. 'I have a nagging feeling that he was among the drinkers singing the Horst Wessel song at the bar in Grünegg.'

'Then he deserved to die. And we have to assume that he is just one of many. Think about it: Collingham and Harper killed in Bavaria, and now an attack hundreds of miles away in Berlin. Someone wants to stop us.'

'You're right.'

Heck touched the side of Wilde's head, his finger tracing the old bullet scar where the hair had never regrown, even nine years later. 'This wasn't the first time someone tried to shoot you, Professor. You want to tell me about it?'

'Another day maybe.'

'I hope you killed the guy who did it.'

The flight was scheduled for early morning, so Wilde had to make do with four hours' sleep. Washing quickly and hurrying downstairs, he stopped to scratch a note of thanks for Richard Helms and left the Minsky caviar to be shared out.

Outside, the morning was grey and had a chill in the air and he cursed the lack of a cup of coffee. The military driver of a large Daimler Benz was already there, waiting to take him to Tempelhof. The road had been cleared of debris so the drive was relatively easy and he arrived with half an hour to spare before the transport plane was due to depart.

A familiar figure was standing outside the airport entrance. Boris Minsky.

Wilde did not try to conceal his astonishment and irritation.

'Comrade Minsky, what in God's name are you doing here?'

'Nothing to do with God, my friend.' Minsky gave a shrug that said, *I had no option*. He was in a civilian suit rather than the tunic and medals of a Red Army colonel general. 'Everything to do with Comrade Stalin and his two attack dogs. When I got back to my quarters last night a summons was awaiting me. I was ordered to report to Viktor Abakumov in Moscow with immediate effect. And we all know what that means.' He held his hand like a gun and put it to the back of his head. 'Boom. Boris Minsky dead.'

'That's bad, but it doesn't answer my question.'

'You have to save me, my friend.'

'Impossible. I'm heading to Nuremberg, and I'm going alone.'

'This is life or death. You're my only hope. It was difficult enough getting here to the aerodrome undetected. I certainly could not make my way out of the Soviet sector of Germany by an overland route. Please, you must allow me to join you on your flight.'

'And how would I explain to the crew that a Soviet colonel general wishes to join me aboard an American transport to Nuremberg?'

Minsky pulled out ID papers and showed them to Wilde. 'My new identity. Tell them I am Sergei Borisov, one of the lawyers representing the Soviet Union in the forthcoming war crimes trials.'

'Sergei Borisov?'

'From now on, I am plain Sergei Borisov, lawyer.'

Wilde studied the papers. He didn't know if they would appear genuine to a Soviet checkpoint, but they certainly seemed professionally produced. 'You didn't fix this overnight.'

Minsky smiled. 'My job has its advantages. I have known this day was coming for many weeks, so I made preparations.'

'And was I part of these preparations? Is that what your assistance has been about?'

'Such a cynic, and you a renowned professor of history.'

Wilde didn't think of himself as cynical, but realistic. He looked Minsky up and down. Without his uniform, he did look quite different. The bald head and the proud belly might give him away in Moscow, but in the West he wasn't well known and would probably get away with it.

'You are going to Nuremberg to interrogate von Schirach, the Nazi Youth leader. I am going to look at the physical arrangements for the trials – the layout of the courtroom and the seating of the Nazi criminals, and the custody details of our sole defendant, Hans Fritzsche. And then I will report back to Nikitchenko. It's a convincing story, so have no fear. We are allies and you offered me a lift, that is all – so you are in the clear.'

'I'll see what I can do.'

It was simple getting Boris Minsky aboard the Lockheed Lodestar; nothing was too much trouble for America's new best friend, Russia.

The day was gradually warming up and the sky was clearing. There were only ten passengers but Wilde and his new companion didn't speak a word to each other during the flight. Boris Minsky insisted it should be that way. He didn't want any of the other passengers knowing he was Russian, nor did he want them overhearing his conversation. Instead he spent the time looking out of the window at the peaceful fields and urban ruins of Germany.

Two hours and two hundred and fifty miles later, they came down to an easy landing at an airfield just outside Nuremberg. Once disembarked and clear of possible eavesdroppers, Wilde said, 'So what now, comrade?'

'You have to get me to England. There are other Russians here in Nuremberg. I must not be seen.'

'We'll have to find you some sort of lodgings – pension or small hotel on the outskirts, well away from the Palace of Justice because that place will be crawling with people who could recognise you. Then I'll call Philip Eaton. He can arrange to come to Nuremberg or fix transport for you to Bad Oeynhausen. By the way, when you said you were being followed and watched last night I thought I saw your shadow – it turned out he was shadowing *me*. What would you know about that?'

'A man, you say?'

'Small, slender, like a dancer, but with a hint of Goebbels.'

Minsky shrugged. 'My shadow was a woman. She was blonde, easily identifiable for those with eyes to see. I knew she was there, but of course most men would have noticed only her breasts and her legs and would have offered her a drink.'

Wilde wasn't totally convinced. 'If you say so, Minsky, or Borisov or whatever you wish me to call me.'

'Borisov. From now on call me Sergei Borisov. Let's make it English – *Mr* Borisov.'

Heck woke up a lot later than Wilde and after a good break-fast made his way from Foehrenweg to the British zone, and from there on to the district of Wedding in the French sector. The sight that greeted him on the corner of Exerzierstrasse and Schulstrasse astonished him. Somehow the magnificent Jewish Hospital, three miles directly north of the Branden-burg Gate, had escaped the bombing almost intact. The only damage seemed to be the windows, which had gone the way of almost all glass in Berlin, such was the shuddering power of the blast waves released by thousands of tons of high explosives.

A religious man might have taken the survival of the Jewish Hospital as a sign from God, but Heck knew there was no God. Auschwitz was the proof of that.

He had come here at the suggestion of Richard Helms after mentioning his search for Miriam. 'I think that's probably as good a place as any if you're looking to find out what happened to your friend. Anyway, it must be worth a shot. Good luck finding your young lady.'

Helms's indication that the hospital was still standing did not tell the half of it. Amid the wreckage of central Berlin, Heck had not expected to find a building in such good condi-tion, and still operating as a hospital, as it had done through-out the war.

It was a remarkable neoclassical structure built just before the First World War and its wide imposing facade spoke volumes about the high status of Jews in those long-gone days. Heck felt nauseous.

He thought of all the people whose lives had been saved by this place over so many years.

Now, it seemed but a monument to the one hundred and fifty thousand Jewish Berliners who had been carried away to their deaths in squalid camps. Few had escaped and survived underground in this city in the long years of war. A handful at the most, perhaps a few hundred.

Was Miriam one of them?

Inside the entrance hall, he found a whole wall covered in pieces of paper with names and locations of survivors, and pleas for any knowledge of members of their family or friends. Every displaced persons camp had a similar wall and he had studied many of them. Now, he went through these new names, line by line, word by word, for a full fifteen minutes, then moved away, head down.

All those names. It was unbearable. And no sign of a Rabinowitz.

Other than that, it was like any hospital in Europe. Busy corridors, low voices, trolleys with patients being moved. At the front desk, he asked if he could speak to someone about a friend of his and was directed to a ground-floor office. He was admitted immediately and a middle-aged doctor introduced herself as Matilda Kuhn.

'I survived,' she said. 'I say that every day but instead of feeling joy, I feel nothing but overhwelming guilt and despair.'

'Yes,' he said. 'I feel the same.'

'But there is someone you wish to find, so there is still hope. Until a death is confirmed, we must all keep looking. What is this person's name?'

'Miriam Rabinowitz. She would be twenty-two, like me.'

She gave him a strange look. 'If you don't mind me saying, you look a lot older than that.'

He tapped his eyebrow. 'This helps. Also I grew up fast, and I'm glad that I did – for I was able to join the British Army and fight the fucking Nazis. Please forgive my language, Doctor.'

'Don't worry. They deserve all the adjectives you can throw at them.'

'So anyway, I really am just twenty-two and I am an army officer. Lieutenant Mozes Heck.'

'I can tell you are not a Berliner. Let me guess – Bavaria?'

'I lived there as a child, but I am Dutch, from Amsterdam. I fear my family all perished. I have been looking for them in the DP camps, but no sign as yet.'

'Don't give up hope. It's all we have. And this Miriam Rabinowitz, is she in your family?'

'No, we met on holiday and exchanged letters. I am in Berlin on another matter and wished to see if she had survived.'

'The name means nothing to me, I'm afraid. Have you looked at the notice wall?'

He nodded. Yes, he had studied every name. 'Not a single Rabinowitz, nor a Heck, nor any other name I know.'

'Well, you must put your name up there along with an address and any other means of getting in touch, such as telephone numbers or regimental details. Also put the names of anyone you are looking for. Your friend Miriam, all your family.'

'Is there anyone else here who might know her. I believe this place somehow kept working throughout the war. She might have sought work as a nurse.'

'I have been here throughout the war. I was classified half Christian and somehow escaped the transports. If she had been here I would know her. Do you have a picture?'

He pulled the photograph from his pocket and presented it to the doctor. He instantly saw the knitting of her brows, as though the face meant something to her.

'You've seen her?'

The doctor nodded but said nothing.

'Well?'

'I know the face, but I don't recognise the name.'

'Perhaps she was using a false name. I imagine many of the invisibles were.'

'Perhaps.' Her response was curt and unfriendly.

'Is something the matter, Doctor? Do you know something?'

Dr Kuhn handed the photograph back to Heck. 'Forget about her. Forget she ever existed and get on with your life, Lieutenant. And please, never show that photograph around here again.'

'You think she's dead? Was she discovered by the Gestapo?'

'I don't know. She had changed her name to Miriam Berenbaum.' Dr Kuhn rose to her feet. 'I'm afraid I have nothing more to tell you, Lieutenant Heck.'

'But when did you meet her? Did she come to the hospital as a patient or did she work here? When did you last see her? Surely you must have heard or seen something?'

'Good day, Lieutenant. I'm sure you can find your own way out.'

'No! You cannot just leave it like that. You know something, Doctor. I would rather hear the truth than be left in limbo. Was she deported, or killed?'

'There is nothing more to say. Now, please, I am very busy.'

'Her father was a doctor, so it is entirely possible she came here to work. Perhaps you knew him – Herr Dr Rabinowitz?'

'No, I never met your Dr Rabinowitz.' She was moving towards the door to open it for him.

He couldn't allow it and pulled out his pistol. 'Tell me what you know.'

She stopped and gave him a look of utter disbelief and scorn. 'You would shoot me? Then you are just like them. You are just like her.'

He was stupefied by her words. How could drawing a gun be remotely similar to Miriam? 'What do you mean?' he demanded.

'You really don't know, do you.' She let out a long unhappy sigh and walked back to her chair behind the desk. 'Put away your gun, Lieutenant. I will tell you everything I can about Miriam Berenbaum.'

Heck felt a chill of horror. 'What is there to tell? I don't understand.'

'Please, sit down. This is hard for me, and it will be hard for you.'

Slowly, he took the seat, his eyes fixed on Matilda Kuhn's face, but she wasn't meeting his eyes. 'Doctor?'

'Lieutenant, I have to tell you that Miriam Berenbaum is – or was – a *greifer*, God rot her wicked soul.'

'*Greifer*? Catcher? What do you mean by that?'

'She betrayed Jews, her own people, to save her skin. Hundreds of them. She lured them with promises of food and shelter, and handed them to the Gestapo for transportation to the death camps. I did not wish to tell you, but that is what your friend did.'

'No, I don't believe it, not Miriam.'

'I'm sorry, I understand why you don't wish to hear this, but pictures don't lie, and the photograph you showed me is of Miriam Berenbaum.'

'The picture was taken in 1939. She must have changed.'

'No, it's her. I would swear to it before a court of law in this world or to Jehovah on the Day of Judgement.'

'You knew her well?'

'This hospital was one of her favourite hunting grounds. Yes, I knew her. She was so sweet, so beautiful and so treacherous. We were all taken in by her for a long time. It was only when one of her victims escaped from the assembly camp for deportation and returned here that we learnt the truth.'

Heck couldn't believe it. Yes, he had only met her that once in Switzerland but they had corresponded for three years, and this Miriam Berenbaum could not be the same person. Could it?

'I can see what you are thinking, Lieutenant. But I am older than you and I perhaps know more about the human heart than you. In extremis, people will do terrible things to save themselves. We are already learning how Jews in the camps helped the Nazi extermination machine in the hope of living a little longer themselves.'

That was true enough. Heck had heard many such stories in his journeys around the DP camps. It was said that some Jews had been formed into special commandos to push the Jews into the gas chambers and burn their bodies afterwards. But Miriam? No, it could not be. For if *she*, the love of his young days, was guilty of such betrayal, then what was the point in life itself?

He put away his gun. 'Please, forgive me for threatening you like that.'

'I confess I didn't enjoy it.'

'Did you see this Miriam Berenbaum again after her duplicity was discovered?'

'Oh, indeed, yes. She denied it at first, but then she laughed and said that we would have done the same in her place. She had been promised her life and her freedom in return for her work. She spat at my feet, and then went away, still laughing.'

'Have you any idea where she is now?'

'In hell, I hope. But that is just wishful thinking. I did hear a rumour that she is in Russian hands and even that she may be put on trial. If that is the case, I will weep no tears for her. I have never been a vengeful person, Lieutenant Heck, but in the case of Miriam Berenbaum, I hope she gets her just deserts.' Her eyes closed, her mouth tightened as she thought back to the horrors of the past. 'Two of my closest friends, one a nurse, one a doctor, died because of Miriam Berenbaum, or Rabinowitz, or whatever her true name is.'

Chapter 26

With the help of the driver who was at the aerodrome to collect Wilde, they found a small hotel in the southern suburbs of Nuremberg. The drive through the ruins of the city – ninety per cent of the buildings had been destroyed – was poignant for Wilde. He knew of its magnificent place in history. This was the birthplace of Albrecht Dürer and Johann Pachelbel, the site of the Reformation and the German Renaissance. Perhaps the most German of the country's great cities. All brought to dust and ruin. It was said that the corpses of thirty thousand men, women and children were still unrecovered from beneath the rubble.

However grotesque Nuremberg's recent history as the place where Hitler staged his menacing rallies, it was still a sad scene, especially for a historian.

Now at the modest little pension, Wilde stood beside the Russian at the front desk while he was checked in. The manageress, dressed in local costume, looked at them both with obvious suspicion, but she was clever enough to realise who was the victor and who the vanquished, and offered Borisov her best room. Her obsequious manner did not fool Wilde for a minute. This woman had been a paid-up Nazi and was not happy about the result of the war. The thought of having a Russian guest made her sick to the stomach.

Wilde accompanied him up to the allotted room, which was basic but clean. 'Just stay here, Mr Borisov,' he said, stressing the new name. 'I'll make contact with you as soon as I hear from Eaton.'

'Don't worry, I'm not going anywhere.'

'Well, you're a free man, but there may be those who recognise you.'

Wilde took his leave and the GI driver conveyed him through the ruins to the Grand Hotel near the Palace of Justice. This hotel – once the hang-out of Hitler and his gang during the Nuremberg rallies – had been damaged in the massive bombing campaign, but enough was still intact to provide comfortable lodging for the influx of lawyers, military men and journalists gathering ahead of the trials. It was still overly ornate with ugly, heavy German furniture, but importantly it had a cocktail bar.

Settling in to his room, his first task was to break his promise to Borisov, something he should have done in the first instance.

A couple of calls located Allen Dulles in Wiesbaden. The OSS chief was impressed by what Wilde told him.

'Minsky's defected, eh? That's quite a coup, Professor Wilde. But why does he want to go to England – why not America?'

'He likes England. In particular, he likes Cambridge.'

'I take it you haven't told Richard Helms about this otherwise he would already have passed on the message.'

'No, I'm already breaking my promise to Minsky by telling you.'

'Why would you keep a promise to a damned Commie, Wilde?'

It was a good question. Why had he? 'I guess it's because he helped me. But you're right, Mr Dulles, and that's why I'm telling you now. I've got Minsky holed up in a small hotel well away from the comings and goings around here.'

'Keep in touch then. I want to keep an eye on Comrade Minsky. I'm not as dewy eyed about the Russians as some of our friends back in Washington DC. Who else have you told about this?'

'Only Philip Eaton.'

'Ah yes, Eaton. Can't say I warmed to him. Old-fashioned British public school snob. But you know the guy going back a long way. Do you trust him?'

'That's another difficult question. He has helped me in the past but I'm not sure it's possible to trust anyone in the British secret service. Happy to talk at length about him when we meet. For the moment, though, I need your help on this other matter. I want access to one of the top-level prisoners held here: Baldur von Schirach. Preferably today or first thing tomorrow.'

'Shouldn't be a problem. I'll get on to commandant Andrus and come back to you soonest.'

Colonel Andrus walked Wilde through the echoing silence of the four-storey prison attached to the damaged grey-stoned walls of the Palace of Justice. The only sounds were their footsteps and the clanging of doors and keys as they climbed the stone steps to the upper storey, but from a distance they could hear the muffled hammering of workmen – former SS men mostly – repairing and refurbishing the main building to house the courts where their recent masters would stand trial for their lives.

'Here we are,' Burton Andrus said when they reached a range of identical cell doors, each with a GI standing to attention outside. To Wilde, the guards all looked bored witless. 'Just a reminder, Professor Wilde. We don't give these prisoners an inch. No cigarettes, no extra food, no privileges.'

'Understood.'

'They are defendants in a criminal trial and will be treated as such. They may have lost the war but most of them are still arrogant sons of bitches and I won't tolerate that. I want them to have a little taste of what they did to their own prisoners. Now, Professor, I know you have left your pistol in my office, but I am afraid you will have to be searched again. We have the strictest security here.'

Wilde allowed himself to be intimately searched by a GI and then Andrus looked through the ten-inch peephole. At last he nodded to the guard to open the heavy oak door. Von Schirach's cell was tiny, exactly the same as everyone else's. Rank in the Nazi hierarchy brought no privileges here.

Inside, the prisoner was sitting on the edge of his bed. It had a straw mattress, a plain pillow and two tattered blankets folded at the end. There were no books or papers to read, but there was a small wooden table with a single chair. The prisoner immediately stood up and pulled back his shoulders.

Wilde nodded to him to sit down. Baldur von Schirach's mother was American and his first language was English, so that was the way Wilde addressed him.

'Have you been told who I am?'

'You are a professor of history, that's all I know. I presume you intend to write a book about us.'

Wilde noted the curious clipped accent. He was weighing up how to deal with this man. He had the arrogance of his upper-class heritage, but he was clearly knocked back by his reduced circumstances. He probably didn't fear the firing squad, but he would certainly fear dishonour. That was the way to play it.

'No, I am not writing a book, not about you and the Nazis anyway. I am here because I am presently working with American intelligence. I'll get straight to the point Mr von Schirach. I am looking for a friend of yours named Julius Boden.'

'Is he alive then?'

'That's what I'm hoping you'll help me with.'

'What do you want with Julius?'

'That is my business, Mr von Schirach. The question is, are you willing to help me find him?'

'How can I help you find him if I do not even know if he is alive? I have been imprisoned both here and in Luxembourg since my arrest in Austria at the end of the war – I have no contact with the outside world.'

Wilde studied the man. Despite his prison diet and the looseness of his clothes, he had the soft aspect and smooth skin of a man who was used to living well. More than that, there was something feminine about him. Was this truly the founder of the Hitler Youth, the organisation designed to turn boys into manly fighting machines? He did not look a good role model. And yet the boys had apparently loved him. Wilde changed tack.

'Tell me, Herr von Schirach, why did you choose Germany over America given your dual nationality?'

He shrugged as if the question was ridiculous. 'I believed in Hitler, of course. But he fooled us all, and it was the worst mistake of my life.' His face broke into a momentary half-smile, more a tic than a true expression of good humour. It vanished as soon as it arrived.

'It seems it took you a very long time to discover your mistake.'

'Professor Wilde, how could I have known twenty years ago that there would be extermination camps, massacres, hostage shootings, invasions? No one knew. Statesmen and royalty throughout the civilised world believed in Adolf Hitler. When I first met him at the theatre in 1925, I found him to be a man of great culture with a wide knowledge of music. My mother was extremely impressed by him and perhaps she helped cast a spell over me. I was just one of many taken in by his vision and his oratory. We believed we were building a magnificent new Germany. I taught my boys – my Hitler Youth – about hard work and loyalty. I did not teach them cruelty.'

'But somehow they learnt it.'

He nodded sadly. 'My country has paid a heavy price, and so shall I.' That half-smile again, there one moment, gone the next.

'And the Jews, they paid the heaviest price of all. You deported sixty thousand of them to their deaths when you were Gauleiter of Vienna.'

'*Nein*, that was the SS. I had no say in such things. Kalten-brunner assured me they were to be given homes and work and food in a safe place, far away from the anti-Semitism of Vienna. I thought they were heading for a better life. When I tried to make further inquiries, I was told it was none of my business.'

'They were heading to their death.'

'How could I have known that? Himmler and Hitler did not tell me these things. And there was no reasoning with a man like Kaltenbrunner. Ask him, he's here in these cells.'

'I have no interest in him. Anyway, you were the top man in Vienna, you should have stood up to him.'

Schirach let out a long slow breath. 'That's easily said, but it was less easy to do. Those who defied the SS and the Gestapo were likely to end up against a wall. Anyway, I am ashamed of myself, and I am ashamed of my country for what was done.'

'You didn't care about the Jews. Your anti-Semitism was well known and documented.'

'I confess it and once again I am ashamed. I spoke with ill-judged hostility against the Jews, and I am not proud of my prejudice, but I was one among millions. The funny thing is my family never had a problem with Jews. My parents had Jewish friends. My wife even denounced Hitler to his face for the treatment of the Jews in Amsterdam, and was banished from his presence.' He shook his head. '*Jah*, I am ashamed. I was a coward – I closed my eyes to things I should have seen. Those people did not deserve their fate. We all have much to be ashamed about . . .'

'So perhaps you might begin to atone for your transgressions by telling me what you know about your friend Julius Boden, the famous SS officer.'

'What do you want to know?'

'Let's start at the beginning. How did you come to know him?'

'We lived not far from each other in southern Bavaria. I have properties in Kochel-am-See and nearby on the banks of Walchensee. His hometown – village really – is a few miles to the south, in the Alps.'

'Which village would that be?'

'Schwarzenkirche – Black Church in English. In the mountains, just on the German side of the border with Austria. His family has lived there for generations and is very wealthy. They are dairy and beef farmers with large holdings. Before the war, he was talking about branching out into ski tourism. It would be a good spot, perhaps the new Kitzbühel or Alpbach – it is very beautiful.' He paused, then gave a full smile. 'Professor, I am happy to tell you everything I know. I very much want to cooperate with the Allies, not just to save my neck, but because we must admit our sins if ever we are to regain our place among the civilised nations. But can I ask you one thing: who suggested you talk to me?'

'Hans Fritzsche.'

'Really? But I hardly know the man. Is he interned some-where?'

'He's held by the Soviets. He is to be brought here to stand trial alongside you.'

'On what charge? He was nothing but a voice on the radio.'

'I am sure all will become clear when the indictments are read out.'

'Fritzsche, huh? If he is a war criminal, then every German adult is a war criminal. He is a nobody. An unpleasant char-acter, yes, but of no importance in the hierarchy of the Third Reich. Hardly in the league of Goering, Ley, Ribbentrop, Stre-icher and the generals.'

'To get back to Julius Boden. Where exactly did you meet, and when?'

'Have you heard of Colin Ross?'

'Yes, I've heard of him. He's a travel writer.'

'He *was* a travel writer, a man who went to many countries and counted many great men among his acquaintances and friends. He's dead now. Five months ago, as the Allies closed in, he and his wife dug graves for themselves, then killed them-selves with poison and bullets. They had been living in a lit-tle wooden house on our land near Walchensee and they are interred nearby in the woods. He wanted no stone, no memo-rial. His books sold in millions, but I predict that the Allies will not allow him to be remembered, for he believed wholeheart-edly in the National Socialist cause.'

Wilde looked at his watch ostentatiously.

'Forgive me, Professor, am I boring you? You asked how I met Julius. That would have been 1936. Colin Ross hosted a dinner party and Julius and I both happened to be invited. We hit it off and were great friends ever since. I rather think Colin was trying to get us together, as though we had a similar world view. Certainly I took to Julius immediately, as did my wife, Henriette.'

'Where is Boden now?'

'I told you. I don't know if Julius is even alive.'

'And his wife?'

'He has never married.'

'What about his parents? Where are they?'

'I heard that his father had died, but I imagine that Ilse Boden is still living in the family home in Schwarzenkirche. Go and talk to her. She should know her son's fate.'

'Does the house have a name or number?'

Schirach laughed. 'It is called the Bauernhof Edelweiss. A rather quaint name for such a grand farming enterprise. It is not difficult to find. There are not more than forty or fifty houses in Schwarzenkirche and everyone there pays homage to the Boden family. In England you would call them liege lords.'

'I believe Julius Boden was also seen as a bit of a war hero.'

'Indeed. The greatest of war heroes and much decorated. Iron Cross First Class, Knight's Cross with Oak Leaves and I don't know what else.'

'And he was SS?'

'*Jah*, he was.'

'They were the cruellest of the cruel. Real savages. War criminals to a man. How come an urbane fellow such as yourself counted him as a friend.'

'Julius was a soldier, but I do not believe he was a savage. I cannot believe it.'

'I bet they all say that now.'

'But in the case of Julius it is true. He is – or wàs – a man of great honour and courage. He believed in the military code, as did I. It was something we tried to inculcate in our Hitler Youth.'

'One more thing. Where is Hitler?'

'A question I have been asked many times. I was not in the bunker, but I have been told that he is dead and I have no reason to disbelieve the reports.'

'If your friend Boden had rescued him from the bunker, where would he have taken him to hide?'

'Ah, so that is what this is about. But why would you suspect Julius of being involved in such a thing?'

'Just answer the question, Schirach. Helping me may even help you when it comes to being sentenced.'

'I am not trying to save my neck.'

'Of course you want to live. You're not even forty. You have young children, a beautiful young wife. Would you not wish to stay alive for them?'

He shook his head slowly. 'I will not be allowed to live. We will all be shot by firing squad. The Russians are involved in this forthcoming trial and they will not allow anyone to survive. And even if drawing you a map to Hitler's hideout were to be the difference between life and death, then I would have to die, because I have no idea where Hitler is.'

'Where would you hide him?'

'In a prison cell in the deepest dungeon in Germany. And I would leave him there to rot.'

'Don't get funny with me. You clearly know southern Bavaria and the Austrian Tyrol as well as any man. I have reason to believe that Hitler is hidden there, probably high in his beloved mountains. The question is where?'

Schirach looked helpless and uplifted his palms. At that moment Wilde felt certain he really didn't have a clue, either about Hitler's fate or the whereabouts of Julius Boden.

'I think of needles and haystacks, Professor. If Hitler is hidden in that region, you could take an army and search for years and you would not find him. If he is there, he will be in a specially made bunker, *jah*? So someone must have made it. Find the person who made it.'

Or find Boden.

Wilde stood up. The cell was cramped and airless and he was going to get no more out of the self-satisfied aristocrat whose remorse was about as genuine as ersatz coffee. 'Thank you, Herr von Schirach,' he said.

'Please, before you go, could you somehow get a message to Henriette – my wife – and our children?'

'Where are they?'

'Perhaps at home in Kochel, perhaps in an internment camp. I wish I knew.'

'Well, I don't know if Colonel Andrus would allow me to do that, but I will ask him.'

'Just tell them that I love them and send them kisses and let them know that I am in good spirits.'

'I'll do my best.'

'You know I am sure you are talking to everyone who was in the bunker, but don't neglect Hitler's secretaries. Sometimes these women overhear things. If anyone knows Hitler's fate, it could be one of them – particularly Joanna Wolf and Christa Schroeder. They were at the heart of Hitler's secret world for many years. They are probably still loyal to him, but they might let some piece of information slip.'

'Where are they?'

'I don't know. Wolf was a Munich girl and Schroeder certainly lived there as a young woman, so maybe there, or perhaps still being interrogated by one of the four powers. I wish you luck in your quest, Professor. And please . . . my family.'

'One last question: have you heard of a man named August Jaeger?'

'Of course. He is a fine man and the greatest mountain guide of his generation. Why, do you think he has something to do with all this?'

'Would Boden have known him?'

'Without doubt. Jaeger is an extremely important person in the Alps.'

Chapter 27

The note was written in blue ink in a neat hand and said 'Thanks for the lift'. The single sheet of paper with its meagre message was all Colonel General Boris Minsky, now known as Sergei Borisov, had left in his hotel room. But there was a P.S. 'You want Boden, try Dachau.'

'Herr Borisov didn't check out,' the manageress said huffily. 'We served him food and drink but he didn't pay us a pfennig. Ah, *Gott*, these dirty Russians. They will be the death of the world.'

'Don't worry, lady, the bill will be settled.'

The question was: why in hell had he simply taken off, and where had he gone? Was it even Wilde's concern anymore? He had agreed to help the Russian in return for an interview with Hans Fritzsche. Both Wilde and Minsky had got what they wanted, so that was an end to it. What the Russian did now was his own business.

Wilde would call Dulles and Eaton because they had both become involved. If they were worried that a senior SMERSH officer was loose in the West, let them deal with it. Wilde simply wanted to get back to Bavaria and track down Julius Boden. Maybe, he'd be sitting with his feet up at home in Schwarzenkirche, smoking a pipe, wearing slippers and drinking schnapps while telling tales of derring-do to anyone who could bear to listen. Or maybe, as Borisov suggested, he would be interned in Dachau with other former SS men.

Now all Wilde needed was the presence of Lieutenant Mozes Heck. He was a difficult man, but he had his uses.

*

He found him back at the Grand Hotel, in the lounge near the concierge, cup of coffee at his side, cigarette in hand, writing in his journal.

'I wasn't expecting you quite so soon, Lieutenant Heck.'

'No, well, things didn't work out as I hoped in Berlin. How about you?'

'We need to go to Bavaria first thing in the morning. I know a bit more about Standartenführer Boden. I have a strong feeling that he could be the man we want, and we're getting close.'

Years before Auschwitz and the other death factories came into existence, Dachau had become a byword for brutality and murder. In the late summer of 1945 – twelve years after it was built as the first German concentration camp and three months after the war's end – it was still used to incarcerate thousands of prisoners.

But the nature of those inmates had changed.

Now the SS guards were themselves held prisoner, along with many members of the Waffen SS – the fighting arm of the organisation – and other suspected war criminals.

Those guarding them were US Third Army soldiers and military police.

Wilde looked at the main entrance with dark fascination. The Nazi insignia of swastika and eagle had been torn down, but the impressive stone facade was still intact. On the right, there was a wall with tall trees behind it, as though this were some kind of rural holiday retreat, and on the left, a broad-fronted building that could have served as comfortable accommodation or an administration block. Jeeps and other US Army vehicles were parked haphazardly on the wide tarmac frontage.

So this was the brutal place that had helped terrify Germany into submission. He turned to Heck and saw the deep well of anger in his eyes. How could the man not be thinking that it was in just such a camp that his own family had been murdered?

Wilde and Heck had driven to this place, a little way north of Munich, in a large open-topped supercharged Mercedes, which had once transported senior Nazi officers and was now part of the US Army car pool at Nuremberg for the use of officers. Allen Dulles had arranged for it to be delivered to the hotel with a full tank and Wilde and Heck had left soon after breakfast. It had not been the easiest of journeys. A couple of river bridges had not yet been repaired and the crossings had to be made by ferry, which caused delays. But now they were outside the main Dachau gate, Wilde still at the wheel, both men alone with their thoughts.

'You'd like to burn the place down, Lieutenant?'

Heck nodded. 'With every fucking Nazi locked inside, pleading for their lives as the flames licked their arses. I can smell the bastards from here.'

Wilde reached out and put his right arm around the Dutchman's shoulders. 'I wish I had words to bring you comfort, Mozes.'

'Words will never wash away what was done.'

'Come on, let's go and see if Boden's here.'

Dulles had called ahead and they were immediately escorted through to the duty officer's quarters. He was an amiable major named Clausen, who immediately ordered a pot of coffee and sandwiches for his guests.

'Now then, fellers, I'm told you want to talk with one of our prisoners. I wasn't given a name, though.'

'The name's Julius Boden, SS Standartenführer, which I think is something like colonel.'

'Ah,' Major Clausen said, 'then you have a problem. Or rather *we* do. Boden was here, but he has gone AWOL.'

Wilde and Heck looked at the major in disbelief. 'Missing?' they said as one.

'Yup. Hell of a thing.'

'Tell me this isn't true,' Wilde said.

'I'm ashamed to say it really is true.'

'We have travelled the length and breadth of Germany and you've let him escape? What happened?'

'I wish we knew, Professor. He wasn't in his bunk; he didn't make roll call. We have asked the others in the block and none of them are saying a thing. The bastard just vanished and we don't know how.'

Wilde had a pretty good idea. Who would know the weak points of this place better than the guards who used to run it – the very men who had become Boden's fellow inmates?

'When was this?'

'Couple of weeks ago. As it turned out, he's a native of Bavaria, so we sent a squad to his home village, but there was no sign of him. We're not quite sure where else to look.'

'Perhaps he was hiding in the barn?' Wilde suggested.

Clausen bridled. 'Are you making fun of me, Professor? I can assure you our men would have made a thorough search of the premises and asked stern questions throughout the village. His mother was there and seemed dismissive in the extreme. Apparently her words were "Do you think my son would be stupid enough to come here when he must know he is being hunted?"'

'Fair point,' Wilde said.

'Anyway,' Clausen continued, 'an inquiry is under way. But he'll probably turn up eventually.'

Wilde wished he shared the major's optimism. 'Where and when was he originally taken prisoner?' he asked.

'I don't have that information to hand but I will check for you.'

'I want to talk with the other men in his barrack room,' Heck said.

'You'll get little enough out of them. Their only regret is that they lost the war. Few if any of them have any remorse or even acceptance of guilt.'

'I want to go to the barrack room anyway, to see the belongings Boden left here. He could not have taken everything when he escaped.'

'The barrack room is easily organised, but the inmates are allowed very little in the way of personal possessions. There is nothing left to see, I'm afraid.'

'This is an outrage,' Heck growled. 'Call yourself guards? What sort of incompetent joint are you running here?'

'Don't take that tone with me, Lieutenant,' Clausen said. 'We may be in different armies, but I am your senior officer and I will have your respect.'

Wilde tried to calm the situation. 'Lieutenant Heck has a personal interest in this, Major. Given that the Nazis murdered his family, I think you might agree that his anger is understandable.'

There was silence. The coffee came in. Clausen poured three cups of strong black coffee and handed one across to Heck. 'I'm sorry, please accept my heartfelt condolences. And I admit that there has been an unforgivable security lapse. The only thing I can say in our defence is that the great majority of our inmates have not the slightest interest in escaping. They are a pathetic, beaten-down, no-hope bunch of inconsequentials. Maybe we let our guard down in the case of Boden.'

Heck nodded, nothing more, but his fury was still barely contained.

'There is one other thing, which might be of interest to you,' Clausen said.

'Go on.'

'You are not the first people to come here looking for Julius Boden. Three days ago, a woman arrived asking if he was here and if she might be permitted to speak to him.'

'What woman?' Wilde demanded.

'She was French, short-haired and extremely beautiful. Her name was Lilly Marais.'

Chapter 28

January 1945

Lilly Marais kept her head up as she was marched through the village and commune of Ste-Estelle-sur-Seine. The placard around her neck was all that covered her, but she was defiant and met the eyes of all those who stared and spat and barracked. At the edge of the village, the mayor, Jean Étienne, tossed a threadbare blanket and a pair of her clogs in her direction. They landed on the ground, in the mud at her feet, and he told her to pick them up and go.

With the blanket wrapped around her body, covering her modesty and affording her a little warmth, she walked away without once looking back. When the baying of the villagers diminished, she removed the *collabo* placard and threw it into a ditch.

She walked eastwards simply because that was the road they had put her on, but then the road turned south and she followed it. She knew it was the Rouen road, but the city was twenty-five kilometres away and she was ill-equipped to walk that far in such bitter cold.

Anyway, she had no thought as to where she might go. All she knew was that she could never return home.

Her feet and lower legs were becoming numb, yet still they moved forward, mechanically. Slowly her head drooped, as metres turned into kilometres, and she began to stumble. She could no longer feel her frozen fingers. A British armoured car trundled to a halt at her side and a sergeant leant out. '*Parlez vous, mademoiselle?*'

She knew what they meant and walked on without responding. She was horribly cold, but she wasn't ready to sell her body. The people of the village, her own father, might despise her and banish her and call her a whore, but they didn't know her if they thought she would ever stoop so low. Better death than dishonour. Her love for Julius was real, yet they couldn't see it.

'Suit yourself, sweetheart,' the sergeant said. 'But it's cosy and warm in here. Where do you want to go? Rouen? We'll take you, darling. Find you a nice wig.'

She spoke almost no English and did not know exactly what he was saying, but she could guess the import. The sergeant shrugged and disappeared into the depths of the vehicle. The armoured car geared up and gathered speed and soon it was a speck in the distance.

The trees were bare and the vast expanse of farmland was flat and white and bleak. The furrows of the ploughed fields were frozen hard. All she could think of was Nathalie. Her breasts were so swollen, so painful, and her nipples chafed against the blanket. What had Papa done to the baby? His eyes had strayed to the well. He had threatened on more than one occasion to throw her down there.

In mid-afternoon the wind grew stronger and the temperature dropped sharply. It occurred to her that she would die out here and the thought gave her comfort. She had nothing to live for and oblivion had to be preferable to pointless struggle. This would be a good place to die; simply slip away into endless sleep. Her body would disappear into a snowdrift, to be a feast for crows and foxes when the thaw came.

Her progress slowed and became more erratic. What was the point of walking when she wasn't going anywhere? Darkness fell and she lay down in the snow. It was easy to die, the cold didn't hurt so much now. The numbness was complete and her eyes closed.

In the morning she woke in a hospital bed. A large nurse in starched uniform came over to her. 'You are lucky to be alive, *mademoiselle*. A farmer found you and brought you here.'

Lilly said nothing. She had been aware of the farmer, a powerful man with a large handlebar moustache, lifting her gently into his wagon and covering her with a tarpaulin, and then she had slipped back into unconsciousness.

'I see from your lovely new hairstyle that you are a collaborator,' the nurse continued.

Lilly did not meet the nurse's stern gaze, but she had seen her face. It was angry, masculine and strong. She was about thirty and her mouth was set in disapproval and she seemed to be looking down at her from a great height.

'And from your breasts it seems you have been feeding a baby,' the nurse continued. 'Where is the child?'

Lilly turned her face away and buried it in the pillow.

'Have you killed it? Have you killed your German bastard? Well, *mademoiselle*, you will be out of here this morning, and good riddance to you. You disgust me.'

An hour later, a doctor arrived. He was white-haired and ancient, as though he should be at home smoking his pipe by the fire. But he was kinder than the nurse and made sure Lilly was given some coffee along with half a baguette and a piece of cheese. He told her that if it was in his gift, she would be allowed to stay, for she had been very close to dying out there on the road. 'You were very fortunate that the farmer found you when he did. Any longer and you would have suffered frostbite and severe exposure. Beyond that we might not have been able to do anything for you.'

'Thank you,' she said.

'Your child? Can you talk to me about it?'

'She is dead. My father killed her.'

'I'm sorry. And I am sorry that you cannot stay, but our priority is soldiers coming back injured from the front, you see. We do not have spare beds for those who can walk.'

He found some clothes from a charity box – a skirt, blouse, men's woollen socks, an overcoat, a scarf and some old shoes. Then he escorted her to the door of the hospital.

'Where will you go, Lilly?' he asked.

'Germany,' she said.

'You can't go there. War is raging.' He fished in his pocket and gave her a few francs. 'Go to the Red Cross. They may be able to look after you. God be with you, whatever you have done.'

She had decided to live. Her only reason for life was the chance that Julius was still alive, but it was enough. God must have meant her to live, otherwise why would he have sent the farmer to save her from the snow. So perhaps he intended Julius to live too.

Julius had told her that he was from Bavaria, which she understood to be in the far south of Germany, and that his family were wealthy farmers somewhere in the mountains. Beyond that she knew nothing other than that it was a thousand kilometres to the west and south of here. In the early days of their affair, she hadn't needed to know his life story, or where he came from. She wanted nothing but his body and his company. Stretched out sated in the the great four-poster bed in the chateau requisitioned by the SS, she had touched his brutal scars and knew what devastating injuries he had already survived and it was enough. So perhaps he would survive again, whatever this war might bring. If so, she would find him.

But first she needed to earn enough for food and find a way through the chaos of war.

She tied the scarf around her savagely shaved head in such a way that it would not be obvious that she was bald, then wandered around the town centre, asking for work. The city had been half destroyed by Allied bombing raids, so that many shops, businesses and cafes were put out of business. Potential employers were few and far between, but she did not give up. As darkness fell in the late afternoon, she wondered about the farmer who had saved her. Perhaps he would give her some work and shelter. Perhaps she could go back to the hospital and ask the doctor for the farmer's name and the location of the farm. But then she realised she didn't know the doctor's name either.

Lilly waited in the cold outside the front entrance of the hospital. She had the coat wrapped tightly around her and she stood in the yellow light of a lamppost. The receptionist had refused to help her and told her she could not wait inside the hospital, so all she could do was stand here outside and hope that the kindly old man would emerge and give her the information that she needed. She would happily do farm work for a little food, shelter and a few francs. Something to tide her over until she could travel into Germany.

The doctor didn't come but the surly, judgemental nurse appeared. Lilly looked away, not wishing to make eye contact with the woman. The nurse walked on by without a word and then turned back.

'You know,' she said, 'it is not right that you have a German baby and you are alive, while my sister is murdered by the Germans. It is not right. God should not do these things.'

Lilly stiffened and ignored her. Please let the doctor come out.

'How old is your baby?' The nurse shook Lilly, demanding she meet her eyes. 'I ask you again, how old is your baby?'

'Four weeks, but she is dead.'

'And you have fed her yourself?'

Lilly nodded, desperate for the woman to leave her alone.

The nurse grabbed her arm. 'Come with me.'

Lilly tried to wrench her arm away, but she was tired and weak and found herself being manhandled and dragged along the road.

'Stop, I need to see the doctor.'

'I tell you what you need, Mademoiselle Marais – you need to do something useful with your worthless life.'

The nurse was strong and brawny and she was not going to release her grip, pulling Lilly around the corner from the hospital, along a bomb-devastated street. Halfway down, she stopped outside a tall house that had escaped the bombing. For a moment, she let Lilly go and turned the handle on the front door. Lilly moved away, but the nurse grabbed her again and pulled her inside the hallway, then pushed her roughly into a large front room.

'Wait here. If you try to get away, I will do you harm. Just sit down and wait.'

Lilly had no fight left. She sank into an armchair. The nurse went out into the hallway and shouted something. Then again. It sounded like '*Maman*'.

A minute or two later, the nurse returned followed by an older woman with grey hair and a brown shawl about her shoulders.

She was carrying a baby of about two weeks in her arms, and a bottle. The nurse took the baby from the old woman and thrust it into Lilly's arms.

'This is my nephew, Maurice,' she said. 'His mother is dead, thanks to your German friends. Her husband, also named Maurice, was lined up against a wall and shot dead as a hostage on the day of the Allied landing. It was too much for Mireille. Three days ago she threw herself into the Seine and drowned. She killed herself, but to all intents and purposes, the Germans killed her. So now you will feed Maurice with your milk. And if you do this, I will feed you.'

Lilly at last met the nurse's eyes and saw only bitterness. But her breasts were swollen and the warmth and the smell of the baby touched her to her core. He had the same smell as Nathalie, and the same soft skin. She opened her coat and unbuttoned her blouse and offered a nipple to the baby's mouth. At first it seemed bemused, as though it had never done this before.

'Let me help you,' the older woman said. 'Come, the boy is accustomed to the breast.' She stepped forward and knelt at Lilly's side. Gently, she moved the baby's mouth to the nipple and extracted a little milk with her fingers, like a farm wife milking a cow. At last the baby's instinct took over and he latched his little pink mouth on to her nipple and began to suck.

Lilly looked down on the baby with overwhelming love, and tears began to fall from her eyes.

Late summer, 1945

'Is this some strange attempt at humour, Major?'
  'No, this really happened.'
  'But who was she? You must have asked.'

'Of course, but she wasn't very forthcoming. All she told us was that her name was Lilly Marais and that Boden was her fiancé. She asked us to tell him that she could be contacted at the Apfelwald Displaced Persons camp. She didn't seem to understand that Julius Boden was a wanted man. She said she would wait for him however long it took.'

'And she suggested they were to get married?'

'That was her version. He might have had a different view of things, of course. He wouldn't be the first soldier to promise a girl marriage and then leave her in the lurch.'

'Anything more? You said she was from France, but where exactly?'

'Yes, I asked that, too, but she wouldn't say. It wasn't helped by the language barrier. I've got a bit of French but she has no English and little German.'

'Tell me about Boden. What does he look like? What do you know of his background?'

'Oh, on the surface, he's remarkably charming and urbane. Pretty good English, fair haired, quite tall. The perfect Teuton warrior. He was in the SS Das Reich – the 2nd Panzer Division. Served in both east and west theatres at various stages of the war. The Das Reich was implicated in atrocities, the worst of which is the infamous Oradour-sur-Glane massacre. Boden was a senior officer, but what part he played in that slaughter and others is not yet known. It was one of our priority inquiries ahead of the trials.'

'He clearly came to the attention of Hitler and Goebbels.'

'Well, yes, I heard he was considered a hero. He was said to be responsible for some astonishing act of courage on the eastern front. Led charges against Soviet machine gun posts on two occasions. Of course, it would all have been played up by

Goebbels for propaganda purposes, so one never knows how daring he really was. I think Boden rather fitted the bill as the all-German action man.'

Wilde listened intently. He realised that such things had happened in Britain and America, too. Countries needed heroes to boost morale, and the Allies were no exception: figures like the infantryman Audie Murphy in America, the legless pilot Douglas Bader in Britain, the female sniper Lyudmila Pavlichenko in Russia. And now Julius Boden in Germany. Such warriors helped to sell the glory of war to impressionable youngsters. It was the way of the world.

'What else, Major?'

'Well, he had his big publicity tour of Germany, and then he returned to the front and was wounded. Took two bullets, one in the shoulder, the other in his thigh. That just made him even more the big hero, and then things really changed for him. Following his recuperation, he was used for a few more publicity tours. After that Goebbels decided Boden was too valuable alive to be risked in the front line. It was a good look to have a few heroes actually survive. So he was assigned to some senior administrative role in northern France, strengthening defences against the inevitable Allied invasion. He was there – Rouen, I think – throughout 1943 until the Normandy landings in June last year when he rejoined the Das Reich as they drove north from the South of France. He was certainly with them at the time of Oradour-sur-Glane, but whether he played a part in that massacre is still to be determined. There was one other thing . . .'

'Go on, Major Clausen.'

'I heard a whisper that his service in the east wasn't quite all it seemed. There is word from the Soviets about some enormous atrocity inflicted on the Jews in Kiev. His name came up although there is a bit of confusion because Das Reich wasn't mentioned in that connection. Our problem in investigating such matters is that officers can be posted on a temporary basis between regiments, and verifying atrocities committed in the east can be difficult at the best of times. It's certainly something I'd like to ask him about. If you find him, do bring him back because I'd rather like to see him hang.'

'Where was he arrested?' Heck asked.

'Zell am See in Austria, along with a few other notables. He had become detached from Das Reich.'

That, thought Wilde, might well be because he was no longer with his regiment, but engaged on special business – the business of relocating his Führer from a bunker in Berlin to a sanctuary in the Alps. 'Has he received any other visitors or letters since being brought to Dachau?'

'No visitors that I know of, but I could check the records. I'll ask in the post room about letters. I'll also get more details about his arrest, plus papers relating to his service record as we have it. Can you stay a while or would you like me to phone you?'

Wilde turned to Heck. 'What do you think, Lieutenant?'

'We could wait an hour. I'd like to visit his quarters. Will his neighbours be there?'

Clausen checked his watch. 'They're parading. One of my men will help you find those who were in the bunks in his vicinity. No rough play, though, is that understood?'

'Of course,' Heck said.

Wilde raised an eyebrow. This might not end well. Clausen left them to finish their coffee while he went to find them an escort. When they were alone, Wilde gave a direct order. 'I'll look after your pistol, Lieutenant Heck.'

'Come on, Professor. Don't you trust me yet?'

'Not in this case, no. You out there with your pistol among a lot of unarmed SS men would be a bit like letting a lion loose in a closed compound full of gazelles.'

Reluctantly, the Dutchman took out his weapon, gripped it by the barrel and proffered it to Wilde.

'Thank you. You'll have it back as soon as we're out of this hellhole.'

Chapter 29

Colonel John Appache waved the request through with barely a murmur. 'You want a hundred troops to raid some village? Sure. Make it two hundred. You think Adolf's there?'

'Probably not. But we have reason to believe there could be a man who knows his whereabouts,' Wilde said.

'Well that's what we need. Who is this guy?'

'A man named Boden. Standartenführer Julius Boden.'

Appache looked surprised. 'You're looking for Boden? Why exactly?'

'Have you heard of him, Colonel?'

'Sure. Of course. He was an important guy in the Third Reich, a hero.'

'Then you'll be alarmed to know that he managed to escape from Dachau.'

Appache was thoughtful for a few moments. 'And you think you'll find him in the village – what was it, Schwarz something?'

'Schwarzenkirche. It's his home village.'

'Well, goddamn it, that's a hell of a thing.'

'And we'll be OK with the troops?'

'You think this is good use of their time?'

'We'll find out, won't we.'

'OK, let's go in just before dawn. I'll be with you.'

'Thank you.'

'Oh, and keep me in the loop with developments like that. Don't spring stuff on me, Professor. That was the problem with Collingham and Harper. Their death left us in the dark. Proper up-to-date briefings, OK?'

*

The soldiers came to Schwarzenkirche in the last of the twilight. A company of two hundred American troops, heavily armed, and led by Colonel John Appache. Their vehicles had been parked two miles distant and they made their way to the village on foot, splitting into four groups to approach the settlement of pretty Bavarian chalets from east, west, south and north.

Their boots were silent on the lush grass of the flowery meadow that surrounded the village. Mountains towered on three sides and pine forests bordered the meadows with ancient rocky paths through to the higher pastures.

At a signal from Appache, the soldiers came to a halt fifty yards outside the village. They all knew their role. A quarter were to remain outside the village to prevent any escapes, while the main body moved in as one, three men to each of the forty-eight houses.

Heck was leading the squad from the north, while Wilde was second in command to Appache in the southern squad coming from the alm above the village. It had to be that way, Appache had said. 'I'm afraid I can't ask my men to obey orders from a college professor, so in theory I will be leading. In practice, you will take the lead because this is your mission. As Lieutenant Heck is an officer in the British military, my men are obliged to accept his command, even if it's under sufferance.'

A detailed outline of the village had been supplied at Dachau, having been sketched by the small squad who went to Schwarzenkirche in the initital search for Julius Boden. Major Clausen had led that raid and he had answered all Wilde's questions. Now he was in the team waiting outside the village.

The village itself was another of those exquisite Alpine resorts that had somehow escaped the bombs and shells of the war. It encircled a small, still lake, with a black-domed church at one end and the ruins of a schloss at the other extremity. Just to the east of the church there was a stone building that served as a village hall and meeting place. It was fronted by a square paved with smooth old cobbles.

Appache gave another signal and the troops began their final incursion, moving faster now, their boots silent on the dewy grass. The village was sleeping and the only light came from the torches carried by the soldiers and the merest hint of daylight across the high peaks. Wilde had memorised the map and made directly for the Boden chalet, easily the most imposing in the village, a large building of ancient, age-blackened wood – very like the one they had been to in Almrosen when looking for Jaeger the mountain guide. This house was even larger and was backed by two vast barns and a stable for a dozen or more horses.

This village looked quaint in the twilight but it was still a place where men and women worked at the age-old tasks of sowing and harvesting, tending the cows and the sheep and the pigs, sending milk, cheese and butter far into the towns and cities of Upper Bavaria.

There was no gentle waking for the villagers today. No knocking on doors or ringing of bells. The troops burst into the buildings without warning. If the doors were unlocked, which many were, the handles were simply turned. If not – if a bolt had been slotted home at bedtime – the doors were sledgehammered.

Wilde stood in the main room of the Boden house as his uniformed men fanned out through the property, pushing uninvited into bedrooms. From outside there were the shouts of men and the farmyard sounds of pigs and chickens and goats being woken and scattered. Within two minutes, Wilde's men had brought out two women – one a striking, fair-haired woman in her mid to late forties, and a younger woman in her early twenties or teens, both in nightgowns and hastily donned cotton robes.

'Who are you? What is this?' the older woman demanded.

'Are you Frau Boden?'

'Of course I am, this is my house. The question is, who are you?'

She really was a remarkable creature, her face carved from palest marble. Her fair hair was loose and tangled from sleep, but that could not disguise her natural good looks. Not pretty, or soft, but noble and imperious, like a warrior queen out of a Wagner opera. All she needed was a horned helmet.

'And you?' He indicated the younger woman.

'She is my maid,' Ilse Boden said, answering for the young woman. 'How dare you come into my house like this. You have no right.'

'We have every right. Read the terms of the occupation. We are looking for your son, Standartenführer Julius Boden. He has escaped internment as well you know.'

'Well, clearly he is not here. As I told your men when they came before, he would not be so stupid as to come here.'

Wilde saw a family picture on a shelf near the ceramic-tiled wood stove, the centrepiece of many Alpine homes. 'I take it he is in this picture?'

'You barge into my house like a burglar and you expect me to answer your questions. Who do you think you are?'

Wilde shrugged. 'I'll take that as a yes.' He examined the picture closely. There were five people in the picture. A younger Frau Boden in smart Bavarian clothes, a man who must be her husband, wearing an expensive jacket and Tyrolean hat with obligatory feather, and three children. A boy of about sixteen, who he imagined must be Julius, and a younger boy and girl aged five or six, perhaps twins. Wilde removed the photograph from its silver frame. 'And I'll take this so I know what I'm looking for.'

'That is theft.'

'Sue me.'

'And you call yourselves liberators. You are lower than swine.'

'I suspect your son and his comrades probably committed worse crimes than taking possession of a photograph. And now, Frau Boden, I must ask you and your maid to go out to the square and assemble with the other villagers.'

'And if I refuse to leave my house?'

'Then you will be marched there or, if necessary, carried.'

'This is outrageous, you know. You come here accusing us of all sorts of crimes, and then *you* act like gangsters.' She turned to the maid. 'Come, Ingrid. I suppose we must obey these dirty Americans.'

When they were gone, Wilde examined the property at his leisure. As well as the extensive outhouses, there was a massive area beneath the house used as a cattle shed in the cold winter months when the cows were herded down from the high pastures and snow settled on the land.

Their warmth and animal odours might have taken a little getting used to for anyone in the house above who was new to such living conditions. But it was a practice that worked, and went back many generations.

Wandering through the bedrooms, Wilde found nothing but the crumpled bed of the mistress of the house and, in a much smaller room, her maid's. There was no sign of Boden, or anyone else.

Twenty minutes later, eighty or ninety men, women and children were assembled in the square by the village hall, which was

THE MAN IN THE BUNKER | 284

attached to the small school. The morning was dry and the sun was coming up. Most of the villagers were boys and girls or the middle-aged and old. Only five of those present were young men of working or military age, and even then at the lower end – perhaps sixteen at the most. An older man of about sixty with a large bushy moustache and an ornate pipe hanging from his mouth stepped forward and announced himself as the mayor. He was one of the few to have found time to put on trousers and a jacket. He stood at the front of the group beside the communal water trough, his hand on the pump.

A dozen American soldiers stood facing them, weapons trained on the ground with implicit menace.

'OK,' Wilde said to Clausen. 'Look them over if you would, Major. None of them looks like your description of Boden, or the man in the picture I found in his house, but I'll await your verdict.'

Clausen walked slowly along the lines of sullen villagers, stopping before each one to examine the face. When he had finished, he shook his head. 'No, he's not here. No one even vaguely like him.'

Inside the buildings, the soldiers continued their search. The sound of the clattering of boots on wooden floorboards and the occasional crash of broken glass or crockery could be heard in the square, to be met by yet more sullen glares from the crowd of disgruntled villagers.

Wilde joined the house-to-house search, trying doors, ensuring the men were doing a thorough job in going through cupboards, outhouses, attics, seeking trapdoors and hiding places. It became plain to him that the Boden house was a great deal more sumptuous than any other home in the village. It was also the only house without a Catholic crucifix in evidence on any of the walls.

The soldiers found plenty of incriminating property, including hidden swastikas and photographs of Hitler, along with military rifles and pistols which should have been surrendered. Curiously, the cleanest house of all was the Boden property. There was no evidence that the family had ever had any connection to the Nazis.

'Well, Wilde?' Colonel Appache said. 'There doesn't seem to be any sign of our man. What now?'

'Keep your men looking. I'll address the villagers.'

Appache stood aside. 'Do your worst, Professor.'

Wilde stood in front of the gathered Germans and clapped his hands to get their attention. He spoke in their language, slowly, to make sure he was fully understood. Heck was at his side, stepping in with a correction if he misspoke or failed to get the Bavarian dialect right. There were no soft words, no *'sorry for getting you out of bed and breaking down your doors'*. Wilde went straight for the throat.

'We make no apology for this visit to your village. We're looking for one of your people, an SS officer named Julius Boden. I must tell you that if anyone has knowledge of his whereabouts it is your duty to come forward now and tell us all you know. By the same token, if you gain any information at a later date, you must make contact with the Counter Intelligence Corps in Garmisch. Do you understand?'

They made no sign that they understood.

'I ask again, do you understand?' He addressed the mayor personally. 'Tell your people to respond to me, Herr Bürgermeister.'

The mayor simply shrugged. One of the soldiers prodded his chest with a rifle and the mayor turned and addressed a few desultory words to the villagers. Finally, there were a few reluctant nods of the head. All the adults stood with arms folded in front of their dressing gowns. Not utter defiance, but not cooperative.

'Good. Because failure to give us any relevant information regarding Standartenführer Boden will result in your removal to an internment camp. Again, do you understand?'

A few more nods.

'You should all be clear that whatever your former loyalties to Hitler and the National Socialist Party, they have been defeated and will not rise again. It must now be your mission to build a new Germany, ruled by law not fear. To do that, you would do well to assist the occupying powers. We have your best interests at heart. To help you, though, we have to tear Nazism out at its roots. That means that men like Julius Boden must face up to their actions during the past six years. If they are innocent, they will be freed. If they are found to have committed war crimes, they must face the full force of the law. I have no thoughts on the guilt or innocence of Boden, but as an SS officer, he must be investigated. So help us find him, for the sake of the new, civilised Germany.'

He stepped back. There was no applause, no noticeable reaction of any kind. Wilde signalled to Boden's mother. 'Come with me.'

'And what exactly do you want with me this time?'

'I want to talk with you, in your property.'

'Very well, but I will talk better with a coffee. Perhaps Ingrid could come with us and make it?'

'Yes, I will allow that.'

Wilde gestured to Heck to join them, and together they walked back to the Boden house. The interior of the property was not as they had left it. Tables and chairs had been turned over, rugs lifted, sideboards pulled away from the wall. In the big front room, Heck and Wilde returned the chairs to their upright position and indicated Ilse Boden to sit down. They sat facing her and the maid went off to prepare coffee for her mistress.

'You haven't told me your names,' Frau Boden said.

'My name is Wilde. I do not have military rank. And this is Lieutenant Heck, a British Army officer.'

'So you're not a military man, Herr Wilde. That must make you a spy, I suppose.'

'You don't need to know anything more about me.'

'As you wish.' She allowed herself a smile, but her carapace remained ferociously hard. 'That was quite some little speech you made.'

'I meant every word of it. In particular, it was addressed to you, Frau Boden, and by extension to your son. It would be better for him to give himself up.'

'You could well be right, but as I haven't the faintest idea where he is I don't really see how I can assist you.'

'Are you a Nazi?' Heck demanded.

She gave him a withering look. 'My politics are my own business, don't you think? Isn't that what you democrats say? Isn't that what the lauded secret ballot is all about? But if you really must know, I don't have any politics. That is men's work.'

'Women brought Hitler to power.'

She shrugged and looked past him to the window. Contempt oozed from every delicate pore of her handsome face.

Heck got up and walked over to her. He pushed his face within an inch of hers and gave her a look as scornful as her own. 'Well you're clearly not ashamed of your fucking Nazi son, so that makes you a piece of dogshit, lady. When I find him I will take great pleasure in killing him and I will invite you to watch as he grovels and begs for his life.'

She did not reply, would not even acknowledge him, save to turn her face sharply away from his. Heck stalked away and began pacing the room.

The maid brought a single cup of coffee to her mistress. None for her visitors.

'Is he like you, your son?' Wilde asked.

She stirred cream into her cup, then turned to Wilde. 'In what way?'

'Does he consider himself better than the rest of humanity?'

'If he does, I would say he has cause. He *is* better than the rest of humanity. He would rather die than beg or grovel to either of you two, or anyone else. Perhaps you'll meet him one day, Herr Wilde, and then you will find out for yourself.'

'Where is your husband?'

'Dead.'

'Did he die in the war?'

'I'm not sure I wish to talk about my husband or his death. You are here trying to find an escaped prisoner, my son, not to pry into my personal grief.'

'And the younger children, where are they?'

'With their grandfather, though I have no idea what business that is of yours either.'

'And where does he live?'

'Find out yourself.'

'You are not helping yourself, or your son, Frau Boden.'

She shrugged. 'I have to say, you are going to a great deal of trouble to find one SS officer among thousands. Why is he so important to you that you bring a small army here?'

'We take every potential war criminal seriously. Let me ask another question pertaining to your son. Have you heard of a Frenchwoman named Lilly Marais?'

Frau Boden stiffened. Her cup was halfway to her lips, and stopped. She put the cup down. 'Who?'

'Lilly Marais. A French refugee, at present living in the Apfelwald displaced persons camp near Garmisch. She's a friend of your son. A very good friend, I suspect.'

'The name means nothing. This is preposterous.'

Wilde's eyes locked with the German woman's and he saw something other than pure loathing. A sliver of anxiety, perhaps. The name of Lilly Marais most certainly meant something to her. Wilde rose to his feet. 'Would you please leave us now, Frau Boden. I wish to speak alone with your maid.'

'No, I won't allow that.'

'I'm afraid you have no option. Perhaps you would escort Frau Boden to her bedchamber, Lieutenant Heck. And make sure she stays there until I am finished.'

'I'd be happy to, Professor.'

'Professor? You call this man "professor"? Of what are you a professor, Herr Wilde? Uncivil behaviour, perhaps.'

Wilde didn't bother to reply. 'Get her out of here, Lieutenant.' As the Dutchman pulled the lady of the house from the room, Wilde wondered what it was about her that engendered such feelings of hostility in him. Perhaps it was her total lack of remorse. Or was it simply that somehow she fulfilled the Nazi stereotype of idealised womanhood – an image Wilde had always found profoundly loathsome? With such a mother, how could Julius Boden have been anything else but an SS officer?

Ingrid, the maid, was clearly in thrall to her mistress. Wilde went to her in the kitchen where she was busy tidying up the mess the soldiers had made in searching the house.

'What is your name?'

She bowed her head nervously. 'Zinke, Ingrid, sir.'

'Sit down at the table, Ingrid.' She did as ordered, and folded her large hands in her lap. She was a plump, ungainly young woman with a pleasant though slightly bovine face. Wilde estimated her age at about nineteen. 'Well now, Ingrid, you realise that we are looking for Frau Boden's son, Julius. When did you last see him?'

'I don't understand the question.'

Wilde pulled out a chair and sat at the table looking directly at her. A black and white cat snaked past his legs. 'How long have you been employed by Frau Boden?'

'Two years and two months.'

'So I presume you have met Standartenführer Boden quite a few times?'

The maid's glance drifted towards the area of the house where her mistress had disappeared.

'Answer the question.'

She nodded uncertainly.

'So how often has he been home in the past two years?'

'Please, sir, I cannot answer these questions. I am just a servant here. It is not my place to answer questions. If I do so, I will lose my job.'

'If you don't answer questions, you are liable to be interned. You don't want to be sent to a camp, do you?'

She looked down at her lap.

'Fräulein Ingrid?'

Her head was shaking and Wilde wondered whether she was weeping. She was clearly more terrified of her mistress than of him or the soldiers.

'Where do you come from, Fräulein?'

'Innsbruck, sir.'

'And how did you find this job?'

'I was approached by a friend of my family. My father was brought up here before moving to Austria.'

'Are you a Nazi, Fräulein?'

She looked startled. 'Of course, sir. I am a good party member and was in the Band of German Maidens.' Her shoulders went back proudly. 'I was a group leader.'

Wilde wasn't surprised. The poor girl was too simple to realise that most of her fellow Austrians and Germans would now be denying that they ever had anything to do with the Nazis or Hitler. 'It must have been a big day for you when you met Julius Boden. He is a hero.'

'Yes, he is a very brave man.'

'Perhaps you are a little in love with him.'

'Oh, sir, he would never look at a plain girl like me. He could have any woman he wanted.'

'Have you heard of Lilly Marais?'

She looked puzzled. 'No, sir. Who is she?'

'That doesn't matter. But tell me, where do you think Herr Boden is now?'

'I don't know.'

'He's been hiding here, hasn't he?'

She shook her head again, terror in her eyes. 'No.'

Wilde knew a lie when he heard it, but it was pointless pursuing the interrogation. Nothing short of torture would get this young woman to disobey her mistress and reveal information about Boden. 'You can go now, Fräulein Ingrid. Go and tell my companion to bring Frau Boden back here.'

'Please, don't tell the mistress that I have said anything. I really can't afford to lose this job. She will be angry.'

'You sound scared, Fräulein.'

'Things aren't easy, sir. I need the money from this job. My father has a temper . . .'

Ilse Boden had dressed and done her hair. She wore smart Bavarian clothes – dark green woollen skirt with a fitted, waist-length jacket with with green piping, turned-back collar and cuffs and deer-horn buttons – and her hair was tied up in blonde plaits. This woman was clearly more landowner than farmer; Wilde could imagine her holding court among the Strausses or Wagners at a Bayreuth concert. If anything, her demeanour was even more overbearing than before.

'Have you finished with us now, Professor?' She stressed the word *professor* as though it were an insult.

'Almost. Your maid Ingrid Zinke tells me your son has been here very recently,' he lied. 'I was hoping you would tell me more about the precise date and your knowledge of his plans.'

'If my maid said that, she was mistaken. Julius has not been here this year.'

'Thank you, Frau Boden. That will be all.'

Chapter 30

Wilde arrived at the displaced persons camp alone and went straight to the medical hut. Dr Angie Gray was in her office teaching Jerzy some English. Her door was open and she ushered Wilde in with a warm smile. 'Well, well, if it isn't Tom Wilde.'

'A great pleasure to see you again, Angie.' He had almost forgotten how dramatically red her hair was, and her profusion of freckles almost seemed to have been painted on her face. 'And you, Jerzy.'

'Hello, boss. Has Mo shot more fucking Nazis?'

Angie was horrified. 'You can't say that, Jerzy!'

'What, I can't say "Nazi"?'

'The word before that. It's not a nice word.'

'But Mo says it all the time.'

'Well Lieutenant Heck is a law unto himself. You'll get into trouble if you copy him.' She grinned at Wilde. 'Stupid, isn't it? Which of the two words has caused more harm in the world?'

'Better ask Mo Heck.'

'Have you brought your trigger-happy friend with you?'

'No, he's elsewhere.' In fact he would probably be halfway up a mountainside by now, but the doctor didn't need to know that.

'It's probably safer that he stays away from here,' she said. 'Mr Heck may or may not be pleased to know that the man he shot in the arm survived and has indeed been transferred to an SS holding camp. I really understand the need for revenge – Mozes Heck is not alone in that – but it has to end. And now is a good time.'

'I agree, but I need to work with him.'

'Somehow I can't quite imagine you two working together. Still, I'm looking forward to hearing all about your tourist trip around what remains of Germany.' She turned back to Jerzy. 'If you want to go out, we can continue our lesson later.'

'No, I stay with you and boss Tom.'

'It's OK,' Wilde said. 'Let him remain. Look, I've got something I want to talk to you about, Angie. I know there are hundreds of people here, probably thousands, but I need to know whether you've come across a refugee named Lilly Marais.'

'Indeed, I have, Tom. She is a most unusual case. Our refugees come mostly from Germany itself or from the East. I know that other DP camps have been looking after liberated French slave labourers, but she is the first French person we have had, of any age or sex. What exactly do you want with her?'

'She is looking for the same man as us. It's just possible that he might try to make contact with her here. I want her watched.'

'I hope you're going to give me a better clue than that. What man are we talking about?'

'He's an SS officer.' Wilde gave her the story about Boden's escape from Dachau and his significance in their own quest. 'The fact is, we have reason to believe Hitler is hiding out in this part of Bavaria or the Tyrol, and we have cause to think that Boden might know where he is. Problem is, we can't find Boden.'

'So that's what this is all about? Well, then, of course I will do everything in my power to assist you.'

'Thank you.'

'Just keep Mr Heck under control. As to Lilly Marais, I can tell you that she has talked to me about this man Boden, her so-called fiancé. She was asking me what she should do – how she might find him. I suggested that if he was an SS officer, he might be at Dachau. And then it all came gushing out – her love affair, the promise of a fine wedding. A few days ago, I actually drove her to Dachau.'

'I must say I had wondered how she got there.'

'Well, it was a pleasant day out for me, but a terrible disappointment for Lilly.'

'What more do you know about her?'

'I know that her affair with Julius Boden has had a tragic outcome.' Angie Gray's face fell. 'She had his baby, and it is now dead.'

'I'm sorry to hear that.'

'Last winter, a few months after the liberation of her region, her village – even her own father – turned against her. They shaved her head, threw her out of the community and, worst of all, killed the baby, probably by throwing it down a well. A terrible story, which I fear has been repeated many times over throughout the Continent. Hundreds of thousands of babies have been born to German soldiers in the occupied territories, and many of the mothers and children have faced retribution.'

Wilde nodded. From what he knew about the events in Berlin, it occurred to him that the shoe was now very much on the other foot; there would be many Russian babies born to German women. Perhaps the same would happen with the millions of British, French and American soldiers stationed here. Non-fraternisation might be the order of the day, but the reality would always be very different. How would this all end? How would the wounds ever heal?

'For months she survived as a wet nurse to an orphaned child,' Dr Gray continued. 'When the war ended and the child was weaned, she made her way eastwards – walking, hitching lifts – trying to find Julius Boden. All she knew was that he lived in the mountains in southern Bavaria, which isn't a great deal of help in the present chaos. He had told her that she would be welcomed with open arms by his people, that she would be feted like a queen. Highly unlikely, I think. Don't you?'

'I can imagine she might be disappointed.'

'I feel sorry for her, because she's a lovely young woman who has had an extremely hard time and she has obviously invested a great deal in this man. Probably too much. She truly loves her German – it wasn't a case of selling herself for perfume and food. Whether he loves her is another matter. Soldiers promising marriage to young girls is a story as old as warfare. Lilly's only crime was to be an incorrigible romantic, incredibly beautiful and not terribly bright.'

'The perfect target for a soldier on the prowl for some fun.'

'Yes. And I'm still concerned for her.'

'Well, I don't wish her any harm. So will you help us?'

'The thing is, it might not end well.'

'I'll do everything I can to protect her.'

'What do you want from her? Are you planning to interrogate her, to persuade her to help you?'

Wilde shook his head. 'Absolutely not. Her loyalty clearly lies with Boden, so if she has a chance to tip him off, she will. I don't want her to know anything about us or this conversation. All we can do is observe her and hope she leads us to him. His family knows she is here. If they have contact with Boden, there is every chance they will pass on this information. Whether he will want anything to do with her is another matter, but it's our best shot.'

'OK, I'll help. If there's any hope of bringing Hitler to justice, count me in. What do you want me to do?'

'In the first instance I'd like you to talk to her. Find out if anyone has approached her from outside. Just talk casually – nothing to alert her to your true motive. Could you do that?'

Angie Gray looked uneasy. 'I suppose so.'

Wilde wasn't sure what to say, because he understood the doctor's fears. It was not his aim to reunite the Frenchwoman with her love. He had other plans for Boden. 'I can't claim I have any perfect solution for Lilly Marais.'

She smiled and touched his arm. 'You're an honest man, Tom. I will help you, but will you do one thing for me: try to take Boden alive. It is just possible he *does* love Lilly. And it is also feasible that he's not a war criminal. In which case, there would be a tiny outside chance that one day he will be freed and they will be together.'

'One other thing.' He turned to Jerzy, who had been listening intently without saying a word. 'I need your help, too, Jerzy.'

'You do, boss? Sure I help you.'

'Angie will point out the Frenchwoman – then I want you to watch her, like a spy.'

'Don't worry, I know who you mean. Seen her before. She don't speak to nobody.'

'To *anybody*, Jerzy – she doesn't speak to anybody. Remember what I told you about the double negative?'

'Sorry, Doc.'

Wilde held out a present, hastily wrapped in brown paper and string that he acquired from the Garmisch CIC post room. 'This is for you, Jerzy, for your help. Payment in advance.'

'For me?'

'Open it.'

Jerzy looked puzzled. His gaze turned to Angie Gray and she nodded. 'OK, boss.' He carefully unwrapped the brown paper and revealed the box camera that Heck had been given by the woman at the roadside stall. 'It's from Mo.'

'Really?'

'He thought you'd like it.'

Jerzy took the camera and looked at it wide-eyed. 'Thanks, boss.' He turned it this way and that, cleaned the lens and view-finder. He grinned at Wilde and at Dr Gray.

'Sorry I've got no film for it, but maybe it'll help you watch Lilly Marais.'

'This is a good camera. I'll get film one day, then you'll see.'

'You're clear about the Frenchwoman?'

'Sure. Mostly, she just sits alone. Always there by the gate. Except at meal times. She pretty woman, but maybe a little crazy in the head.' The boy tapped his temple with his forefinger.

'Does she notice you when you're watching her?'

'I think she don't notice nothing.' He caught Angie's eye guiltily. 'Anything.'

'Do this and I promise I'll find some film for your cameras,' Wilde said.

'Even better, boss.' Jerzy saluted Wilde and gave him a wide grin, complete with a couple of broken teeth.

'Good lad.'

Wilde took the photograph of the Boden family from his pocket and pointed at Julius. 'That man in particular. That's the man we're looking for. But even if he doesn't come himself and someone else comes, you must tell us. Yes?'

'Best job I ever have.'

'Everyone knows you go around with your camera watching people. Just carry on like that, as normal.'

'Sure, boss.'

'I'll be here as much as I can, but I have other things to do. If I'm not here, I want you to alert the doctor. And you, Angie, perhaps you could put a call straight through to me at CIC Garmisch.'

'Yes, I'll go along with that. But if he leaves with her, I'd have no way of stopping them.'

'I don't want him arrested. I want to follow him. Just make a note of their direction of travel. I'll be on a motorbike and I'll catch them.'

The Hungarian woman raised her skirts. Her thighs were pale and mottled, her skin saggy, her pubic hair thick and dark. Jerzy fixed his eye to the viewfinder of his Kodak 8 Cine camera and watched with astonishment and rising interest as she squatted down over the man's naked belly. The man's penis was engorged and hard and she lowered herself onto it so that it disappeared inside her.

What were they doing? He had seen animals do this at the farm in Poland, but these were human beings.

Now they were moving as one. The woman was arching her back, grinding the man like a millstone grinding corn. And he was responding by pushing upwards into her. What was happening? This scrawny dark-haired woman and the big man seemed to be mating like livestock.

It felt like a transgression to be watching these things, but they were doing it in the middle of open land between two of the camp's huts in broad daylight so that anyone could see. There were hundreds of people about, but no one else showed any interest in what was happening. They walked past the couple with scarcely a glance. Yet he, Jerzy, could not take his eye away.

It didn't last long. After two minutes, the man shuddered. Perhaps she had harmed him. Then she shuddered, too, and collapsed on him. At last Jerzy took his eye away from the cine camera and switched to his new box camera.

The woman rose from the man, smoothing down her skirt as she stood up. The man was on his knees now, putting away his penis and buttoning his trousers. The woman walked away without a word.

Jerzy was no longer interested. He looked around the dusty camp parade ground and his focus returned to the pretty Frenchwoman he had been watching earlier. He had noticed her before and she was certainly a strange one, kept herself to herself. Not like most of the people here in Apfelwald.

She spent most of the day sitting against the fence by the main gate, alone. Jerzy had an idea that it would be good to go and introduce himself to her, but Tom didn't want that.

With his attention now on the box camera, he slung the Kodak 8 around his shoulder on a strap made from a piece of string he had picked up from the ground outside the canteen. He had found the cine camera itself back in July. It was in a roadside ditch on the long walk here from the countryside between Oswiecim and Krakow, from the place where he had worked as a farm boy since 1942.

Life had been hard on the farm, but he was never beaten and, though food was sparse, there was always something to eat. The farmer's wife was kind and the farmer himself, though morose, was fair. They had lost their own son in 1939 and so they needed Jerzy's assistance with the chores. They never asked him if he was Jewish and he never told them. When they went to church, he went with them and tried to mouth the words. He was a quick learner and he knew better than to ever allow anyone to see his circumcised penis.

He had grown strong, but was still short for his age. At the end of the war, the farm couple wanted him to stay because they still needed him, but he simply walked away, westwards.

Even at the tender age of eleven he knew there was nothing left for him in Poland. There never could be, because everything had been taken away.

He had to cut himself adrift and never try to return to the time before.

The time before . . .

The time when he had a family and a home and a name. The name he refused to remember because it would mean something inexplicable and terrible had happened.

He couldn't explain it to himself, let alone anyone else. He remembered the cinema, of course, because he loved it. The films every week. Cowboy films and Charlie Chaplin films were the best, but he loved them all.

Now he saw the world and everything that had happened in a fractured narrative – staccato scenes, like a black and white film on the screen. He saw his mother ladling grey soup into a grey bowl, then the camera moved to his father and he was shouting at Jerzy for not shining his shoes or for looking out of the window during his English lessons. The scene changed to the narrow street and he saw his own hand holding his older sister's as they walked together to the schoolroom. The soundtrack grew louder and the music turned to the drone of aeroplanes and the stamp of a thousand black boots.

Cut to Jerzy on the thin single mattress that he and his sister Aggie and their small brother Robert shared in a corner of the little room. The air is filled with another sound now: the cracking of wood. The camera shot is reversed and he is looking from the mattress to the door, which is now broken open. Two giant men in alien uniforms with massive guns fill the doorway. Mother has snatched up little Robert and is cowering in the corner. The camera cuts to Father's face. He seems to be afraid.

That is something new, something he has never seen before. Father has never been afraid; it is Father who instils fear in the family with his rages and his beatings, so how can *he* be afraid?

Cut to a long line of families with suitcases. Yellow stars on their chests, though not for Jerzy. He is only eight back then, so too young for a star. Cut to the face of a man with the SS flashes and the hooked cross emblem on his uniform. One of many, but one he remembered, captured on the film of his brain for ever. A face he would see again, here at Apfelwald. The man he told Mo about. The man Mo shot in the arm. The soundtrack now is hushed, light murmuring from the men and women in the line, the occasional shout and whip crack from the men in uniform, and the barking of their dogs as the line is driven onwards, down to the trains. Mother and Father are talking quietly to each other. They are arguing. They have argued all Jerzy's life, but this argument seems to be of a different order; there is no shouting, no fists, no broken crockery.

Father grabs Jerzy by the arm. His fingers dig deep into his muscle and he is in pain. Father's face is right up close, so close that he can see the pores of his skin, the follicles of his beard and he can smell his fetid breath as he growls in his ear. 'Run, Jerzy. When we turn the corner, run. There is an alley to the left. Run there and stay alive. Leave Krakow. You are eight. Go and be a man and survive.' It is a whisper, but it is a shout, too. A command of such urgency that Jerzy does not dare disobey.

The film is speeding up. His mother kisses his head. They turn the corner. He runs. There are shouts in the strange language used by the men with guns and hooked crosses. He hears the crack of gunfire. He knows that sound, for he has heard it in the ghetto. He has seen what it does, how men and women crumple to the ground when they are shot. Now they are shooting at him, but they don't hit him, because he is too fast and he zigzags, like in the films. He runs to the lane, runs down the lane and realises he is not being pursued.

He stops. The film is dark now, the buildings above him on both sides are closing in on him. He creeps back in the shadows to the main road where the people are still marching. Across the road, he sees Father and Aggie and Mother with Robert in her arms. They have been taken out of the line and are being held at gunpoint against the wall of a shop. Two men in uniform are shouting at them. Then there is a crack and Robert falls to the ground. Mother screams and then she is shot. Another shot and Aggie slides sideways. The moments tick by, a pistol is held to Father's face. Then the trigger is pulled and blood sprays up from Father's face and he falls on Mother.

The four of them, his family, are lying together in a heap, joined together in death. No more shouting for them, no more tears. They have died because they let him escape, as a warning to other families. He has nothing left. All he can do is obey Father, and live.

It was a hot day, and Heck was sweating profusely. His throat was parched and he took long swigs from his water flask. He had thought he was fitter than this after his years in the British Army, but the climb was tough in places and he was out of breath. He resolved to give up smoking. But not yet.

The route he was taking was picked from the beautiful hand-drawn map of the Alps they had found in August Jaeger's house in Almrosen. The chart was minutely detailed, full of mountains, forests, rivers, glaciers, huts, houses, villages and tracks through the high meadows and passes of the Alps. All complete with precise contours to show altitude. The complexity of the chart and the harshness of much of the terrain only served to show how impossible it would be to locate someone without some good clue to their whereabouts.

Heck and Wilde had studied the map with a magnifying glass for an hour before they decided on this route. It seemed perfect for Heck's purposes, an obscure rocky way that went nowhere except to what looked like a hopeful observation point above the village of Schwarzenkirche. A place where he just might have an eagle's eye view of the Boden house and anyone who came to it or left. A place where no one was likely to go when on their daily business of herding goats or heading for the high meadows to scythe the grass and oats.

Colonel Appache had been summoned to Flint Kaserne at Bad Tölz by Patton, so Heck had gone straight to the Garmisch quartermaster for equipment: a small radio transmitter, mountain camouflage, sleeping bag, binoculars, weapons and C-rations. A driver had dropped him two and a half miles from the village, and he had hiked from the valley along difficult rocky terrain, through forest land, well away from the routes the villagers were likely to take.

It wasn't a long hike, but he was taking it slow because he had to be sure he wasn't observed. Every ten minutes he stopped and spied out the lie of the land.

All was clear. From above and below he could hear the comforting clanging of cow bells in the high meadows and the occasional bleating of sheep. The dominant colours were the dark green of the needle-laden fir trees, the lush green of the grass, the grey of the rock faces and the blue of the sky.

According to the map, he was at an altitude of just over 1,600 metres when he came to a platform of rock. This was the spot they had decided would be the perfect observation post, but he was in woodland and at first he thought he would have no view.

He moved on a little further, across a narrow escarpment and came to an even better rock platform. It was about eight feet in width and went back about twenty feet into the cliff face. Above him there was nothing but an overhang and then a sheer ascent, below him, woods on a steep slope. But this time he had a clear view over the top of the trees.

He had found what he wanted – a panorama of the village about four hundred feet below. No one would see him from down there unless they were specifically looking for him, and no one could approach him unless they came along the path marked on Jaeger's map.

Removing the radio pack and the rest of his equipment, he stretched out on his back, looking up into the sky and the towering peaks. A pair of alpine choughs caught his eye and he watched them dance and play in the air.

When he was rested, he turned on to his belly, clutched the binoculars to his face and looked down to the Boden house – the Bauernhof Edelweiss as it was prettily called.

He watched the house steadily for a few minutes, then ranged his view around the village. He recognised the mayor with his ornate pipe in his hand, striding past the ruins of the schloss, and he saw various other faces he recognised from their earlier visit. Far below the village he saw a red speck on the road, some sort of vehicle making its way towards Schwarzenkirche.

Heck took out his flask and poured himself a small, strong coffee, keeping his gaze vaguely on the village. He had enough food and water to last three days at most, but he hoped this would be settled long before then, for the coffee certainly wouldn't last. He lit up a cigarette and drew deeply of the smoke. It occurred to him that if he saw Frau Boden's son, he might have a clear shot with the rifle. But that wasn't the point, was it? He couldn't shoot the bastard. They had to either take him alive and question him – or follow him. Either way, he had to lead them to Hitler.

Letting Boden live would be hard. It went against the grain not to shoot an SS man, but maybe his chance would come later, when they had found their true quarry.

They had invested a great deal in Boden and there was no doubt that he was their best bet at the moment, but the truth was there was no solid evidence that he had helped Hitler escape the bunker. At the very least, however, he was a filthy Nazi who deserved to die.

There was movement at the Boden farmhouse. Frau Ilse and her maid had emerged and were standing on the doorstep, talking animatedly. The way the girl hung her head it seemed she was being chastised, as if she still hadn't been forgiven for daring to answer any of Wilde's questions. Heck stubbed out his cigarette

Suddenly, the mistress of the house slapped the girl around the face with brutal force and she fell to her knees, holding her head in her hands. The older woman pulled her roughly to her feet and shook her violently.

A rickety van – the one he had seen a few minutes earlier on the road up from the valley – was drawing up nearby. It was bright red and bore the legend *Reichspost* on the side. The driver stopped it beneath some fruit trees.

Frau Ilse took the girl by the collar and dragged her towards the van. The driver got out. Heck recognised him instantly. This was almost certainly the slender man who followed him in Berlin, the one working with the sniper outside the Kabaret

Lola. Now he was helping Frau Ilse Boden push Ingrid Zinke into the passenger seat of the van. The man then nodded as the mistress of the house gave him instructions. Finally, she picked up a small valise from the doorstep and handed it to the driver.

He got back into the van and drove off out of the village onto the road past the lake, then back down into the valley.

Heck stubbed out his cigarette and removed the radio transmitter from his backpack.

Chapter 31

'As Hitler's secretary, you must have been extremely close to him, Frau Schroeder.'

'Of course, Professor Wilde. I was at his beck and call day and night.'

'So you would have known all his secrets?'

'Well, no, not all of them. But, yes, I was privy to his thoughts, and I was required to type up battle orders on his behalf. Not that I understood everything. These were matters for men, not women.'

'You were in the bunker until the very end, I believe?'

'The end? No, he ordered me to leave on April twentieth, ten days before his death. I was instructed to go with others to the Obersalzberg in Bavaria.'

Wilde smiled at Christa Schroeder. She was a plain, unprepossessing woman who was probably very efficient as a shorthand typist, but narrow and unimaginative. He doubted whether she would have much insight – either into those around her, or herself. They were in an interview office at Garmisch and she was sitting very primly, very upright, with her hands crossed in her lap.

'Are you being looked after well?'

'I am being held captive at an internment camp, though I have no idea why. I am a secretary, not a prisoner of war. And certainly not a criminal.'

'Indeed, but you knew a lot of criminals, so perhaps your incarceration is understandable. You must have known things.'

'I merely took a shorthand note and typed. Beyond that, nothing.'

Wilde nodded, as though he was in full agreement with her. And perhaps she was telling the truth – perhaps she really did have no idea about the multitude of crimes committed by Hitler and his infernal machine. Was that feasible? 'Tell me about the Führer – how were you chosen to work for him? You had an important job in the Third Reich.'

'That's easy and not very glamorous. I simply replied to a job advertisement in a Munich newspaper in 1930 when I was just twenty-two years old. I was not a party member and knew nothing of Hitler or politics, but I was experienced in office work and had good references, and so I got the job. I think he liked me very much, for he was always kind to me and talked to me at length about his childhood, both the good parts and the less happy parts, such as his father's vicious temper. He loved his mother dearly.'

That was too much, and Wilde laughed out loud. 'So he was simply a jolly good fellow, not at all the type to invade other countries and order the deaths of millions of people?'

Her jaw tightened. 'If you talk to me like that, then you will get nothing from me, sir.'

'Forgive me, but it sounded as if you were making excuses for him – as though he must have been a good man because he loved his mother. I wonder, Frau Schroeder, perhaps you were a little in love with him?'

She considered this for a few moments. 'No, I didn't love him, but I admired him greatly and I think we all had a great belief in him, that he was doing his best for Germany. He gave us back our pride. He promised bread and work – and he gave us bread and work.'

And brought you all to destruction, thought Wilde, but stating the obvious would be of no benefit here. 'Tell me about the man you knew. Was he stern with those around him?'

'Oh, he had his moods. What man doesn't? For much of the time he was charming and good natured, but then the devil entered his soul and he raged. His blue eyes told everything. At one moment, they were warm, the next they were ice-cold and you did your best to avoid the fury that you knew was about to erupt.'

'Where is he now, Frau Schroeder?'

'He is dead.'

'Why do you say that?'

'Because he told me he would never be taken alive, that he would shoot himself or take poison – or do both simultaneously.'

'But saying that and doing it are two different things. You were not there in the bunker at the end. Just imagine for a moment that he is still alive, where would he be, do you think?'

'In the mountains, of course. He loved the mountains more than anything. He was always happiest at the Berghof. He would take his morning tea on the terrace alone, looking out across the Alps, lost in his own world.'

'Apart from the Obersalzberg, what were his other favourite places in the Alps?'

'Well, of course, he loved the Tyrol, also Salzburgerland and Upper Austria.'

'Any particular towns or villages?'

'I'm afraid I couldn't say.'

'Did you ever meet a man named Julius Boden?'

She beamed. 'Standartenführer Boden? Oh yes, a wonderful man. A true German hero.'

'And he was close to Hitler?'

'The Führer had great admiration for him. He considered Boden the ideal German, an *Übermensch*. "Frau Schroeder," he said to me, "if I had ten thousand Bodens, I could conquer the world."' She smiled at the memory. 'Such a handsome man, and charming too. He would always have a kind word for me and the other secretaries and would kiss our hands like the gentleman he was. But tell me, Professor, why do you ask about him?'

'Because he has escaped custody and we wish to find him.'

'You think he has something to do with Adolf Hitler's disappearance? That is crazy, Professor. The Führer has gone to a better world.'

'Did you ever meet Boden's mother?'

Her brow clouded. 'Yes, I did.'

'But you didn't like her?'

She hesitated, choosing her words carefully. 'She was not my sort of person. The Führer, however, had a lot of time for her. I believe they first met at the opera.'

'Did he ever go to her home in Schwarzenkirche?'

'That I couldn't say.'

'Can't say, or won't say?'

'If he did, I cannot recall the occasion.'

There was a knock at the door. A young uniformed officer came in and honoured Wilde with an extravagant salute. 'Lieutenant Witton, sir. We have received a radio message from Lieutenant Heck.'

Wilde turned to Christa Schroeder. He had no more use for her. The woman was no actress and unless he was badly mistaken, she was telling the truth. As far as she was concerned, Hitler was dead; if she believed for a moment that Adolf was still alive, she would sing it from the rooftops. 'That is all, Frau Schroeder. Thank you for your time.'

He left her and followed the lieutenant from the room. 'So what's the message?'

'He says the maidservant has been sacked by Mrs Boden. Sent packing in an old red German postal van. The *Reichspost* has been disbanded, so it shouldn't be hard to spot the vehicle. The lieutenant says it's likely to be taxiing her home to Innsbruck and we might do well to intercept her, for she may well have a grudge against her erstwhile employer. Also says he recognises the driver from Berlin.'

This was important news. A breakthrough. 'Better get me a vehicle.'

The lieutenant grinned. 'All our checkpoints have been alerted, sir, and we've already had a sighting. I'd be honoured to drive you there.'

'Good man.'

'Hell, I could do with the outing. Goddamn office work gets me down.'

The red Reichspost van was parked at the side of the highway in front of a checkpoint, within a couple of miles of the historic village of Oberammergau. The driver was lying flat on the road with a rifle pointing at his back.

'Pick him up, I want to see his face,' Wilde said to the lieutenant as they climbed out of the jeep.

'Sure thing, Mr Wilde.' He signalled to the soldier guarding the driver. 'You can let him up now, Corporal.'

The soldier winced. 'Better look in the back of the van first, sir.'

The body of Ingrid Zinke was curled up like a foetus. She had been strangled with a belt, which was still tied around her neck. Her eyes were wide open and bloodshot, her tongue protruding between her blue lips. Her hands were bound behind her back with thin cord and her pretty dirndl skirt rode high around her thighs. The poor girl had been in no position to fight off her killer or struggle against death.

Wilde gazed at the pathetic sight for a few long moments, then returned to the prostrate driver and dragged him to his feet and slammed his fist hard into his face. The man grunted and fell backwards, blood spewing from his nose and mouth. Wilde pulled him up and hit him again, then threw him to the ground.

'Bind him tight,' he said to the corporal. 'We're taking him back to Garmisch. Get one of your men to drive the van with the body.'

The lieutenant looked concerned. 'Isn't this a matter for the military police, Professor Wilde?'

'No.'

'But a young woman has been murdered.'

'Yes, and we have the killer in custody – and I know his motive and who ordered the killing. The dead girl is named Ingrid Zinke. She was killed to silence her. I believe her family lives in Innsbruck, so perhaps you could ask your French counterparts to seek them out and get them to come and identify her. It's possible they might even have useful information to impart.'

'Understood, sir.'

The killer's ID papers gave his name as Andreas Stock, and his profession as postman. His address was given as Grünegg. He was a small, undernourished man of twenty-eight and Wilde had seen him before, on a rubble-strewn street in Berlin just before a sniper opened fire. Had he also been among the men and women singing the Horst Wessel song in the Kuhhaus?

Other than that, no information was to be had. Andreas Stock refused to say a word. He didn't even confirm his name.

Wilde had been through the dead woman's valise, which was found beside her body. The contents were what you might expect of a serving girl of limited means – a few cheap items of clothing, the stub of a lipstick, a toothbrush and hairbrush, a wooden crucifix, a few letters from her mother, Marthe, complete with her home address in Innsbruck. And that was it.

'I have seen you before, Stock.'

No response.

'Perhaps more than once. Certainly Berlin, both inside and outside the Kabaret Lola. I suggest you talk – otherwise things will not go well for you. You know what – who – we want because you have been doing your damndest to hide him.'

Wilde had an interpreter with him in case of difficulties with the local Bavarian and Austrian dialects, but his presence was pointless, for nothing was going to come from the lips of Andreas Stock.

He fired questions at the killer for two hours, but got no reply. Finally, he ordered a doctor to be brought in to put a couple of stitches in his nose and lip, then tried one last time.

Wilde had gone equipped with cigarettes and when he slid them across they weren't even acknowledged. Finally, he asked the interpreter to leave the room.

'Herr Stock,' he said now they were alone together, 'you have one last chance. I know that you were ordered to murder the girl by her employer, Frau Boden. If you are prepared to talk to me and tell me all you know, I may be able to save you from the hangman's noose. But you have to do this now because I won't make this offer again, and nor will anyone else. You know we are looking for Julius Boden and, more than that, for Adolf Hitler. Help me with this.'

They were in a stone-walled cell with an iron bed, two wooden chairs and a small table. The air was chilly, but not as cold as the gaze of Andreas Stock, which remained directed to somewhere in the middle distance. He still said nothing. Wilde was thinking hard. In other circumstances, his instinct would be to go to Schwarzenkirche and bring Ilse Boden in for some tough interrogation. He had no doubt that she was behind the poor girl's death.

But he couldn't go there. He didn't want her to know that her assassin was now languishing in a US Army cell block. He wanted her to think she was in the clear and unobserved, so that her son would feel secure and come to the village. And from there? He had to be their best hope of leading them to their ultimate target.

It was a long shot, but so was this whole quest.

Wilde walked out of the cell without another word to the prisoner. He slammed the iron door shut and told the guard to keep Stock in solitary. No visitors, no information from outside – and his presence was to be disclosed to no one apart from the girl's family.

He went to Appache's office and found the colonel lounging at his desk. He offered Wilde coffee and seemed almost light-hearted. 'You know, Professor, sometimes I love my job and sometimes I hate it. Today, I am in a good mood because I had a difficult meeting with Patton at Bad Tölz and it occurred to me that however bad things seem, at least I'm not General George S. Patton. Great war leader, but the war's over and there's nothing left for the sad son of a bitch, so he just wants to make things tough for his subordinates. As for me, I've got a life to go back to one day soon.'

'Glad to hear it.'

'Enough about me. How's it going with you?'

Wilde told him about Andreas Stock and the murder of Ingrid Zinke.

'And this is all something to do with Julius Boden?'

'Clearly.'

'Well if you're getting close, that's good. But not good enough. You've got to find the man. Boden might possibly be a conduit, but he's not the endgame. We need Adolf Hitler himself, so don't close your mind.'

Wilde sighed. He didn't bother to reply.

'Where's Lieutenant Heck?'

'He's out pursuing another lead.'

'What does that mean?'

Wilde found himself not wanting to tell Appache that Heck was observing Boden's home from a mountainside eyrie. He was beginning to understand why Collingham and Harper had kept information close to their chests.

He was saved from answering by a knock at the door. The colonel's secretary walked in. 'Excuse me, sir. I have a call for Mr Wilde.'

'Who is it?'

'It wasn't a good line, but it sounded a bit urgent.'

Wilde nodded an apology to Colonel Appache and went out of the room to the secretary's deskphone. 'Hello, Wilde here. Who's calling, please?'

'I heard you wanted to speak to me.'

'Who's this?'

'Jaeger. August Jaeger. You have something of mine.'

It was the missing mountain guide, cousin to Himmler's deputy Walter Schellenberg, friend of Julius Boden. The man Schellenberg had suggested as the ideal architect of an Alpine retreat or fortress. He was speaking in English, but heavily accented.

'Thanks for calling, Herr Jaeger. Yes, I certainly did want to speak to you.'

'You have my map – my life's work. You have stolen it.'

'Borrowed. Come here to Garmisch and talk to me and I will be happy to return it to you.'

'No, you must come to me. Come to my house in Almrosen, just before dawn tomorrow. I'll be there then. Please, don't breathe a word about this call. Not to anyone.'

Wilde heard fear in Jaeger's voice. 'Let's talk now.'

'It's not safe. The death of your friends should tell you that. You come here – come alone and don't be seen.'

He felt a chill. 'My friends?'

The line went dead. Wilde handed the telephone back to the secretary. 'Thank you.'

Appache was at his side. 'Some sort of movement?'

'Maybe. Just another line of inquiry. I'll let you know if anything comes of it.'

'You OSS boys like to keep things under your hats, don't you?'

'It won us the war, Colonel.'

'You know, Wilde . . .'

He held up a hand to stop the colonel in his tracks. 'Forgive me. Superstition. Chickens hatching, that sort of thing.' He looked at his watch. 'I've got to go.'

'Goddamn it, Wilde, this isn't good enough.'

But Wilde didn't hear him. Or didn't want to. He was already out of the office, heading for the jeep. He wanted a few hours alone, to study the map in greater detail and to get it photographically copied. He had a powerful feeling that it meant something more than just a mountain man's life's work. It was a key that might unlock a door. Or snap closed like a gin-trap.

Chapter 32

Mozes Heck slept in snatches. Even in his army-issue sleeping bag he couldn't get comfortable on the rocky ground. The temperature fell sharply, and by the early hours, he was cold.

Every time he woke up, he reached for the binoculars and peered down into the village. When the cloud cover lowered and enveloped the mountainside, he could see nothing. Not that there was much to see anyway, even during the daylight hours.

After the farewell scene between Frau Boden and her maidservant, nothing other than the daily routine of alpine life occurred. The harvesting of potatoes, the bringing home of the goats, the storing of hay in barns, the gossiping in the street, the feeding of chickens, the cutting of lumber for winter warmth. There was little or no fuel to be had, so the old men, boys and women worked by hand or made use of their old horses and carts. All the men and boys wore leather shorts of varying lengths and shades, and elf-style hats, often with a feather. All the women wore skirts and aprons and covered their hair in scarves. The children ran barefoot and there was much laughter.

It was a gentle, bucolic pattern of life that must have stretched back hundreds, perhaps thousands, of years and could almost make a man forget that he was here watching for evil.

Now, at midnight, he was alone with his thoughts, and these continually strayed back to Berlin. He had begun to doubt himself. If Miriam Rabinowitz, his first love, the sweetest girl in the world, had turned into the malevolent *greifer* Miriam Berenbaum, then what judge of character was he? If he had been wrong about Miriam, then how could he think he was right about anything? All his beliefs and all his values were as dust.

And what of Maria Dienstag, the woman with the dead baby? It had been an other-worldly encounter, and he still could not adequately explain to himself why he had helped her rather than turn her aside and leave her to go on her merry way to insanity and self-destruction, like so many others in this god-forsaken wasteland. A crazy woman, driven to madness by the death of her child . . . it was just one grim story among millions in this year of unfolding horror.

He had helped her within a couple of minutes of shooting dead a fellow German for the crime of being a Nazi. Perhaps that was the clue. Perhaps he had needed to prove to himself that he was capable of mercy, so was better than the enemy. Yet for all he knew at first sight, she might have been a rabid Nazi, too; many women were – and often as culpable as the men.

But he *had* helped her and, in doing so, he had discovered by chance that she and her husband had resisted Hitler and had paid a heavy price for their doomed heroism. Not only that, but they had actually assisted Miriam and had given her shelter.

Here on this uncomfortable rock ledge, in the damp mist of a low cloud, he worried that he had not done enough for her, that he could have done more than leave her to the tender mercies of a priest with a little money for her keep.

He knew what his father would have done, of course. The old man would have taken Maria into their home and he and Mother would have cared for her and fed her until she was well in body and soul. That had always been the way of Good Dr Heck, as everyone called him, both in Munich and Amsterdam. What sort of people thought it right to kill Good Dr Heck and his family? Had they gone to the gas chambers with words of forgiveness for their murderers?

Father had wanted Mozes to be a doctor, but he had always known that it wasn't for him. His nature was wrong. He did not love all humanity. He wanted to be a writer.

He turned over on the rocky ground in a hopeless attempt to get comfortable. It didn't matter; he'd sleep anyway. He had slept in shallow foxholes, behind tanks and in ruined buildings on the way eastwards from Normandy, this past year. He could sleep anywhere at any time. The only thing that intruded tonight was the thought of his family, and that made him want to weep. But no tears came and he wanted to rage at the sky in his wrath and frustration, but not here where he would be heard by those below.

Were they all Nazis in the village of Schwarzenkirche, and all privy to the secret? All complicit in Boden's plot? Or were they just simple farmers, going about their daily lives like his own family had gone about theirs?

He poured himself the last of the coffee, though it was no better than lukewarm and listened to the sounds of the night, the distant rushing of water and the whisper of the wind.

Wilde parked down a short track away from the main road, just by a fast-flowing stream. It was 4.30 a.m. and still dark. He was wearing a pair of plimsolls to deaden the sound of his feet as he walked the last mile up the mountain road to Almrosen. On his shoulder he carried a lightweight leather document bag containing Jaeger's map of the Alps. A precise photographic copy remained in safe keeping back at Garmisch.

The village was dark and silent. No dogs barked, no cocks crowed. The houses were nothing but black shadows against a slightly less dark sky. He was walking more carefully now, expecting at any moment to be confronted by an armed guard.

It was a foolish thought; alpine villages were not patrolled by law officers. But the darkness plays tricks with a man's mind as well as his vision.

His grip was tight on the Walther pistol in his jacket pocket. The air was chilly, yet fragrant with the scent of geraniums in the boxes that decorated the balconies of all the chalets.

Now he was outside Jaeger's enormous house, beneath the vast array of antlers that adorned the wooden wall above the door. He had a flashlight, but wanted to avoid using it. All it would take was one insomniac at a window and the covert nature of this visit would be gone. He turned the door handle and was not surprised to find it unlocked.

'Herr Jaeger,' he said in a low, urgent voice. There was no reply, so he stepped inside anyway. Perhaps Jaeger was watching him, to make sure he really had come alone.

Once inside, he had to switch on the torch, but he kept it low, the beam cupped by his hand to diminish the light. It was not perfect, because the windows had no curtains and the shutters were open. He pushed the door to, but did not close it properly.

The floorboards were ancient and he knew they would creak as he walked, so he measured his steps with care. It all looked the same as the last time they were here. Nothing seemed to be out of place. And yet he sensed a difference. He stood in the big hall area and waited. When no one appeared, he began to walk through the rooms of all three storeys, including five bedrooms, taking particular interest in the biggest, which he assumed must be Jaeger's. The beds were all made and had not been slept in.

Returning to the main room, the living area adjoining the kitchen, he took a corner seat, switched off the torch and put his pistol on the table in front of him to wait. And then he felt it – the warmth. He was close to the tiled wood-burner and he could feel a soothing heat in his shoulder. Placing the palm of his hand flat against the tiles, he confirmed for himself that there was a little fire left in the burner, just a few embers perhaps. By no means hot, certainly not enough to heat the room, but someone had been here in the past day.

Had he arrived too late or misunderstood the timing? Had August Jaeger disappeared into the mountains again? He was certain now that Jaeger had been in the village all along when he and Heck came here before, and that he had simply slipped away at their approach or perhaps had been warned to make himself scarce, perhaps by someone from the guest house down in Grünegg. Well, this time Wilde would stay, and see what transpired.

He didn't have long to wait.

Half an hour later, with the first rays of sunlight touching a white peak in the east, the front door opened and a figure stepped inside, directly in Wilde's line of vision. But it wasn't August Jaeger.

It was the woman they had met before, the plump farmer's wife who had been severing a chicken's head. She stopped suddenly, as though sensing his presence

'*Grüss Gott*, Fräulein.'

She gasped in shock and held her hand to her breast.

'I'm sorry, did I startle you?' he said in German.

'What are you doing here, sir?' She was breathing heavily and her eyes were wide, but she was doing her best to regain some composure.

'I came back to see Herr Jaeger.'

'But you can't just walk into a man's house in the night, like a thief!'

'He called me and told me to meet him here. Where is he?'

'I don't know. I have just come to do my cleaning. I look after the house.'

'But he *was* here. And you must have told him my name and location – otherwise he would not have called me.' He placed his palm against the tiles of the stove. 'Warm.'

'The heat is from yesterday. I saw him yesterday morning, but not since.'

'Did he say where he had been or where he was going?'

'No, sir. He never does.'

'But you talked about me?'

She hesitated, then nodded. 'Yes, sir, I mentioned your visit.'

'How did he react?'

She didn't reply.

'Fräulein?'

'Sir, if I am honest, I would say that he was angry that his beloved map had been taken, and nervous. Anyone would be nervous when secret agents seek them out.'

'So you think we're secret agents?'

'Of course. What else would you be?'

'When you were here before, I don't think you told us your name.'

Once again, she was reluctant to reply.

'Well?'

'Paula, sir, my name is Paula.'

'Do you have a second name?'

'Why do you want to know?'

He patted the seat at his side. 'Come and sit down. Talk to me a bit while I wait for Herr Jaeger.'

'I can't, I have work to do and then I must go home to feed the chickens and turn out the goats on to the pasture.'

'You still haven't told me your second name.'

'It is . . . it is Jaeger.'

'Well, I am very pleased to meet you Fräulein Jaeger – or should that be Frau?'

'Yes, I am Frau Jaeger. And before you ask, my husband Peter was August Jaeger's nephew, the son of his younger brother. Peter died in May, defending Berlin.'

'I'm sorry to hear that.'

She looked down and smoothed her apron.

'Forgive me for asking, but are you with child?'

She shook her head sadly. 'No. And I never will be, for the few men left alive have their choice of women, and I am no movie star.'

'I'm sorry, Frau Jaeger. But perhaps you are unhappy to find me alive?'

'Why would I think such a thing?'

'My colleague and I were almost killed when we were last here. Two other vehicles seemed keen to make a sandwich of us, which suggests they might have known who we were. As it happened, their drivers died for their troubles. You must have heard of it?'

She nodded. 'Yes, of course. It was an awful tragedy. But I don't understand what you mean by *sandwich*?'

'I mean that one or both of them were trying to kill us – either crush us or force us off the road.'

'No, that can't be so. I was told the brakes failed on the timber lorry.'

'Did both the dead men come from this village?'

'No, sir, one was Richter from Grünegg, the other was a stranger. Richter's brakes failed as he was going down hill towards his farm. It is assumed the driver of the other vehicle wasn't paying attention to the road, for they collided and both went into the ravine. But it sounds as if you know that? Did you see what happened?'

'Yes, and it wasn't quite the way you describe.'

'But why would they want to harm you?'

'They knew who we were and didn't like us asking questions. And they're not alone in that. Take you, for instance. You told us you had never heard of Walter Schellenberg, yet you were married to his relative – some sort of cousin, I presume.'

She came forward at last and tentatively sat down on the bench seat by the table, keeping her distance from Wilde at a couple of feet, her hands crossed in her lap, meekly like a supplicant. 'I'm sorry, it is true. I should not have lied to you. I said confession in church later that day because I am not accustomed to telling lies, sir.'

'So you do know about Schellenberg. Regular visitor was he?'

'I believe he came here quite often as a child, for the holidays in summer and winter, but I only knew him as an adult, when he came less frequently – once or twice before the war, and then once last year.'

'The last time he came, was he alone?'

'No, there were other men with him.'

'Anyone you recognised?'

She shook her head. 'All I can tell you is that they were SS officers. Six of them.'

'And they came to see August Jaeger?'

'Yes.'

'I'm interested in another man, Standartenführer Julius Boden. Do you know him?'

'I know the name, of course. Everyone does. His home is not more than forty kilometres from here by road, perhaps half that hiking. It is called Schwarzenkirche, a very pretty village. People say it will become the next Kitzbühel.'

'You remember what you said about lying? I was born a Catholic, like you, and I'm pretty sure it's a mortal sin here in Austria, just as it was in America.'

She closed her eyes and nodded her head. 'I have met him. He came here a few times because he was – is, I suppose – good friends with August.'

'Was he with Schellenberg's little SS group?'

Again she hesitated.

'Well?'

She nodded. 'Yes, he was with them. But, sir, can I not ask you what this is all about?'

'You tell me, Frau Jaeger, what do you think it's about?'

She met his eyes. 'You asked me to be honest with you, so perhaps you will extend me the same courtesy.'

'Try me.'

'I think you are looking for Hitler. Everyone in the village thinks that. No one has been talking about anything else since you came before.'

'Carry on.'

'You think Uncle August knows where he is, don't you?'

'From what I'm told, he'd be the best man to find a secure hideout up here, so yes, in that case I think he might know where Hitler's secreted himself. Why else would your husband's uncle have been talking to Boden and the other SS men in 1944?'

'But we hate Hitler, here. No one would do anything to help that filthy man. He was the Antichrist.'

'Are you sure about that? Your neighbours down in Grünegg still sing the Nazi anthem.'

'We are not like them. They were all Hitlerites there and maybe they still are. We despise them. Two of our men were denounced as communists by them and were taken away to Dachau, where they died. But they weren't communists. It was simply a stupid argument about a horse they sold at market. The man in Grünegg who bought it claimed they had lied about its age. As for Hitler, he is a stain on our land.'

'And you all think like that here in Almrosen? What about Uncle August – does he hate Hitler?'

Her face creased up. This was clearly torture for her. 'I don't know, sir. I really don't know. He seemed on good terms with Schellenberg and his men, and he was an old friend of Julius Boden, so perhaps he was helping them. Uncle August goes about things his own way. He is a strange man.' Her voice lowered. 'Some say he has fathered at least one child in every valley in Austria. And the war has been good for him, for the husbands were almost all away fighting. But the men in the villages know his ways and they don't trust him near their wives – so he has enemies.' She crossed herself hurriedly. 'I'm sorry, I should not have said that, sir. It is a terrible sin to spread such gossip.'

Wilde was beginning to feel sorry for Paula Jaeger. Her bulky farmer's wife strength concealed a sensitive soul – and her loyalties were torn. She was, perhaps, too honest for her own good. He hoped she would not pay a heavy price for talking to him like this.

He was growing tired. He had had no breakfast and badly wanted a coffee, even the acorn version. And why had August Jaeger not turned up? They were supposed to meet before dawn, and it was now daylight. Damn it, the elusive mountain guide wasn't coming after all.

'Let's go to your house, Frau Jaeger. Perhaps you'd make me a cup of ersatz coffee again. I'd pay you for it, of course.'

'People will see us.'

'People will see me anyway when I go back to my car. Better to be open about it. Brazen it out. You've nothing to hide. Anyway, if everyone here is so anti-Hitler, they'll be cheering you on.'

Reluctantly, she accepted his point of view, but he could tell she wasn't convinced because she looked up and down the road with apprehension as she exited August Jaeger's house. An old woman hobbled past and Paula said a hasty '*Grüss Gott*' before ducking back inside, trying to shield Wilde from the old woman's line of vision. Only when the road was clear did she allow Wilde to follow her out and hurry the few yards down the path to her own much smaller chalet.

She bustled around nervously as she brewed him acorn coffee and gave him breakfast. He sat at her table and tucked into some black bread spread with wonderful butter, all the time wondering what to do next. August Jaeger's phone call had seemed like progress, now he felt empty.

'Frau Jaeger,' he said when the coffee arrived in a small cup. 'Answer me one question if you would. In all your conversations with Uncle August, did he ever talk of his idea of a perfect hiding place in the Alps.'

'No, of course not. We didn't have conversations like that.'

'OK.' He sipped the coffee. It was growing on him. 'But you must know these mountains pretty well yourself. How far would you say it is from here to Schwarzenkirche, for instance?'

'Across the mountains and high pastures? I suppose twenty kilometres. A long day's walk because the terrain is hard and dangerous in the high mountains and glaciers. By road is far longer, but assuredly quicker and safer.'

'So a day's hike.'

'Yes, for an extremely fit man or woman. But it's not a route for amateur walkers and ramblers.'

'And if you were going to hide someone?'

She laughed for the first time. 'The *Einsiedelei*. When we were children, my friends and I used to go up there to give bread to the *Einsiedler*. We thought he was so funny, hiding away from the world like that in his little house with his little chapel, half carved into the rock wall.'

Einsiedler. Hermit. There was a hermitage in the mountains near here.

'Tell me more about it.'

'Oh there is no one there now. Not since the war.'

'But you think it would be a good place to hide?'

She shrugged. 'I suppose so. We used to love the place. Luckily the old hermit was a kindly man or he would have been driven mad by us kids playing around his mountain retreat. Oh yes, the caves in the cliff there are good to hide in. You know we're not the only village in the Alps with a hermitage. It was a custom going back many hundreds of years. The village was expected to feed the man and in return he would pray for the community and the health of their livestock. I am not sure whether any other hermitages are left, but maybe there are. Surely you cannot believe that Adolf Hitler is hiding there . . .'

'When were you last there?'

'Seven years, eight years maybe. No one has any cause to go there. Maybe the children play there still, I don't know.'

'Will you take me?'

Chapter 33

The eyes of the whole village were on them as they walked up from Paula Jaeger's little chalet towards the woods. No one said a word, either to Wilde or the woman guiding him, but they stopped and stared.

She had protested that she had too much work to do and couldn't take him, but he knew that the truth was she didn't want to be seen with him. An offer of money did not change her mind, but his persistence wore her down and she succumbed. 'Your shoes are stupid, though,' she said. 'They look like tennis shoes.'

'Well, they're all I've got with me.'

'Are you a married man, Herr Wilde?'

'I am.'

'Well, I am sure your wife would agree with me.' She smiled at him. 'I have an old pair of Peter's boots still. They look about your size.'

'That's very kind, Frau Jaeger. Thank you.'

'His smoked glasses, too. The sun can be extremely bright and damaging to the eyes when you go high in these mountains.'

Wilde accepted both offers. As they walked up the track, he had his hands in his jacket pockets as a precautionary measure. The villagers might not have known whether he was gripping a gun butt, but these were ordinary farming folk and they weren't likely to take any chances with him.

When they were away from the settlement and climbing steeply on a woodland path heading north-west, Wilde removed his left hand from his pocket and took her by the upper arm. 'I wanted to thank you, Frau Jaeger.'

'It is a small enough thing.'

'Are you OK? Are you worried about your neighbours?'

'I will be fine.'

'Won't you be seen as a traitor?'

'I don't know, but it's too late to change my mind now. Anyway, there have been too many lies these past seven years. Too many cowards.'

Wilde understood, but he was worried about her. The woman was patently honest with a strong sense of morality.

'Tell me, sir, did the Nazis really do all those things that are now said? Kill all those Jewish people in the camps? Women, children and the old?'

'They really did that.'

'I don't know what to say. I am so ashamed – the whole world will spit on us and shun us. We will all be counted as guilty.'

Wilde didn't know what to say either. He couldn't accept her contrition on behalf of the dead and bereaved, but nor did he condemn her out of hand for crimes committed by others. 'Come on,' he said. 'This is no time for such discussions. How long is the walk?'

'An hour and a half, maybe a little more depending on the state of the paths. They have not been maintained so well during the war years. It is more than just a walk, you see. In places, it is a difficult climb, particularly the final section – probably to discourage casual visitors. After all, the hermits wished to be alone and undisturbed.'

They continued and the ascent became increasingly hard going. Every quarter-hour they stopped to take water from a flask. At last they arrived at a narrow pasture with towering peaks on three sides, and the hermitage came into view. It was more than Wilde expected. He had imagined a hut, but this was rather more grand – a little whitewashed building made of stone and, beside it, a pretty little chapel, also painted white. Both buildings nestled into the rock face.

A long path of stone steps led up almost vertically from the meadow. Paula Jaeger led the way and Wilde immediately realised it was going to be as tough as she suggested, because there were no handholds, nothing like a handrail, not even a length of rope to grip. One slip and you could do yourself serious damage.

He was already sweating as the morning sun began to burn into the nape of his neck. The air was getting thin and he was breathing heavily, his eyes fixed on the grey stone of each step and on her boots, a couple of feet above him. At the top, he stopped and caught his breath. What now? Why had he even come here? What was he expecting – a cordial welcome from Adolf Hitler in his mountain retreat?

'You are out of breath, Herr Wilde.'

'I live in a place called Cambridge – it's very flat with plenty of oxygen.' He noticed that she wasn't even panting.

'Come on, I will show you around. Though I can't think what you are hoping to find. If Hitler was here, we would already have been machine-gunned by his SS guards.'

Maybe, he thought. But he took the Walther from his pocket anyway. She walked towards the door of the little house, which was in good condition, with glass windows intact, but he held her back. 'I'll go first.'

He pushed open the door and stepped inside a dark hall-way. As his eyes adjusted to the gloom, he realised it was the one and only room in the house. The view from below had been deceptive, making it seem a bit larger. A small table with a hard-backed chair backed onto the rear wall and there was a fireplace with ashes in the grate and two blackened pans hanging from hooks. By the door there was a tin washbasin. Beneath the window stood a single bedstead; surprisingly it had a mattress and blankets, crumpled up as though someone had slept here.

And that was it. This was the austere home of the hermits. A place to find God or drive you insane. The strange thing was it still felt lived in. No dust, no cobwebs.

'Why is there bedding?'

'For mountain travellers,' she said. 'I think someone has been here.'

He turned around. 'I thought the same. Who?'

'Someone hiding. I have heard of former SS and Gestapo men concealing themselves in the mountains and forests to avoid internment.'

Wilde lowered his voice. 'We should be careful. Whoever was here might be around still. Is it just this tiny house and the little chapel?'

'There is a woodshed at the back, with room for a broom and other tools. And the caves behind.'

Wilde took a last look around, even gazing into the cooking pans. There really was nothing here. God, what a miserable, spartan existence. Surely, the beauty of the mountains would never compensate for the absence of human contact.

He looked at the woodshed behind the house. A few logs were scattered on the ground, nothing else. To his right, the chapel was twice the height of the house. It had a tall arched doorway, which opened easily. His eyesight struggled to adjust to the dim interior. At first he just saw an altar and a carved cross with Christ in a loincloth.

And then he saw the corpse, stretched out along the stone-paved nave. Its head was soaked in blood and unrecognisable as human.

In the first two weeks of liberation, many souls were lost to malnutrition and disease in the Apfelwald camp, but after that things improved quickly and dramatically. Living skeletons became vibrant human beings again, women regained their menstrual cycles, sexual desire returned. Now, in late August, Dr Angie Gray had been counting the days since the last death, and the figure stood at ten. That was yesterday.

Today, she had lost a patient. An old Jewish woman had been brought to the medical centre in a state of collapse the evening before, having been found curled up on the dusty ground near her barrack-room dormitory.

The words 'old Jewish woman' were not quite right. The truth was, Anna Brand was only in her forties, but her hair was white and thin, her skin was sallow and deeply lined and she looked twice her age.

She had survived the war, but not the peace. Angie had tried many times to talk to her, but she was trapped in a shell of memories from which she could not escape. Angie very much wanted to help her migrate to England or America, but it was difficult without contacts or relatives in those countries to sponsor her, and Anna Brand was never forthcoming with information to help the process. The only clue to her life came when she said that her sister lived in Palestine, but when Angie probed for details, such as the sister's name and address, Anna Brand had clammed up. Now she had finally found peace, but Angie Gray was distraught.

'What did she die of, Doctor?' one of the nurses asked as they stood looking down at the woman's pathetic remains.

Angie shook her head. In her examination of Anna Brand when she was brought in, she had found no specific diseases, or evidence of cancers or TB. Yes, the woman was underweight, but certainly not dangerously so. 'I don't know.'

'I think she died of a broken heart,' the nurse said.

It was not a condition that you'd be likely to find in any medical book, but Angie couldn't disagree. 'You may be right,' was all she said.

Another nurse came in. 'That boy wants to speak to you, Doctor. He says it's urgent.'

'Thank you.'

Jerzy was beside himself with excitement. 'She spoke to someone, Doctor. I watched them.'

'Who did she speak to? Anyone you recognised?'

'No. New man. He just walk into camp and she see him immediately because she always sit by the gate. Then he see her. I watch them through the lens.'

'What did he look like?'

'I don't know – a man. He had big coat on, like an army coat, though I don't know why because day is not cold. And a hat.'

'Is he still there?'

Jerzy shook his head. 'No, he gone away. I think she want go with him, but he make her stay.' He grinned. 'The man gave her big kiss. It was funny.'

'Did you get a picture?'

'Oh yeah, Dr Angie, I got good pictures with the film you gave me. When film is finished I give you.'

She held out her hand. 'Give me the film. I have to get it developed.'

'No. Not finished.'

'Please, Jerzy, I need it now. Tom will want it processed in a hurry. I'll do my best to find you another roll.'

'OK. Five minutes – I go shoot some snaps around the camp. Can I take your picture, Doctor?'

'Go on then, if it speeds things up.'

Chapter 34

The corpse itself was not the worst thing. Everyone who had survived the war had already become inured to the sight of bodies, either in bombing raids, in the camps or on the battlefield. But this was different; this was grotesque mutilation.

The corpse was on the tiled floor of the chapel, but parts of the body were laid out like holy relics in a dish on the altar.

The dead man's tongue, his eyes and his ears were there, on the silver paten – the platter used by priests at mass to hold the Eucharistic bread. The amount of blood both on the paten and around the dead man's head suggested he was still alive and bleeding profusely when these organs were cut from his face. He would have been defenceless, for his arms and legs were tightly bound with thick rope.

'Dear God in heaven, it's Uncle August.' Paula clasped her hands to her cheeks in horror. 'What have they done to him? Who has done this terrible thing?'

'You tell me.'

Paula's gaze swivelled between the corpse and the platter on the altar, then she turned away and fell to her knees. 'I can't look. The eyes stare at me.' She lowered her head and began to pray.

Wilde's own heart was pounding from the inhuman obscenity of what they had found. He took deep breaths to calm himself and tried to make sense of the blood and cruelty. Even the grey stone walls seemed to lose their solidity and the floor was moving like a vessel in a storm. His teeth were clenched, every muscle taut, his mind numbed.

Get a grip, Wilde, you've seen blood and death before. You have to act. Now.

He had to take it all in, to search thoroughly for any clues that might lead to the killer. *Find the killer, find Hitler.*

While Paula prayed, Wilde placed his hand on the dead man's forehead and arm and found a little warmth. The blood was coagulating, but still had a bright sheen. Wilde was no expert but he reckoned the man had been dead a couple of hours.

He walked around the little chapel, taking everything in. Apart from the altar with its defaced paten and its crucifix, it was an austere space, lit by a single plain glass window. No ornamentation here. Nothing to distract the meditations of the hermit. In a corner, he found a rucksack, a coil of climber's rope and an ice axe. They were all smeared with blood. The body itself had been bound with similar rope, perhaps cut from this coil.

He tried to imagine the way it had gone. The killers had come here and overpowered Jaeger at gunpoint, then tied him up and carved him to death with the axe and a blade. From the shape and size of the corpse, it seemed he had been a strong and healthy man in his fifties. But no one, however physically powerful, could counter the threat of a firearm.

The reason for his murder was obvious. This was nothing to do with vengeful husbands from the valleys of the Tyrol taking retribution on the man who had seduced their wives. This was all about the telephone call to Wilde at Garmisch.

Whether he had inadvertently revealed his intentions, or the phone had been bugged, someone must have known that Jaeger had made contact with him.

The severing of a tongue was a universally understood warning to others to keep their mouths shut. The eyes and the ears? That meant he had seen and heard too much.

One thing was clear: Wilde and Lieutenant Heck had been on the right track almost from the start. The answer lay here in the Alps, and August Jaeger had been the key. It was his name that slipped from the lips of Himmler's henchman Walter Schellenberg in London, and it had been sound information.

But that line of inquiry was dead. Literally, he thought, gazing once more on the terrible remains of a man. The only thing Wilde was left with was a growing certainty that Hitler was alive, and that he was hiding somewhere in these mountains.

Not only that, but he was protected by men, and perhaps women, too, who would always strike first at anyone making inquiries, even if they were nowhere close. No chance was to be taken. Cut out the threat at the onset.

That was why he and Heck had nearly been crushed to death on the mountain road down to Grünegg, that was why a sniper had tried to kill him in Berlin and why agents Randy Collingham and Denis Harper were shot in the back of the head on a pretty Bavarian road.

And it was almost certainly the reason the poor maidservant Ingrid Zinke was killed by the driver of a red Reichspost van. To shut her up.

Wilde was certain now that Jaeger had held the answer. With his demise, however, there was still one trail left: Julius Boden and the village of Schwarzenkirche.

If anyone knew the whereabouts of Adolf Hitler it had to be Boden or his mother. But Wilde was under no illusion that Hitler would be anywhere near their home. People like the Bodens didn't soil their own doorstep. Nor would they talk, even if arrested. So Wilde would have to outwit them.

Gently, he pulled Paula Jaeger to her feet. 'Come on, let's go.'

'What do we do, Herr Wilde?'

'There's nothing we can do here.'

'At least let us put a blanket over him.' The next words were little more than a whisper. 'And something to cover the items on the altar.'

'Yes, we'll do that. Then we return to Almrosen and make contact with the French military. It's their responsibility now. Where's the nearest telephone?'

'There's one in my house.'

Was that a reproachful look she was giving him? Maybe his presence had resulted in August Jaeger's death, but Wilde hadn't brought the evil; it had been here already, an infection every bit as deadly as the Black Death. The scourge of Nazism.

'Well, we'd better get back to the village and let the mayor or whoever's in charge deal with this. You and I can't carry him.'

After covering the corpse and taking a last look around, both inside the hut and chapel, and in the shallow cave, they began the trek back down to Almrosen.

First, they had to negotiate the stone steps, which were even more difficult going down than up, but Wilde led the way and reached the flat grassy meadow safely. Paula was a little way behind him. He knew she was weeping and shaking from the horror of her uncle's death, and that she could barely see where she was going for the tears she kept brushing away.

He caught his breath and looked around the glorious alm. This was too idyllic a spot for such wickedness.

Way beyond the little lake, he saw two figures. At first, he thought it must be a pair of mountain goats or wolves but then he became certain that it was two men, walking steadily away.

His blood ran cold. The killers.

Paula was at his side. The sobs were choking her and he put a comforting arm around her shoulders. 'Can you look over there?' he said.

'I don't want to see anything, ever. I will never sleep again.'

'I know, but please – look across the lake. Do you recognise those men?'

She raised her eyes and followed the direction of Wilde's outstretched arm. 'What men?'

Wilde screwed up his eyes. 'Can you not see them?'

She held her hand flat to her brow to shield her eyes from the sunlight. 'Ah yes, now I see them. But it's just a couple of kids.'

'Are you sure?'

'Yes, Mr Wilde, look again. A boy in leather shorts and a girl in dirndl, skipping through the meadow.'

He peered into the distance. Maybe she was right. They didn't look very old or tall. 'Do you recognise them – are they from your village?'

'No, sir, but these mountains are accessible from other villages.'

'I want to talk to them. Maybe they saw something. You stay here.'

'You're going to leave me?' She sounded horrified.

'Go back to the village. Talk to the village elders. Tell them what's happened. They'll organise everything and call in the French authorities.'

'But there is a killer somewhere in these mountains. I think Uncle August has not been dead long, and so the murderer could still be around. I would rather stay with you.'

'As you wish.'

They set off along a path to the north of the lake. Its waters were mirror still and pure. The sun cast a reflection on its surface of the towering mountain behind.

As they circled the little lake, they lost sight of the two children.

'Where do you think they've gone?'

She shrugged. 'That's hard to say.'

'But where does this path lead? You've lived here all your life, you must know this place.'

'There are lots of tracks, but they just go up into the higher mountains and beyond.'

It was an easy walk on stone and grass. Wilde felt increasingly uneasy and kept his hand on the butt of his pistol in his pocket. At the far side of the lake, there was still no sign of the young people. For twenty minutes he explored the boulders and the last of the straggly trees. This was the limit of the forest. Above this there was nothing but bare mountain. His view was reasonable in all directions, but there was nothing. No boys, no girls, no secret lair. Just the towering mountains, the rocks, the wildflowers and the sky.

With so many paths to choose from, it was pointless going further.

Chapter 35

Lydia sipped her coffee and read the letter yet again. It had arrived on the doormat that morning and every time she read it, her heart sank a little deeper. 'Dear Mrs Wilde,' it began, 'thank you for your application to study medicine at St Bartholomew's Hospital Medical College, but I am afraid I must tell you that you will not be offered a place. Yours faithfully, etc.'

It was short and to the point. She had immediately telephoned the hospital and asked to speak to someone in the admissions department. The receptionist had told her bluntly that women were never accepted. 'I believe the last female physician at Bart's was the famous Dr Elizabeth Blackwell about a hundred years ago. I'm most terribly sorry, Mrs Wilde.'

She wanted to tear the letter into shreds and throw it into the bin, but something held her back and she simply slapped it angrily down on the table. She'd keep the bloody thing as a reminder not to get her hopes up about anything important ever again.

Since Tom had gone off on his jaunt to Germany she had been living in a heightened state of anticipation. She had been certain she would get a place at Bart's. Dear God, she had the academic background and she had been brought up in a medical household. More importantly, perhaps, her father had served as a houseman at Bart's. After dabbling in poetry, publishing and left-wing political debate, this was the career she had been waiting for all her life. She had always done well at chemistry and human anatomy.

She had been so certain of success that she had placed an advertisement in the *Cambridge Daily News* for a nanny to help with Johnny when she was away in London. She had received a good number of applications and had already interviewed half a dozen of the more likely ones.

Her thought was that it should be someone young, clever and full of energy; perhaps a war widow who needed work and a place to live. Maybe someone with a young child of her own to care for; he or she would be company for Johnny.

And now this. She had placed all her eggs in the one basket. What would Tom say? Well, of course, she knew very well what he would say – he would tell her to apply to the other medical schools sharpish. He was right, of course. But she had a horrible feeling she would get the same reply elsewhere.

Perhaps she should wander down to the college. Someone there might know about places that accepted women and girls. Yes, she'd do that. The senior tutor would point her in the right direction. Or talk to their good friend Rupert Weir; as a GP and police surgeon he might have some insights.

There was a knock at the door. Her first thought was that it must be Doris come to do the cleaning, but she had a key of her own. Anyway, it was her day off. So if it wasn't her, who else would be calling on her? Had she forgotten about an appointment with a would-be nanny? She looked out of the window and her blood ran cold. Philip Eaton was there.

Why would Philip Eaton be calling on her – and who was that man with him?

Only one thought came to mind: it was bad news. Something had happened to Tom. She opened the door. 'Yes, Philip?' She couldn't hide the tension in her voice.

'Ah, Lydia, how are you?'

'What's happened? Something's happened, hasn't it?'

'To Tom? Good Lord, nothing. He's fine, drinking the German bars dry of beer no doubt.' Then, perhaps fearing he had overstepped the mark, 'And missing you and the boy dreadfully, of course. I spoke to him not so long ago and all was well.'

She closed her eyes with a sigh of relief. 'Damn you, Philip, you should have called ahead. Everyone knows what the knock on the door means.'

'The war's over, Lydia – but yes, of course I should have called ahead. Forgive me.'

'Well, you'd better come in.' She held the door wide for him and the stranger at his side. Once inside the door, Eaton introduced them.

'This is Sergei Borisov.'

'How do you do,' she said, sizing up the bald stranger with a bulging belly beneath a brand-new sports jacket that really didn't suit him, and a loud yellow and blue striped tie that looked even worse.

Sergei Borisov, the former Boris Minsky, gave her a charming smile. 'I am very well, thank you, Mrs Wilde.' He bowed his head graciously as he shook hands. 'It is my very great honour and pleasure to make your acquaintance, dear lady.'

'Well, I'm sure I'm pleased to meet you, too,' she said, withdrawing her hand from his. She turned to Eaton. 'I suppose you'll eventually tell me why you're both here, but in the meantime, perhaps you'd like a cup of tea?'

'Coffee,' Eaton said, handing her a large bag of beans. 'Fresh off the boat from Kenya. And there's more in the car, along with a peach, a bar of chocolate for the boy, a bottle of Scotch for you and a whole hamper of unobtainable foodstuffs for the family.'

Lydia knew she was being softened up, but she happily accepted the coffee and took them through to the kitchen where she sat her visitors down and began to grind the beans. The aroma was exquisite.

'And where is young Johnny today?'

'He's playing with one of his friends across the road. He starts elementary school in a couple of weeks. Look, Philip, it's always a great pleasure to see you, but I'm pretty sure you're here with some purpose in mind.'

'Are you suggesting I only ever arrive when I want a favour?' She raised an eyebrow.

'Well, I must confess that often is the case. I will make amends one day and simply turn up with a motive-free picnic. Anyway, you are as always extremely perceptive. Lydia the practical poet – a wonderful combination.'

'And you can stop buttering me up, because it won't work. If you have a favour to ask, just ask it.'

'Which brings me neatly to Mr Borisov here. Despite his passable English, you will probably have observed from his accent that he is Russian.'

'Carry on.'

'He has defected from the Soviet zone in Berlin to seek asylum in Britain.'

Lydia frowned. 'Why would he defect? I thought we were allies.'

'We are. But there are tensions and they're growing. Not that that is the reason he felt obliged to leave Russia. He believed he was marked down for execution by Comrade Beria and so, understandably, he hoped to avoid a bullet in the head. As you might imagine, he brings with him a wealth of information of life inside the Kremlin. Now he needs a safe house for a very short time.'

'What does that have to do with me?' she demanded, knowing very well what it meant.

'Well, you see, it was Tom who got him out of the Soviet zone.'

'Let me guess: you're suggesting that you want him to stay here with me and Johnny.'

'I confess that was the idea.'

'Oh no, Philip, that's really not on. Anyway, I happen to know that the secret service has its own safe houses. In fact, I seem to recall there's one not far from here, used by Five. You've used it yourself.'

Eaton and Borisov exchanged a meaningful glance. 'This is difficult for me to admit, Lydia,' Eaton said, 'but I have to tell you that we have a problem. I can't use any of our safe houses for one simple reason – they're not safe. It seems we have at least two traitors, one in Five, one in Six. It is possible that there are more.'

'Well, why don't you charge them?'

'Because we're not sure who they are. Mr Borisov is or was a member of the Russian intelligence service SMERSH, and he has a great deal of information on them, but he has only ever known them by their code names. We are hoping by intensive questioning and deduction that we will be able to narrow down our search for the traitor. In the meantime, I have to keep him safe. Tom and I are the only two who know he has defected. Actually, you make that three now.'

'Well, keep him in your own house, Philip. You have a lovely home in Chelsea – survived the Blitz, didn't it?'

'There's another matter, of course. As you pointed out, the Soviet Union is our ally. If they hear we have Borisov here, they will demand his return and we will be obliged to comply. We can't allow that.'

'You didn't answer my question.'

'How's that coffee coming along? You know, I could keep you jolly well supplied. I wouldn't expect you to do this for nothing.'

'You sound like a bloody black marketeer.'

He shrugged with a guilty smile.

'Does Tom know about this plan?'

'I can't make contact with him at the moment. Do you think he'd object?'

'The question, really, is whether I object, isn't it?'

'Yes, of course.'

Sergei Borisov put his fat, rough hand on the table. 'Please, Mrs Wilde, I realise this is asking a great thing of you and I will understand completely if you turn me away. There will be no hard feelings. But allow me to tell you a bit about myself. I studied at Cambridge before the war – the first war, that is. As you can see, I am not a young man. I know and love this town very much and it is my heartfelt desire to teach here one day, if one of the colleges would accept me. But in the meantime, I am homeless and I badly need a bed for a few nights. I promise I would be no trouble to you or your son. I would add that I did your husband a very great favour in Berlin, and one day I am sure he will confirm that to you.'

She looked at Eaton and shook her head in resignation. She knew when she was beaten. 'How long is *a few nights*, Philip?'

'No more than a week. This has all been done in an immense hurry, but I will find a suitable place for Mr Borisov sooner rather than later, I promise you.' His eyes strayed to the letter on the table.

'Read it if you like,' she said. 'Or burn it.'

'I confess I noticed the Bart's heading.'

'They've turned me down because I'm a woman. Probably too old as well. Oh, and the worst crime of all, I'm a mother. It doesn't say so there, but I rang the receptionist and she confirmed that the men-only rule is a matter of policy. You'd have thought the question of brainpower and commitment would be rather more important than sex and age, but there you go.'

'I'm truly sorry to hear that, Lydia.'

She snorted, then screwed up the letter and tossed it towards the wastepaper basket, missing it by a couple of inches.

'That's life, Philip.'

'But it's not good enough. Let's just hope Mr Attlee sweeps away all that sort of nonsense.'

'Good God, don't tell me you voted Labour? I had you down as Tory to the marrow.'

He smiled. 'Really? I thought you knew me rather better than that.'

'You're a dark horse, Philip.' But, of course, she had always known that. And she hadn't for a moment put him down as Tory. In fact, she had never been quite sure what he was, and she was still confused. Obviously, he was good at his job, for if a senior intelligence agent couldn't keep his feelings secret, what use was he?

'Well?'

'Well what?'

'You haven't actually said no to my proposition.'

'One week, no longer.'

'I'll go and get the hamper and Mr Borisov's meagre belongings.'

Chapter 36

The radio was dead. Mo Heck was stuck halfway up a mountain with no way of communicating with Tom Wilde or anyone else. Not that he had anything to report for it had been a long day of nothingness. Nothing but watching farm folk going about their daily grind. No vehicles arrived in the village, none left.

He was isolated and the day had become cold. There was a feeling of snow in the air, which was not uncommon at these altitudes in late summer. Heck was well aware of this, because he knew the Alps from his boyhood summer holidays in Switzerland. The question he couldn't get away from was the problem of what exactly to do if he saw Standartenführer Julius Boden. By the time he got down to the village, Boden could well be gone. And with the radio kaput there was no way of summoning help to block his exit or pursue him.

To hell with it, for the moment there seemed to be no alternative but to stay where he was and continue to observe; he'd give the stake-out one more night and then, if nothing happened, he was getting out of here.

He smoked a cigarette, certain that they'd never see the thin, dissipating wisps of smoke from down there. And then he had an idea. At first it seemed crazy and he dismissed it.

But, as the day wore on, he kept returning to the same thought. Was it really so crazy? Wilde wouldn't approve, of course, but it had to be better than this. He would force the issue. He'd make one of the Nazi-loving bastards talk.

'But I thought he didn't have any film. How did he get these pictures?'

Angie Gray smiled at Wilde's bewilderment. 'You'd be amazed what you can get here, Professor. I think I told you this camp was turning into a little town, and so it is. There's a flourishing marketplace and all sorts of industry going on. Some of the refugees have started a newspaper, there's a make-shift restaurant with kosher specialities – thanks largely to the American Jewish Joint Distribution Committee – and then there's the theatre and the band. Anyway, I heard that a camera club had started. They sold me a roll of film at a fair price and then developed it in their little darkroom – a corner of their blockhouse.'

Wilde studied the small black and white photographs of the man with Lilly Marais, comparing it with the picture he had taken from the Boden house in Schwarzenkirche. Even though the man in Jerzy's pictures was wearing a heavy overcoat and had a hat pulled down over his brow, it was quite clearly Julius Boden.

Jerzy was looking on, beside himself with excitement. 'Is OK, boss?'

'It's good, Jerzy. You're a fine photographer. Did you hear anything they said?'

'Sorry, boss, wasn't close enough. The woman, she want go with him but he shake his head and push her away. Made her stay. I think he come back for her. Maybe tonight after dark.'

Wilde had the same thought. But in the meantime, he needed to get a message to Heck, to bring him up to date. The problem was the wireless operator at Garmsich said he had lost contact. Nor could he go up the mountain to Heck at the moment, because he had to stay here and wait for darkness.

'You're right, Jerzy. Great work. Get out there and watch her. Run in as soon as you see the man.'

The boy saluted – the way he had seen the GIs salute – and disappeared.

'Are you going to seize him at gunpoint?' Angie asked when they were alone in her office.

'That was my initial thought. But I doubt he'd say a word. I'd rather follow him. He's not the target, just the means to an end.'

'Well, be careful – please.'

Wilde nodded. He had a very good idea of the sort of people they were dealing with; the mutilated body of August Jaeger in a mountain chapel and the corpse of the maidservant Ingrid Zinke in a red van had made that clear enough.

He had not felt good about leaving Paula to deal with her neighbours and contact the French authorities, but he could see no option. There was nothing he, Wilde, could do to assist her. His presence in Almrosen would only confuse the issue.

Paula had accepted his decision with good grace, but he could see that she was terrified and lost. He hoped to God that her community was as close-knit and anti-Nazi as she had claimed.

Now, with Jerzy outside watching Lilly, he explained all this to Angie Gray and she listened without comment. When the whole story had spilled out, she smiled reassuringly. 'I've got a bottle of whisky tucked away in my office if you're interested.'

'Angie, I can think of nothing I'd like more right now. But today, I'm going to have to decline the offer.'

'Well if you need one later, it'll be here, and so will I. We can get tight together and tell each other secrets.'

'You're asking an intelligence officer to tell secrets?'

'Not military secrets, love secrets. The best kind.'

He laughed. 'Why don't you tell me what's next for you. You said you're posting was almost up – so where are you heading?'

'Oh, I'll just go where the wind blows me.'

That sounded very romantic, but he wasn't sure he believed her. She'd want a family one day. Didn't everybody? And then a regular job at a local cottage hospital somewhere in the Home Counties when the children were old enough for school, or perhaps join a general practice. He looked at her bright eyes and chided himself for such conventional thoughts. Angie Gray was never going to marry and settle down. Such things could not be talked about, but he had seen that much in her and hoped she would find happiness anyway.

'Actually, if you must know I'd like to move into psychiatry, do some research on the long-term effects of this bloody war. What are the lasting effects of concentration camps? What do constant bombing raids do to the brains of human beings? There's also a great deal of work to be done on shell shock and battle fatigue.'

'You have plenty of material for your research here.'

'You're right. Their bodies heal quickly, but their minds are another matter. I spend a lot of time talking to them. Some of them won't talk, of course. They can't bear to remember. The past is the past and they want to build new lives. But some let me in – and I have kept extensive notes.'

'Enough for a book?'

'I'll see. But, please, don't mention that to anyone. I'd want to use case histories, but not real names, so no one will get hurt more.'

The door swung open. Jerzy was standing there, arms raised. 'He's here, boss!'

Already? Wilde looked through the window. The time had gone fast. It was dusk and it was raining.

'Wish me luck, Dr Gray.'

'Good luck, Professor Wilde.'

The motorbike was parked just outside the camp gate. A Harley-Davidson WLA in US Army livery. Not the fastest bike on the road – well short of his own Rudge Special back home in Cambridge – but it should do the job.

He sat astride the machine, the engine purring beneath him as he watched Lilly Marais and the man he believed to be Julius Boden duck through the rain and quickly climb into the back of a soft-top Mercedes. A driver was already at the wheel.

Wilde had borrowed an army waterproof and goggles from the GIs in the camp guardroom, but he doubted the outfit would keep him dry in this downpour.

The Mercedes pulled away. Wilde watched it gather speed for half a minute, then he turned the throttle on the Harley and began to follow it. The bike still had wartime blackout headlights, but he wasn't going to use them until necessary. He would use the lights of the car ahead to show him the way.

He wasn't surprised by the route Boden was taking. They were heading south, past Garmisch towards the high mountains.

The road was familiar to him, but it became increasingly difficult as the rain turned first to sleet and then light snow when they gained altitude. As the snow drifted and swirled, becoming heavier for a while and then lighter again, the tail lights of the Mercedes became hard to make out. The problem wasn't just visibility. The snow wasn't settling, but it was making the road slippery and treacherous.

The tyres of the Harley had little tread and were losing grip.

Wilde lost control completely on a right-hand bend. The bike just slid away beneath him and there was nothing he could do to stop it. He was thrown clear, but the Harley careered into the cliff face, spun around and stopped.

Swearing as he picked himself up, he brushed the snow off his jacket then walked over to the motorbike and raised it up onto its stand. By the light of a torch from his pocket, he saw that the front wheel was slightly bent.

Sitting astride the machine, he kicked the starter, but there was no response. Either the engine was flooded, or worse. He waited a minute, then tried again. The engine spluttered, then roared into life.

Heading on up the steep, twisty road, the damaged wheel made the bike tougher to manoeuvre and he soon realised he had lost touch with the Mercedes. But that didn't matter now, because he knew where it was going. This road led to only one place – Schwarzenkirche. Boden was taking his bride home.

Julius Boden stroked Lilly's hair. She was nestling into his arms in the back of the car, holding him as though she would never let him go. He kissed her again, then whispered words of love in French into her ear.

Ahead of them, snow swirled in mysterious patterns in the headlights of the Mercedes.

Not for the first time, he thought back to the time he met Lilly Marais in the summer of 1943. He had been in the back of a Mercedes like this one, driving from the Normandy coast to Rouen. It had been a long day. He had been inspecting improvements to his sector of the vast system of fortifications known as the Atlantic Wall and he had not been happy with what he had seen. There were still gaps – blind spots on the shoreline that the machine-gunners could not cover. Such over-sights mattered; one had to be prepared for all eventualities – even the unlikely arrival of an enemy landing force.

Bored, reluctant officers and engineers had had to be cajoled and threatened with unpleasant deployments elsewhere if they didn't rectify the problems in short order. Of course, they all recognised him and watched him as though he were a film star. His fame had travelled far and wide in the Reich. The upshot of that was that there were those who didn't take him seriously as a soldier. *Good for a picture in the papers, nothing more.* Well, they'd soon learn the truth when he sent them east to face a bombardment by the Ivans.

Though weary from his day's work, he had been happy and in a good mood as they drove through the village of Ste Estelle-sur-Seine. It wasn't a particularly memorable place. Just another northern French farming community and, anyway, his mind was elsewhere – the prospect of a few drinks and a bit of dancing at the midsummer ball.

But then, out of the corner of his eye, he saw her.

Standartenführer Boden had enjoyed the company of many beautiful women in his young life, including the finest beauties of Berlin and Munich. But Lilly was different. This was like chancing upon a Michelangelo sculpture or a Mozart symphony for the first time.

She was with a group of four other girls, running down the street, laughing, until suddenly they saw the open-topped staff car with its swastika flags and came to a sudden halt as if struck by a bullet. They stood rigid at the side of the road and waited for it to pass.

But Boden spoke in the driver's ear, telling him to stop. Slowly, the car backed up until the vehicle was alongside the five girls. Boden summoned them to him with a curl of his gloved fingers.

The girls were all in summer dresses. Scraps of bright material that swayed in the light June breeze and showed off their tanned legs and arms. Their hair was loose and long.

They seemed too nervous to approach him.

'Come,' he said in French, 'I won't bite. Come and talk to me.' And then he pointed at the one that had made him stop. 'You,' he said, 'what is your name, Mademoiselle?'

'Me?' She pointed at her chest, surprised to be singled out.

'Yes, you.'

'Lilly, sir. Lilly Marais.'

'Well, Lilly Marais, you are too beautiful to be shy, come and talk to me.'

She looked around at her companions. They didn't know how to react. Then, shoulders back, hair swinging, she stepped up boldly to the rear door of the staff car.

'Do you like champagne, Lilly?'

'I have never tried it, sir.'

He laughed. 'My name is not "sir", it is Standartenführer Boden, and just for today you shall call me Julius. Would you like to try champagne?'

She looked around at her friends once more. 'I don't know.'

'How old are you, Lilly?'

'Eighteen.'

'Do you like dancing?'

'Oh yes, sir . . . Julius. Yes, we all love to dance.'

'Good. Then my car will come here to collect you and your four friends at six thirty this evening. Wear your finest clothes.'

And now, just over two years later, here she was approaching his home village on the border of southern Bavaria and

Austria, about to meet his mother for the first time – and his people.

Wilde ditched the motorbike in trees close to the pathway to Heck's eyrie, then began the gruelling two and a half mile trek up the mountainside. He carried nothing but his pistol and flashlight, but the conditions were treacherous.

Once the lights of the village came into view below, he could no longer use his torch and stowed it in his jacket pocket. Now he had to walk more slowly and a great deal more carefully.

In a patch between trees, he lost his footing in the snow at the edge of the path and fell.

He tore his palms as he scrabbled to get a handhold on the loose, sharp-edged stone, then came to a juddering halt on a small rock ledge, five foot down from the path.

For a few moments he stopped in the trees, catching his breath. He listened to the night and felt certain he could hear voices from a long way below. He took out the torch, sure that the trees would prevent it being seen, and splayed its beam across the rock face he had slid down. He saw two handholds; they were all he needed.

He switched off the light again and pulled himself up the slope. The angle was about forty-five degrees. Small rocks broke away, but through sheer strength and momentum – ignoring the blood trickling from his wrist – he hauled himself back to the path.

The snow was easing. No more than a fluttering, as he forged on. Half an hour later he reached a wide rock ledge. A little further on he spotted the radio, half buried in snow, along with a pack with C-rations, and a sleeping bag.

There were no weapons.

And no sign of Lieutenant Heck.

Chapter 37

Julius Richard Boden was aware that his mother considered his love for Lilly Marais as some sort of aberration. 'A French peasant girl!' she had exclaimed when first he told her about her in the spring of 1944. 'God in heaven, Julius, what are you thinking of?'

He silenced her with a finger to his lips. 'When she comes here, Mother, you will welcome her with respect and warmth, for she is to be my bride. Is that clear?'

Ilse Boden hesitated for only a few moments, then nodded her head. 'Yes, that is clear.'

'You will take her by the hand and kiss her cheeks in the French manner and tell her how lovely she is. And that will not be difficult, for she is fair like you, and more beautiful than any film star.'

'If you say so.'

That conversation had taken place two months before the Allied invasion. At that time, he had thought he would take her home in style, that she would be waved off by her fellow villagers in Ste-Estelle-sur-Seine and cheered into her new home of Schwarzenkirche.

The invasion changed all that. He had had to leave her without saying farewell, with no way of explaining himself. Now, at last, he could make amends.

But it was still obvious that his mother would not be won over easily.

While Lilly was up in the guest bedroom being prepared for the great welcome, Boden was downstairs with his mother.

'I am disappointed in you, *Mutti*.'

'I shook her hand, Julius. What more do you want me to do?'

'You could have embraced her like a daughter. You could have smiled and made her feel welcome.'

'But she is French. They are the enemy.'

'You will make amends.'

Ilse Boden pulled back her shoulders and tilted her proud chin.

'Do you understand?'

'I always understand you, Julius. But not in this matter.'

'Listen to me. Lilly has shown great courage in braving the wrath of her own people and has had to endure much hardship in making her way here unassisted in the wake of war. Courage and fortitude worthy of a German woman. You will be proud to call her daughter-in-law, and if ever you hear a word said against her, you will tell me and I will deal with it harshly.'

She did not argue, but he knew what she was thinking.

He understood his mother perfectly. She was thinking that she would no longer be matriarch here, no longer the mistress of her own house. And she was mourning her loss. She was thinking that she would happily kill this interloper. But Ilse Boden would be won over. Julius would make sure of that.

She would come around to his decision and accept it, because she had to; it was the way of the world. The wife replaces the mother.

Anyway, she would have something else to console herself. Something far more magnificent than being the great lady of this house and this village. An honour that would resonate down the ages and see her revered above all women.

She would become known as the mother of the second Führer.

*

Wilde peered down to the village. Lights were on in most of the houses and there was some sort of activity in the main street, though he couldn't make out what it was. All he knew was that most of the villagers were outside their houses, some chatting, some with arms folded simply waiting and watching expectantly.

The Mercedes that had brought Julius Boden was parked outside the family home, but Wilde couldn't see him or his mother or Lilly. Was Heck down there? Where else could he be? Wilde didn't like the look of this one bit.

Leaning over the rock ledge, he realised it would be quite possible to get down to the village without using the mountain path. Some of the way down it would be a simple matter of sliding on snow and grass but there were a few short drops which would have to be negotiated with care or somehow avoided. He could move from tree to tree, using them to break his fall. Is that what Heck had done?

All Wilde could think was that the Dutchman must have seen Julius Boden arriving and decided to take matters into his own hands. It was not a good prospect.

These thoughts were interrupted.

Without warning, an explosive flash lit the sky.

Wilde's gaze swerved from the centre of the village up to the gentle, snow-covered meadow as two great columns of fire rose into the air.

The whole area at the southern extremity of the village was illuminated by a pair of huge bonfires that must have been ignited with large quantities of petrol or some other accelerant. In other circumstances, the roar and brilliance of the inferno would have been a magnificent spectacle. For Wilde it was both alarming and mystifying. What was happening?

Next, he heard the beat of drums and saw more lights. A dozen torches, then a dozen more, all held aloft by marching men, goose-stepping down the slope towards the enormous bonfires, heading between them towards the village and the little lake.

It didn't stop there. The numbers grew in waves of a dozen; three, four, five, six – each appearing as if by magic from behind the lip at the top of the alm. For a moment, Wilde expected them to keep coming until a whole army occupied the open meadow behind the village. But it stopped at six – seventy-two men in all. Fewer soldiers than a British Army company.

Their torches and the light from the fires gave the snow a golden-yellow glow, contrasting strangely with the dark uniforms and the black helmets of the marching men.

The drummers led the way, six of them, one for each line, thudding out a pagan beat, which intensified as they approached the village. Behind them came the flag-bearers, carrying vast swastika battle colours.

It was a recreation in miniature of one of Hitler's satanic Nuremberg rallies. But those menacing ranks of men in their hundreds of thousands were long gone. Many to mass battlefield graves in the East, many to the misery and hunger of a POW camp. These few were the dismal, defiant remnants of an army that was supposed to conquer the world.

The word *remnants* was correct. For after his initial shock, Wilde saw that these were not all hard, fighting men. On the contrary, some were boys, most were old men. Their uniforms of helmets, high boots and SS flashes on the lapels should be intimidating, but these were merely ill-fitting.

That said, the men and boys were armed to kill.

A gasp went up from the watching villagers and Wilde looked back towards the Boden house. The front door was open and light streamed out onto the snowy street.

Julius Boden stepped out in full SS officer's uniform and regalia, his cap at a jaunty angle. Behind him, Wilde saw the faces of his mother and another woman, Lilly Marais, holding back in the doorway. Boden left them and marched alone up the village street, looking from side to side, greeting his people with straight-arm salutes as he went. The men saluted him back, the women went down on their knees. Some begged to kiss his hand.

He held his hand to them and they grasped it and planted their lips on it. Then he touched them on the shoulder to raise them to their feet, as though he were a messiah with his disciples.

A hundred metres above him, the men with torches continued their parade, breaking into two columns, each of which marched around the bonfires. Then, in an intricate manoeuvre, they crossed and formed a human swastika.

Boden stopped at the end of his solitary progress. A small dais had been prepared for him and he stepped on to it. He wasn't an enormous man – perhaps six foot, about the same as Wilde – but he had the lean power of an athlete and, more importantly, he had presence. Erect and still, he placed his left hand on the hilt of his ceremonial dagger, and thrust out his right arm in salute.

The swastika of men broke apart into two lines and they marched past him, eyes left and saluting as they came near to their master.

Wilde was bemused. Was Hitler here somewhere? There was no sign of him; in fact, these people almost seemed to be treating Julius Boden as their führer. And then Wilde saw Heck, moving low from behind a barn, heading straight for Boden. His hand was coming out of his jacket and even from this distance Wilde realised with dread that it was gripping a pistol.

Heck had been waiting in the dark shadow of the barn for an hour. What for? What had he expected? He had seen the Mercedes arrive and had seen the two men and a woman emerge. From their body language, he knew that the taller one – proud, chin tilted with inborn arrogance – was Julius Boden. And surely the beautiful but shabbily dressed young woman clutching his arm and gazing at him with adoring eyes must be Lilly Marais.

As he saw the build-up of activity, the old men and women in the street, the splashing of petrol on the high wooden stacks that he had noted being built during the day, he realised that some sort of strange event was about to unfold.

He began to understand what he must do. For all his family and all the other families, there must be retribution. The only question was who to kill? He still hoped that Hitler, the architect of the horror, would appear, but in his absence then Boden would pay the blood price.

Heck knew he could be discovered at any moment. The villagers were all out on the street now and there were few places of concealment from people who knew these buildings so well. All he could do was crouch low and keep still.

Then the whole world was lit by fire and the air was filled by drumbeats and the soft thud of stamped boots on light snow and grass and the reek of flaming petrol. He saw the gathering of the enemy and the arrival on the scene of Boden in the uniform of the devil.

He could hold back no longer.

*

Just as he had called Lilly to his car that first day at Ste-Estelle-sur-Seine, Boden now curled his fingers again and summoned her from the front door to join him on the dais.

He could see her reluctance. These people were all strangers to her and the high-Bavarian clothes his mother had laid out for her were not at all the style she was used to. He smiled encouragingly and gestured again for her to come and join him.

Tentatively, she stepped from the doorway onto the road. His mother followed her and took her arm, firmly guiding her between the gauntlet of curious villagers.

They gazed at the Frenchwoman in awe. Her beauty in itself was remarkable and would turn heads anywhere in the world, but the fact that she had been chosen by Julius Boden made her something more, a princess or a goddess.

Boden felt a surge of pride as he looked at her and gazed on the assembled people he had known all his life, and the loyal cohort of men and boys in uniform who had concealed themselves and their uniforms and weapons here in Schwarzenkirche and other nearby villages and mountain refuges.

To an outsider or to one who had been at Nuremberg in the glory days, this might not seem much. But these men and women were the embers of a fire that still burned, deep in the ashes.

All that such embers needed was fuel and a gentle breeze to grow into a raging fire once more. He, Julius Boden, would provide that fuel. No one, the Führer had said, would ever extinguish the German flame.

It was the Führer himself who had chosen him for this role. 'They have all betrayed me,' he had said, clutching Boden's arm. 'Himmler, Goering, the generals . . . cowards and traitors every one. And so it must fall to a younger man to finish what I have started. I know you share my commitment and vision,

Boden. Take the baton from me and carry it to glory. Do this for your Führer and for greater Germany.'

'*Mein* Führer, I am unworthy.'

Hitler's watery blue eyes had penetrated deep into Boden's soul. 'I am not asking you to do this, Standartenführer, I am commanding you. You have never once disobeyed a Führer order even though enemy fire rained down on you in the inferno of battle, so I know you will obey this. You are the chosen one, Boden.'

Boden had clicked his heels and bowed. '*Jawohl, mein* Führer.'

From his hiding place, Heck watched the two women – mother and putative daughter-in-law – gliding along the little road, past the ancient chalets that had probably been here for centuries, all of them repaired and renovated by each generation. The women wore smart Bavarian jackets and skirts and the younger one looked extremely nervous as the eyes of the little crowd devoured her.

Boden was preparing to greet them, his arms wide. Lilly hesitated but Frau Boden urged her forward with the palm of a hand on the younger woman's lower back.

Without a plan, guided only by bottomless hatred and a need for vengeance, Heck was moving now, gun in hand . . .

Chapter 38

Wilde was already scrambling down through the trees when he heard a muffled shot. He couldn't see what was happening, but he could hear the shouts and screams. A few seconds later, he heard more shots.

He fought his way down, past trees, through thick beds of pine needles and light clouds of snow drifting down from the shaken branches. He stopped momentarily on the lip of a ten-foot drop of sheer rock face, then slid over, cutting his hands and wrists and tearing his clothes as he grasped at sharp outcrops.

Now he was at the woods at the edge of the village. A hundred metres of meadow separated him from the mayhem, all lit by the raging fires and the guttering torches. The formation of troops had collapsed. Men and boys were running or crouching, some firing and shouting as they identified the fleeing man as the enemy, others cowering like a frightened rabble.

On the dais, Wilde saw that Boden had fallen and was curled up clutching his abdomen. The two women were kneeling at his side, the mother holding his face in her hands, Lilly pressing an article of clothing to his stomach, staunching a wound.

In the distance, he was certain he saw Mozes Heck, running from a dozen uniformed men with guns. He heard more shots. There were dogs, too, large Alsatians. They were to the north of the village, near the lake. Within seconds, they vanished into the woods.

Wilde had to get there, to find Heck before anyone else did.

Heck was injured. He had fired his shot – just the one, into Boden's belly – before he was attacked by a woman with a knife.

He hadn't seen her or recognised her until the very last moment when she emerged from the small crowd, screaming, lunging at him. He tried to parry her blow with his pistol, but the blade sliced deep into his right arm, just above the elbow.

It was the woman from the stall on the road. The woman who had given him the box camera and claimed to know nothing about the murders of Randy Collingham and Denis Harper. The thin, one-eyed woman in the torn and tattered dress with a stall full of war souvenirs and a hidden stash of cigarettes. Birgit Zimmer, that was it; that was what she had said her name was.

Goddamn it, they should have taken her in and locked her up. She *must* have been involved in the murders of Randy and Denis.

At least he had shot the fucking SS guy, Boden. Shot him in the stomach. It could be a nasty, slow way to die. Hopefully he would leave this earth in the same pain that he and his kind had inflicted on so many innocents.

The look of fear on his arrogant, self-satisfied face as he saw the gun. That had been worth seeing. He didn't have time to plead for his life, but his eyes were wide in terror. If Heck died now at the hands of these people, it would be worth it to have seen the terror in those eyes.

Heck hadn't stopped to inspect his handiwork. With pain searing through his right arm where he had been cut, he transferred the pistol to his left hand and ran along the bank of the lake. He was fast and strong and had the element of surprise. But it was only a matter of moments before his pursuers were on his tail, shouting in guttural German, firing wildly in his direction.

Once in the woods, he crashed through the undergrowth, heading downhill all the time. He didn't have any idea where he was going, only that he would move until he was sure he had lost them – or until they caught him and killed him. If he could take some of them before they got him, so much the better.

He would shoot as many he could. And for as long as he stayed alive, he would stab them with his knife or beat them to death with his fist, with a fallen branch, a rock, anything.

Blood was seeping through Lilly's fingers. She spoke to him softly in French. 'Julius, please live, my darling. You must live.'

He was conscious but his pain was great and she had no way of easing it. All she could do was stem the flow of blood with the cloth of her skirt. He was breathing fast and seemed to be trying to speak, but no words emerged from his mouth.

What had just happened? Why had someone attacked her beautiful Julius?

For a moment she thought this whole night must be a bad dream. When he came for her at the camp, he held her tenderly and told her that he was taking her home to meet his family and his people.

It sounded the most natural thing in the world. Why wouldn't the man she loved want to introduce her to his mother and siblings?

But then, at his great house in this high alpine village, his mother received her in a cold and haughty manner and despatched her to a bedchamber with a woman from the village who proceeded to spend an hour bustling around her, bathing her, dressing her in fine clothes and making the best of her short hair. She hadn't asked for any of it and nor did she want it.

Why hadn't Julius eased her in more gently?

She felt trapped and helpless. She was a lone foreigner among these people, and she had no power to resist. She was supposed to be a bride, but it occurred to her that she was their prisoner.

Here on the dais, with all the blood and horror, his mother, Frau Boden, was kissing her son. Suddenly, she turned to Lilly with loathing etched in her face. 'You brought this on him. This is all your doing. Dirty French peasant.' With her right arm, she thrust Lilly away. 'Get this woman out of here,' she shouted at those who had gathered around her.

Two women began to drag Lilly away from Julius and away from the dais. She tried to stay with him, to hold her bunched-up skirt at the wound to keep his precious blood inside him. The blood that had flowed through their lost child, Nathalie.

But she didn't have the strength and could do nothing to prevent them tossing her aside like a bag of garbage.

Wilde was skirting the village, staying in the trees. In his favour, the men and women of the community were either crowded around the dais or were heading towards the woods at the far side where Heck disappeared.

He was angry beyond words. Heck had not only endangered both their lives for no good reason, but he had ruined every-thing. This was never supposed to be about confronting Boden, let alone shooting him. They had one mission: to find Adolf Hitler and Boden was to have been their conduit to him. Well, how did killing him help that?

Wilde had given Allen Dulles and Colonel Appache the benefit of the doubt when they selected the hot-headed young Dutchman for this operation, now he knew it had been a bad choice all along. Heck was in a blood-red world of his own, and no amount of reasoning was going to alter that. Even worse, it looked as though he was about to die for his foolhardy actions.

For the first time in his life, Mozes Heck realised he was not immortal. Blood was spilling from the savage wound to his arm and he was becoming weaker. Struggling in the near-darkness, he had crossed a stream in an effort to throw the barking dogs off his scent and now he was in a hollow, deep in the woods beside rocks and an icy waterfall.

Behind him, he saw the flickering lights of his pursuers and heard their shouts and speculative bursts of gunfire.

Very little snow had penetrated the canopy of branches, so his footprints could not be seen or followed and the rush of the water deadened other sounds.

He needed rest. The snow had stopped and the cloud cleared and some light came from a sliver of moon. Carefully, he slumped down on a thick carpet of pine needles. He had some cover from the trees and, with his left hand, he swept pine needles across his legs and torso in an attempt at concealment. All he could hope was that he would not be seen and that the hunt would die away, but the darkness would not help him if they came close to him with their torches and dog. Unlike him, they would know these woods intimately. His chances were slender.

There was another factor, though: fear. Few of the men in SS uniform could be true battle-hardened soldiers. At first sight they had been alarming, but closer inspection showed that many were grey-haired men or just boys. Also, the more they fanned out into the depths of the woods, the thinner their lines became. How much courage did they have alone in a dark forest, faced with a desperate gunman?

He sensed soft footfalls, saw the flickering glow of a torch and his body tensed. The throb of excruciating pain in his right arm momentarily forgotten, his left hand slid towards the dagger in his belt. He couldn't afford to take another gunshot, for it would be a certain giveaway of his location.

The light of the torch shifted, guttering and casting strange shapes through the branches. Then, at last, it intensified. Heck's eyes were wide open and he was staring straight into the muzzle of a short carbine no more than two feet from his face.

Incongruously, he felt like laughing. The weapon looked as though it had been old when the Great War began. Above the barrel, he met the torchlit eyes of the man with his finger on the trigger – a man who seemed as ancient as his gun. His peasant features were worn and thick from a surfeit of sausage fat, his eyes were hooded and blank; a lifetime of slaughter on the battlefield and in the farmyard left a man without qualms or sensitivity. To this old farmer and soldier, the shooting of a man was no more remarkable than the wringing of a fowl's neck or the bayonetting of a Tommy in the trenches.

Heck raised himself into a sitting position and put his one good arm out above his head in surrender, the knife dropping from his grasp. Waiting to die, he heard a click and recoiled. But he wasn't dead; the carbine had misfired. Another click.

He didn't wait for a third click. The dagger was back in his left hand and he lunged upwards, thrusting the blade deep into the old soldier's navel. A look of astonishment crossed the old man's wrinkled brow.

Heck pulled out the dagger blade and pushed it in again, and again. Stabbing with all the speed he could muster, to make the man die before he could call out to his comrades. The blade snapped off deep inside the dying body, but it mattered nothing, for the German had already crumpled. Heck was on his knees now and had dropped the useless hilt of the dagger, taking hold of the carbine with his uninjured left hand and cracking it down hard into the enemy's face.

The German lay silent. His torch had fallen to his side but was still alight, illuminating his face, now no more than a bloody pulp.

Heck picked up the torch and stabbed it into the earth to extinguish it. The dead German's friends were certain to be close by and he had to move from here fast.

He hadn't seen the second man.

Chapter 39

At first Wilde didn't understand what he was seeing. Two men struggling with low groans in the light of a torch flame, fizzling in a soft damp cushion of pine needles. One of the men had to be Heck, but which one? Wilde used his own flashlight sparingly, afraid that it would be seen.

He descended to his belly and crawled wormlike through the forest. Then, at last, he saw one of the men stand up and knew instantly that it was Lieutenant Heck. He watched appalled as Heck smashed a rifle butt into the prone man's head. Wilde flashed his own electric torch and whispered urgently, 'Heck, it's me – Wilde.'

Heck turned in his direction. He was holding the gun with one arm. Wilde spoke a little louder. 'It's OK, Lieutenant, it's me.'

'I need your help.' He was stumbling and seemed about to fall.

Wilde rose to his feet and loped across to his companion. His flashlight showed the bloody remains of the German but also the vicious cut that Heck had suffered.

'You have to bandage it.' He nodded to the corpse. 'His shirt.'

Wilde tore open the dead man's tunic and ripped some of the blood-soaked material from his shirt and quickly bandaged Heck's arm, stemming the flow of blood. He also found a rusty bayonet in the waistband and transferred it to his own belt.

'The carbine?'

Heck shook his head. 'It misfired. That's why I'm still here. Tell me, did you see anything? Did I kill Boden?'

'I saw it all, but I'm not certain he's dead. Jesus, Heck, what were you thinking?'

'I wasn't thinking. I could just smell the gas, feel the panic and terror of my mother and father and brother and sisters. The gas flowing into their poor, beautiful lungs. I felt the tears running down their cheeks and I felt their hands holding mine . . .'

They were both silent for a moment, then Wilde put his arm around Heck. 'Come on, we have to get out of here.'

'I'm lost, Wilde. My arm . . . it's bad.'

They took it slow, going deeper and deeper into the woods before circling back towards the road and the corner where Wilde had hidden the Harley-Davidson. It was after midnight, almost two hours since the events at Schwarzenkirche, and the gunfire and calls of the hunters had died down then ceased.

Wilde's companion was weak, but he couldn't take the risk that the bike had been discovered and ambushed, so he made Heck sit against a tree while he watched the road from cover.

'Stay here,' he said. 'Come out when you hear the engine fire up.'

Heck was barely awake. Wilde slapped the sides of his face. 'Don't black out on me, Lieutenant.'

The bike hadn't been found by the pursuers. He quickly inspected the damage sustained on the mountain road. The front wheel was slightly buckled but the tyres were still sound. She roared into life straightaway.

Heck stumbled from the undergrowth. Wilde helped him onto the pillion, and they were gone.

Colonel Appache was not pleased to be woken in the early hours of the morning. He was a great deal unhappier when he discovered what had been happening at Schwarzenkirche.

'You mean you staked out the place without telling me, and then that goddamn Heck tried to kill Julius Boden? Are you totally insane, Wilde?'

'It wasn't the way we planned.'

'Where is the Dutch bastard now?'

'Sickbay. He suffered a bad wound.'

'Shame they didn't kill him. Goddamn amateurs the pair of you.'

Wilde wasn't going to take this. 'We'll talk about this later if you want. Lieutenant Heck made an error, but he showed extreme courage and I won't have him called an amateur by you or anyone else. For the moment, we have to plan our next move. We have to go in force to Schwarzenkirche and pick up Boden, if he's alive.'

'No chance, Wilde. We did that before, if you recall, and it was a fiasco. Anyway, do you really think Julius Boden's people would be dumb enough to keep him there?'

Wilde turned on his heel and left the room without a word.

He grabbed a bottle of rye whiskey from the PX then borrowed another motorbike from the pound and rode the three miles to Apfelwald. He found Angie Gray doing her last rounds and about to turn in for the night.

'Care to share a couple of glasses with me? I need company.'

'My bottle not good enough for you, huh?'

They sat together in her office, drinking steadily into the night. Wilde told her the whole story and she listened in silence. Only when he had finished did she put forward a thought.

'What about Lilly? What's happened to her?'

'I really don't know. I saw her briefly, but after that I don't have any idea what happened.'

'Well, I'd like to find out – wouldn't you?'

'I'm going to sound heartless, Angie, but I have to say that she wasn't my immediate priority. She went there of her own accord.'

'But she couldn't have had any idea what she was getting into. Is she safe?'

He shrugged. 'OK, I'll see what I can do, though we have to face it that she might be happy in the company of a bunch of fanatical Nazis. Who knows? One way or another we'll find out.'

She looked at her watch. 'Tom, I've got to turn in now.'

'Of course.' He smiled. 'Thanks for listening to me. I couldn't talk to Colonel Appache. Gets my goat.'

Angie Gray left him with the remains of the rye, a pot of strong black coffee and a sleeping bag. He sat at her table and unfolded August Jaeger's map. It was a metre and a half wide and a metre deep and Jaeger's handwriting was minute but perfectly legible. Wilde had never seen such an intricate chart.

Once again, he studied it using a magnifying glass, but this time he was concentrating on a select area – the high mountains and lakes between Almrosen and Schwarzenkirche. He had no evidence to suggest that this area might be significant, just a hunch.

For one thing, it was remote. A few villages were dotted around both Almrosen and Schwarzenkirche, but nothing in between – just harsh terrain at lung-sapping altitude, broken by what were probably rushing streams, dark lakes and meadows. No roads, no communications.

His eye kept going back to one small area, which he took to be a pasture in a mountain bowl. It was the name that August Jaeger had written there in tiny black letters that caught his attention: *Die versteckte Alm.*

The hidden meadow.

The height of this meadow was 2,000 metres, which Wilde converted to 6,500 feet. A mountain hut or something similar was delineated without any accompanying legend. It seemed absurd, of course. Perhaps the rye whiskey was melting his brain. But why not that place? If Hitler was alive, he had to be somewhere.

And August Jaeger had wanted to tell him something, hadn't he? Why else would he have made that phone call and arranged a rendezvous?

Wilde worked out that the hidden meadow was four or five miles from the hermit chapel where he and Paula Jaeger had found the mutilated body. Had Jaeger regretted finding a hiding place for the murderous tyrant? Maybe he had already helped Collingham and Harper and was aware of their deaths. That could be why he had made himself scarce in the mountains these past few days.

But then he had had second thoughts and called Wilde. He had paid a terrible price for that fateful phone call.

According to the map, the hidden meadow was a little closer to Schwarzenkirche than to Almrosen. It was difficult to tell from the chart which route might be best to get there, because the paths were not rated for difficulty or danger.

Wilde had to get some rest. Heck was out of commission with his wound and Colonel Appache appeared to be in no mood to help, so somehow he would have to make his way to the hidden meadow alone. He swirled the whiskey, inhaled its smoky sweetness, then put the glass down unfinished.

He rolled out the sleeping bag on the floor, stripped to his underwear, climbed in and fell asleep in an instant.

Chapter 40

None of this was as Lilly had imagined it. As she and Julius lay entwined in each other's arms in those sweet nights in Normandy, she had never for a moment doubted his devotion to her.

But now, for the first time, she was not sure of *her* love for him.

In the back of her mind she had always known that he was an important man and that he had some darkness in his past, but somehow those issues never intruded on their own quiet, domestic bliss. She asked him no difficult questions and she never thought of him as *the enemy*.

Instead, she concentrated on their similarities. She came from a farming village, and he told her that he did, too. All she wanted from life was the beat of the seasons and the routine of a rural day, and he said he would give it to her.

And then she arrived here in his home village, and there was a parade to greet her. She didn't ask for it and didn't want it. She wanted to curl up and die as she walked along the little street to the sound of drums, watched by the inquisitive eyes of the villagers, all sparkling in the light of flaming torches. 'They are expecting this of you, *liebling*. I am their chief man and they must meet my bride.'

That was bad enough. The attack was worse – and changed everything.

She knew she was in trouble. She had already seen the loathing in his mother's eyes. Now, she truly believed that she was safe only as long as Julius was there to protect her. What would happen if he died?

Again that thought: did she love him? She loved the memory of him, but among his own people he didn't seem quite the same. He still professed his love, but now the darkness was more than just a distant shadow.

His mother would kill her in a heartbeat. These people were as unforgiving as her own father.

After the attack, she had been dragged away and consigned to a large bedroom with pine panelling and a pair of single beds with fresh white sheets and eider-feather duvets. It was a beautiful room, the sort of room that tourists might pay good money for. But Lilly was keenly aware that this was no hotel room; this was a prison cell.

Ilse Boden hadn't said another word to her after the terrifying assault on the dais when the stranger came out of nowhere and fired at Julius. All Lilly wanted was to help him, but the other women pulled her away.

On instructions from Ilse Boden in a language that Lilly was a long way from mastering, her two teenaged children, Brünnhilde and Siegfried, had marched her here and put her in this room. The girl had brought her a plate of bread and cheese and a glass of beer. 'Eat, sleep,' she said in French with no hint of a smile, then backed out. Lilly heard the key turn and realised she was locked in.

She had met these two briefly when she first arrived with Julius. She was struck by their welcoming smiles. Their faces so innocent, fresh and sweet – but their whisperings so sly.

The window opened on to a balcony. Lilly stood out there in the cold night air. She was still wearing these dark green Bavarian clothes that were so unfamiliar and wanted to take them off. They felt expensive but she hated them. And now, they were stained with Julius's blood. And yet her own clothes had been taken away from her, so this was all she had.

She looked out at the dark waters of the lake and the forbidding mountains all around her. The room was high up on the third floor of the Bauernhof Edelweiss, but perhaps she could climb down from here. Then where would she go? A woman could die alone in these mountains. The alternative was to stay and pray that Julius lived. She wondered where he was. Was there a doctor in the village or would he have been driven to hospital?

She had many questions, and no answers.

Wilde was woken by Angie Gray. 'Good night's sleep, Tom?'

'I needed it.'

'And you didn't even finish the whiskey. I had thought better of you.'

He clambered out of the sleeping bag. 'Forgive my sorry state,' he said.

'Well, I'm shocked. I have never seen a man in his underwear before.'

He laughed. 'And you a doctor of medicine.'

'Breakfast?'

'Angie, you will make some man a wonderful wife one day.'

'And that, Tom Wilde, is where you're more wrong than you could possibly imagine. Come on, coffee and good fresh bread awaits us.'

Two hours later, Wilde found Mo Heck sitting up in bed, his arm bandaged and in a white sling. A US Army nurse was checking his pulse.

Wilde hung back in the doorway until she had finished, then approached the bed. 'Well, Lieutenant, looks like you're out of commission for a while.'

'I'll be up in no time.'

'That was one hell of a ride back from Schwarzenkirche. You were so out of it, I was worried you'd fall off the bike.'

'Then you don't know me very well, Professor.'

'Anyway, I'm glad you're alive.'

'Any word on Boden?'

Wilde shook his head. 'Our friend Colonel Appache won't spare me any troops. I don't think it's too advisable to go there alone.'

'Appache's no friend of mine. Bloody pen-pusher. As an army colonel he'd make a great shipping clerk.'

Wilde didn't disagree. 'I came to tell you that I've got an idea. We've spent all this time trying to find Boden and watching the Frenchwoman, but maybe there's another way to find Hitler. It's possible Jaeger's map holds the key.'

'Go on.'

'I've been studying it with great care and there's a place that interests me. A place called the Hidden Meadow, slotted into a high mountain bowl between Almrosen and Schwarzenkirche. There's some sort of mountain hut there. I'm going to take a look at it.'

'Then I'm coming with you.'

'Uh-uh, no chance.' He indicated the wounded arm. 'It'll be a difficult trek through high, treacherous terrain.'

'There's nothing wrong with my legs.'

'You'll need both arms. And you're weak. You lost a lot of blood.'

'It's nothing. It's been stitched up. Come on, show me the map – point out this place. You think Hitler's there?'

'I don't think that for a moment. If I'm honest, I came into this operation thinking he was probably still alive. Now, I have no idea. Let's face it, the bastard probably shot himself in the bunker. But I've got to take a look.'

He pulled the map from his bag and spread it on the bed in front of Heck, then pointed out the hidden meadow – *Die versteckte Alm.*

'He's there,' Heck said.

Wilde simply shrugged.

'Fucking Hitler is there, Wilde. Why didn't we see this before?'

'Because we didn't know where to look.'

'I'm coming with you.'

'I'll give you twenty-four hours. If the doctors say yes, we'll give it a go. If not, then you're staying here.'

Chapter 41

Twenty-four hours kicking his heels. He was like a wild cat in a cage. The only relief was getting a telephone call placed home to Lydia, but even that didn't go as smoothly as he had hoped.

'Tom, where are you?'

'Counter Intelligence Corps, Garmisch. There's too much to tell you. How's Johnny? How are you?'

'Well, not perfect actually.' Her voice turned to a whisper. 'We have a visitor, name of Sergei Borisov. I believe you know him.'

'Good God, what's he doing there?'

'Eaton brought him. Apparently he doesn't trust the safe houses used by the British secret services.'

'You should have said no. Is he there now?'

'Yes, he's here now. Eating our food, drinking our coffee.'

'Happy to accept the charity of my beautiful bourgeoise wife then?'

'What?'

'Never mind. Just something he said that stuck in my mind.'

'Well, on the plus side, Eaton brought a good supply of comestibles. On the minus side, I really don't feel comfortable with this man in the house. I think he's done bad things . . .' Her whispered words tailed off.

Of course he had done bad things. He was SMERSH. Part of Stalin's killing machine. 'Can you put him on the phone?'

'Why? What are you going to say?'

'I'm going to tell him he needs to find somewhere else. This is an outrageous misuse of your good nature.'

'No, don't do that. He'll be gone in two or three days. Anyway, you'll be home soon . . . won't you?'

'Yes, I'll be home soon. I have to prepare for Michaelmas. But has he done anything untoward? Has he tried anything on?'

'No, nothing like that. He's actually very cheery and plays on the floor with Johnny. Goes out a lot, too. Eaton has provided him with a motorbike. But you know me, if there's something rotten in a man's soul, I see it. And I see it in him. I see the crawling worms beneath the skin.'

'Don't take any risks. If you have the slightest cause for concern, call Rupert Weir or go straight to the police. Don't call Eaton. Got that?'

'Come home soon, darling.'

'I love you with all my heart, Lydia.'

His next call was to Paula Jaeger. He trusted her, but he didn't trust that her phone wasn't tapped, so he said nothing about the hidden meadow. 'What's happened about Uncle August?'

'The French military police came and organised the removal of the body for autopsy. They questioned everyone in the village. And that's it. What else can they do unless someone comes forward and testifies against the killers? And that's not going to happen, Professor Wilde.'

'Will you be around tomorrow?'

'Where else would I go?'

'Well, I might come to see you. I have a favour to ask.'

'I wish you wouldn't say things like that.'

'Have you got a gun?'

'Only Peter's old hunting rifle.'

'Keep it loaded and keep it with you.'

He had a nagging worry about Lydia; Eaton should not have imposed the Russian on her. But while there didn't seem to be an immediate threat to his wife, the same could not be said about Paula Jaeger or, indeed, Lilly Marais. In different ways, both women were trapped in the heart of a conspiracy of blood.

Wilde needed to find answers. All he knew was that Heck had shot Boden and had killed a man in the woods. But he couldn't be sure whether Boden was alive or dead, or how that might affect Lilly's safety or the hunt for Hitler.

Nor could he be sure that the assassins who had killed August Jaeger might not now go after his brother's daughter-in-law, Paula. So he needed help, boots on the ground to stamp out this insurgency.

He went to see John Appache again. If anything the colonel was in a worse mood than the night before. He sat with his feet on the desk eyeing up Wilde as though he were some unpleasant insect that needed swatting.

'What?'

'Just give me half a dozen men, Colonel. I have to see what's happening in Schwarzenkirche. We know a senior SS officer – a wanted man – is wounded or dead. We know that someone up there ordered the murder of the maidservant, Ingrid Zinke. We know that there are dozens of uncompromising Nazis stamping around in jackboots and helmets. This is something the US Army has to look into. This is your job, Colonel.'

'Dozens of uncompromising Nazis? The way I understood your testimony, it was a bunch of old men and Boy Scouts play-acting. And as for the murder of the maidservant, we've got her killer interned. He'll hang, end of story. Look, Wilde, you heard me last night and the answer's the same today. If you think you've got unfinished business at Schwarzenkirche then go there yourself. My men have more important matters to deal with.'

'But what if Boden's alive – we can get information from him. If anyone knows the whereabouts of Adolf Hitler, Boden is the man.'

'Oh really? You think he would have stayed there after what happened? You and that goddamned Jew lieutenant blundering in like a couple of crazed buffaloes would have scared him off good and proper.'

'Let's find out then. You have to act, Colonel.'

Appache's brow darkened. 'No one but a US Army general or the President himself tells me what I have to do, Wilde. When you have solid evidence that you've found Hitler's hideout, you can have all the troops you want – tanks, planes, a thousand airborne, you name it. Until then, forget it.'

Wilde was not intimidated by this man. 'Your role in this is to help me and Heck, give us all assistance necessary. I say again, we need to find out what happened to Boden.'

'Fuck you, Mr Wilde. Get back to your books and leave the real work to the professionals.'

Consumed with rage, he went to the guard house and made his way to the cold, bare cell housing Andreas Stock. The German was sitting on the edge of his bed, one foot on the floor, his other foot swinging. He didn't look up or stir when Wilde entered.

'Herr Stock, I am here to inform you that Julius Boden was shot last night. You no longer owe him any loyalty.'

Stock slowly raised his eyes but still he said nothing.

'Silence until death, eh? Well, that will do you a fine lot of good. I also have something to show you.' He took the map out of his bag and laid it out beside Stock on the bed. 'Here.' He stabbed his index finger at the words *Die versteckte Alm*. 'Recognise it?'

The thin German didn't move his head, but his eyes strayed sideways to the map and Wilde's finger. Wilde was certain he saw him stiffen. It meant something to him.

'Perhaps you know the place? The hidden meadow. I imagine it's extremely pretty up there with mountains all around, nice cool air. Wildflowers in summer, a roaring log fire in winter. Perfect place for an old tyrant's retirement home.'

At last Andreas Stock spoke. 'Are you going there?'

'Of course.'

He gave Wilde an enigmatic smile, 'Good luck, Ami.'

Ingrid Zinke's father, Joachim, was in the reception area at the entrance to the camp. He was a tall lean man with the gnarled features of a prizefighter who had lost too many bouts. Wilde offered his condolences for the death of his daughter, but they were meagre words given the depth of the man's loss.

'I have come to collect Ingrid's body,' he said plainly.

'And you will be given every assistance. You know that we have the killer in custody.'

'Yes, I heard. Andreas Stock. I would like to see him.'

'Do you know him?'

'Of course. He is Ilse Boden's brother. Please, let me see him.'

Somehow Wilde was not surprised to learn of the familial link. It made sense. 'I don't think that will be possible.'

'Give me five minutes with him. Please.'

'I would like to, but I can't.'

'He will hang, though?'

'Without a doubt.'

Joachim Zinke nodded his head slowly. 'Thank you, sir. I trust you. You know I never wanted Ingrid to go to those people. But she needed the work. That woman . . . she is a devil.'

Did he believe Frau Boden was behind his daughter's murder? Surely no one could have told him such a thing. 'Why do you say that?'

- 'I have nothing more to say. God will punish that family.'

In the afternoon, Wilde returned to the single-bed ward where Mo Heck was being looked after.

'Two visits in one day, Professor? I feel like royalty.'

'Give me your right hand.'

Tentatively, Heck slid his right arm out of the sling. The whole of the arm was bandaged save the hand. Wilde took it in his own right hand and squeezed. Heck pulled back sharply and suppressed a cry of pain. There was no strength in the Dutchman's arm or hand.

'This is hopeless, Lieutenant. You'd only be a hindrance in the high mountains, and nothing is going to change before tomorrow.'

'Then wait, Wilde. You can't go there alone.'

'I'm just going to scout the place out. After that, we'll take it from there. In the meantime, eat well and sleep.'

Chapter 42

Just as aristocrats talk indiscreetly in front of their servants, never for a moment thinking they will hear or understand the conversation, so medical staff confer together in front of their patients.

Mo Heck's eyes were closed, but he wasn't asleep. The bandage had been taken off his arm by a nurse so that the doctor could examine the wound and she was now re-dressing it. The doctor was talking to the nurse in a casual way, sharing some scandalous gossip about a mutual friend and an intelligence officer newly arrived from Des Moines, Iowa. They were laughing and joking and wondering whether the new guy had a wife back home.

And then there was another voice, a second doctor. 'Oh, Fred,' he said, 'sorry to interrupt but I was wondering if you could come take a look.'

'Sure, Garret. What is it?'

'The German who came in last night, the one with the bullet in his abdomen. We removed it OK and there's an outside chance he'll live, but I'd like your opinion on treatment. Colonel Appache is taking an interest in the guy.'

'I'll come with you now.'

Wilde spent the early evening with Angie Gray and Jerzy. The strange thing, given their surroundings and the terrible circumstances that had brought the three of them together here, was that they managed to laugh a lot.

Jerzy was a good lad – very intelligent and easy in his ways. He might have been only eleven but the way he looked at the doctor, Wilde knew the boy was in love with her. She, too, was smitten with him in a motherly sort of way.

Wilde had acquired another Harley from the motor pool at Garmisch and, at ten o'clock, he took his leave of Angie and Jerzy and rode south to Almrosen, reckoning to arrive around midnight. The roads were empty save for a couple of American roadblocks in Germany and a French military checkpoint at the Austrian border. It had begun to rain again and the damp, despondent soldiers waved him on with a couple of questions about the purpose of his journey and a cursory glance at his papers. American passports carried a lot of clout in Europe in the late summer of 1945.

As before, Wilde parked in woods well away from the village of Almrosen. Given what had happened to August Jaeger up at the hermitage, it was impossible to rule out the possibility that Paula was a target and so he couldn't take a chance that she was being watched or that her phone was tapped. The village was in darkness and the rain still fell, which helped him approach her house with stealth.

Skirting Paula's neat little chalet, he went around to the back and found a dry place near her outhouses where she kept her goats and chickens. His body tensed at the sound of the animals bleating and clucking when they sensed his presence, but they soon stopped and went back to sleep.

He put his pack of weapons, rope, and binoculars down and crouched beneath the overhanging roof and watched her house. An hour later, he moved through the rain to her back door and knocked. There was no reply and he guessed she was asleep. All around the world, farmers always went to bed early and rose early. They lived their lives in the same rhythm as the seasons and their livestock.

The door was unlocked so he went in and lit his torch. She was sitting facing him, a long-barrelled hunting rifle pointing directly at his chest.

In the early hours, Mozes Heck slipped out of bed. Barefoot, wearing only pyjama trousers, he left his room and padded along the corridors. He was aware that at least one night nurse would be on duty, so he had to proceed slowly and carefully.

Prowling, like a night predator.

He moved from room to room, ward to ward. It was a small military hospital, with fifty beds, only a quarter of which were occupied. There was no form of identification on the doors, so he had to move silently to each patient to check the clipboard at the foot of each bed and, when possible, the face of the invalid. His only light was the low-wattage illumination from the corridors.

Julius Boden was in the last room. He was alone, flat on his back, either unconscious or asleep.

Heck stroked his brow to see if he would wake. Boden was burning up, and he continued to breathe heavily – his chest heaving as though every inhalation would be his last – but did not stir. For a minute Heck studied the face. He was young, fair-haired and handsome, with soft skin and no hint of stubble from a day or more without shaving. Not just handsome, but pretty. And there seemed to be a slight smile on his perfect pink lips.

On his way here, Heck had chanced upon a trolley with medical equipment and found a pair of sharp scissors. Now his left hand held the point of one of the two blades to Boden's throat. 'Where is he?' he whispered into the SS officer's ear. 'Where is Hitler?'

Boden didn't respond and Heck pressed the point of the scissors harder into his throat. 'Talk to me, Nazi.'

The patient's eyes opened. He was staring straight past Heck, his expression blank with no semblance of comprehension.

'Now tell me? Where is he? You have one chance.'

Heck felt a hand on his shoulder and swung around. A nurse in a crisp white uniform was standing there. She reached out and gently removed the scissors from his hand.

'I'll take those, my dear. Now, what exactly do you think you're doing, Lieutenant?' She spoke the words softly and with a kindly accent that seemed to emanate from America's Deep South.

He didn't say anything. What could he say?

'Oh dear,' she said, 'night terrors, I suppose. I've seen a lot of men like you in the war. Come on, let's get you back to your own bed, shall we?' She smoothed Boden's sheets, then put an arm around Heck's shoulders and moved him towards the door. 'Don't be alarmed, there's no harm done, Lieutenant. Mr Boden is sedated – he won't remember a thing.'

Paula Jaeger lowered her rifle. 'Oh, Mr Wilde, it's you. My heart was pounding so much I thought my chest would burst.'

'I'm sorry, Paula.'

'But why are you here? Why have you come back?'

'I told you. I want a favour. You know these mountains.'

'Of course, I have lived here all my life.'

'I want you to be my guide for a day. I'll pay you well – in dollars or cigarettes or whatever you like. Will you do that for me?'

'It's dangerous, isn't it? The killers of Uncle August are still out there.'

He couldn't lie to her; she wasn't stupid. 'Yes.' He nodded. 'It's dangerous. And I have already put you in peril, but I'll do my best to protect you. Once we get near to our goal, I'll go on alone.'

'Is this something to do with Uncle August's map?'

'It is. I want you to take me to a place he's marked called *Die versteckte Alm*. Do you know it?'

'I have heard of it. I am sure I could find it with the map, but it will be a hard trek. Do you think Hitler is there?'

He shrugged. 'It's a long shot, but I have to look. Are you sure about this?'

She smiled at him. 'I feel I have no option.' The other words, the ones in her head, remained unspoken, but they both knew what they were. *We have kept silent, done nothing for far too long. These people have heaped death, misery and destruction upon us. They must be stopped for ever.*

'I think we should leave before the village wakes.'

'Let me make you some coffee.'

Chapter 43

They set off an hour before dawn while the village slept, walking silently across the damp meadow grass at the side of the settlement and then up the same mountain path they had taken on the way to the little hermitage where August Jaeger had died.

The rain had stopped and the light, when it came, was grey and the peaks were shrouded in dark clouds. Most of the snow had now melted, save at great height.

Both of them wore strong boots and Paula had discarded her traditional woman's costume for a pair of her late husband's trousers, held tight at the waist with a belt and tacked up then secured with string around her boots. They both had ropes and axes, and Wilde had two holstered pistols, an M3 sub-machine gun strapped to his backpack and a pair of hand grenades in his jacket pockets.

Their route took them past the hermitage. When they saw it, Wilde decided it was worth a short detour and climbed up the steep stone steps alone while Paula waited below. He walked through the little house and chapel in the lee of the rock face, in case something had been missed. The place had been left undisturbed by the French military. All that had changed was that the body and body parts had been removed. To the French occupying force, this was a crime of little interest, an argument among their enemies. No one cared that a man had died, nor were they interested in the identity of the killer.

He rejoined Paula and they carried on, past the little lake to the high mountains beyond. The path she chose was hard. For most of the trek, they were above the treeline and the grass was becoming sparse. The rocks were jagged and grey and, in places, loose and deadly. Every half-hour they stopped and studied the map together, and she pointed out their location. Progress seemed grindingly slow.

Paula had been worried that the weather would deteriorate, but the clouds had cleared and they were walking in full sun which, in a way, was worse. In his jacket, with his pack and weapons on his back, Wilde was drenched in sweat. The M3 was a lightweight weapon compared to other sub-machine guns, but carried uphill for hours on end its weight took a toll.

They made frequent stops to drink water and their canteens soon emptied and had to be refilled from ice-cold streams, which only served to burn the throat.

More than seven hours later, they came to a high ridge of sharp-spiked rock, a razor's edge of a crest.

'I think we're just about there, Professor Wilde.'

He raised an eyebrow. He couldn't believe anyone could live here or even close by.

'Look over the ridge. If the map is right, you will find a self-contained valley below, with a small lake and a house.'

Wilde crawled forward on his belly to the craggy rim and peered down a few hundred feet into the most perfect scene he had ever witnessed. The lake was a small oval of still black water, surrounded by the green of a pasture. The solitary building was more like a small farmhouse than a traditional single-room shepherd's hut. Smoke spiralled from a single chimney.

Cows munched lazily at the grass and flowers.

Almost-verticle peaks rose on all sides of the meadow, so that it made more a vase shape than a bowl. This, he reflected, could be Hilton's mythical Shangri-La.

No one could stumble across this place by mistake. It was, truly, a hidden meadow – *Die versteckte Alm*. The sun was high and the whole valley was bathed in light. It was all simply beautiful.

Wilde turned and gestured for Paula to come forward and look for herself. She gasped as she looked down.

'It is wonderful,' she said, 'so peaceful. Hitler cannot be here.'

'I was thinking much the same. Is this Austria still, or Germany?'

'According to the map, it is close to the border. It seems to be Germany. What will you do now?'

'Well, someone has to be there – look at the smoke. I'll watch for a while and see who comes out of the house, then we'll see what – or who – we're dealing with. Perhaps you should go back to Almrosen.'

'No, you'll need me to help you find your way back.'

'Are you certain, Paula?'

She unpacked her bag. 'Let's eat – bread and cheese. And cold coffee.'

Mozes Heck slept fitfully. Every time he drifted into wakefulness he considered his options. He had lost his second chance to kill Julius Boden and he badly wanted to get back there and finish the job. But the nurse had made it clear that she would be observing him.

'No more night terrors, please, Lieutenant. No more somnambulism. OK, my dear? I'll be outside the room, so just call if you need anything.'

What most kept him awake was trying to solve the puzzle of the part being played by Colonel Appache. It was obvious from the snatch of conversation of the two doctors that the colonel

not only knew that Boden was here, but had somehow facili-
tated it. Why would he do that? And why would he keep such a
thing secret from the two men hunting him?

Heck knew his mind was foggy, that nothing was making
sense, but something was not right. He knew that much.

When the nurse arrived again in the morning and asked
whether he was well enough to eat a little breakfast, he told her
he needed to speak with Colonel Appache urgently.

The nurse looked doubtful. 'I can pass on a message, of course.'

'Just tell his secretary that Lieutenant Heck has a proposition
for him.'

'Just that?'

'Just that.'

At ten o'clock, the colonel was at his bedside, bristling with
hostile indignation. 'You wanted to see me, Lieutenant?'

'Yes, sir. Perhaps you already know what it's about.'

'Well, why don't you try giving me a clue and we'll take it
from there. I believe you said you had some kind of proposition for me.'

'Actually, I just want to know what the deal is with Boden.
Why is he here in this hospital being treated? And why didn't
you tell me or Wilde that you had him?'

The colonel didn't try to conceal his anger. 'I don't know
what you're talking about.'

'No? I saw him last night. I held a blade to his throat in a bed
not a hundred paces from here.'

'I think I'd better call the doctor, soldier. You're delusional.'

Heck had risen from the bed and was moving towards the
door. 'Come with me, Colonel, let's go talk to him now.'

Appache reached out to stop him. 'Where the hell do you
damned well think you're going?'

Heck slipped from his grasp and ran along the corridor. The movement shook his injured arm and the pain was intense, but he didn't stop until he was at the door of the room where he knew Boden was being treated.

Appache was three steps behind him. 'Have you taken leave of your senses, Heck?'

'Open the door, Colonel. Show me what's inside.'

'God damn you, Heck, if you were in the US Army I would have you court-martialled for your insubordination. As it is, I am going to relieve you of your mission with immediate effect. You will return to your regiment as soon as you're out of here.'

A nurse and a doctor had heard the commotion and had joined them.

'OK,' Heck said. 'I'll do it myself.' With his left hand, he pushed the door open and stepped into the room. The bed was empty, just a bare mattress where Boden had lain.

There was movement at the door to the mountain house. Wilde screwed the binoculars tight to his eyes. A dark-haired woman was coming out. She had some sort of tool in her hand.

Wilde quickly realised it was a pair of secateurs. She was deadheading geraniums in boxes along the front verandah. At first sight he had thought she was quite young, but now he estimated she was about forty or fifty, a plain-looking woman, but healthy and strong.

She turned back towards the door as though she had been called, but it was impossible to hear anything up on the high ridge.

Wilde had a good view of her face, and he had seen photographs of Eva Braun. He was certain this woman was not her. Could it be one of Hitler's secretaries or a relative? He had no way of knowing.

The chances, of course, were that the woman was a simple housewife, living here herding cattle on a beautiful high pasture before returning down to the valley in the winter.

Wilde handed the eyeglasses to Paula. 'Do you recognise that woman?'

She studied her for half a minute, then handed the binoculars back to Wilde. 'No, I am certain I have never seen her.'

'I have to go down there,' Wilde said. He took out the map and they studied it together. Three paths were marked, two of them from the direction they had come. 'Which one looks best to you, Paula?'

'Best in which way? Easiest to negotiate, or best for not being seen?'

'Oh, the latter. It won't be a good idea to announce my approach.'

'You really think he's down there?'

'I don't know. What do you think?'

She shrugged. 'I don't know either.'

'Well, if he's not dead he has to be somewhere. Why not here?'

'Then he will have protection. Armed men. So you have to be wary – see who is guarding him.'

Wilde smiled at her. He moved back from the ridge, stood up and stretched, then donned his backpack and weapons.

He handed the binoculars to Paula. 'Watch the house. If anything happens to me, get out as fast as you can and report to Lieutenant Heck. You'll find him at the American Counter Intelligence Corps base in Garmisch. Wish me luck.'

'Good luck, Professor Wilde.'

He soon realised that he had picked the toughest possible route down to the house; much of the path was loose scree and there were no trees for cover. He was open and visible against the rock face if anyone cared to look. But at least the woman at the house had gone back indoors and no one else was outside. The only witnesses to his descent were Paula Jaeger above and the grazing cows below.

Like a mountain goat picking its way from ledge to ledge, he stopped every few steps. The climb down took twenty minutes. And finally his feet touched the lush grass and bright flowers of the hidden meadow.

He crouched down and rested a few moments, then unslung the M3 from his back and cradled it in his arms. The weapon had a thirty-round stick magazine and no safety catch. He rested his right index finger lightly on the trigger.

Chapter 44

The woman with dark hair came out of the house again, but scuttled back inside as soon as she saw him approaching. Wilde was not surprised by her reaction. Anyone would be alarmed to see a stranger striding towards them with a sub-machine gun in their arms.

He moved faster. Now he was on the verandah where she had been dead-heading. 'Excuse me, lady,' he called out in German.

When she didn't emerge after a few seconds, he pushed the door open and stepped into the house. He found himself in a small hallway or anteroom with three doors facing him – one to the left, one straight ahead and one to the right. He pushed them open one by one.

The first gave on to a short corridor with two doors visible and a picture window overlooking the verandah to the west, the second opened on to a large sitting room with armchairs, a traditional ceramic wood-burner, an open fireplace and various other decorations and pictures. The third door opened onto a narrow kitchen. The woman was standing there, a long-bladed carving knife in hand, defensively. She wore a brightly coloured apron. A pan was boiling on the range.

'Put the knife down,' he said, not bothering to point the M3 in her direction. 'I'm not going to hurt you. I just want a cup of water.'

'Then why are you here armed like a soldier? Why do you walk into my house uninvited?' She did not sound as frightened as an innocent woman should.

'I'm on a military exercise.' He wasn't about to give her any further explanation. 'What is this place? This isn't just a herder's hut.'

'No, it is a summer retreat. A holiday home.' She wasn't relaxing, but she had placed the knife down on the wooden table, within easy reach of her right hand.

'Who else is here?'

'No one.'

'Someone called you. I was watching . . .'

'Oh, that was just Opa.' She tapped her temple with her index finger, the international signal of dementia or insanity.

'Opa?'

'That's what we call him. An old grandfather. He's not all there, a typical greybeard. I look after the place for the owners, and I look after him. The owners come here for several weeks every year in the summer months. Not during the war, you understand, but before that – and now they have started again this summer. They are wealthy people. I am their housekeeper.'

'Are they here now?'

'No, they have returned to Munich.'

'What's their name?'

'I'm not sure that's any of your business. I will give you your glass of water and then I must insist you leave. Opa would not be happy to see a stranger with a gun. He is a timid old man.'

'I think I'll go and say hello to him. Just to reassure him.'

She moved forward. 'You can't go wandering around this house. This is private property.'

Wilde ignored her entreaty and moved away, keeping her covered as he backed towards the door. He raised the angle of the M3 fractionally so that its short barrel was pointing directly at her chest.

She sneered at him. 'You're American, yes? You think you scare me?'

'I don't know. Do I?'

'No, because I know you're not going to shoot me, Ami. Americans don't shoot women, do they? You're here to protect us from the criminal Nazis. That's what all the newsreels tell us. Good old Uncle Sam, saviour of the world.' She spat the words.

Wilde ignored her and backed further away into the wood-panelled hallway. With his foot, he pushed open the middle door into the large sitting room. He had thought before that it was empty, but now he realised that there was another door on the far side of the room and he could hear sounds from beyond. And then a voice came – a gravelly German growl that he couldn't decipher. Keeping one eye on the woman, he moved towards the inner door.

'Don't go in there,' she whispered urgently. 'Go away and leave us alone.'

Another growl from beyond the door, this time discernible. 'Frau Fuchs, where is lunch?'

She cupped her hands. 'Five minutes, Opa.'

Wilde opened the door into a gloomy room, jabbing the muzzle of the M3 before him. The shutters were closed, but there was some light – the flickering of a moving image on a white canvas screen. The clicking and humming of a small cine projector was the only sound.

An old man was sitting at a large square table, laden with small objects. It was low, like a coffee table. Beyond this was the screen, which he was watching intently. It seemed to be some sort of horror film. A thin wire noose was being tightened around a man's neck.

Suddenly, the old man turned around and Wilde saw his face for the first time. It was framed in a full, tangled beard of iron-grey. His hair was an uncombed mass of thin grey locks. He wore a pair of heavy spectacles, which he immediately pulled down his nose to get a better view of the newcomer. In doing so, he revealed his eyes – hooded, tired and icy blue.

'Where is Bormann?' the old man said, pulling the glasses back into place. 'I told you to find Bormann. He is the only one who would never betray me. He will save Germany. I need him. Now!'

'*Bist du Hitler?*' Even as Wilde asked the question, he realised how foolish he must sound. What a crazy thing to ask a bearded old man in a mountain house. But not so crazy really, because of course this *was* Hitler. The severe downturn of the thin mouth, the slight sharpness of the nose, a forward hunch to the shoulders – all characteristics seen around the world in newspapers and films, but greatly exaggerated since the old days of triumph. Gone was the brisk Charlie Chaplin moustache, of course, transformed into a full set of grandfatherly whiskers.

But the eyes remained unchanged; the cold blue eyes.

'I told you to bring me Bormann. Get me Bormann or I will have you shot. I will shoot you myself. Do you think I won't? Get me Boden, too, I want Boden. This is a great day, for I have decided to raise him up to the rank of field marshal. He will command the reserve armies in Pomerania, the third SS Panzers. Kesselring will take over the Ninth Army and move from the south. In tandem, they will drive eastwards through Prussia and sweep Zhukov's rabble aside in a mighty pincer. Come, young man, look here.'

He patted the table and Wilde realised he was looking at an intricate relief model of Europe complete with tiny toy soldiers, aircraft and tanks.

Hitler thrust his open hands forward until the fingers joined to illustrate the pincer movement. It was the sort of dramatic display he might have made from the podium at a million-man rally. 'We must seize this moment of destiny. The final thrust – first Leningrad, then Moscow.'

Wilde watched him bemused. Hitler's arms were down at his side now, shaking with excitement and palsy.

Behind him, the film flickered on in all its horror. Wilde didn't want to look, but nor could he tear his eyes away; the images were repulsive. A stool was kicked from beneath the feet of the man with the wire noose about his neck. Now he was swinging helplessly in space, the tips of his toes inches from the stone floor, his legs and arms bound tight. The camera moved onto his face, close up on his bulging eyes, his hopeless resignation and longing for death. Who was this man?

The woman in the apron – Frau Fuchs – had joined him at the door. 'Is this really Hitler?' Wilde asked her.

'This is Opa,' she said. 'He has a taste for old Hollywood horror films, and he imagines things. Now please go.'

'No,' the bearded man said. 'I need him. He is to bring Bormann and Boden to me. Together we will save Germany. This is our destiny.' He stopped and his watery blue eyes bored into Wilde. 'Who are you? Have I seen you before?'

'My name is Wilde. I have come to arrest you.'

'Then you will be shot. Frau Fuchs, bring me my pistol.'

This was not going to be easy. Before coming down here, Paula had studied the map and pointed out what she believed would be an easier, quicker way out of the hidden meadow, a route down to a village to the north avoiding both Schwarzen-kirche and Almrosen. But even the route she suggested would not be simple. There would be some difficult climbing, some streams to cross, treacherous inclines, even a small glacier that would be tough to negotiate without crampons.

How was he to get this man down along such mountain paths? It was a problem that had nagged away at the back of his mind during the trek here. But he had not given it serious thought, because in his heart he never expected to find Adolf Hitler.

Could he bind him and leave him here until he returned with a force of men? That might be a better option. But he would also have to incarcerate his housekeeper. And perhaps other people came here – people like Ilse Boden or other die-hard Nazis from Schwarzenkirche or further afield. If they arrived before Wilde's return, then Hitler would disappear once more.

Even as these thoughts surged through his mind, the decision was taken out of his hands. He heard footsteps and voices from outside.

And then they appeared: two of them, a boy and a girl in their early teenage years. A boy in leather shorts and a girl in traditional dirndl, with all the joy of two young people skipping through the long grass. Both of them were about thirteen and fair-skinned. The boy with short hair, the girl with thick blonde braids tied up. The family connection was plain to see. These two were undoubtedly the younger children of Ilse Boden, siblings of Julius. The boy and girl were of an age; perhaps they were twins. Wilde had seen them in the old photograph he had removed from their mother's home. The years had not changed them much. He also rather thought they were the two that he and Paula had seen from the hermitage.

They had a confident air and they looked strong and athletic.

Hitler gazed at them briefly, seemingly without interest, and sat down without saying anything more. He began to move soldiers and tanks from northern Germany along the Baltic coast through Poland.

'Frau Fuchs, Opa – you have a visitor!' the boy said, keeping his eyes on Wilde's face, studiously avoiding the sub-machine gun. Then the boy smiled at the housekeeper. 'Won't you introduce us, Frau Fuchs?'

'I don't need introductions, I know who you are,' Wilde said. He turned to the housekeeper. 'Frau Fuchs, explain to these children that I wish them no harm, but nor will I be deterred from my purpose. If that means locking them away with you while I take my prisoner into custody, then so be it. I have this right under the law as laid down by the Allied Powers, and I will brook no interference from any of you.'

It was a straightforward declaration of intent, but as he said the words, Wilde knew his statement carried no power unless they believed he was prepared to use violence against them.

And there was another matter of an equally practical nature – he had no idea whether this place contained a lockable room. This dark den of the the former Führer would certainly not serve such a purpose; even if the door could be locked, the shutters could easily be opened and the windows broken to make their escape.

The boy was grinning at him. Wilde's blood ran cold. There was a gun in the boy's hand – a Luger by the look of it. He had his finger in the trigger guard and he began to spin the pistol slowly like a gunslinger in a cowboy movie.

'Will you shoot us?' the boy asked, then he and his sister doubled up laughing.

If Heck was here he would kill the boy and girl and the two adults in a heartbeat. But Tom Wilde was not Heck. He could no more shoot these two children and the housekeeper than his own wife and son.

'My name is Siegfried,' the boy said. 'And this is my sister Brünnhilde.'

'Siegfried, you look like a sensible boy. I don't want anyone to get hurt. Not even him.' He indicated Hitler. 'He must face interrogation and trial. So cooperate, and no harm will come to you. Do you understand?'

'Oh yes, we understand, don't we, Hildy?'

Now Wilde saw that she, too, had a pistol. It weighed heavily in her dainty child's hand, but he had no doubt that she knew how to use it.

'You must know of course that we could never allow Opa to be taken prisoner,' the girl said. 'Do you imagine that we could allow him to be displayed in some cage for the crowds to gape at, and then be slaughtered like a hog?'

'Perhaps it would be better if you put your weapon down,' the housekeeper said to Wilde. 'There's really nothing you can do.'

'We know every metre of these mountains and this alm,' the boy continued. 'And I can promise you that no one is coming to help you.'

Wilde had backed away so that he was now standing within inches of Hitler. He could smell the man's unwashed body, almost feel the globules of sweat on his pale, unhealthy brow. He was simply sitting there, playing with his toys like an infant, unaware of the real-life drama being played out by the others in the room. Wilde wasn't even sure that he understood the conversation or its implication for him.

Instinct told him that the children would kill without hesitation; so would Frau Fuchs. Perhaps they had done so before. He was facing three killers and some inconvenient spark of civilisation prevented him from doing to them what they would do to him.

He lunged for Hitler, dragging him up from the couch. In a single, seamless movement, he had drawn his dagger from his belt and curled his left arm around the former Führer's neck so that their faces were almost touching and he was using Hitler as both shield and hostage.

The honed blade touched his cold, perspiration-soaked trachea. One sideways move and the blood would rush forth. Oh yes, he could do that. It would not weigh on his conscience to kill the murderer of millions in cold blood.

It was the others that posed the problem.

He thrust the muzzle of the M3 beneath Hitler's arm, covering the housekeeper and children. One tug of the trigger and they would be riddled with bullets. But even if his brain told his finger to fire, he knew his finger would disobey.

Hitler was making no noise. He wasn't exactly limp, but nor was he straining to get free.

Siegfried Boden shrugged. 'Think about it, Ami, you don't have to do this. You don't have to die today. We can pay you big money to walk away. Imagine how much money is behind us. Millions in Swiss accounts. Just put down your weapons and walk away. You have our word that you will be safe.'

'What is Opa now anyway?' Brünnhilde said. 'Look at him. He's just a harmless old greybeard. He is like a grandad to us. A very special grandfather – and we have sworn to look after him.'

'This is madness. He is nothing to you. You're young. A new Germany is about to be born and you should be a part of it.'

Suddenly the full, hideous enormity of his situation hit him. He had found Adolf Hitler, the most wanted man in the world, the worst mass murderer in history, and he was standing here with a knife to his throat, holding him in his arms, confronted by two lethal children.

With two split-second motions he could kill the Führer and those protecting him and the world would applaud.

The history books would say that he was the man who had rid the world of the tyrant. And the others? Collateral damage, just like the innocents killed in the bombing of Hamburg and Rotterdam, London and Warsaw.

And he couldn't do it. The bomber crews had done it every day, and he couldn't.

If only Hitler had been guarded by SS men. That would have been easy. He would have shot them without hesitation.

The housekeeper gave a heavy sigh and shook her head. 'There will be no bloodshed in here.' She addressed Siegfried and Brünnhilde. 'Go and wait outside. The American will have to leave at some stage, and he can't get past you. Let his blood feed the wildflowers and the grass.'

'I don't know, Frau Fuchs,' the boy said doubtfully.

'You have no say in the matter. Get out, both of you. I will deal with this.'

Siegfried laughed again and then, slowly and reluctantly, he thrust his Luger into the waistband of his leather shorts. He put his arm around his sister's shoulder. 'Come, Hildy.'

They walked away, with their backs to him. They had no fear of Wilde or his weapons.

'What about you, Frau Fuchs?' Wilde said after the brother and sister had departed, closing the door after them. 'You want to live, don't you? Help me with this, and I will put in a good word for you. It's all over – the war, this, everything – you know that surely.'

'You don't understand, Ami. I have bought you a little time, so now, please, do something for me – leave Opa be. I don't think he knows what is happening, and he can certainly do you no harm.'

Wilde pushed Hitler back down onto the couch and put the dagger back in his belt. He kept his finger on the trigger of the M3.

Hitler was in a world of his own. He moved more soldiers forward then, with a sweep of his arm, he pushed a dozen or so soldiers from Leningrad into the sea. 'Finished. We have done it.' Then he turned his gaze on his housekeeper. 'Where is my spaghetti? Bring it to me.'

She raised her eyebrows. 'One minute, Opa. Just one minute.' She switched her gaze to Wilde. 'It is almost cooked, Ami. Can I get it for him? Perhaps you would like some, too. I make the best sugo in Bavaria.'

What could she do that hadn't already been done? Wilde almost laughed at the preposterous situation, then nodded. Even criminals or deserters were allowed a last meal before they faced the firing squad. 'Get him his food.'

He followed her to the door so he could continue to watch Hitler and cover him with the M3 and keep half an eye on Frau Fuchs's movements.

A couple of minutes later, she returned with a steaming bowl of pasta on a tray with a spoon and fork and a little jar of olive oil. 'We have no Parmesan,' she said. 'Ah, so many things are lost for ever.'

Wilde didn't trust her. He watched as she put the tray down on the table in front of her master and placed a napkin on his lap as if he were a child. Then she dribbled a little oil over the tomato sauce and handed him the fork and spoon.

She was looking at Wilde as though sizing him up.

'You want to say something, Frau Fuchs?'

She began speaking in good English. 'I merely want you to know that he is not the man you seek. No longer the Führer of old. These past months . . . the loss. You can tell that he is not all there. These days he has long periods of silence, then rages. He plays with toy armies and watches those hideous films of the July traitors being executed. Over and over. He is fifty-six, but he might as well be eighty-six. He is not the man we loved.'

Wilde could believe it. This was certainly not the war leader who once held the whole of mainland Europe in his cruel grip of iron. 'What are you to him, Frau Fuchs?'

'Oh, nothing but an old forgotten friend from quieter days in Munich. I am a nobody.'

'He still needs to face justice for his sins. You know that?'

'God will judge him.'

Wilde stared at the bearded, bespectacled man. A hollowed-out monster.

'Do you like music, Ami?' Frau Fuchs continued. 'Can I play a little Wagner on the gramophone? It soothes him, you see.' She paused. 'You must understand that this is his last meal. We are all going to die here. There is no way out. You do not have the stomach to kill children, and so Siggy and Hildy will kill us all rather than let you take him.'

'Put the music on.'

She found the record immediately from a stack beneath a shelf, placed it gently on the player and dropped the needle into the groove. From the very first notes Wilde recognised it as the prelude to *Götterdämmerung*. 'The Twilight of the Gods.'

Wilde saw a smile on the woman's face for the first time. Hitler remained unmoved; he simply continued eating, slowly, chewing every mouthful with exaggerated care. It would not have been a surprise to see Frau Fuchs spooning the food into his mouth, but that didn't happen.

When, at last, he had eaten enough, he pushed the plate away and Frau Fuchs stepped forward as if to pick it up.

Instead, she knelt before him and embraced him. 'Forgive me, *mein* Führer,' she said softly.

Wilde couldn't work out what was happening, but then – when it was too late – he realised that she had slid a knife into him, for he let out a gasp and fell forward onto her. She didn't attempt to move away, but held him closer to her breast, like a mother with a child. Blood was dripping from his mouth and he became still.

She smoothed his hair with her palm, stroking him gently, whispering to his dead body. Then she pulled herself away. The bloody carving knife in her hand. It had a long blade and must have gone deep beneath Hitler's ribcage into his heart, killing him within moments. A clean death, not the agony-filled, screaming one he deserved. She dropped the knife.

'That is all,' she said. 'It is over. It is the proper time and place for him to die. The succession is assured and he has gone.'

'You have cheated justice, Frau Fuchs.'

'But this way I give *you* a chance to live, and to return to your family. You have at most ten seconds to get out of this house.' Her eyes drifted to the gramophone at the side of the room and suddenly he noted the contraption half hidden behind it. A clock, exposed wires, explosives. A large box full of dynamite.

Wilde grabbed her hand, but she fought him off. 'I stay with him. Go.'

He wrenched open the shutters and crashed out through the window. He was just beginning to pull himself up when the blast came. He heard nothing, saw nothing, as he was propelled into oblivion.

Chapter 45

'Mrs Wilde, I cannot tell you how much I appreciate your hospitality these past few days. I have spoken with Mr Eaton and he tells me I will be collected the day after tomorrow. So I will finally be out of your hair.'

Lydia was dishing up lunchtime soup to Johnny and Borisov. She was surprised by the news he had just imparted. 'Has Philip found you another safe house then?'

'I believe so. And may I say that this soup looks and smells quite delicious, just like all your marvellous cooking.' He patted his stomach appreciatively. 'You will make me fatter than I am.'

'You will have to thank Philip Eaton for the food. We don't usually eat this well, you know.'

'I understand completely. We, too, have rationing in the Soviet Union. Much more severe, I think. But I have good news – I gave your husband some caviar, so I am sure he will bring it home to share with you. In the meantime, let us eat and drink at Mr Eaton's expense while we may.'

Lydia could do without the fish roe, but she had grown less offended by the Russian intelligence officer's presence in her house over the past couple of days. He could be quite charming, in fact, and seemed to know how to flatter her even if she didn't really believe a word of it.

This was the skill of the spy: gain people's trust, worm your way into their affections. And Borisov was good at it. He almost made her believe he was on her side. Also, as a house guest, he was clean and attentive – and Johnny liked playing with him.

'What will you do in the long-term, Mr Borisov?'

'That is in the lap of the gods. I am still a Russian at heart, but I had to come here to save my life. Once someone above you turns on you, there is no way back. It was Beria or Abakumov, maybe both. Have you heard of them?'

'I have heard of Lavrentiy Beria.'

'They are as deadly as each other. Not men to cross, but how can a man avoid that when they turn on everyone?' He laughed darkly. 'No one gets out of the NKVD or SMERSH alive.'

'Except you, perhaps, Mr Borisov.'

'Indeed, that is my hope. But it means I must live out my days in exile. At least your country is beautiful. It has always felt like a second home to me.'

'And where in Russia do you call home?'

'Moscow.'

'You have a family there?'

'A wife, two children.'

'What will happen to them?'

He shrugged. 'Olga will be questioned about what she knows. But she has nothing to tell them. I protected her by keeping everything to myself. I hope they will not torture her, but I know she will be sent to the Gulag. The children will go into the care of the state. That is life in Soviet Russia.'

'I don't know what to say.'

'You think I have done wrong – abandoning them to such a fate. But what you don't understand, my dear Mrs Wilde, is that the same fate would have awaited them if I had gone back to Moscow for the last bullet. The Soviet state does not leave the families of the accused untouched. This is the system backed by all your idealistic communist friends in Cambridge.'

'What makes you think I have communist friends?'

He laughed out loud. 'How do you think, my dear? I know their names because they work for Mother Russia, that is how I know. Some call them fellow travellers; the NKVD calls them useful idiots. They are dangerous to the West.'

'Then I had better be more careful who I confide in. Don't want to give away any state secrets, do I.'

'Ah, Mrs Wilde, now you make fun of me. You are too clever.'

Yes, she thought, perhaps I am too clever. Which might be why I don't swallow this story about Sergei Borisov fleeing a death sentence. Tom might like to think he was the intelligence officer in this household, but that didn't prevent her having ideas of her own. And she was certain of one thing: Borisov and Eaton were up to something.

Paula Jaeger saw the house disintegrate through Wilde's CIC-issue binoculars. The blinding flash came first, then the splintering of a house – great beams, furniture, roofing, a mass of glass – fragmented and thrown across a wide area and, last of all, the thunderous roar, echoing around the mountains.

In the split second before the explosion, she saw something else. A figure crashing through a window, shattering the glass. Her first thought was that someone had thrown out a large object or animal, but then came the blast and her cognitive powers went numb.

A grey-black pall rose from what had once been a rather lovely wooden chalet. It now lay flattened, though much of it was still airborne: sheets, shrapnel, paper, carpet, wooden planks, all floating through the air then drifting to the earth. Above all, though, there was the smoke, blanking the sky and the mountains.

Before the explosion she had seen the two children waiting outside on the verandah. She had also watched them arrive but had no inkling as to what had occurred indoors or why they had emerged again.

Now she could see no human beings at all. Some of the cattle had fallen to the ground and were struggling to get up, others were scattering.

The air was thick with acrid smoke as she made her way down the path that Wilde had taken no more than half an hour ago. Her heart was full of terrible foreboding. Only as she was close to the bottom of the steep and rocky track did she see a human being. One of the two children was out on the meadow, perhaps fifty metres from the house; it was the boy and he was trying to pick himself up, clearly stunned.

He was on his knees, gasping for breath. He rose shakily to his feet and looked about him. Paula stopped, shielded from sight by a boulder, and watched him as he limped towards a prone figure. It was the girl. The boy knelt beside her and tried to bring her around. He cradled her in his arms and Paula feared that she must be dead, for she could see no movement.

Gradually, the boy lifted her up. He was saying something to her but she didn't seem to respond. Her fair hair and pretty dress were blackened and torn and her arms hung limply by her sides. The boy managed to get her over his back and held her across his shoulders like a collier bearing a sack of coal. Then, still limping badly, he began to carry her past the lake and away from the wreckage.

After an initial glance at the hopeless ruins of the house, he didn't look back. Didn't check whether anyone else had survived and might need help. Nor was he aware of Paula. He hadn't seen her, but she had seen his gun and had no intention of approaching him.

Within minutes, the two children were gone, in the direction of the path that must lead down to Schwarzenkirche.

Hesitantly, Paula made her move, pistol in hand, watching all around her as she advanced upon the ruins of the building. It was on fire, flames leaping and black smoke billowing. No one could be alive in there. The fire would consume everything and she had no way of extinguishing it.

To the north of the meadow, at the edge of the lake and far from the window that had shattered moments before the blast, she saw a mound. She broke into a run; it was a human figure, half in, half out of the water. When she was within twenty metres she knew it was Tom Wilde, but she could see no sign of life.

His feet and legs were in the water, his head twisted sideways on the grassy edge of the water, his arms stretched out wide.

Paula felt his neck and wrist for a pulse, and found one. He was alive, but unconscious.

In the afternoon, Heck woke from a drug-induced sleep. He vaguely remembered the needle going into his arm a couple of seconds after he gazed with astonishment at the empty bed where he knew Boden had been lying. The tranquilliser took effect quickly, and the last thing he felt was his legs buckling beneath him. He supposed he must have been carried back to this bed, because he could not have made it here alone.

As he came to, he felt groggy. His body was so heavy he could hardly move. He lay with his eyes closed, trying to make sense of Boden's disappearance and Colonel Appache's part in it. He simply couldn't understand why Appache or anyone else in this place would protect an SS officer.

Little hints began to register. It seemed like an insane thought, but was it beyond the bounds of possibility that Appache had warned Boden to make himself scarce when the raid on the village was planned? Was it even possible that Appache had effected his escape from Dachau in the first place?

Heck's head throbbed, but he rose from his bed and made his way painfully and slowly along the corridor to the nurses' station. 'I'm discharging myself,' he said to the first nurse he found. 'I have things to do.'

'But you must still be in pain, Lieutenant.'

'Well, I'll live with it. Now, if you could find my clothes and shoes, I won't take up any more of your time.'

'I'll have to check with the doctor, sir. He'll want a last look at the wound to be certain it's healing properly. Can you return to your bed and give me ten minutes, please?'

What option did he have? He wasn't going out into the middle of Garmisch in a surgical gown and bare feet.

Five minutes later, the nurse reappeared. 'I'm afraid the doctor is busy right now, but he asked you to wait half an hour for him.'

'Goddamn it, nurse, this is wasting my time.'

'I understand your frustration, believe me. But there is something else, sir. It seems you have a visitor. A young lady is here to see you. Can I show her through?'

Who the hell could be visiting him here? The only person who came to mind was Dr Gray from the DP camp. 'Does this visitor have a name?' he asked.

'Mrs Lazzaro, but she says you would know her better by another name, Miriam Rabinowitz.'

'She's here?'

'Just outside, Lieutenant.'

'How did she get here?'

'You can ask her yourself. I'll bring her in.'

Miriam? His brain was still a fog and he wondered if he was dreaming. Was this a nightmare? Would her lips – the lips that had betrayed countless Jews – drip with blood?

He had almost erased her from his memory. The tale of her treachery was more than a young man could bear; Dr Kuhn at the Jewish Hospital in Berlin had insisted she was a catcher of Jews, sending her own people to their deaths and using the name Miriam Berenbaum.

But what of Maria Dienstag's testimony. Maria had been Miriam's neighbour and she had told him that Miriam had been saved by a group of anti-Nazi dissidents called the Red Orchestra.

'Hello, Mozes.'

She was there at the door to his ward, almost exactly as he remembered her from their holiday in Switzerland. It seemed like a lifetime ago but it was what, eight years? The dates were fuzzy in his head.

Her hair was tied up like a woman of substance. She wore a suit of fine wool and a fashionable hat. Her face was full and her girlish figure had developed curves. Her mouth was smiling, but her eyes were etched with concern.

'Miriam, is it you?'

'Of course it's me. I got a message from the Jewish Hospital in Berlin, via the Red Cross. You went there looking for me.'

'Your name . . . why have you changed your name?'

'Silly, I am a married woman now. My husband and I live in Zurich with our small daughter. I had to come and see you though.'

'Married?'

She nodded and, for a moment, he thought her eyes were a little watery. 'Yes,' she said, 'very happily married. We have a good life, and I feel guilty for it every day. My parents were murdered. I think my elder brother is alive – and I am on my way eastwards to a displaced person's camp near Theresienstadt. Please God he is there and safe.'

Suddenly he felt foolish, standing here in this surgical gown. 'Forgive me,' he said. 'I can't find my clothes.'

'That's all right, Mozes, you look just fine. Shall I sit beside you on the bed?'

Now she was there, at his side, and he could smell expensive perfume. 'I went to your apartment,' he said. 'A foul Nazi woman lives there. Name of Ursula Ganzen. She moved in as your family was being moved out. You must evict her and claim your home back.' *Not that you would want it*, he thought. *Who would want to live amid rubble and dust?*

She took his left hand in hers. For a minute, they simply looked at each other, lost for words to fill in the gap. Their lives had changed so dramatically; neither of them was the carefree, besotted young idealist of their days together in the Swiss mountains.

'I heard something,' he said at last.

Miriam nodded again. 'Yes, I know. Dr Kuhn made a terrible mistake but fortunately one of her colleagues pointed it out to her. She then went to great lengths to make contact with me. She had confused me with another woman named Miriam with similar features and is deeply apologetic about her error. She told me that you were in the British Army, and they said you were on secondment here.'

'That doctor told me that you were a *greifer*. A catcher of Jews.'

'I can promise you that wasn't me. I was in Zurich long before those events. I got married in December 1943; my husband was an Italian businessman who had sought asylum in Switzerland.'

It was information he didn't want to hear. Nor did he want to hear about her child. 'How did you get out of Germany? The Red Orchestra got you out?'

'An underground group of anti-Nazis. I don't know what name they went by. It's a long story, for another day.'

'Maria Dienstag told me they helped you. I didn't know what to think.'

'You have spoken to Maria? She is still alive?'

'She has had a bad time. Her husband was arrested by the Gestapo and executed. Then her baby died. I found her outside your old house, half crazy with grief, trying to find help for the child – but he was already long dead, there in the pram.'

'Dear Maria, she took me in and saved my life. Where is she now?'

'I got her to a British military hospital, where she was helped. When I left her, she had finally accepted that her child was dead. She found lodging and food, in return for helping at a church. Hopefully life will improve for her.'

'Oh, you will give me her address, won't you?'

'Of course.'

'And you, Mo? Your family?'

He tried to tell her they were all dead, but he couldn't speak. The words stuck in his throat and the tears welled up; for the first time in all these years of war and horror, he wept.

When Wilde regained consciousness, he was aware of only one thing – the stench of fire, smoke and metal. Then came the roaring in his ears. He was trying to speak but if any words emerged he couldn't hear them. Last of all, he saw the face of a woman, Paula, also moving her lips without sound.

He pointed at his ears. 'I can't hear,' he said, though he wasn't certain the words had actually come out of his mouth.

Her hand was outstretched so he took it and let her pull him to his feet. He had no idea how long he had been out cold. The last thing he remembered was the prelude to *Götterdämmerung*. And then he remembered something else; the death of the tyrant.

Now he was standing, but he immediately fell to his knees and vomited. He stayed like that for half a minute, then wiped his sleeve across his mouth and got up again. He felt dizzy but he was aware enough to know that he must be concussed.

Wilde surveyed the meadow and the flattened house, the panicked cattle, and the fire and the billowing cloud of black smoke, blanking out the sun. Where was his sub-machine gun? He looked down at his own body. His clothes were torn and covered in soot. So were his hands. He supposed he must have cuts, but he wasn't in pain and couldn't see any injuries.

He got to his feet again and took a couple of steps. He was unsteady, but the fact that he didn't fall was promising; he could walk. And he could think. He was aware that Paula was watching him with concern and so he smiled at her to reassure her. He gestured with his hand for her to follow him as he walked towards the burning ruins of the house.

It had been spread over a wide area by the explosion. In the blackened wreckage at the perimeter he saw a charred body; there was just enough left to identify it as Frau Fuchs. The fire was dying down, but he couldn't see Hitler's corpse. Perhaps he had got his wish to disappear without trace and not be displayed for gawping eyes. That must have been the purpose of the massive bomb waiting to be detonated in his room.

An insurance policy. The ultimate guarantee that he would not be displayed to the world, alive or dead.

Wilde saw the M3 sub-machine gun. As he was picking it up, he felt a hand on his shoulder and turned. Paula tapped her wristwatch then pointed towards the track that had brought them here. She mouthed words and he read her lips. *There's nothing more we can do here.* He nodded, yes, the day was drawing on; they had to get back to her home village and the only way out was to walk the high trails.

It was a strange day. Adolf Hitler was dead.

Chapter 46

The bride was wearing white. Her new husband, in an ill-fitting black suit, gazed at her with adoring eyes. It was a day of joy. In the absence of family, Angie Gray and another doctor gave the woman away and Jerzy played the role of photographer.

Beneath the chuppah canopy, the bride walked around the groom seven times, then the rabbi read the marriage words and the groom placed the ring on his new wife's index finger, before stamping on a wine glass to signify the destruction of the temple.

Everyone applauded and the dancing and drinking began.

Not everyone was interested. A group of young men huddled around a tight chess game without giving the newly-weds so much as a glance. There had been weddings here at Apfelwald every day this month. What was one more?

Wilde stood a few moments and watched the wedding. He still had ringing in his ears, but he had regained most of his hearing after a night asleep on a couch in Paula Jaeger's spare room. They had arrived back at Almrosen long after dark, and they were both exhausted. Paula's main concern was that the animals needed feeding, but then she found a note from a neighbour, telling her that everything had been taken care of.

And so, after glasses of schnapps but no conversation, she and Wilde both fell into deep sleep in their separate rooms. Not once did she ask who he had met inside the house on the hidden meadow, or what had happened. And nor did he tell her.

Now he was back at Apfelwald. When Angie Gray and Jerzy spotted him, he smiled and waved to them and they left the ceremony to join him near the medical centre.

Dr Gray smiled back. 'Well, you're alive, Professor, but what's happened? You smell like a battlefield and you look like you've just crawled down a chimney.'

'You'll have to speak up.' He realised he was probably shouting, so he pointed at his ears. 'Explosion.'

'What happened?' She raised her voice and enunciated the words with exaggerated clarity.

It was a good question. He was still trying to process the events of the previous day. It all seemed like a dream sequence. He had found Hitler and watched him die. No, that couldn't be right; it sounded insane. But then again, it had happened.

So why, he wondered, did he have this unpleasant sensation that his business here wasn't finished?

Taking his leave of Paula Jaeger at Almrosen after a quick breakfast, he had felt a surge of hope. She was a remarkable woman. To look at, a sturdy farmer's wife but beneath the surface, a heart of gold and steel. There were good Germans and Austrians. The future would be fine.

But something was still not right.

'I really can't talk right now, Angie.'

'Let's get you inside and have a proper look at you.'

'I'm OK – even managed to ride a motorbike here from Austria.'

'I'm the doctor, so I'll decide if you're OK or not. Apart from which, I'm extremely glad you're here because I'm worried about Lilly. There's been no word from her, and Colonel Appache says there's nothing he can do. Says she's a free agent. But I don't buy that.'

Wilde rather thought the colonel had a fair point. 'I'm afraid he is probably right.'

'We have to get her away from that place. I heard what they did to the poor maidservant. We know these Nazi bastards *kill* people.'

Standartenführer Julius Boden was awaiting the promised use of the telephone. He was very weak and couldn't move from bed, so it would have to be brought to him.

The doctors had been giving him morphine for the pain. It took away the physical agony of the wound, but it did not induce euphoria. Instead, he found himself in purgatory.

He was back in Kiev in 1941 with his Waffen-SS company, at that time deployed as part of Einsatzgruppe C – Task Force C. For two days his troops had manned the machine guns along one side of a gully near the city, a dark, forested place known by the local people as Babi Yar. The dates – 29th and 30th September – would be imprinted on his brain for ever.

It was the date of lost innocence. The day he became death.

From childhood, he had helped take the cattle and goats into the mountain pastures near the family home in Schwarzen-kirche. Now he was herding babies, children, women, men. They were undressed and trembling, knowing they were about to die, yet still modestly trying to cover their genitals and breasts with their bare hands.

On and on they came, hour after hour, into the burning hot rattle of the machine guns, into the cauldron of death. Their bodies white and splashed with red in the gully that became their grave.

The thrill of guilt had been beyond anything Julius Boden had ever experienced. He was born and baptised a Catholic and had expected to be struck down by God. But he wasn't. God stood idly by and did nothing.

Nor had nightmares come to Boden. Not then. He was able to laugh and find love. And in the four years since Babi Yar he had slept every night in perfect peace. Until now.

Why did the dead visit him now? Why, when he closed his eyes, was he assailed by their stained white flesh? Why now, when he lay between life and death, did their tens of thousands of eyes rise from the earth to judge him?

Of course, he knew the answer. He had sold his soul like Faust. Lilly was both his Helen and his Gretchen. Beauty and innocence that would haunt him as he fell to damnation.

The devil was coming to claim his debt.

In his lucid moments when the morphine had worn off, he knew he had to talk to his mother. Something had gone terribly wrong and he was bereft of information.

And there at last was John Appache, telephone in hand, trailing a long wire into the makeshift bedroom in his own quarters. 'Here you are, Boden,' he said. 'One call, that's your lot. You understand?'

Boden struggled to sit up in bed and winced at the intense pain. 'Of course, and thank you for everything, Colonel.'

'Don't thank me, thank my superiors.'

The American CIC man turned on his heel and walked out.

When the door was shut, Boden tried to get comfortable. He had been shot in the stomach. The American surgeons had saved his life thus far, but he knew from their faces that the prognosis was not good, and he did not expect to live. He knew from the battlefield that it was often not the initial wound that killed, but the infection that followed. He was burning hot. His torso was bandaged heavily and the pain coursed through him in waves as he tried to ease himself into a position to make this last call. Finally, he settled back on the pillows, lifted the handset and got the exchange to put him through to his home number.

He had an important message to pass on to Siegfried. He would have to take the torch and carry it forward to the next generation. Siggy would be the bearer of the flame that had been lit by Adolf Hitler. A fire that must never be extinguished.

His mother answered, her voice as brusque as ever. 'Bauernhof Edelweiss.'

'It's Julius. We have to talk.'

'Julius, you're alive. Thank God. Hildy is dead. So is Frau Fuchs. And Opa.'

'Opa dead?' Opa – grandad. Their private name for Adolf Hitler. He wasn't anyone's grandfather, of course, but the few people charged with concealing him had had it drummed into them that he must never be referred to as anything but Opa. You never knew who might be listening. Only the Bodens and Frau Fuchs must ever know about Hitler's presence in the hidden meadow. That was why August Jaeger had had to die. He had found the place for them, but his loyalties were questionable.

'The Ami got to him. Fuchs set off the device. It must have been all she could do, but Siggy has other ideas. He blames her. He is angry, Julius. He says you should never have made him defer to Frau Fuchs. He also blames the Frenchwoman, too. He even blames me.'

'I'll talk to Siggy.'

'Julius, you don't sound well. Your breathing is not good.'

'I think I do not have much time. Give me Siggy.'

The boy's voice came on the line. 'When will we see you, Julius?'

'You won't, Siggy. The torch passes to you. You know what to do.'

'And the Frenchwoman?'

'Leave her. She knows nothing.'

'I'm not sure, Julius. She led them to us.'

'You've got it all wrong.' Boden's voice was growing weaker. His breathing was shallow and laboured.

'Have I, Julius? Have I? Are you sure? Hildy is dead because of her. Opa is dead. All because of your infatuation for the stupid, treacherous French bitch.'

'Do you really believe this?'

'You're becoming faint, Julius. I can't hear you.'

'Do what you have to do, then, Siggy.' His eyes were closed, he was slipping away into the night, into the ravine at Babi Yar, where the dead white flesh would welcome him, and torment him for all eternity.

'That looked a beautiful wedding,' Wilde said, stretched out on the bed while Angie Gray gave him the once-over. Jerzy had followed them in and was watching Wilde through the lens of the box camera.

'They have weddings every day,' Angie said. 'Often more than one. Desperate to replace their lost families and find a bit of affection, and who can blame them.'

'That could be you one day, Angie, a blushing bride.'

'Now you're making fun of me, Professor. Obviously I am never going to be a bride, but I can tell you this – I *am* going to be a mother.'

'Really? Well that is good news. Tell me more.'

'Jerzy has very kindly agreed to let me adopt him. Haven't you, Jerzy?'

'I want to marry her but she says I'm too young.'

'Just take what's on offer, Jerzy. She'll make you a fine mother.'

'Maybe, but she's very strict already – says I have to go to school and then college. I just want to take pictures, boss.'

'No reason you can't do both. Just listen to your mother. Mothers are always right. Now, Dr Gray, if you're done with me, I have an urgent telephone call to make. May I use your office?'

'Go ahead – but take it easy.'

Allen Dulles did not sound ecstatic at the news. 'You saw him die? Why the hell couldn't you capture him, Professor Wilde?'

'I'll give you all the details when we meet.'

'And you're certain it was him?'

'I have no doubts.'

'Then where is the body?'

'There was an explosion, a conflagration. I don't imagine there is much left. Teeth maybe – but we saw how easily dental records could be manipulated with the jawbone supposedly found outside the bunker in Berlin.'

'Well, I want to congratulate you, but this still seems horribly inconclusive.'

'Not in my mind it's not, sir.'

'What was he like, the great dictator?'

'Like a bearded, bespectacled, senile old man. If you didn't know his history, you'd say he was sad and pathetic and you'd almost feel sorry for him. But I say good riddance to the Nazi bastard.'

'I'll drink to that, but I would have loved to have seen him paraded to the world in a cage. I'll fix a flight for you to get you home. First thing tomorrow suit you?'

'That'll be fine.'

'Via Wiesbaden if that's OK. You can give me a full briefing. By the way, who else have you told about this?'

'No one.' Not even Paula Jaeger, though she might have made a guess.

'Well, keep it that way for a while. We'll work out how to play it. President Truman might want a say. In the meantime, give me the coordinates and I'll get a squad up there to examine the scene. Your job is done, Professor Wilde.'

Wilde put down the phone and it rang immediately. Wilde guessed it was for Angie, but picked it up anyway. 'Apfelwald medical centre,' he said.

'Is that you, Wilde?'

'Colonel?'

'Thank God I got you, Wilde. I had no idea where you were,' Appache said.

'What is it?'

'Professor, we have a problem.'

Chapter 47

Wilde was incredulous. As he listened to Appache, he realised his hearing was almost back to normal, but he held the phone hard against his ear because he simply couldn't believe what he was being told.

'And that's it,' Appache said finally.

'You've been protecting Julius Boden?'

'I had no option. This was orders from on high – maybe right the way from the Oval Office, though they'll never own it.'

'But why would you do that?'

'I've explained this all to Lieutenant Heck, who's standing right beside me here at Garmisch, and he is as angry as you, Professor. I've got a bruised jaw to prove it.'

'Did he slug you?'

'I got off lightly. With his right arm out of action, he had to hit me with his left. I guess I deserved it,' Appache said. 'There will be no report made. To tell the truth, I'm pretty mad myself. I should never have been put in this position.'

'You're going to have to explain this better,' Wilde said. 'Why would anyone protect an SS officer?'

'Because I was ordered to. Because word has come down from on high that we are to recruit and protect the more biddable senior Nazis, however vile their past. The world might not know it yet, but it seems that Nazism is no longer enemy number one. Communism is, and these guys will help us root it out in the new Germany.'

'That just sounds crazy.'

'I'm not going to argue about that, Professor.'

'But why Boden in particular?'

'He was young and he appeared willing to change. He said the right things. In particular, he made it clear from the start when he was arrested at Zell am See that he was eager to work for us. His name went forward, he was approved and I received orders to protect him. No internment, no investigation into possible atrocities, no prosecution.'

'Dear God, you're supping with the devil.'

Appache shrugged. 'I can't argue with that. But I'm a soldier. I do what I'm told.'

'I suppose it was you who sprang Boden from Dachau.'

The colonel grunted. 'Boden's not even the only one, nor perhaps the worst. I know of at least one Gestapo torturer who has agreed to spy for Uncle Sam in return for liberty and immunity from war crimes prosecution. It makes me sick to my stomach.'

'And I guess you warned Boden about our raid on Schwarzenkirche?'

'I had to, Wilde.'

'He really did play you like a trout, didn't he? So why are you telling us this now?'

'Well, for one thing, he's dead.' Appache was breathing heavily. He sounded close to broken. 'Let me put Lieutenant Heck on the line. I've said enough.'

'Professor?'

'What the hell's going on, Lieutenant? It sounds like a madhouse over there.'

'I, uh, forced the issue.' He briefly told Wilde about his night excursion – finding Boden and then his disappearance. 'Two hours ago, I gave the colonel an ultimatum. Unless he told me what was going on, he could shoot me or I would go to British High Command and let them know exactly what their American allies were up to. Fortunately, he chose to come clean. In truth, I think he was beginning to fear the project might come back to bite him one day. That's the problem when you obey unwritten orders.'

'Then what?'

'He admitted Boden *was* here and being protected. It seems that after I shot him, he was driven here from Schwarzenkirche and left at the door.'

'Go on.'

'Boden was dying and he knew it. He asked to phone home to his bitch of a mother. The colonel acceded, but he was already becoming queasy and so he bugged the call.' Heck chuckled. 'That was most enlightening. Boden spoke to *Mutti* and his brother Siegfried. We heard all about the death of someone called Opa, a woman called Frau Fuchs and a girl called Hildy.'

Wilde wasn't about to tell them that he knew all this. Nor was he going to mention his confrontation with Adolf Hitler. These were matters for Allen Dulles to consider and rule on. 'And Boden's dead now?' he demanded.

'Died of a bullet wound. A shooting incident of unknown origin.'

'Unknown origin? Really, Lieutenant?'

Heck laughed. 'It will have to satisfy Mr Appache's chiefs when they ask him what happened to their asset. But there was something else in the phone call. He wasn't just saying good-bye. He authorised a murder. The Frenchwoman. She led us to them, so she had to die.'

'How long ago did you hear this?'

'Ten minutes.'

'Then we have no time to lose.'

*

Wilde slung the M3 over his shoulder, ran from the office and grabbed the Harley. A few minutes later he pulled up outside the CIC base at Garmisch. Heck was there waiting for him, his arm in a sling.

'You can't ride pillion with one arm out of action, Heck.'

'We've got the colonel's Packard Sedan, and a couple of his men. They'll be here with it any moment, along with a bunch of small arms and ammo.'

When they arrived, Wilde took the wheel and they drove up the now-familiar roads to Schwarzenkirche at high speed, stopping only briefly for army checkpoints. He knew this was almost certainly a lost cause. If the Bodens had decided to murder Lilly, why would they wait?

The village was in turmoil. Men and women were standing in groups around the Bauernhof Edelweiss. As Wilde jumped from the car, he saw a man sitting on the doorstep, covered in blood, his head hung low.

A bloody dagger lay on the ground at his feet. At first Wilde didn't recognise him, but then the man slowly unfolded his body and their eyes met. It was Ingrid Zinke's father, Joachim. Tears were rolling down his cheeks, streaking the blood.

'What have you done?'

'I couldn't wait for God's justice.' The grief-stricken father held out his hands like a criminal waiting to be cuffed.

'You must tell me what has happened, Herr Zinke.'

'She wanted to silence my daughter. Well, I have silenced her.' He smiled through the blood and the tears. 'Have you come to arrest me?'

Wilde signalled to one of the two soldiers who had accompanied him to go into the house with Heck. He told the other soldier to control the assembled crowd of villagers. 'Stand back and don't interfere,' Wilde barked. 'This is a US military matter and will be dealt with in accordance with the law.'

Even as he looked at their sullen faces, he wondered what roles they had individually played in the torchlit events here when Boden had been shot and Heck stabbed. He quickly searched their faces for clues, but they were blank. Where, he wondered, had they hidden their uniforms, their swastika pennants and their Nazi insignia? What had they done with the body of the man killed in the woods by Heck?

He turned back to Zinke. 'You're going to make this easy, yes?'

'I have done what I came to do.'

'You've killed Frau Boden?'

He nodded.

'Is there anyone else in the house?'

'I don't know. I didn't look.'

'Get in the car.'

Zinke stood up. He was as tall as Wilde, but thinner. At Garmisch, he had cut the figure of a fighter; now he looked a gaunt, defeated creature as he stepped into the back seat of the car and stared stone-faced ahead. It would be a shame to hang him after what he had been through, but that was his likely fate. Wilde would put in a word for him, but perhaps it would not be welcomed.

Heck was at the door of the huge old house. Lilly Marais stood at his side, her eyes wide, her hands clenched in front of her. Wilde guessed that it was Herr Zinke's arrival that had saved her life.

'It's a bloodbath in there,' Heck said. 'House of death.'

'Just Frau Boden?'

'The only one murdered by him. He sliced her up pretty bad. But there is another body – laid out in an open coffin ready for burial. A pretty young girl, looks like the daughter.'

'That would be Brünnhilde – Hildy.' *What a bloody waste of lives*, Wilde thought. *The Nazis are done for, yet still they find a way to kill young and old and destroy families.* 'What about the younger son, the girl's twin?'

Heck shook his head. 'No sign of him.'

Chapter 48

Wilde postponed his journey home by twenty-four hours and took his last motorbike ride up into the mountains of the Tyrol, through Grünegg to the little village of Almrosen. The day was warm with a light breeze. Paula Jaeger was sitting out at the back, peeling potatoes.

She smiled broadly at his arrival. 'You want me to take you up into the high Alps again, Professor Wilde?'

He laughed. 'Not this time. I just came to thank you. You showed great courage, Paula. There's hope for Austria with people like you.'

'I don't know. It just made me mad, what they did to Uncle August.'

'Have you had any trouble? Any threats?'

'No. The people here have always treated me with respect and continue to do so. They have their suspicions about what happened, but no one says anything. And secretly, I think they are a little proud of me. All I want now is a new man so I can have babies before it is too late. But there are no men to be had.'

'Well, you've got a friend in me, which probably isn't much consolation. Perhaps one day you could visit us in England and meet my wife and boy. There are plenty of young men in my hometown.'

'Oh, I can never leave here. Who would look after the animals?'

'Maybe I could bring my wife and our little boy up here to meet you.'

'You can stay in my new guest house.'

'You're opening a guest house?'

'It seems I am to inherit Uncle August's property. I am the sole beneficiary in his will. It will make a perfect pension or small hotel, don't you think?'

'Indeed I do.'

He stayed for lunch and they sat outside eating black bread and mountain cheese and drinking home-brewed beer.

As he was leaving, she touched his arm. 'Will you not tell me what happened in the house up at the hidden meadow, Professor?'

'Better you don't know.' He squeezed her hand, then kissed her cheek and bade her farewell.

At Apfelwald, he found Angie Gray and her new unofficial adoptee Jerzy packing up.

'So your mission is complete, Professor?'

'That's for others to decide. What about you?'

'Yes, this is the end of my posting. Let others take over, I must continue with my medical career and earn some money. I now have a child to raise and educate.'

'Where are you planning to go?'

'Paris. We are taking Lilly back to France. She plans to get work as a waitress or a seamstress and rebuild her life. You know, she may not be the cleverest young woman in the world, but she's very sweet and with those film star looks, I rather think she'll survive – and probably prosper. I also think it would be good for Jerzy to learn some French. He is good at languages. We leave this afternoon.'

'Is Lilly around? I haven't really met her properly.'

'I'll get her. I'm afraid she doesn't speak English and has very little German.'

'Then I'll rely on you to interpret.'

For such an astonishingly beautiful young woman, Lilly Marais appeared remarkably shy and diffident as she approached him. Something told him that she had not always been like that, however. That recent events had knocked her confidence.

He tried to put her at ease with a warm smile and a lingering handshake. 'It is a pleasure to meet you,' he said in schoolboy French.

'I feel such a fool, Professor Wilde,' she said, using Angie Gray to translate.

'Love makes fools of us all.'

'But you know he was very handsome and charming. He told me there would be a great welcoming party for me in his village, that I would be honoured as his bride. The true nature of the welcome was awful.'

Wilde felt a pang of sympathy for the woman. Like many thousands of other young women in the occupied territories, she had suffered abuse and worse from her own family and friends. Many had had their heads shaved, others had been banished from their villages and communities. Their crime? Falling in love with the enemy.

'I always knew Julius was in the SS, but I was naive – I didn't know what it meant. I still don't know what he did in the war – and I don't want to know – but he was never cruel to me.'

Cruel enough to order her death, though.

Had Angie or anyone else told her about the bugged phone call between Boden and Siegfried? Wilde wasn't going to be the one to tell her.

'His mother was another matter. I knew the moment I met her that she hated me for loving her son. I knew that she would kill me if she could.'

'Well, you're with good people now. I hope you find a better life for yourself in Paris.'

Wilde clutched them all by the hand. 'It has been a great pleasure to meet you, Angie – and you, Jerzy. I know you will always miss your own mother, but I think you will find that Dr Gray has great qualities of her own. And you look after her, too, OK?'

The boy grinned. 'Don't worry, boss. She's safe with me. You like one last picture?'

'Why not?'

Jerzy grabbed a passing nurse by the sleeve, handed her the camera and showed her how to press the button. Then he lined up with Wilde and Angie Gray and Lilly Marais and the nurse took a couple of snaps.

'Send me a copy, Jerzy,' Wilde said. 'I'll leave you my address.'

His final visit to CIC Garmisch was not easy. 'Are you going to tell me what happened up there, Professor?'

'I'm not entirely sure, Lieutenant.'

'Was the Hitler bastard there?'

Wilde shrugged. 'I'm not sure we'll ever know.'

'Come on. We're in this together. You and me, a team from the word go. I saved your life, remember?'

'And I paid my debt. All I can say is that I no longer believe a hunt for Adolf Hitler would be a productive use of time or manpower.'

'So you killed him?'

Wilde simply smiled.

'I'll take that as a yes. My only regret is that I didn't get to fire the bullet.'

Wilde shook him warmly by the hand. 'You're not the easiest of men, Lieutenant Heck, but somehow we muddle through, I think.'

Heck grinned. 'You're saying I'm difficult? Well, that makes two of us, Professor.'

Wilde hitched a lift to the Schongau airbase and joined a military flight to Wiesbaden. He found Allen Dulles in his office, digging the ashes from his pipe. He stood up as soon as Wilde entered and shook him by the hand.

'Well, who would have thought it, Professor Wilde. You found the bastard.'

Yes, he had. And yet it still felt unreal. He was the man who tracked down Adolf Hitler and witnessed his death.

'Just a shame there was nothing but ashes and a couple of bones. Not even a damned dental plate to identify him.'

'But you believe me, Mr Dulles?'

The OSS bureau chief tamped in another wedge of aromatic tobacco, then loosened it with his metal pick. 'I certainly do. But what do I do with the information? How do we prove it? Who do we tell? The newspapers will want proof, and you don't have it. Should I send you back to Bavaria to find the missing boy? Well, we both know that's not going to happen.'

'So what now?'

'You go back to Cambridge and hammer some history into young heads. Or maybe you want to stay in the OSS?'

'No, I prefer the first option. I just don't like being left with the feeling that I somehow failed.'

'Oh, you didn't fail, Wilde. We now know the truth about Hitler, which means I don't have to waste any more time or energy looking for him. Case closed.' He reached for a decanter. 'Care for a whiskey?'

'Thank you, that would be very welcome. There was something else, though.'

'Oh yeah?'

'The matter of Julius Boden being recruited by the Counter Intelligence Corps. Colonel Appache came clean.'

'Yes, I heard.' He poured two large whiskeys into crystal glasses.

'Well, I don't like it. We lost hundreds of thousands of good men to rid the world of brutes like Boden. We shouldn't be doing deals with them.'

'I agree. It's scandalous. Unfortunately, the CIC is outside my jurisdiction, but I sure as hell will be making my feelings known in Washington. I've already spoken to Bill Donovan, and he's as one with us in this matter. He also sends you his congratulations.' He clinked glasses. 'Here's to you, Professor. And to the death of dictators.'

'Has he told the President about Hitler?'

'He has. And it goes no further. You, me, Bill and Harry. I can't stop you telling your gorgeous wife, of course, but she knows how to keep a secret, doesn't she?'

Yes, Lydia knew how to keep a secret.

'There may even be some sort of decoration in the offing for you.'

Wilde drank the whiskey down. It was American rye, which he liked almost as much as Scotch. But he didn't need medals. 'Tell Bill that a case of single malt will suit me fine.'

'I'll do that.' He poured him another. 'Now finish your drink, get back on the plane and go home.'

Chapter 49

Back in his British Army uniform, but with his arm still in a sling, Mo Heck took his leave of Dr Gray and young Jerzy.

'You're not going to shoot anyone, are you, Mo?' Angie Gray entreated him.

'No, that's over. I've had my fill of vengeance. I thought it would numb the pain, but it doesn't.'

'Where are you going then?'

'I have to rejoin my unit. I'm still in the British Army, you know. But first I have something I must do.'

He caught the train from Munich and settled back as they rattled slowly northwards across the American and then Soviet-occupied ruins of Germany. Gazing out of the window as the afternoon wore on into evening, he looked dispassionately on the unspoilt hills and forests and farmland, interspersed with the rubble of towns, the casually scattered burnt-out tanks and artillery pieces and war planes, the tangled wreckage of bridges and factories.

As the train clattered on into the night, he tried to make sense of this devastated but still beautiful country. The country of Bach and Beethoven, Schiller and Heine, Einstein and Goethe. What had got into these great and civilised people that they should turn into a nation of ravening beasts?

Fellow passengers came and went. At Leipzig an old German man with one arm and a walking stick entered his carriage and sat opposite him. He grinned at Heck and pointed at the sling and bandaged arm. 'At least you still have your arm, soldier,' he said in broken English.

'Where did you lose yours, old man?' Heck replied in German.

'Verdun, fighting the French.' As the train pulled out of the town, he indicated the ruins outside the carriage window. 'Your bombers did quite a job.'

'So did yours. Go and have a look at London.'

'Yes, I know.' He was silent for a couple of minutes and tears began to well up in his eyes. 'My son was in the Luftwaffe, shot down and killed by your Spitfires. What a waste. What a crazy waste. No more wars please, Englishman.'

'I'm not English, I'm Dutch. I'm a Jew.'

'Then I apologise twice over to you.'

'What did you do to bring down Hitler?'

'What could I do? I am a brewer by trade. We were powerless.'

'Then I can't accept your apology.'

The old man nodded slowly. 'I understand.'

'You are all guilty. You should have stopped them.'

They spoke no more until the train arrived in Berlin. The old man hung his head as he prepared to depart, but Heck stopped him. 'Wait,' he said. 'I can't forgive you, but at least you tried to apologise, and I am sorry for your loss.'

'Thank you, sir. That means a great deal to me.'

Maria Dienstag was sweeping the floor of the church. At first she shrunk back alarmed at the arrival of a man in uniform, but then she recognised him.

'Mr Heck, why are you here?'

'I came to see you Frau Dienstag, to see how you are.'

'Me? Oh I get by. I have food, though not much, and I have a bed to sleep in.'

'And the priest, he looks after you well?'

'Not bad. He is a kind man, but he works me hard. Not that I mind. I am used to work. It's better than thinking.'

'You look well, much better.'

Her bald head was still covered by a scarf, but a smile lit up her face; she was prettier than he remembered her. Less gaunt.

'You look a little worse, though,' she said. 'Your arm is injured.'

'It's nothing. A scratch. Come on, put your broom down, I'm taking you out for a cup of coffee. I noticed that someone has opened a cafe in the ruins near here.'

'I have to finish my work.'

'It's all right, I've spoken to the priest.'

She held back. 'I don't know if I should, Mr Heck.'

He took the broom from her and leant it against the wall, then he took her small hand in his and led her from the church. She did not resist, but she insisted on taking off her apron and leaving it by the main door.

They found a table outside the bar, in the sunshine. Heck asked the waitress if she had real coffee, but she shook her head.

'Would you have real coffee if I gave you ten American cigarettes?'

'That would be different, sir. I think we might manage that.'

When the coffee arrived, they both spooned in milk and sugar. 'I can't believe it,' Maria said. 'I haven't tasted this in five or more years.'

'I've got good news,' Heck said. 'Miriam is alive. You and your husband saved her life. She lives in Zurich with her husband and child.'

'Oh, that is wonderful news. But, of course, I am sorry for you . . .'

He shrugged. 'It was a youthful infatuation, nothing more. The important thing is that she is alive and happy.'

'Well, if you ever talk to her or see her, please give her my best regards.'

'I will do that.'

'And you, Mr Heck, what will you do now? Will you stay in the army?'

'No, I will resign my commission as soon as possible. And then I am going to make myself very rich.'

She laughed. 'And how will you do that?'

'To start with I am writing a book about the war, and the tragic fate of my people.' He placed his journal on the table. 'Much of it is already in here. And with the money I make, I shall start a publishing company.'

'That's a very good plan. I wish you luck.'

'I also want a family, with many babies.' He reached across the table and took her hand. 'I am sorry, Frau Dienstag, but I don't have time to woo you properly, so I must ask you straight out: will you marry me?'

The question stunned her, but then she burst into tears.

'Well?'

'You want me to marry a man with just one eyebrow?' Her tears were tears of laughter and joy.

'I know you are still mourning your husband and child. We are both grieving. But I think we have a spark – and we have hope.'

'Yes, Mr Heck, yes I will marry you. I have been thinking about you all day and all night.'

'And I you.'

'I can't believe it. Things like this don't happen to me.'

'And the babies?'

'Yes, many babies.'

Chapter 50

Wilde flew into Northolt in north-west London, then took the train up to Cambridge. It was midday and he found Lydia in the back garden, but she did not look her usual welcoming self.

She was in her old green corduroy trousers – the ones she wore for gardening – and a large white men's cotton shirt. In one hand she had a wood-handled trowel and in the other, she had Johnny's hand. Her hair was tangled, her face was grimy and sweaty and she was scowling.

'Daddy, Daddy!' the boy said.

'Johnny.' He reached out, picked him up and tickled him so that he squealed.

'Well?' Lydia said, still not smiling.

'I'm home,' Wilde said.

'So I see. And what happened? Did you find the horrid little man with the toothbrush moustache?'

'That's a bit complicated.'

'Tom, I have been stuck alone in this bloody house with a demanding toddler and a Russian spy for God knows how long, I can do without your riddles. Did you find the Nazi swine or not?'

'Yes, I found him. But he no longer had the moustache. He had a bushy grey beard and thick glasses and a stoop and looked like everyone's idea of a grandfather.'

'Where was he? More the point, where is he now?'

'That's the problem. There was an explosion, a fire, and he was burnt to a cinder. There's nothing left of him. And no one else saw him. No one alive anyway. So I'll never be able to prove any of it.'

'I thought you were working with someone else?'

'I was. A guy named Mozes Heck, a lieutenant in the British Army, Dutch Jew by birth. But he was in hospital at the time recovering from a wound. Look, can we go indoors and have a cup of something and I'll tell you the whole story. It's been one hell of a journey. Germany's a smoking pile of rubble.'

'You know, Tom. I really don't want to hear it. I'm sure you have had the time of your life among the willing Fräuleins. They offer their services for two cigarettes or a Yankee dollar, I believe.'

'That's not fair.'

'Maybe not. But life isn't fair, is it, Tom? For instance, I have been told by the senior tutor at your college that my chance of getting a place at one of the big medical schools is precisely zero. Our good friend Rupert Weir said much the same, though rather more kindly. And do you know why? Because I am married and I have a child and I am in my thirties. Oh, and because they will be awarding almost all the places to young men returning from the war. So it seems my useful life is now over. I can bring up children and that's about the size of it.'

'I'm sorry, Lydia. Truly I am.'

'He did suggest, however, that if I was very lucky, even with my advanced years, I might be accepted into the London School of Medicine for Women. Of course I had already thought of that, but I always had my sights set on Bart's.'

'What about Addenbrooke's?'

'I don't know. I suppose I was avoiding Cambridge because I'll just find myself looking after hearth and home. Edinburgh was a thought, though. They have been accepting women since the last century. Again there's that question, however – will my age be held against me?'

'Try, try and try again.'

'The senior tutor did suggest I might be qualified to teach children at elementary school or a local prep school.'

'That's a useful career, Lydia.'

'Yes, it is. But it's not what I wanted.'

For a moment he thought she was going to burst into tears. Instead, she threw the trowel into the soft earth, and put her arms around her husband and her son.

'You owe me, Mr Wilde.'

She smelt earthy and he instantly felt aroused. 'I'll see what I can do.'

'Not like that,' she said. 'I mean you owe me big time. I'm talking nights out dancing, holidays in far-flung exotic locations.'

'Then we'll talk to Thomas Cook. By the way, you mentioned the Russian. Where *is* Borisov?'

'Gone. Went this morning. He thanked me, handed me a bunch of flowers and kissed me on both cheeks and walked away. I've no idea where he went.'

'What about Eaton? Does he know he's gone?'

She shrugged. 'I've no idea. I suggest you call him. Anyway, I thought you two had progressed to first-name terms.'

Wilde felt that chill of unease again. This wasn't right. Sergei Borisov, otherwise known as Boris Minsky, senior officer in Stalin's lethal intelligence service SMERSH, should not be on the loose in Britain without a minder. The war might be over, but only a fool or a naive innocent would think that all was well with the world and that everyone was friends.

He would make that call to Philip Eaton, and follow up with another one to Allen Dulles.

What worried him most was that he, Wilde, was the one who had effected Borisov's defection to the West. The thing was, he had been so preoccupied with the primary mission in

Germany, that he hadn't bothered to question the Russian's true motives. Well, he was beginning to question them now, and he felt uncomfortable.

'By the way,' Lydia said, 'What was that stuff about your beautiful bourgeoise wife?'

'Oh, that was bloody Borisov taunting me with the Marxists' old sneering shibboleth about the middle classes. Forget it.'

'So it was supposed to be an insult? Well, I like bourgeoise. Shakespeare was bourgeois.'

Separated by hundreds of miles, a man and a boy walked along unfamiliar streets with very different thoughts in their heads. In the little town of Godmanchester in England, Sergei Borisov strode along with his hands in the pockets of his tweedy trousers, whistling jauntily like a well-fed English countryman.

He went down West Street. Outside the imposing facade of Farm Hall, he stopped and pulled a packet of Du Maurier cigarettes from his jacket pocket. He put one cigarette in his mouth and lit it with a lighter, meanwhile holding the cigarette pack firmly in the other hand, its neat red cover pointing at the house. His finger clicked a little button on the top and the secret camera took a picture.

He moved on and took more pictures, from every angle, nodding in silent greeting to a passing grandmother. He knew that ten German nuclear scientists were held prisoner behind the walls of this house. The Soviet Union needed such men working for them; Hiroshima and Nagasaki had made their acquisition imperative. That was his task; that was why he was here.

In Munich, meanwhile, 700 miles to the south-east, Siegfried Boden negotiated the broken streets in search of work or, at least, a piece of bread. His clothes were torn and tattered from the explosion, but he had regained his hearing and he still had his pistol.

He was alone now. *Mutti* was dead, so was Hildy and there was no word of Julius. So that left only him. He was the heir and his destiny awaited him. All the while as he walked, a single thought ran through his mind, as if on an endless spool. *I am the man now, and I will rise from the ashes.*

Chapter 51

The letter arrived just over two weeks later. It contained the photograph of Wilde with Lilly, Angie and Jerzy, and a two-page letter from Angie.

Dear Tom,

I have some news that you might like to hear. We arrived in Paris as planned and, after a couple of nights in a rather drab hotel, I managed to secure a short lease on a pleasant apartment in Montparnasse (see address). My intention is to see if I can find any employment in the local hospitals or perhaps as a locum. I am not sure how things work in France, but I believe I have enough of the language to see me through. Also, looking at schools for Jerzy (again, not totally sure of the French system).

Anyway, back to the news. When we were settled in our new home, I took the liberty of leaving Jerzy with Lilly, telling them I had to visit old friends in the country and would be back in two or three days. I rented a car, found some black market petrol at an exhorbitant price and headed for Normandy, to the village of Ste-Estelle-sur-Seine. This was Lilly's home village. Without alarming her, I wanted to establish the situation there, and whether there would be any hope of reconciliation between her and her family and the other villagers. Time, of course, can sometimes heal.

It turned out that a great deal has changed. In particular, her father (the local blacksmith) had taken his life during the summer, hanging himself from the rafters in his smithy. Whether it was guilt over his treatment of his daughter I have no idea.

Her mother was not unhappy to see me and talk to me. She had clearly been under the thumb of her husband and I rather think she was glad to see the back of him. She was very keen to learn about Lilly and seemed terribly guilty for what had happened to her.

Did she think the village would accept Lilly back? She wasn't sure. One of their number had been taken hostage by the Germans during the war and had been shot in reprisal when the Resistance attacked a Wehrmacht patrol just before D-Day. So there is still bad feeling.

I did, however, learn something else from Lilly's mother. It seems her baby, Nathalie, was not killed (as she had believed), but was placed with the nuns in a convent near Rouen. And this is where the news comes in. To cut a long story short, I drove to the convent and discovered that the baby was, indeed, there — and was thriving.

The nuns seemed reluctant to part with the child. They don't approve of children being brought up by young single mothers. But I know a bit about the way the world works, so I made an offer of a fair-sized donation to their funds and suddenly they were all sweetness and light. 'Of course, little Nathalie must be returned to her true mother. Would Madame Gray wish to take her now, or will the mother come to collect her?'

I took the latter option, not being at all sure that I could look after a baby and drive at the same time. Two days later, mother and child were reunited, tears of joy were shed and now our apartment in Paris is filled with the sound of gurgles, wailings and much laughter.

I hope you like the photo. Please accept our regards and pass on our felicitations to you and your family. I wish your wife every success in securing a place at medical school.

Your friend,

Angie Gray

What Happened to the Witnesses?

WALTER SCHELLENBERG
SS intelligence chief

Smooth, highly educated, multilingual and one-time lover of Coco Chanel, Schellenberg was the ultimate Nazi fixer, acting as both efficient bureaucrat and spy. Despite his later protestations, Schellenberg was up to his neck in organising the annihilation of the Jews. In one memo, he even refers to 'The Final Solution' and he played an important role in persuading the army to support the *Einsatzgruppen* – the mobile murder squads who slaughtered hundreds of thousands of innocent people in Eastern Europe. He was at the heart of Himmler's SS machine before and during the war, rising inexorably to be his master's second-in-command. But he played a dangerous game at the end, conspiring to do a deal with the West by offering the lives of Jews in return for favourable peace terms. He also urged Himmler to depose Hitler – and even maintained later that Himmler had poisoned the Führer. Schellenberg was captured in Denmark by the British and was interrogated over a long period. He was accused of war crimes but mitigated his sentence by testifying against other SS leaders. He was sentenced to six years for complicity in the murder of Soviet captives, but was freed early because of ill health. He died aged 42 in 1952.

HANNA REITSCH
Celebrity aviator and test pilot

Small, smiley and tough as steel, she was endowed with astonishing skill and courage, breaking numerous records as a pilot of war planes, civilian aircraft and gliders – and even becoming the first woman to fly a helicopter. But she was also obsessed with Hitler and would never hear a word said against him. Perhaps her most remarkable feat was her flight in and out of central Berlin in the very last days of the war (as described elsewhere in this book). She was subjected to intensive interrogation when held prisoner at Oberursel because it was assumed by the Americans that she had flown Hitler out of Berlin and so must know where he was. When she was freed and permitted to fly again in 1952, she broke yet more records and travelled abroad to set up gliding schools, first in India, then in Ghana. Despite never renouncing Nazism, she was feted by world leaders including President Kennedy, Indian premier Nehru and Ghana's president Nkrumah, with whom she may have had an affair. She never married and died in 1979, aged 67. Cause of death was given as heart attack – but some suspected she finally took the cyanide pill given to her by Hitler thirty-four years earlier.

HANS FRITZSCHE
Propagandist

He was the sole Russian-held defendant at the main Nuremberg trial, where he was charged with crimes against humanity – allegedly using his frequent radio broadcasts to incite the German people to commit atrocities. He broke down in tears on more than one occasion during the trial. He was clearly in emotional agony when terrible films of the suffering in concentration camps were shown in court. Prison psychologist Gustave Gilbert, who conducted extensive interviews with all the accused, recalled one lunchtime: 'I saw Fritzsche struggling to avoid crying and he put on dark glasses to hide his eyes. I noticed him again during the afternoon intermission and he was still choking back tears.' After one film of the atrocities, Gilbert visited Fritzsche in his cell. 'He spoke haltingly, choking with every phrase – "I have the feeling I am drowning in filth. I am choking in it . . . I cannot go on. It is a daily execution".' No one really understood why he was on trial, because he was considered a very junior member of the Nazi regime compared to the other defendants. As a young man, Fritzsche studied history, languages and philosophy at university and became a newspaper journalist. In 1933, he joined the Propaganda Ministry under Goebbels. The Nuremberg court found him not guilty, but he was sentenced to eight years by a separate denazification court. He was freed early but died soon after, in 1953, of cancer. He was 53.

ERICH KEMPKA
Hitler's driver

He had an incredible escape from the Bunker along Berlin railway tracks, assisted by a slave girl from the Balkans. She had found him, injured and desperate, still wearing his SS officer's uniform. Even though he was her natural enemy she helped him out of the uniform into civilian overalls and – when they were discovered by Russian soldiers – held his hand and told them he was her husband. The Russians embraced them as friends and gave them vodka and food. They parted when he was safely clear of the city. 'Many men would do well to use that girl as a shining example of humanity,' he wrote later. He was eventually taken prisoner by the US Counter Intelligence Corps in southern Germany and was held until 1947. He testified at the main Nuremberg trial, but was not himself accused of war crimes. Yet he never really renounced his Nazi past and attended SS reunions for many years. He also made excuses for Hitler. 'It is not my purpose to decide between right and wrong,' he said in his memoir. 'As a simple man, what mattered to me was how men proved their class. Almost without exception those around Hitler enjoyed only the best from him. Perhaps history will make this its greatest reproach of him, that he was too trusting of those around him.' Kempka died in 1975, aged 64.

CHRISTA SCHROEDER
Hitler's secretary

When she left the Bunker on April 21st 1945, Schroeder was given a cyanide capsule by Hitler, the man she had served faithfully for 12 years. As his secretary she had followed him from Munich to Berlin, then to his eastern headquarters, the Wolfsschanze, then back to Berlin and the Bunker. In 1938, she became engaged to a foreign diplomat, but Hitler forbade the match and she never married. Almost every day she had tea with Hitler, other secretaries and Eva Braun and watched his health deteriorating dramatically in the final weeks. She said that towards the end he talked only about dogs, which drove Eva to distraction. She told Schroeder: 'I'm really fed up with Blondi (his Alsatian). Sometimes I give the beast a good kick under the table. That is my revenge.' Schroeder had been ordered to leave the Bunker and Hitler said he would follow her and the others to southern Germany, but she didn't see him again. She was arrested by the Americans a month later and was held until 1948. She kept the poison pill for a long time, but never took it. She later wrote her memoirs – *He Was My Chief* – and worked as a secretary for a Munich building firm, dying in 1984, aged 76.

BALDUR VON SCHIRACH
Founder of Hitler Youth

While imprisoned at Nuremberg, Schirach went to great lengths to distance himself from the horrors of the Nazis. But in truth he had lived the high life as one of their most senior members, marrying Henriette, the beautiful daughter of Hitler's great friend Heinrich Hoffman. In her memoir, Henriette recalled the heady days when he ran the Hitler Youth: 'On Baldur's birthday, the house was besieged by members of the BDM, the Nazi Girls' Association, who came with flags and flutes to bring their gifts – plovers' eggs and live geese, or once, an outsize nutcracker from Sonneberg, together with a pair of hand-knitted gloves from Saxony, one embroidered with the word *Heil*, and the other with *Hitler*.' But after the war, Schirach would try to excuse his devotion to the Führer by saying 'Before 1934, Hitler was human; from 1934 to 1938, he was superhuman, from 1938 onwards he was inhuman.' Schirach, who had been responsible for sending thousands of Viennese Jews to the death camps, was convicted of crimes against humanity but was spared the rope and served twenty years in Spandau Prison. Henriette divorced him. Two years after his release he gave a fascinating but gruesomely self-serving TV interview to David Frost, which you can find on YouTube. He also published his memoirs and lived out his days in comfort, dying aged 67 in 1974.

KURT DIEBNER
Nuclear physicist

Having studied experimental physics in Innsbruck and Halle as a young man, he went on to join the Nazi party and, in the war, headed Germany's nuclear energy project. Despite the

Allies' fears, this actually never came close to developing an atomic bomb. Diebner later claimed that he had never voted for Hitler and that he actually 'suffered under the Nazis'. He said the only reason he stayed in the party was that science jobs were restricted to Nazis. Along with nine other scientists detained at Farm Hall, Huntingdonshire, after the war, he was released on January 3rd, 1946, and returned to Germany. He worked in private industry in Hamburg, trying to develop nuclear-powered merchant ships. He died in 1964, aged 59.

Acknowledgements

Thanks to my wife, Naomi, who had to put up with even more of me during the writing of this book, because of lockdown. Thanks to all at Bonnier Zaffre – particularly my editor Ben Willis, art director Nick Stearn, the sales and marketing teams, my publicist Clare Kelly and editorial assistant Ciara Corrigan – for keeping calm and carrying on in tough times. And thanks to my agent, Teresa Chris, the voice of sanity and good humour at all times.

If you enjoyed *The Man in the Bunker*,
why not join the
RORY CLEMENTS READERS' CLUB

When you sign up you'll receive a free copy of
an exclusive short story, plus news about upcoming books,
sneak previews, and exclusive behind-the-scenes material.
To join, simply visit:
bit.ly/RoryClementsClub

Keep reading for a letter from the author . . .

Hello!

I want to tell you a little bit about the background to *The Man in the Bunker*.

Some of the action takes place in a displaced persons camp in Bavaria. There were hundreds of such camps throughout Europe because millions of people had been driven from their homes by persecution and the ravages of war.

Conditions varied greatly between these camps. There were still shortages of food and not all the establishments were run with kindness. Some were even based in former Nazi concentration camps, such as Bergen-Belsen. But despite this, there was one element that had been missing during the Nazi years: hope.

Young people who had lost their families were desperate to rebuild their lives. They fell in love and married at a remarkable rate. In one camp up to six couples were getting married every day (sometimes they divorced a couple of days later). Babies quickly appeared – in Bergen-Belsen alone there were 555 births in 1946.

The camps that lasted the longest became little towns with their own theatres, cinemas, newspapers, schools, religious centres, football teams and orchestras. Incredibly, many of the refugees still hadn't found a permanent home ten years later. The last two camps didn't close until the late 1950s.

If you would like to hear more about my books, you can visit my website **www.roryclements.co.uk** where you can join the Rory Clements Readers' Club (**bit.ly/RoryClementsClub**). It only takes a few moments to sign up, there are no catches or costs. Bonnier Books UK will keep your data private and confidential, and it will never be passed on to a third party. We won't spam you with loads of emails, just get in touch now and again with news about my books, and you can unsubscribe any time you want.

And if you would like to get involved in a wider conversation about my books, please do review *The Man in the Bunker* on Amazon, on Goodreads, on any other e-store, on your own blog and social media accounts, or talk about it with friends, family or reader groups! Sharing your thoughts helps other readers, and I always enjoy hearing about what people experience from my writing.

Thank you again for reading *The Man in the Bunker*.

With best wishes,

Rory Clements